Carolina Hideaways

*There Is No Hiding from God and Love
in Three Contemporary Romances*

Terry Fowler

BARBOUR
PUBLISHING

Published by Barbour Publishing, Inc., P.O. Box 719, Uhrichsville, Ohio 44683,
www.barbourbooks.com

*Our mission is to publish and distribute inspirational products offering exceptional
value and biblical encouragement to the masses.*

 Member of the
Evangelical Christian
Publishers Association

Printed in the United States of America.

Dear Readers,

One of my favorite verses is Psalm 46:1—"God is our refuge and strength, an ever-present help in trouble." Like the characters of these stories we all deal with situations that make us want to run and hide, but we soon learn that with God by our side, we will survive. A kidnapped child, a health condition that at times seems hopeless, even the murder of loved ones—these can be survived if we lean on God and trust Him to get us through.

I love calling North Carolina home. I've lived here my entire life, pretty much within an hour of where I grew up, and can't think of another place I'd want to be. Beaches and mountains are among the state's most popular destinations, and I've used both in these stories. I hope you feel the sand beneath your feet and stand at the top of the mountain as you experience North Carolina with me.

As always, I pray you have accepted the gift of salvation. It's yours for the asking.

Terry Fowler
www.terryfowler.net

PEACE, BE STILL

Dedication

To the lost children and those who search for them.
Thanks to Tammy and Mary for all your help.
Special thanks to Mark Young and Mike Overton
for your police expertise.

Chapter 1

*M*ommy! Mommy! Mommeeeeeeee!"

"No! Leave her alone." Katy Sinclair beat at the stranger's arm. "Let her go." His fist. A punch to her face. Pain. "Help us!" she moaned as she struggled up from the ground and ran after them.

Katy moved restlessly on the bed, her head moving from side to side as the image changed. *Another man, this time gentle and concerned. "No leads, Mrs. Sinclair," the agent said. "I'm afraid she's. . ."*

"No!" Bethie wasn't dead. Katy knew she wasn't.

Another change, this time her husband's familiar face filled with loathing.

"I don't know why I ever married you. Good riddance."

Another place, the local detective, sympathetic as he said, "There was no child with Jack Sinclair."

Katy stirred when the new sound entered her world of darkness. Pounding. Frenzied and relentless. Each thud jarred her further into wakefulness. Forcing open heavy lids, she looked at the ceiling of a strange room in semi-darkness. Where was she?

So dark. She rolled her head to one side and caught sight of the clock on the nightstand: 3:00 p.m. She never slept that late. Katy shifted and her back objected to the exertion. Sucking in a deep breath, she tried again, this time easing her legs over the side of the bed. She attributed her disorientation to the pain medication. Vague recollections of nightmare-riddled sleep and waking long enough to take more pills surfaced and disappeared like feathers in the wind.

The beach. She'd come here on Wednesday. A visit to the Wilmington Police Department only verified Bethany hadn't been with Jack. Then she'd injured her back when she tripped on the stairs dragging her duffel into the cottage. Unable to drive herself, she'd struggled back down the stairs to take a cab to the emergency room. There had been another cab and a late-night stop at the all-night pharmacy to pick up the prescriptions after being diagnosed with severe back strain. That last excruciating climb up the stairs had been miserable.

Holding on to the nightstand, Katy pushed herself upright and shuffled toward the window. She pulled back the curtain and stared at the plywood covering. No wonder the room was so dark. Confused, Katy pulled on her robe and continued her slow trek to the kitchen only to find the french door covered as well. What was going on?

She moved like a woman three times her age, each step causing her pain. Katy navigated her way through the great room and opened the front door, fully expecting to be met with another wall of wood.

Finally escape. The screen door closed behind her with a thud. Katy stepped out onto the covered deck and stilled. Where were the rockers, and why was plywood propped against the house? An unyielding breeze whipped her hair across her face. Something wasn't right here.

Coming around the corner, Richie Taylor swiped water from his eyes and paused when he spotted the woman on the deck. His gaze widened as he stared at Mr. Lennon's houseguest. Striking, she stood tall and model thin. Her long auburn hair flashed like a sunbeam in the otherwise dreary day. She looked young, maybe in her midtwenties.

Placing the hammer into his tool belt, he moved up the stairs and took shelter underneath the overhang. "I figured you'd already headed for higher ground." Suspicion touched her solemn expression, and he hastened to explain. "Mr. Lennon asked me to board up the place. They're predicting this one will take our breath away."

"Board up? Take our breath away?" She parroted his words.

"You do know we're under a hurricane watch, don't you?" Richie asked.

Her pale green gaze widened with something akin to terror.

How could she not know? Hurricane Kirk had made the national news. From what he'd heard before leaving the office, they were saying the severity of the storm could turn Interstate 40 into a one-way highway out of the city. Beach police had informed residents of the mandatory evacuation, and the deadline was fast approaching.

"What day is this?"

Strange question, but then people often lost track of time on vacation. "Friday," Richie said. Her wide mouth formed a rounded O. "Is something wrong?"

"Apparently Rip Van Winkle has nothing on me." Self-derision touched the full lips. "I've nearly slept away two days."

A wind gust caused the robe to balloon about her slim form. Rain pelted his back and reminded Richie there wasn't time for idle chatter. "You need to get off the island. This place will be flooded in a few hours."

"Flooded?" she repeated, sounding dazed.

"I wouldn't waste time. Once they close the bridge, you won't be able to leave."

Richie caught her just as her legs gave way. Her face turned pink as he pulled her upward. "We have to get out of here. Do you need help?"

Shaking her head, she steadied herself against the doorframe.

"I'm Richie. I've got a couple of things to finish up out here. Yell if you need anything."

"I'm Katy."

Slightly stooped, she crept toward the door. Richie frowned. At the rate she moved, the hurricane would arrive before she made it inside.

Fighting the urge to carry her into the cottage, he moved along the deck.

Richie lifted the sheet of plywood over the window and nailed it into place. Covered windows would not make much difference with a Category 3 or 4 storm, but he'd promised Mr. Lennon.

He pounded the last nail, unhooked his tool belt, and ran for the truck. Richie wished for a towel as he shoved the worn leather belt across the cowhide-patterned seat cover and climbed inside. The khaki slacks and striped polo he'd worn to the office that morning clung to him.

Richie caught sight of the car parked underneath the house. What could she be doing? Hadn't she understood? While his heart and head battled between self-preservation and Christian duty, he knew he couldn't just drive away. He twisted the key, thinking he'd take shelter underneath the house and run upstairs to check on her. Nothing happened. "Come on," he coaxed, patting the steering wheel before twisting it again. Still no response.

Nothing had gone as planned today. After oversleeping, he'd hurried to the office only to realize he'd left his cell at home in the charger. His last appointment ran over, and he'd been late getting back to the beach.

He fiddled under the hood and tried again. The old truck wasn't going anywhere. A heavy wind-driven downpour pushed at him. Richie dashed toward the stairs. Tapping on the screen door, he called, "Katy? Are you there? Katy?"

"Come in."

"Can I. . ." The words trailed off. The lights blazed in the room. Dressed in shorts and a T-shirt, her hair brushed and makeup refreshed, she sat in the armchair. "Why aren't you packing?"

Shrugging, Katy indicated the suitcases around her feet. "I never unpacked."

"I wasn't kidding," he ripped out impatiently. "You have to get out of here. Now."

Katy struggled to her feet. "I don't have anywhere to go."

Frustrated, Richie asked, "Why didn't you say so earlier?"

"It's not your responsibility."

The way he figured it, Mr. Lennon wouldn't appreciate him leaving his guest behind to die. "Then I'm making it my responsibility. You can barely stand. The first strong breeze will take you away." Richie took her arm. "Let's go."

She stared at him, wide-eyed and shocked. "What do you think you're doing? Take your hands off me." Katy twisted away. "I'll call the police."

He barely heard her above the torrential downpour but could see the movement caused her pain. He let go. "No judge in the world would convict me once I told them about your physical state."

"Why are you doing this?"

She looked so fragile, defeated. "Because you need help and I'm the one He sent."

"Who sent?"

"God."

Raw hurt glittered in her eyes. "Please don't tell me I'm your good deed for the week."

He shrugged. "I'm willing to be yours. My truck won't start. Can I use your phone?"

Katy indicated the cordless on the table. "It wasn't working Wednesday evening."

Which makes it difficult to carry out her threat, he thought wryly. Richie hit the ON button and sighed. No dial tone. Things just kept getting worse.

Katy pulled a cell from her purse and checked the display. "Battery's dead. I forgot my charger."

"And I left my phone at home. Just proves technology isn't infallible, doesn't it?"

The sigh came from the depths of her soul. "Where do you need to go? I'll take you."

"The shelter. I'll load your bags," Richie said. "Don't forget your medications, and find some blankets. A flashlight if you have one, identification, and important papers."

"I saw camping gear in the closet."

"I'll take a look. A sleeping bag would be more comfortable for you."

~

Exhausted and in great pain, Katy watched Richie cram the pillow and sleeping bag into the backseat of her car.

"Want me to drive?"

Though tempted, she shook her head. "Can't. Rental. What about your truck?"

He slid into the passenger seat and adjusted it to fit his long legs. He pulled the seat belt over his chest and clicked it into place. "No time."

"But it's your transportation. . . ."

"Our lives are more important. Let's go."

She backed from underneath the cottage and drove toward Lumina Avenue. "Where?"

"Head for Wilmington. I'll direct you to the closest shelter."

Once they learned she was coming to the area, the Lennons had insisted on loaning her their vacation cottage. Any other time, she would have eagerly anticipated a stay on a four-mile-long beach island along the North Carolina coast. But this visit had nothing to do with fun in the sun.

A couple of others pushed the deadline, but most places were deserted, exterior decorations removed to safe places. Plywood covered window after window. One resident had taken time to spray paint a message instructing Hurricane Kirk to go away. Katy seconded the sentiment.

Already there was a police presence at the drawbridge over the Intracoastal Waterway. No one would be coming back onto the island. Richie waved as they drove past.

Strengthening wind and worsening visibility made driving difficult. The steady *thwack* of the wipers barely affected the downpours that came more regularly. Flooding forced them to backtrack and take a different route.

Richie explained their destination was one of the schools that opened as a Red Cross shelter earlier that day. "It's up here on your left." He gestured toward the driveway and Katy felt relieved.

He pointed to the shelter. "Stop here. I'll park and unload your stuff. No sense in you getting soaked."

Too fatigued to argue, Katy joined the line of people going inside. Richie drove to the far side of the lot and then dashed back. He carried the folding chair, sleeping bag, and pillow. Wiping his face against his shirtsleeve, he said, "The car's safe there. No trees and not too close to the ditch."

They registered and went to their assigned space. He made additional trips outside to bring in the cooler, exercise mats, blankets, and the wheeled duffel bag she insisted be kept safe.

Katy propped herself against the wall and surveyed the room. Bedding and items brought along for comfort lined the area while battery-operated radios and tiny televisions ran constant storm coverage. "Looks like they know what to do."

"They understand the urgency." Richie grabbed the canvas chair and jerked it open. "Hey, you don't look so good." He took her arm and helped her cross the area.

"All this activity isn't good for a recuperative patient." She managed a pained smile and lowered her body into the chair.

"What happened?"

"Strained my back pulling that duffel up the stairs." Katy didn't share that the lingering aftereffects from an auto accident years before made her more susceptible to recurring problems.

"And you've moved junk like a pack mule?"

She grimaced. "Careful there or you'll turn my head."

He chuckled. "Sorry. You're more of a beautiful filly."

"Thanks. I think." Katy managed a tiny laugh.

The grooves about his mouth deepened with his grin. Though they'd never met before, something about his smile seemed very familiar. She tried to focus, but the pain wouldn't let her think.

Richie squatted next to her chair. His whole face spread into a smile. "I meant it strictly as a compliment. Do you have your pills? Are you supposed to eat with them? Can I get you something to drink?"

It took her a moment to sort through the questions. "There's soda and water in the cooler."

He handed her a bottle and busied himself with the exercise mats and sleeping bag. A frown set into his features. "I'm not sure this will be enough for your back."

He had the most expressive face. And the same cornflower blue eyes as Bethany. Perhaps that was why he seemed familiar.

Katy wouldn't complain. If not for his help, she might be sleeping on the cold hard floor. "You take the mats and blanket. I can use the sleeping bag."

Richie shook his head. "Doubt I'll sleep. I hate night storms. Can't see a thing."

Katy glanced at the block walls. There wasn't much to see from this vantage point day or night. She swallowed the pill with a couple of sips from the bottle. "How long will the storm last?"

"It could be hours or days. The hurricane passes, but there's no way to predict what will happen to the island. We won't be able to go home right away."

He spoke with confidence, and Katy wondered what she was going to do. Where would she stay if she couldn't go back to the cottage? Maybe she could ask Richie for a recommendation. Or even have him take her to a hotel.

He shook out the sleeping bag. "My sister was born during a hurricane. Dad says gale-force winds and pouring rain don't compare to a woman in labor."

He chuckled, looking like the original boy next door. Rain plastered his brownish blond hair to his scalp, and it developed interesting spikes as it dried. Katy suspected he used hair wax to style that spiky cut on a daily basis. A sprinkle of the same freckles she hated on herself ran across his nose.

Slim, not overly muscular, she estimated his height to be just over six feet. He reminded Katy of a live wire, in constant motion as he organized their space.

"How's the back?"

"The pills take awhile."

She felt guilty. Their relationship had zoomed from zero to ninety in a short time, and she doubted he'd formed a good opinion of her. "Richie, about the way I acted. . ." She paused, too embarrassed to continue.

"Forget it. You were afraid."

Katy couldn't deny that. The back injury made her feel insecure. "Have you always lived here?"

"Grew up at the beach. My parents leased me their place when they moved to Charlotte to be close to my sister. Lucy gave them their first grandchild a few months ago."

Katy perked up. "Boy or girl?"

"Boy. Little guy has some name half a mile long. They call him Trey."

"Do you have pictures?"

His grimace highlighted the grooves around his mouth. "Not with me. Bad uncle, huh?"

"Only Trey can attest to that," Katy said, deciding Richie was probably a wonderful uncle. "Do you do carpentry work full-time?"

He shook his head. "I have a couple of other part-time jobs. I counsel part-time at a local practice, and I'm the youth minister at New Hope Church."

"Oh."

"It's not that bad."

"I. . .I didn't mean. . . ," she stuttered, embarrassed.

Richie forged on. "You know I'm going to ask, so we might as well get it out of the way now. Do you know the Lord?"

Katy had known God. Then she'd lost her reason for living and managed to lose her connection to Him as well. "I've had more than a nodding acquaintance."

"But not now?"

Katy willed him to drop the subject. She didn't want to break down before a room of strangers, and her current mental state would not withstand a repeat of the story. "So it's your parents, a sister, and baby Trey?"

"And a brother-in-law. My brother died recently."

Waves of nausea rose up in her throat. "I'm sorry."

Richie's head tilted in acknowledgment. "I just got back into town yesterday. My dad suffered a mild heart attack after the funeral. I had to come back to prepare for the storm."

"I hope he's okay."

"Better. The doctor plans to release him in a day or two. What about your family?"

"Pretty much the same as yours. Parents, one sister, and a brother-in-law." Katy didn't mention Bethany. She couldn't.

"Husband?"

Katy thumbed the rings on her left hand, the huge diamond Jack insisted she wear. She'd always considered them much too ostentatious and only wore them now to validate that she was married.

"Dead."

Another look of shared sympathy passed between them.

Her light-headedness increased. "I don't feel well."

"You should lie down." He helped her stand. "When did you last eat?"

The move zapped her remaining strength. She remembered eating a handful of grapes Wednesday afternoon as she explored the cottage. "There's soup and crackers in the bag." While he loaded the car, she'd microwaved soup, dumped it into a thermos, and tucked it in the duffel along with some of the snack items.

Richie looked at her over his shoulder. "Mind if I take a look?"

Katy burrowed into the comfort of the sleeping bag and mumbled, "No."

When he tried to give her the mug of soup, she shook her head. "Just crackers."

As the sad memories encroached, Katy compared the tempest raging in her heart and soul to the one outside. Both had the power to destroy. Could she survive yet another storm?

⌒

Katy's distressed mumbling drew Richie's attention from the borrowed Bible. He wondered what demon she fought in her sleep and supposed the storm troubled her. The powerful force of the wind and rain battering the building only hinted at what was going on outside. Praise God, the strength had dropped from Category 3 to 2. That blessing could save them from total devastation.

Over the past couple of hours, he'd prayed with many church members. Richie wanted to reassure them that their homes and possessions would be safe but knew there would be destruction somewhere. He prayed for God to give them the strength to withstand whatever the outcome might be.

"Bethany!"

Katy's anguished cry brought Richie to his feet. He touched her shoulder, taking care not to cause her pain. "Katy, wake up. You're having a bad dream." Awareness came slowly as she focused on him with surprise and confusion. "It's okay," he whispered. "We're at the shelter. Do you remember?"

She nodded and rubbed her face.

"Feel better?"

"Yes. What about the storm?"

"Kirk's still out there. It's poured rain for a while now. Listeners are calling the radio station to report flooding with downed trees and power lines. Are you hungry? I ate your soup." Richie shrugged apologetically. He'd been cold and wet, and it had been too tempting.

She looked almost ethereal in the dimmed lighting. "I don't like soup. Just thought it might be something I could stomach. I'd rather have the cookies I stuffed in my bag."

Not a healthy meal, but from their earlier encounter on the porch, Richie doubted Katy worried about weight. He pushed the wheeled duffel in her direction.

"What time is it?" she asked as she tore the packet open and offered him a chocolate chip cookie.

"A little after seven." Two small children drew his gaze. "They're so restless. I usually stick games in the truck. I feel so unprepared."

"I could entertain them."

He looked at her with interest. "What did you have in mind?"

"I packed my—" She broke off. "I have puppets and balloons in my duffel."

"Great idea," Richie said, jumping to his feet. "I'll gather the kids around the bed."

"Better make it the chair."

❧

Richie approached the shelter attendants, and their smiles and nods were sufficient to prompt Katy's attempt to rise. A sharp pain reminded her just how long the road to recovery was for a back injury. Of all the stupid things that could have happened, this was the worst. She didn't have time to recuperate.

What had she said in her sleep? The idea of anyone witnessing her fears made Katy consider foregoing medications and sleep until she returned home.

"Okay, Mrs. Katy, your audience is ready." He noted her plight and moved forward to wrap an arm about her waist and help her stand. Katy settled the pillow into the back of the chair and sat.

Richie waited along with a good-sized group of children and parents. She pointed to the bag while the kids scrambled to get as close as possible.

He pulled back the unzipped sides. "Tell me what you need."

"There are puppets in a box marked CINDY ELLA GOES TO THE FARM. Let me have that one." She turned to the group and announced, "I need a volunteer." Several hands shot up. "Who has lungs strong enough to blow up hundreds of balloons?" Most of the hands dropped. She glanced at Richie. "What about you? Are you full of hot air?" Laughter filled the area.

"Probably more than my fair share."

Storytelling was a performance art, and Katy prided herself in her ability to retain the children's attention. Her only hope was that the few minutes of pleasure would help block their fear of the outside elements.

"Is everyone ready?" she asked in her most theatrical voice. The kids chorused "yes." "Okay, it's adventure time."

Their excitement touched Katy in a way few people could understand. Not only the painful remembrance of all she'd lost, but also their happy giggles were a piquant reminder of the memories that kept her going.

They sat enthralled as she used hand puppets to tell the story of the little city girl who went to visit her grandparents' farm. When her grandfather left Cindy Ella alone in the barn, the animals came to life. Katy invited interactive participation when she picked a child and twisted the balloons Richie gave her into the animal of the child's choice. Soon he joined in.

"You're a pretty good twister," Katy said when he gave his dog to the last child.

He grinned and enthused, "You're the real pro. You make it look easy."

"Kids love balloons. I like them myself," she admitted.

"Allow me." Richie went to work on a white bunny. She made him an elephant.

The kids milled around showing off their animals.

"How about a parade?" Katy suggested.

She watched from her chair, finding the children's added animations were just what the doctor ordered. The room came alive with laughter. *If only Bethany were here to see this.* Pain shafted through her heart.

The children and parents chorused "thank you" before going off to settle in for the evening.

"G'night, Mr. Richie."

"Night, Scottie." He hugged the little boy who wrapped his arms about his knees. When his mother picked him up, Scottie wrapped his arms about her neck and offered Katy a shy wave. She almost cried.

"You're a hit." Richie started to sit on the floor.

"Take the chair." Katy grasped the arms and stood. "The kids were the real hit. I can't recall the last time I laughed so much."

"Too bad we didn't have a camera. Tell me about the little guy who waved his hand the entire time."

Katy knew exactly which child he meant. "I had to ignore him. The curious ones don't stop once the questions start. One question only leads to another, and soon it's a free-for-all."

Richie nodded. "Where did you learn to tell stories like that?"

"I've been told I have an overactive imagination." Jack and her family had pointed that out more than once.

"You were the curious one as a child," Richie said with a slow grin. "That's why you identify with them."

Katy laughed. "I have been told I ask too many questions."

"I knew it. Those kids and parents won't forget this for a long time to come."

"Me either," she admitted.

Katy lowered herself onto the sleeping bag and pulled a throw over her bare legs. She frowned. She'd forgotten the pillow.

Richie handed it over and dragged the chair closer. "How long have you been at the Lennons'?"

"I flew in from Vegas Wednesday morning."

Interest flickered in the blue eyes. "You're a long way from home."

She nodded and said, "You're very comfortable with kids."

"I love children. Some of these kids attend my church."

If only Jack had loved children. Her spouse was anything but paternal. "Everyone calls you Richie."

An easy smile played about the corners of his mouth. "They're determined I'll never grow up."

"I wondered. . .I mean, most men. . ." Katy hesitated, feeling a sudden desire to remove her foot from her mouth. "Well, they use their full names."

"My dad is Richard Sr. They named me Richard Jr. Their options were Junior, Little Richard, or Richie."

She giggled at his look of disdain.

"Anyway, the name stuck like glue. In college and seminary, I was Rick or Rich. Then I came home and became Richie again."

"Friendly name for a friendly person." She yawned and rubbed her eyes. "Those pills make it difficult to stay awake."

"You should rest. Care to join me in prayer before you go to sleep?"

Not exactly thrilled, Katy nodded.

Richie dropped to one knee and took her hand in his. "Lord, we come to You tonight, thanking and praising You for this safe haven. We appreciate the power of Your works and ask that You bring us safely through the storm. If it be Your will, we ask for minimal damage—but if not, please give us the strength to deal with the outcome.

"Lord, bless Katy. Renew and strengthen her to carry on with the awesome talent You've given her. As always, be with us and guide us. Make us strong in Your service. In Jesus' name, we pray. Amen."

Tears pooled in her eyes. His prayer brought back memories of her precious granny Thomason praying for her. While Dina went off to camp or traveled with her friends, Katy spent summers with her mother's parents. Her granny loved to tell her about Jesus. Katy had been ten the summer she accepted Jesus as her Savior.

Even after she returned home, Katy felt the comfort of her grandmother's prayers. She'd lost her grandfather at twelve and had been seventeen when her granny passed away. How she wished Edna Thomason could be here now to help her make sense of this crazy situation.

She glanced up and found Richie's gaze focused on her. His hand held hers. Unnerved, Katy mumbled her thanks and removed her hand from his.

"Katy, who is Bethany?"

Chapter 2

Richie welcomed morning with the gritty eyes of a sleepless night. He glanced at Katy, glad to find her in a deep sleep, oblivious to the worries that plagued her earlier.

She intrigued him. No doubt about that, but Richie detected a sadness he hadn't fully understood until she screamed her daughter's name. When he asked about Bethany, a tearful Katy asked him to pray for her little girl. His mind whirled with questions of where the child could be and why she was not with the mother who obviously loved her. He wanted to know more but figured she'd tell him when she was ready.

Richie considered the day ahead. He needed to see what he could do to help but found himself hesitant to leave Katy alone. The feeling she needed someone wouldn't go away. She didn't open up, always stopping short of full revelation. Richie suspected she wouldn't welcome his continued presence. He checked his watch and decided to catch a ride to the church and see how things were there.

"Is it over?" Katy brushed tousled bangs from her eyes and yawned widely. She attempted to sit up and paled. Richie nodded as he stood and offered his hands. She slowly levered upward, her gaze intent when she asked, "Can we leave?"

"They've advised people to stay put."

Katy heaved a sigh and said, "Can't blame a girl for hoping. Do you plan to stay?"

She brushed at her wrinkled clothing.

Richie couldn't deny having had the same hope. Stiff from his night in the chair, he stretched his arms over his head and did a few exercises to loosen up. "I need to check in at church and see what I can do to help."

"Wish I could get out of here," she managed in a disappointed whisper.

"You need to rest. How did your back hold up?"

"Not good."

He slid a water bottle from the almost-nonexistent ice cubes and handed it over. "I'll pick up more ice today. Take it easy. You'll need your strength when you go home."

"If there's a home," she countered.

"Think positive," he urged. "At least people will wonder how you can smile in the midst of all the confusion."

"I wish I felt like smiling."

"Aw come on, it can't be that bad," he teased in an effort to lighten her mood.

"If only you knew."

Her cryptic statement bothered Richie. "Do you need to talk, Katy?"

She shook her head. Pulling a brush from her purse, she drew it slowly through her hair.

He watched the silky hair spill over her shoulders before shaking himself into action. "You need anything before I go?"

"I doubt even your God can help you find the one thing I want most."

His heart plummeted to the pit of his stomach. "I believe our God is capable of giving us everything we need."

"Don't mind me. Would you like a PB&J before you go?" He agreed, and she assembled the sandwiches. "I meant to tell you to help yourself before I flaked out last night."

Katy picked at her food. Her gloominess disturbed him.

"Your soup really hit the spot. I owe you one. Maybe I can take you out to dinner one night soon?"

Richie waited for her response. *Say something,* he encouraged silently. He liked the idea of spending some less-stressful time with Katy, getting to know her better.

"I'm the one who owes you," Katy said finally. "That soup doesn't begin to compensate for all you've done."

"I don't believe in keeping count though I do think one good deed deserves another."

She smiled and he felt encouraged. "That's my girl. Keep smiling."

Richie thanked her for breakfast and told her to take care. On the way out, he whispered up a prayer for her and stopped to give the shelter coordinator a brief rundown of Katy's medical situation.

～

She swallowed a pain pill and forced herself to eat. Afterward, Katy put the grocery items away and lay down. The continuous drone of conversation from a nearby radio made her wonder how long it would be before they returned to music programming. The deejays pondered whether the governor would declare a state of emergency while listeners called in their experiences. The more negative reports served as a poignant reminder of just how much she'd already lost.

How could her child have survived this latest nightmare? All along, she'd harbored the hope that Jack loved Bethany enough to keep her safe.

Why had he done this? They were his family. He claimed to love them, but his every action disproved his words. Katy racked her brain, trying to recall anything he said that might lead her to Bethie.

The days since Bethany's disappearance meshed one into another, leaving her even more discouraged. Hope dwindled when every avenue turned into a dead end.

Her best friend, Melody Lennon-Gerald, had been there for her every step of the way. Katy couldn't begin to guess the number of hours the woman had spent on the computer organizing the volunteer program and searching for any clue that might help find Bethany. She'd been as shocked as Katy when a Google alert provided the information that Jackson Sinclair Jr. was dead.

"Do you think the police know?" Melody asked after they read through the news releases concerning a John Doe and the obituary that featured an older picture of Jack.

"If they do, they're not telling me," Katy said. "I have to go."

"It's in North Carolina. Wilmington. We have that cottage on Wrightsville Beach," Melody said. "I'll go with you."

"You can't. You're scheduled to leave for your Disney vacation in two days. J. J. will be disappointed if you don't go. I'll be okay."

"You'll be careful?"

"You know I will."

⤺

She'd arrived at Wilmington International Airport Wednesday morning, rented a car, and gone straight to the police department. There the detective who had been assigned the homicide case greeted her pleasantly.

"The Las Vegas police have been in contact, Mrs. Sinclair, and I can only tell you what I told them. Your husband did not have a child with him."

"He had something to do with her kidnapping. I know he did." Katy wiped her eyes with the tissue he handed her. "This is Bethany." She showed him the photo.

"They sent a photo, too. I'm sorry, Mrs. Sinclair, but he was alone. No ID, no car, only ten thousand dollars cash in his pocket."

The tissue fell apart beneath her trembling fingers. "But surely someone knows something."

"The only witness reported he apparently stumbled into the shootout. We investigated and no one knew him or why he might be in the area. The shooter has been identified and is currently in jail without bond."

Katy stared at him. *A shootout. Where am I? Dodge City?* "But his car," she said. "He has a red Porsche. People notice cars like that."

The detective shook his head. "We haven't found the vehicle. His brother identified him from the John Doe sketch the media issued. After the autopsy, his body was released to the family along with the money."

Fresh tears tracked down her cheeks. Detective Neumann pushed the box of tissues in her direction. Katy sniffed and dabbed at her nose. "Can you give me his number? I never met Jack's family. I don't know how to contact them."

"What if I give him your number? Ask him to contact you."

She nodded. "Thank you. Please tell him I really need to talk to the family."

The detective added Katy's contact information to his file. He promised to get in touch if anything new surfaced. She doubted she'd hear from him again.

⤺

She tried to get comfortable. Why hadn't she told Richie when he asked about Bethany? Was it more than feeling too emotional? Maybe fear he'd make her see God's will in all this. She'd found him to be a very friendly, helpful person, and yet something held her back.

"It broke."

Katy looked into the tearful gaze of the child holding a yellow balloon fragment in his tiny hand. She looked around. Where was his mother? Why would she allow him to play unsupervised with something so dangerous? "Why don't you give me that, sweetie?"

Trading him a package of cookies for the balloon fragment, she learned his name was Blake and enjoyed his company until his mother, holding a crying infant against her shoulder, showed up to claim him.

"I told you not to bother people," the young woman snapped. She grabbed his hand, and Blake cried out when he dropped his cookies. She let go. "Pick them up and thank the lady."

"He wasn't a bother," Katy told the woman. "Send him over anytime you need a break."

The frazzled mother juggled the squalling baby. "My husband's a fireman. I had to take care of the house and the kids all by myself."

Oh for such stress.

Blake looked back as his mother dragged him away. Katy waved good-bye and welcomed the mind-numbing relief of sleep.

Time passed slowly. She sketched, napped, visited with those who remained, and worried. She'd become quite proficient at worrying over the last few months—first because of the situation with her husband, then Bethie's disappearance, and now this. Had her temporary home withstood the powerful force of the ocean?

Richie showed up late that afternoon with food, ice, and news. Rather than allay her fears, he only verified what she'd already heard.

"Any idea when we can leave?"

He stopped eating and shook his head. "I'm hopeful we'll hear something tomorrow."

Katy watched as those with damaged homes returned for the long night that loomed ahead of them. "What happens once the shelter closes?"

"Those who can't salvage their homes find a new place or go to family and friends. I spoke with the pastor earlier. We'll open the church if needed." He yawned. "Last night is catching up with me."

Richie placed a borrowed air mattress underneath her sleeping bag before he stretched out in the sleeping bag he'd brought with him. Although he tried to read, exhaustion soon overcame him, and the Bible dropped against his chest. A handmade bookmark fell to the floor.

Katy picked it up and read, " 'The Lord bless you and keep you; the Lord make his face shine upon you and be gracious to you; the Lord turn his face toward you and give you peace.' Numbers 6:24–26."

The scripture Granny had recited when she tucked Katy in at night. Then, finding peace seemed so simple. Now, it seemed impossible.

Katy marked his page and laid the Bible on the floor next to him. She tried to relax, but the laziness of the day made it difficult. Not even the added comfort of her sleeping arrangements helped.

A baby's cries broke through Katy's presleep stage and brought back the recurring nightmare of Bethany's screams. They had been at the ice cream shop when the stranger grabbed her child. When she tried to stop him, he punched her in the face. The clerk called for help, but it was too late. Katy struggled to her feet as Bethany fought her captor. His mask nearly slid off as he darted through the exit door and jumped into the backseat of an SUV with dark windows and no plates. The last store before the mall exit. Why hadn't she chosen one of the kiosks deep in the center? Maybe then she would have had time to do something.

She buried her face in the pillow to stifle the sobs. Eventually she cried herself to sleep and woke to find Richie preparing to leave.

He invited her to church, but Katy chose to remain at the shelter. A few kids wandered over to request a story, and she obliged. Sitting in the chair made her back ache, so she returned to her improvised bed and drifted off again.

"Katy, wake up," Richie called. "They're letting the residents go home. You can go with me, and we'll try to get back onto the island. I hope there's someone at the bridge who knows me. I left my permit in the truck."

Richie helped her stand. "I'll load the car." He rolled sleeping bags and repacked her suitcases.

"It's my junk," she protested. "Why should you do all the work?"

He glanced up from his kneeling position. "Please. I don't want to risk your injuring yourself further."

Katy sat and pulled on her sneakers. As Richie made his last trip out, she stood and folded the chair. She carried it to the car and handed it to him.

While he packed the car, she settled behind the wheel. Richie climbed into the passenger seat and directed her back to familiar territory. Pulling in behind the long line of cars, Katy braked and tried to calm her growing agitation. Already she'd seen considerable damage. "Was this storm worse than the others?"

"More rain. I suspect some areas along the river will experience significant flooding."

She allowed the car to roll forward and strained to look ahead. She couldn't see the bridge.

"Katy, I meant it when I asked if you wanted to talk."

She found his gaze fixed on her. Katy allowed her gaze to drift to the waterway in the distance and answered, "I know."

"If you'd like to tell me about your daughter. . .I'm a good listener."

Katy wasn't used to such persistence in a man. Maybe it was the counselor in him. "You've already gone far beyond expected to help a stranger. I'm not proud of my behavior."

"You were frightened."

What would he think if she admitted she was still frightened? Nearly strangled by the fear she would never find her child. Afraid she couldn't manage on her own until she did.

They inched toward the bridge. One by one, vehicles were cleared or rejected. When their turn came, Richie climbed from the car and spoke over the top. "Hey Curt, my truck broke down on Friday, and I left it over at the Lennons' cottage. My permit is in the truck."

The officer nodded. "Take it slow. There's extensive damage to parts of the island."

Katy trembled. How extensive? One part of her wanted to know the truth, while another wanted to push back the clock to the time when she'd slept unaware of approaching danger.

Driving well under the posted speed limit, Katy didn't like what she was seeing. Some residents along the waterway had dragged water-soaked furniture outside. Seeing their lives abandoned on the side of the street made her sad.

For the most part, rows of houses stood just as before the storm, some showing the aftereffects of the hurricane, but just one street down from the Lennons' she could see the ocean had claimed one house and another leaned drunkenly toward the water. She spotted Richie's truck resting just underneath the Lennons' deck. The vehicle had taken out a support post, and the deck had dropped over the abandoned vehicle. Debris littered the area.

"Better stop here. You don't want to puncture a tire."

Katy climbed out, her stunned gaze taking in the aftermath of the storm.

On a beautiful, sunny day just five days before, she'd followed the map Melody provided, driven over the drawbridge, veered left past the town complex and museum, and continued to the stoplight. She'd noted the JOHNNY MERCER'S PIER sign Melody indicated as a marker and turned left again.

Following Lumina Avenue, Katy had found the large hotel and read the concrete post markers until she found the street. She ignored the NO TRESPASSING, DEAD END signs and paused to study her temporary home. Not ultrafancy but obviously well loved. She parked underneath the two-storied sea blue cottage. Like most beach communities, the closely grouped houses didn't allow for much privacy.

Grabbing the bag of perishable groceries, she'd trekked up the stairs and let herself into the house. Katy found the kitchen and shoved the food into the fridge. Pulling back the drapes covering the french door, she turned the lock and stepped out on the oceanfront deck.

Sea oats rustled on the dunes. Katy had found the trail and caught her first glimpse of the Atlantic Ocean. Its vastness left her breathless. Beautiful silvery gray water glimmered beneath the brilliant sunlight. Waves rolled in and diminished as they slid back from the white sandy shore.

Sunseekers lay stretched out on chairs and bright beach towels, their bodies glistening with sunscreen. Children and adults frolicked in the waves, their laughter floating along with the cries of the seagulls. One or two jogged along the beach just out of reach of the incoming waves.

That day she'd dreamed of eventually bringing Bethany to this cottage. Now she didn't know what to expect.

Richie uncovered a surfboard and leaned it against the house. "No telling who this belongs to."

His comment jerked her back to the present. Katy spotted an item she recognized.

When she couldn't pick up the flowerpot from the Lennons' deck railing, she let out a frustrated groan.

"I'll get it." He picked up several more items and piled them underneath the house.

The oceanfront side sustained the majority of the damage. From this vantage point, the gaping hole left by the previously boarded and now missing french doors gave no indication of the damage within. The strength ebbed from her body.

Richie's arm slipped about her waist. "Why don't you wait in the car?"

She couldn't hide. Katy shook her head. "I have to see. Let's go in the other side."

"We can try, if the door isn't blocked."

Even after they unlocked the door, it resisted their efforts. Richie jogged around the house. A couple of minutes later, the door opened with more than a little persuasion on his part.

A tidal wave of grief washed over her. The cozy cottage was no more. Upended, the refrigerator lay across the arched entry to the kitchen. The juxtaposition of items shocked Katy even more.

A shelving unit hung on the wall, every item neatly in place while other items tumbled and tilted at odd angles about the room. The wooden table from the kitchen lay top down on the saturated living room carpet. Three of the chairs littered the room, and Katy wondered what had happened to the fourth.

The house reeked, the stench building until Katy thought she'd be sick. She cupped a hand over her nose and mouth. "What is that smell?"

"Fish and sewer. It gets worse."

How could it possibly get worse? Katy thought.

"Is this all rainwater?"

"Probably storm surge. The force of the winds swirling around in the storm combines with normal tides and creates a storm tide. It can increase the mean water level fifteen feet or more. Water is heavy, and the extended pounding waves can demolish a structure." Throw rugs and carpet squished underneath their feet. Even the overstuffed chenille sofa seemed to have sucked up a good amount of water.

One fist came to her mouth, keeping back the scream. "Oh Richie," she sobbed. "What am I going to do?"

❧

He'd witnessed that same anguish in so many following the hurricanes. But Katy's despair hit him hard. He had to help her. "Let's get out of here.

I need to make a phone call."

She followed him out the door, waiting while he locked up. The irony struck him as he considered the open side, but he'd take care of that soon. He took out the borrowed cell phone and moved away. Dialing the number from memory, Richie felt relieved when the frail voice came over the line. He'd talked to his great-aunt before the storm and knew she planned to stay in Wilmington with some of her friends.

"Richie. Thank God. Did your house survive the storm?"

She always placed others before herself. "I don't know yet. Is your place okay?"

"Yes, praise the Lord."

Richie moved on to his reason for calling. "I need to ask a favor. There's a young woman. . ." He paused, realizing he didn't know her full name. "Katy is staying in the Lennons' cottage, and it's a mess. Can I bring her over? I'd take her to a hotel, but she hurt her back, and I don't want to leave her alone."

"You know there's room for you both."

She always had room for him and his friends. "Thanks, Aunt Lucille. See you soon."

He turned back and caught Katy staring at the cottage in abject horror.

"My aunt has a room you can use."

When she didn't respond, Richie took her hand. It felt moist and clammy, and her breathing was rapid and shallow. Katy was nearing a complete meltdown. His arm went about her waist, and he urged her toward the car and into the passenger seat. Rental or not, she was in no shape to drive. He prepared a mental argument, but she remained silent.

"Katy? Are you okay? Did you hear what I said?"

Her head lay against the seat back. "Why would she take in a stranger?"

"Aunt Lucille lives in the old family home. Always has an extra room. Let's drive over there now. You can meet her and see what you think. I hope this works for you. At least until you're feeling better and some decision can be made about the house."

"Your house," Katy said with a gasp. "You don't know if it's okay."

"We'll drive by on the way to Aunt Lucille's."

Tears pooled in her eyes. Katy sniffed and said, "I've been nothing but a bother."

Taking her hand, Richie squeezed gently. "Hey, you could say the same about me. My truck wasn't going anywhere."

As he drove, she stared out the window. "There's no rhyme or reason to the destruction. How can one place be in ruins while the next appears undisturbed?"

"No one but God can answer that."

His home was only one street over. Richie found himself among the more fortunate residents. Like Aunt Lucille, he praised God that his home had received minimal damage.

"Why aren't you worried?"

"It's just a house."

"It's your home," she countered stubbornly. "How can you say it doesn't matter?"

"I'd miss it if it weren't here, but life goes on."

❧

Sometimes it does, she thought. Other times, life drew to a dead halt. One thing for sure, nothing was ever the same after the destruction.

Katy wondered why he didn't experience the same sickening sense of loss as others. A section of stairs was missing, so he grabbed hold of the post supporting the decking and swung himself up. A couple of minutes later, he disappeared inside.

When he returned, Richie placed a bag into the backseat. "Better than I'd hoped." He backed toward Lumina Avenue. "Some missing shingles, and I'll have to dig out underneath the house and replace the stairs. We installed hurricane shutters, so the windows are still in place. Best of all, we still have beachfront property," he offered with a huge grin. "Aunt Lucille's place is down on the north end."

Several minutes later, Richie braked and pointed to the big multistoried pink house that sat on a slightly larger lot facing the beach. The beautifully landscaped area boasted a number of trees and shrubs in pink, lavender, and white. This area appeared to have avoided the worst of the storm.

"It's wonderful."

"I helped Aunt Lucille redo the landscaping last year. She wanted crepe myrtles and palms." He pointed to the side. "Those are oleanders, and the big flowered shrubs are hydrangeas. I don't even want to think about how much those rocks weigh."

"It's gorgeous."

"My dad spent summers here with his parents and Aunt Lucille's family. After my grandparents and Aunt Lucille's husband died, it was just Aunt Lucille and her daughter. Maria and her family died in a car accident about ten years ago."

Katy smiled sadly. "How old is your aunt?"

"You never ask a Southern lady's age," he declared with a broad grin, "but I think she's in her seventies."

She followed Richie inside. He introduced her to Lucille Miller, and Katy soon found herself in an oceanfront bedroom. "Why would you do this? You don't even know me."

Lucille busied herself turning back the bed, smoothing the old-fashioned chenille spread along with the blanket and sheet. "Child, you're not the first to shelter in this old place. When God blesses you, you have to pass it on."

Katy believed in helping others, but right now she could hardly help herself. She fought to concentrate. The stabbing pain tormented her. She sank down on the side of the bed. "The cottage. . ."

The elderly woman patted her shoulder. "Rest, dear. Richie will handle that for the Lennons."

Later Katy came downstairs and found them in the sitting room. The windows and doors were open, and the breeze from the ocean made the room comfortable despite the lack of air-conditioning.

"Looks like I'll need to stay until I get the steps replaced and find a new vehicle," Richie told his aunt. "My truck drowned."

"Was it insured?" Katy asked.

He looked up and grinned. "Hello, sleepyhead. Feeling better?"

Uncomfortably aware of her appearance, Katy smoothed her hair and wrinkled outfit. She'd love nothing more than a shower and change of clothes.

Lucille rose from the sofa. "I'll get our dinner."

"Don't worry about that old truck," Richie said. "It's run on prayer for years."

Katy shuffled into the antique-filled room. Obviously, Lucille crocheted. Doilies dotted every surface. She chose an armless antique rocker and eased onto the edge of the seat. "If you hadn't been boarding up the house, you'd have been off the island."

"Wasn't meant to be." Richie filled a glass from the pitcher on the coffee table. Handing it to her, he said, "I secured the house."

Katy appreciated the tartness of the homemade lemonade. She became aware of the roar of the waves. The same waves that had calmed her stressed nerves now made her fear their power. She carefully placed the glass on a coaster atop the antique table.

"When can I go back?"

"Aunt Lucille won't mind your company for a few days."

They glanced up when the elderly woman wheeled a tea cart into the room. A kerosene lamp sat on the cart, ready to push back the impending darkness. "It's wonderful having you here. Richie, will you say grace? We have sandwiches and fresh fruit for supper."

Katy bowed her head. His prayer was more than thanks for their food. He spoke praise for their survival, their community, and asked for continued blessings as people dealt with the outcome of the hurricane.

Lucille passed around plates, and Katy bit into the cold ham, lettuce, and tomato sandwich. It tasted so good she nearly drooled.

"What brings you to the beach?" Lucille asked conversationally. "Business or pleasure?"

Katy dabbed at her mouth and said, "I've come to find my missing daughter."

Lucille gasped. "Oh gracious, child, what happened?"

Burning agony formed a huge knot in Katy's throat. Her appetite disappeared and she set her plate back on the cart. "My husband and I separated earlier this year. He took Bethany.

"I had no idea where to look for them until my friend found Jack's obituary on the Internet. I came right away. I spoke with the detective, but he said Jack didn't have a child with him. I hoped to talk to Jack's brother, but I hurt myself and Hurricane Kirk moved in."

Richie dropped his sandwich. "Jack?"

Katy nodded. "Jack Sinclair."

Lucille gasped again, and Richie's expression hardened.

"Is something wrong?" she asked, glancing from one to the other.

"Jack was my half brother."

Everything clicked. The brother who died recently was her husband. "Did the detective give you my number? He said he would." In a flash, she moved to where he sat. "Where is Bethany? She's not dead. I know she's not." She grabbed the front of his golf shirt, her tone approaching near hysteria.

Richie pulled her hand away. "Jack never mentioned a child to my mother."

Katy couldn't have been more shocked if he'd slapped her. "You have to know where she is," she whispered brokenly.

Eyes she'd once considered warm and caring now glared coldly. "I didn't know he was here until I saw the John Doe photo on the news."

Her legs gave way, and she sank to the floor. "What did he do with her?"

"There was no child."

"There is. Your parents. Do they know where she is?"

"You leave my parents alone," Richie all but spat at her. "They've suffered enough. They don't know about your daughter. They would have told me. We don't keep secrets in our family."

"Apparently Jack did." Katy grabbed the chair arm and struggled to her feet. "I need to leave."

"No, child," Lucille protested. "You're family. You have a right to be here."

"She has no rights." Richie's vehemence echoed throughout the room. "She's the reason Jack's dead."

Katy stared. How could he think that? After everything Jack had done to her and their daughter, not to mention her family, Richie had no right to blame her for his brother's actions.

"You don't understand. Jack..."

"No, you don't understand," Richie interrupted. "If your child is dead, you'll experience what my mother has gone through with the loss of her son."

Waves of darkness washed over her, and Katy slipped into the void. In her head, she shouted, *No!* but the word locked deep inside and couldn't escape.

Chapter 3

Richie! How could you be so cruel?" Lucille demanded, bending over Katy's still form to pat ineffectually at her wrists and cheeks. "Just think of the damage she's done to her poor back."

Chastened, he said, "Let me move her to the sofa."

"You think we should?"

Her worried question made him feel even more like a heel.

Despite her state of unconsciousness, Katy was light as a feather in his arms. After placing her on the sofa, he stepped aside to allow his aunt access.

"We need the smelling salts."

Richie retrieved the first aid kit from the bathroom. "This stuff has been around since you were her age," he said as he crushed the tiny vial and passed it to her.

Lucille passed the salts beneath Katy's nostrils. She reacted to the strong odor. "It still works."

She steadied Katy on the sofa, smoothing back her bangs. "How do you feel?"

Gripped by such strong emotions that he wanted to put his fist through a wall, Richie started toward the door.

"Where are you going?" Lucille called.

"I need to walk."

"Don't go far. Remember the curfew."

The law-enforced post-hurricane curfew was the last thing on his mind as he ran outside.

Though he wanted to slam it, Richie closed the screen door softly behind him. He ran down the steps and hurried over the dunes. His bare feet pounded against the damp sand of the beach.

The evening sky was clear, the growing moon hanging high in the distance. The breeze cooled his heated skin. Richie tripped over a piece of driftwood, as darkness hid the evidence of the previous night's storm.

He scrambled up. Katy was Jack's wife. Again fury, blacker than a summer thunderstorm cloud, welled up inside him. Why had God brought her into his life now? Hadn't his family been through enough?

Forgiveness.

How could they forgive? They loved Jack, and to tell his mother of yet another loss would only cause her greater distress. He had to be sure before he said anything. He would verify the child's existence. And whether she was Jack's child. Quite possibly that was why his brother never said anything. He wouldn't be the first man to be duped by the woman he loved.

Fresh grief encompassed him. Little more than a week before, his family received the news that devastated them in different ways. Richie felt the los of his brother deeply. The reality of knowing he'd never see Jack again, neve experience the brotherly bond he craved, hurt so much.

His mother grieved as a parent who never expected her child to die befor her. Jack had never returned home after his college graduation. Cynthia Taylo had made excuses for her older son, but she hadn't understood why he stayed awa Their separation had burdened her for years, and now it was too late.

When Richie's dad suffered a heart attack after the funeral, Richie feare his mother might never overcome her sorrow if she lost her husband as well.

Now they could have lost a grandchild. A little girl named Bethany. Hov could they have kept her a secret from her family? And if Jack brought her t North Carolina, where was she?

Richie slowed to a walk as he approached the house. He could run t another state, but he wouldn't find the answers tonight. Nor would Kaitlir Sinclair fool him again.

Richie let himself into the house and found his aunt waiting for him. "I'n sorry."

"You should apologize to Katy. I've never known you to act that way."

"I couldn't help myself."

"Yes, you could," Lucille countered. "You know there are two sides t every story. You can't go off half-cocked and play judge and jury before yo even hear her side of the situation."

"I know her side."

"You know nothing except what your mother said Jack told her," Lucill said. "Hearsay, Richie."

"Why, Aunt Lucille? Why does she have to show up now when we'r grieving for Jack?"

"What about Katy? Is she allowed to grieve?"

"He said their marriage was over."

"You can love someone you can't live with. She's in agony over her child Certain Jack's involved."

"Why wouldn't Jack tell us about his daughter?" Richie asked. "He had t know we'd be thrilled. I want answers."

"You need to remember Katy has feelings, too. Apologize to her anc maybe she'll give you the answers."

Richie fell asleep that night thinking about what his aunt had said. He didn't like this anger that overwhelmed him at the thought of Jack's senseles death. He'd never forget seeing that sketch of Jack. John Doe, they called him

Richie had contacted them immediately and identified his brother. The police released Jack's body, and he confronted the task of informing his parents They were vacationing with friends in Florida, and telling them was the mos difficult thing he'd ever done.

No one contacted Katy. They couldn't. The only phone number they hac was Jack's cell. The only address an old New York address with an expirec forwarding order. Maybe they should have been more motivated to find her.

The news of Jack's death shocked everyone. At first they said it couldn't be true, but as facts came out, doubts crept in. People started to look at him with pity.

Richie was glad his parents weren't around to see that. He'd promised to keep them informed and sent them home after the funeral. Two nights later Lucy called to tell him their father had suffered a heart attack.

Now Katy had shown up, claiming Jack had taken their child. The situation became more confusing by the day. He would discuss this with his boss after his morning appointments at the counseling center. Though he'd never thought he'd need a psychologist, Glenda had become his sounding board since Jack's death.

Richie threw on jeans and a T-shirt and grabbed a change of clothes. He'd shower at the pastor's house. Maybe even ask if he could stay for a few days. Just until he got his utilities restored and some things straightened out at home. Richie sighed. He needed to stay here. After all, he had brought Katy to Aunt Lucille's home.

Downstairs, he found her on the sofa. *Lying in wait,* Richie thought as he picked up his briefcase. He greeted her coolly.

"Your aunt prepared breakfast on the grill."

"I'll get something later."

"I'll find another place today."

He paused. "Not on my account. Aunt Lucille says you're welcome. It's her home."

"You're wrong about me," she said, her voice wavering.

He stared at her. "Why are you here?"

"Because I believe if Jack was here, Bethany's here, too. The Las Vegas police are calling it a stranger abduction, but Jack's involved. I know he is."

"My brother wasn't a criminal."

She didn't back down. "I loved Jack Sinclair with all my heart, but he was no saint."

"Probably had to do with the company he kept."

Her indrawn breath told him the jab had hit home.

"It's possible, though that company wasn't me or Bethany. He took everything I had to give, including my daughter, and threw my love for him back in my face."

Her sad expression made Richie regret his sarcasm. "Did Jack actually take his daughter?"

"No," she admitted, adding, "but I'm certain he was involved with the kidnapping."

Richie stared at her. "Has anyone seen her with Jack?"

"Well, no," Katy admitted, rubbing her hands along jean-clad thighs. "He provided the appropriate alibis and spouted all the expected fatherly words."

"Have you received a ransom note?"

"No. The only one who stood to benefit was Jack. He knew we'd do anything to get her back."

"You said she's a beautiful child. There are people who prey on pretty children."

"They don't grab children holding their mother's hand in an ice cream shop."

"You can't prove it was Jack or that he had anything to do with her kidnapping. Courts don't convict on gut instinct." Richie walked out the door.

Katy followed. "He did it. I know he did. We hired a private investigator to look for Jack. He couldn't find a trace of him anywhere."

"Maybe he didn't want you to find him," he said without turning back.

"If he was such a concerned father, why did he vanish into thin air?" Katy called. "Wouldn't you want the police to know where you were if your child was missing?"

That stopped him. Richie didn't want her logic to make sense. "It's impossible. There are too many ways to track someone. What about his social security number, credit cards, bank accounts, his car?"

"Jack handled our finances. Insisted it was his role and I should trust him. The police went through our files. Evidently he made certain there wasn't one piece of information left that would lead anyone to him." She moved slowly, coming to lean against the deck rail. "He disappeared within a week of the day Bethany was taken," Katy said, counting off points on her fingers. "No one knows where he went. He wasn't working. If his name was on another bank account, they couldn't find it. Believe me, they tried."

"There was no child."

Her face went deathly white. He felt heartless.

"You think lashing out at me will avenge this role you've assigned me in his death?"

Richie knew it wouldn't. "I'm sorry. I didn't mean to upset you last night and I don't want to do so again today." He massaged his forehead. "Could you describe the man who took her?"

"The sketch artist rendered a drawing, but nothing stood out. Muscular, average height, ski mask pulled down over his face. I caught a brief glimpse when Bethany knocked his mask up but not enough to identify him."

"What are the Las Vegas police doing?"

"Amber Alerts. Code Adams. APBs. They even checked me for DNA because the man punched me in the face, but he wore gloves. I'm a suspect too, so they're telling me as little as possible. The day it happened, they set up roadblocks, called in air support, and even coordinated a manhunt, with no results. They tracked the vehicle through traffic light cameras until they lost it and later found it abandoned. Turns out the SUV was reported stolen two days before the incident. They found strands of Bethie's hair in the vehicle.

"They've checked sex offenders and other criminals connected with kidnapping for money schemes. They've interviewed me and my family. Basically everyone we know. And strangers at the mall. Plus the abduction is in the media.

"Jack showed up with his airtight alibi," she said with a sarcastic laugh. "He even took and passed a polygraph. After he disappeared, they started digging into his past. Checking out his associates. Still, it all takes time, and my baby has been missing for two weeks."

"How did you learn he was dead?"

"On the Internet. Melody Lennon-Gerald set up a Google alert, and it just popped up one day."

Richie felt his head would burst. "I have to go."

"We're victims, too," Katy called after him. "Tell me where Bethany is, and we'll get out of your life forever."

"Why won't you listen? I don't know where she is. I didn't even know she existed."

Katy dropped her face into her hands and sobbed. "I know Jack was involved."

"If he was, it was because you forced him to take action," Richie said so coldly it scared him.

"He wasn't a fit father."

"He told Mom nothing he did was enough for you."

"All I wanted was his love."

He couldn't help but look back at her. Richie warned himself not to be tricked by her pleading gaze. "But you took much more."

She looked as though she pitied his misguided thinking. "I wasn't the manipulator in the relationship. I don't know what he did with Bethany, but I know she isn't dead. She's your niece. I don't care if you believe me. You have to know whom Jack trusted."

"If she is my brother's child, I'll help for her sake and because it's what God would expect."

"She's his," Katy said. "I can prove it."

Richie said nothing further as he walked down the stairs to his borrowed truck.

⌒

Richie's skepticism raised doubts. Katy thought back to the day Bethany disappeared. Had she missed something?

"Where is she?" she had demanded, flinging herself at Jack when he finally showed up at the mall. He grabbed her arms and shoved her away, glancing over his shoulder at the officer. "She's been like this ever since she left me."

Katy wanted to wipe the sympathy off their faces. "You know where she is."

"How can you think I'd do that to my baby?"

Jack's pretense made her even angrier. "You've done worse."

"Your welfare has always been my priority."

Katy almost gagged. She might have believed him at one time but never again. "*You've* been your priority. You may charm these men into believing you're innocent, but I know differently. What do you want? Money? Isn't that the reason you tried to blackmail my father? Threatened to make sure he'd never see us again if he didn't fork over the cash?"

"I have an alibi, Katy." He glanced at the young woman standing next to him. "I was nowhere near here when this happened. And if we're flinging accusations, I'd say it's more likely you and your family staged this to keep me from my child."

The police didn't seem to find it strange that Jack had thought to come prepared with proof it couldn't be him. "We don't need to *stage* anything. The court order prohibiting you from seeing Bethany speaks for itself. And if your alibi had the sense God gave a gnat, she'd run as far away from you as possible."

"Mr. and Mrs. Sinclair," the detective called, "this isn't getting us anywhere."

She whirled about. "He knows where she is."

"Don't start again, Kaitlin," Jack ordered, turning to the officer. "What's being done to find our daughter?"

"We've notified the appropriate agencies and put out a description of the vehicle."

"A black SUV with tinted windows. There are a million black SUVs in this town alone," Katy said.

"We're following all leads. Would you be willing to work with an artist?"

Jack looked at her with surprise. "You saw him?"

She nodded. "Bethany knocked his mask up. I got a glimpse of his face."

"That's wonderful."

Katy didn't believe he truly felt that way. "I'm not sure I saw enough to help."

"We think you'll recall more as you work with the artist."

"She is an artist. She can probably draw him herself. Think hard, Katy. Our daughter's life is at stake."

Katy had returned home feeling even more discouraged. The police had too few clues, and nothing changed over the passing days. Katy read that a child went missing every forty seconds in the United States, over 2,100 per day. Her baby had become a statistic. One of the 24 percent kidnapped by a stranger.

There had been nothing until the obituary showed up. The police weren't telling her anything. She had to know. And now Richie Taylor had relegated her to the villain role, and nothing she could say or do would change his mind. She sank into a chair and stared out over the ocean. Tears trailed along her face.

Lucille Miller touched her arm. "Are you okay?"

She glanced up. "I'll never be okay until I find my child."

"I'm sorry, Katy. There was a side to Jack very few people ever saw. Outwardly, he was personable and charismatic but capable of doing great wrong. His family placed him on such a pedestal."

"You're his great-aunt, too?"

"No," she said with a shake of her head. "Richard Sr. is my nephew. Cynthia and Richard married when Jack was nearly four. Jackson Sinclair, her first husband, was always after the fast dollar. Couldn't keep a job."

"Always someone else's fault." Katy spoke softly, recalling this facet of Jack's personality with ease.

"Cynthia got pregnant right away. I think she hoped fatherhood would calm his wild ways."

Is there such a thing as a mirror nightmare? She'd hoped fatherhood would force Jack to grow up.

"When Jackson died in a motorcycle accident, Cynthia and Jack were devastated. Cynthia knew Richard from high school. He'd lost his wife and was raising Lucy alone. They married and made a good life together. Richie completed the family. Don't blame him for being upset. He idolized Jack."

The rockers moved easily on the weathered wooden deck. Katy found comfort in the gentle sway that reminded her of the hours in Bethie's infancy when they rocked away chunks of every night. A roll-out sunshade covered one end of the deck, and baskets of huge green ferns hung from hooks. The breeze off the ocean was pleasant despite the July heat.

"You had sole custody of Bethany?" Lucille asked.

Katy nodded. "Jack's erratic behavior frightened me."

"What happened?"

A vivid recollection of the worst judgment call of her life came to mind. They were both going stir-crazy. Bethie had whined for days. Her daughter liked going places, seeing and doing things. "It was the first time we'd left my parents' house alone in weeks. Jack had stopped threatening me, and I suppose I felt a false sense of security.

"I can still hear her screams." She paused, forced to consider the possibility that someone other than her husband might be involved. "What if Richie's right? What if Jack didn't take Bethany?"

"Surely the police checked every possibility?"

"But what if I endangered her by insisting it was Jack? The police talked to him, and he said he didn't know anything. He had an alibi."

Lucille reached to pat her hand. "Katy honey, you have to prepare yourself for the possibility she might not come back. It doesn't matter how old your child is. It hurts, but you have to be strong."

Katy hovered on the brink of darkness.

"You're looking awfully pale again. Lie back and close your eyes."

She craved the oblivion she'd find in sleep, but Lucille was right. She had to deal with this. "How will I ever survive without my sweet Bethany?"

"One day at a time." Lucille drifted off in her own private thoughts. "When they told me Maria was dead, I didn't think I'd survive. I felt destined to be alone, but God was good. He sent family and friends to help me handle the grief. I still miss her, but I know I'll see her again."

"Being Bethany's mom is who I am," Katy whispered. "Am I expected to start over, to forget her? That's what my father suggested." That he could make such a callous comment speared her heart each time it came to mind.

"Pray for your daughter, Katy. Our God's in the miracle business. If He wants her to come home, He'll bring her. But you need to prepare yourself for either eventuality." They sat in silence, each considering what Katy might have to face in the very near future. After a while, Lucille asked, "Do you think Jack was selling drugs?"

"I don't know. He always had money, and when I asked where it came from, he wouldn't say. I'm so thankful we couldn't get more than the monthly allowances from my trust fund. Jack would have gone through it in no time.

"My father helped him get jobs, but Jack claimed they weren't right for a man with his qualifications. I suggested he find a job he liked better. Apparently he excelled at unemployment."

"Now that sounds like him," Lucille agreed. "My friend taught him, and she told me he was disrespectful and disruptive. Cynthia said the woman couldn't handle a spirited boy like Jack. No one could. Cynthia spent nearly as much time in the principal's office as Jack did."

"But he was a Christian," Katy protested. Just before they met, she'd renewed her own relationship with God and wouldn't have married him otherwise. During their philosophical discussions, she'd been convinced he loved the Lord with all that was in him.

"To say he wasn't would be passing judgment, but I witnessed Jack doing things he shouldn't and told him so. Mostly he ignored me, but when he got older, he called me a nosy old woman and told me to mind my own business."

Jack had excelled in being disrespectful. The number of people who witnessed the darker side of her husband's personality grew daily. "Did you like Jack?"

"What wasn't to like? He was a rascal. He could charm his way out of anything."

Katy agreed. "I was blinded by love." Though she felt very comfortable with the woman, she paused before asking, "Lucille, is Richie lying?"

"Richie never lies. If he knew where your child was, he'd tell you."

"He's so angry."

"All of them hold you responsible for the changes in Jack. He didn't tell them he was back, but he contacted Cynthia after you left. I suspect you and your family were blamed for his failings."

"And he never mentioned he had a daughter?"

"They don't know about your little girl," Lucille said confidently. "I don't envy Richie having to tell them. Jack's death nearly destroyed his parents. It will be hard to tell them their granddaughter might be. . ."

Her head pounded as Lucille's words trailed off. "No," she cried. "Bethany isn't dead. I know that in my heart."

Lucille said nothing more on the subject. "Do you have a picture?"

"In my purse."

Katy excused herself and located the album. Opening it to the most current photo of her precious baby, she touched the picture as though somehow they might connect. She returned to the deck. "This was taken just before she was kidnapped." Thumbing through the pages, Katy lingered over Bethany's newborn photo. "She was a gorgeous baby."

"Did Jack want a child?"

"No."

"Why did you leave him?"

"I overheard him attempting to blackmail my father. He insinuated people would be shocked to learn Cliff Dennison deprived his daughter and granddaughter. When my dad suggested they test his theory, Jack threatened to take us and disappear. I left him, and Jack never got any more money from my father.

"I don't understand why Jack felt we were entitled to live as well as they did. My father worked hard to support his family. I never expected him to support us. I worked until Bethany was born. After that, we lived off the monthly allowance from my trust fund. I didn't ask for handouts. I had enough."

"And Jack never did. Greed was another of his traits."

"You disliked him," Katy said.

"I disliked the way he fooled his family."

"Jack hurt a lot of people in a very short time."

"And continues to do so from the grave," Lucille agreed. "I'm sorry about your little one, Katy. I'll pray for you both."

Prayer didn't help, Katy thought. At least hers hadn't. She started to rise from the chair.

"Where are you going? Lucille asked.

"I thought I might go to the cottage and see what I can accomplish."

"Leave that to Richie."

"He's not going to do anything to help me."

"Try not to judge him too harshly. Richie is the most honorable, kindest man you'll ever meet. He's struggling with this, but he'll come around. You'll see."

"I hope so. I need his help."

"Well, whatever you decide, remember a bedridden mother can't do much for her child."

Katy appreciated the wise counsel. "I need to schedule a follow-up doctor's appointment. I don't suppose a couple more days will make a difference."

Richie hadn't come around by the time he returned home that afternoon. It wounded her to the core, but Katy would never admit that to him. "I'm sorry about Jack," she said when he stepped onto the deck. "I loved him as long as he let me."

His gaze narrowed. "What does that mean?"

"At first, Jack made me feel special. I didn't know it was a pretense. I know even less about your family than you know about me. He said his mother was upset that we eloped, and we needed to give her time. Then we moved to Vegas, and whenever I suggested a visit, he put me off. He talked with her but never indicated she'd like to talk to me. After Bethany was born, he said he wanted us to meet his family but never made the arrangements."

She took a deep breath and admitted, "I didn't know he came from North Carolina. We met in New York. He never talked about his past."

"I don't want to hear this."

Katy noted the tired slump of his shoulders. Why did she always feel responsible? Maybe deep down she feared one rebellion had resulted in nothing but pain for the family she loved and now for the family who loved Jack.

She didn't fit the Dennison mold. Cliff, her father, demanded and controlled. Rachelle, her mother, believed her husband was always right. Her sister, Dina, was a chip off the old block. She understood their father because they were very alike.

In college, Katy opted for a liberal arts degree. Her father expected her to become a lawyer. Then she and Jack had eloped. Not only had she not married an approved candidate, she'd deprived them of the social event of the season. Maybe they would have been more forgiving if she'd let them have the expensive wedding. They disapproved of her wanting a child right away. Then they fought her because Katy wanted a normal childhood for her daughter, not snatched moments between socializing and career.

The argument with her dad was as fresh in her head as the day it happened. Ever since Bethany and Jack disappeared, Katy agonized over finding them, so frantic and desperate that she couldn't eat or sleep. She suffered from constant headaches and lost weight she couldn't afford to lose. She'd remained in her parents' home, arguing with her father over leaving the investigation to the professionals.

When Jack disappeared, her father hired a private detective to find him. He hadn't turned up anything. Katy thought him incompetent, but her father argued he was one of the best in the business.

After the obituary surfaced, the search intensified for a couple of days before her father called off the investigation. Cliff Dennison concurred with the investigator's belief that without a protector the child had to be dead.

That night at dinner, Katy announced, "I'm going to check this out for myself."

"Don't be foolish, Kaitlin."

"Let your father handle it," her mother said.

Katy loved her parents, but the emotional stress of the kidnapping had widened the rift between them. At eighteen, she'd decided not to become an attorney. He might not have sons to carry on the Dennison name, but her father was an equal opportunity parent. He planned on his daughters becoming stars in the legal arena, and her refusal disappointed him.

Instead, she made a name for herself at the art gallery where she worked. Her parents accepted her career choice and even looked to her for help with a couple of art investments. Then she'd met Jack Sinclair. "I don't like him," her father said when she brought him home for dinner. "Does he always talk about himself nonstop?"

She'd been so eager to get to know Jack that she hadn't noticed. "He's nervous," she defended.

Their opinion of Jack didn't change over time. After he proposed, her parents expressed strong reservations. They'd been so unequivocal that Jack suggested they elope.

"They'll come around after we're married. I love you, Katy. God brought us together. Don't let them stand in the way of our happiness. Marry me now."

She'd allowed herself to be convinced and had lived with the consequences ever since.

But marriage hadn't affected her father's attempts to manage her life. Jack assured that with his failure to provide for his family. Every time her parents offered them another gift, Katy refused while Jack accepted with an alacrity she found embarrassing.

"This new lead on Jack could take us to Bethany."

Cliff Dennison shook his head. "No, Kaitlin. It's time you faced facts. You're clutching at straws, hoping for a miracle. Bethany has been gone too long."

She winced at his comment. "I have to go where Jack went. To look for clues. Surely he wouldn't abandon her in a strange city."

"We tried to tell you Jack was no good, but you wouldn't listen."

Katy sighed. The story never changed. The old adage about making your bed had been tossed in her face about ten loads of laundry too many. Yet she'd tolerate it all over again for the one precious gift her marriage had given her. Bethany was the brightest star in her life. "You already know Jack's dead. Who do you expect to lead you to Bethany?"

"I can't stay here until the grief kills me. I loved Jack, and Bethany wasn't a mistake."

His frown showed nothing but displeasure. "The sooner you put this behind you, the better off you'll be."

Her father's words sucked the breath from her lungs. "How can you say that? Don't you love Bethie?"

"Yes, I love her, and I love you, but I've accepted the inevitable. There's little chance you'll ever find her. All you can do now is move on. Rebuild your life."

Katy's head moved in denial. "She's not dead. I'll find her in North Carolina."

"You'll get yourself killed. You have no idea what Jack was doing. With whom he associated."

"I'd rather be dead than live without my child."

"Don't ever say that again," he said sternly. "You will not die." He hugged her close. "I love you, Kaitlin. I know you doubt that at times, but your mother and I only want the best for you."

"Then you should understand, Daddy. Bethany is my life. I love her just as you love me."

"Katy honey, I don't want her to be dead either." He held Katy as she sobbed out her grief. "I wish it could be different."

Chapter 4

A couple of days after they returned to the island, the utilities were restored. Katy plugged the phone into the charger and went off to enjoy a long, hot shower. Then, wrapped in her robe, she settled on the bed and reached for her phone to check her voice mail. Her sister's angry demand that she call them came as no surprise.

"It's about time," Dina snapped. "We've been worried sick ever since we heard about that hurricane."

"A lot has happened since I arrived."

"What could be more important than telling your family you're alive?"

"The phones weren't working, Dina."

"You have a cell phone."

"The battery died, and I forgot my charger."

Katy couldn't help but think trouble followed her wherever she went. "I hurt my back again last Wednesday. Then the storm came in, and my rescuer turned out to be Jack's half brother."

Katy heard Dina's snort and could almost read her mind. How like Katy. She couldn't locate her husband or her child, but she could stumble upon Jack's relatives. "Richie Taylor boarded up the cottage for Mr. Lennon. It was almost three days before we learned of the connection."

"Has he been helpful?"

"Jack never told them about Bethany."

"You're kidding."

"I finally got Richie to admit she's Jack's daughter, but I'm right back where I started. He doesn't know where Bethany is either."

"Oh Katy honey, I'm sorry."

"The Lennons' cottage was damaged. I'm staying with Richie's great-aunt."

"You can't live like this. When are you coming home?"

"Without Bethany, I have no life."

"Katy, you're stronger than that," Dina chided.

Frustrated tears welled in her eyes at her sister's chastisement. "You wouldn't understand. I'd give my life for Bethie."

The silence stretched until Katy called Dina's name.

"Do you really think I didn't love Bethie?" Her voice quivered. "I adored her. I loved being her auntie Dina. I miss that sweet baby so much. It kills me to think she's no longer a part of my life. I wanted to see her grow up with my kids. But I refuse to blind myself to what this is doing to you."

"God's in the miracle business. I have to believe that." Even as Katy spoke the words, she felt remorse. She hadn't turned to God since this happened.

Why would He provide a miracle for her? "Until they find her body, I'll never believe she's dead."

"You need grief counseling."

"I need Bethany."

"Mom and Dad miss her, too. He gets upset when either of you are mentioned."

Katy loved her father but couldn't forget his comment. "He told me to forget them and move on."

"How long will you punish him for words he didn't mean? Words he regrets?"

"Dad never says anything he doesn't mean."

Dina sighed. "Sure he does, Katy. We all do. Is that why you're staying away? Do you want me to talk to him?"

Katy unwound the towel and dropped her wet hair over her shoulders. Dina hated getting involved in their arguments. "I'm following the only lead I have in hopes of finding Bethany. She's here somewhere. I know she is."

Dina sighed again. "And we're here when you need us. We never wanted this to happen. Dad said Jack was no good."

"Please don't start."

"Are you defending Jack after what he did to you and Bethie?"

Dina's incredulous tone stabbed at her. "No. I'm tired of having my poor judgment rubbed in my face. Jack fooled me. I'm not denying that, but maybe I'd have made wiser decisions if Dad hadn't intruded so much in our lives."

"Oh Katy, I don't want to argue with you. Please come home."

She should tell Dina she had thought about finding somewhere away from their parents to start over. "You know I can't."

"We love you, Katy."

"I love you, too. Tell Kevin I said hello."

"Call Mom and Dad, Katy."

"I will. I have to go, Dina."

Outside, Katy paced the wraparound porch. She had to do something. An idea occurred to her, and after getting dressed, Katy told Lucille she needed to run an errand. She drove into Wilmington. Using a map, Katy located the street where the police found Jack's body.

She parked, picked up the photos of Bethany and Jack, and started her own door-to-door search. The few people who responded to her knock either eyed her with suspicion or shook their heads negatively before closing the door in her face.

The last house on the block was a dilapidated structure sitting among knee-high weeds and appearing vacant. Though tempted to skip it, Katy forced herself up the cracked sidewalk and knocked. A man pulled the door open a crack.

"Sorry to trouble you, but have you seen either of these people?" She held out the photos.

The man glanced at them and yelled, "Hey Beau, there's a woman out here who wants to know about your old friend Jack."

Instinctively, Katy took a step back. The door flung open wide, and a more muscular man joined the first. Vague awareness barely registered before Katy took off running. The man cursed loudly and chased after her.

"Please, God," she whispered as she charged down the street, not daring to look back. She knew he wasn't far behind. "Please don't let him catch me."

The car came into view. She hit the UNLOCK and ALARM buttons at the same time. Breathless, Katy put on one last push and jerked the door open.

She barely made it inside before he caught up with her. The locks clicked in time with his grab for the door handle. Katy fumbled the key into the ignition. She screamed and hid her face when he banged his fists against the window. The relentless bleat of the car alarm brought no interested bystanders.

"We know who you are," he roared. "Give us our money."

The tires peeled rubber as she ran the stop sign and nearly hit the first man. The back glass exploded, and something hard thudded against the rear of her seat.

Katy stomped the gas pedal to the floor. She didn't let up for blocks. Let the police pull her over. In fact, she'd welcome a few squad cars in hot pursuit.

The rearview mirror drew her gaze. Had they followed? Katy barely checked traffic before turning onto the main street. A horn blared in warning. "Sorry," she mumbled.

Could that man have been the reason Jack came to this neighborhood? What did he mean by 'Give us our money'?

Shaking like a tree in a windstorm, Katy pulled into a sprawling parking lot filled with cars and stopped. She fumbled Richie's card and her cell from her purse. It took several attempts to dial his number. "Help me. Please."

"Katy," he called sharply. "What's happened?"

Through her tears, she managed to tell him what she'd done. "He said, 'Your old friend Jack.' How did he know that man?"

"Where are you now?"

She told him.

"I'll be right there. I'm calling the police. Don't leave the car."

<hr>

Richie pulled Katy close, shaken by the wash of emotions he experienced. Could Jack be involved as she suspected?

A hazy memory rose up to haunt him.

"Why can't I go with you?"

Jack sneered. "Me and my friends don't want no snot-nosed kid following us around."

"What's going on here?" their mother demanded.

"I told him he couldn't go. He's such a baby."

"Am not." Richie wiped his nose on his shirtsleeve.

"He needs a bottle, Mom."

His mother hugged him close. "You're too young, sweetie."

"But I want to go," he wailed.

"Too bad, kid," Jack said, flashing him a satisfied smile as he walked away.

Richie shook his head. Where had that memory come from? He leaned back and looked at Katy. "Promise me you won't do anything like that again."

She breathed in shallow, quick gasps. "Do you think he took my baby there?"

"I don't know," Richie said. "The police are here. Let them file a report, and we'll call the rental company to pick up the car. I'll take you back to Aunt Lucille's."

Katy stiffened. "I can't risk leading those men to her house."

"They won't know where you are. You have to leave this to the police, Katy."

"How can I do nothing?"

"I'm not suggesting you do nothing, just that you don't go off on your own like this again. There's no telling what would have happened if they'd caught you. You're lucky that brick didn't hit you in the head."

He remained by her side as Katy provided the officer with a statement and answered his questions. The definite thump in his chest was fear for her. Katy acted out of desperation to find her daughter. She didn't care what happened to herself.

He studied her closely. Pale, but the heat of the day flushed her skin to pink. He grasped her hand and noted the tremble had subsided slightly.

"I'm sorry," she whispered brokenly after the officer had gone. "So sorry."

Richie knew he had to help. He hugged her and said, "It'll be okay, Katy. We're in this together now."

❧

They visited the police station the next day.

"I'm sorry, Mrs. Sinclair," Detective Neumann said, offering her a seat. "The men had disappeared by the time we arrived."

"Could they have my child?" Katy repeated what the second man had said.

The detective shrugged. "It's a condemned house. According to the officers, there's no sign of a child."

"Do you think Jack went there to pay him off?"

"Hard to say."

His noncommittal reply didn't stop her. "He could have paid the men to kidnap Bethany and bring her here."

"Without proof, we can only speculate that he might have gone there with the intent of a payoff."

"Or he could have come to pay the ransom to get her back," Richie offered.

Katy glanced at Richie. She didn't want to hurt him or his family, but she refused to look through rose-colored glasses when it came to Jack. There was no ransom demand, and if there had been, Jack would have come to her father for money. They would never know Jack's intentions.

"If that were the case, he might still be alive if he'd trusted us to do our job." The detective cast a pointed glance in Katy's direction. "That includes you, too, Mrs. Sinclair. I realize you're desperate to find your child, but you need to understand your actions can jeopardize the case."

She nodded. "I didn't think. . ."

"Katy promised not to go off on her own like that anymore," Richie said.

"I don't want either of you taking chances."

They glanced at each other.

"Mrs. Sinclair, we need you to make arrangements to look through the mug shots to see if you can ID either of them."

"Yes. I'll do it now." She glanced at Richie. "I can call a cab after I finish."

"We can have an officer drop her off," Neumann countered.

"I'll stay."

Richie studied the books with her. Katy identified the first man.

"We'll bring him in for questioning, but I'd say he and his friend are long gone." Detective Neumann offered his hand. "Thanks for your help. We'll be in touch."

They walked out to the parking lot. "Why does every clue lead to a dead end?" she asked, not expecting an answer. "Do you think Jack brought his girlfriend here?"

Richie unlocked the doors. "Not many women would take on a child without compensation."

"Who said she didn't?" Katy climbed into the passenger seat and reached for the seat belt. "Detective Neumann said they turned the money over to the family. Where is it?"

"In a safety deposit box at the bank. We can make arrangements to pick it up if you need the funds."

Katy appreciated his honest accounting. His offer to give her the money surprised her. They had paid for Jack's funeral.

"I'm okay. So, what if the woman loved him enough to care for his child?"

"I suppose it's possible," Richie said, "but if she exists, why didn't she come forward to identify Jack?"

"I'm frightened, Richie. Surely he didn't leave a small child alone."

"He didn't plan to die, Katy. And you can't be sure he had her." Richie rested his hands on the steering wheel and stared out in the distance. "I'm not trying to be cruel. It's a reality you have to face."

Just brutally honest.

Chapter 5

Richie couldn't get Katy out of his head. There were too many unanswered questions. Nothing about her matched the portrait of the villainess Jack painted for their mother. He ran up the deck steps and found his great-aunt watering the ferns. "Where's Katy?"

Lucille looked worried. "She went to the cottage. I hope she doesn't overdo."

"I'll check on her." He started to leave and then turned back to Lucille. "Do you think she's telling the truth?"

Sadness filled the elderly woman's eyes. She nodded affirmation. "Yes, Richie, I do. Jack hurt her. And if he stole her child, she would hate him for that reason alone."

He rubbed his forehead. "I'm not so sure Jack took the child. Katy said a stranger grabbed Bethany. I agree the man who chased her seems a likely suspect, but how does that connect to Jack?"

"They knew Jack. Katy thinks he might have hired them," Lucille said. "Why didn't someone help her stop the man?"

"It happened too fast. The shop was near the mall exit, and he escaped before anyone could do anything." He paused, the grimness of the situation tearing at him. "I'm worried for her. I can't believe Bethany's survived so long without her parents."

"Pray, Richie. Sometimes that's all we can do."

"I am. I need to talk to Katy." He kissed her soft, wrinkled cheek. "See you later."

He found Katy in the cottage kitchen, looking like a teenager with her auburn hair brushed up into a ponytail. She wore short denim overalls over a pink tee, and bright yellow latex gloves covered her hands as she washed the lower walls with a bleach-scented concoction.

"Richie. Hi." She smiled self-consciously. "I think the smell is beginning to fade, don't you?"

He nodded. "Katy. . .about yesterday. . .I. . ." Richie began, breaking off when she held up her hands.

"Please don't," she pleaded, refusing to look at him. "Do you have any idea how difficult it is to be the only one who believes my child isn't dead?"

"Hope is a good thing," Richie agreed. "It keeps you going, but deep down inside you have to think that just maybe. . ."

"No!" Katy wailed. "I'd rather he have killed me than done this to her."

"Killed you?"

"Jack threatened my life a couple of times."

Surely he hadn't meant it. "Katy." Again, Richie hesitated. He had to know. "I'm trying to sort this out in my head and. . .I don't understand."

"Welcome to my world." Scorn laced her words.

"Aunt Lucille believes you. How did you convince her?"

She squeezed the sponge almost viciously and swiped at the trail of water running down the cabinet. "I told the truth."

"Jack told Mom you were very demanding."

Katy snorted. "And she believed him without question of course."

"Why would he lie? He needed support."

The irritated green gaze pinned him in place. "Did support include a check to cover our exorbitant lifestyle?"

He shrugged. "I don't know. Possibly." Their parents were very generous with their affection and money. "Why don't you take a break? Get some fresh air. Tell me what you've told Aunt Lucille."

She peeled off the gloves and hung them over the edge of the bucket. After removing two bottles of water from the small cooler, Katy followed him to the porch. He watched her gulp fresh air. After a couple of minutes, she sat in a rocker and pressed her foot to the floor, setting off the rhythmic movement.

"We lived in the house my parents bought and drove the vehicles they supplied. They even paid for the clothes Jack charged regularly on their store accounts. I don't imagine he shared those truths with his mother."

Richie frowned at her emphasis on *truths*. According to his mother, Katy was the big spender. "Did he work?"

"Now and then, but he had a million reasons why the jobs never worked out."

"How did you live?"

"After I gave up my job, the monthly allowance from my trust fund bought the groceries and kept the utilities on. Things were tight, but I wanted to be home with my child."

"But Mom said. . . He said. . ." Richie trailed off, not sure what to believe anymore.

"Please don't tell me any more of his lies. I don't want to hate Jack more than I already do."

"You hate him because you believe he stole Bethany?"

"Among other things," she said. Her voice thickened. "He was my husband. He promised to love me, but he lied."

"I'm sure he loved you both. Some men take longer to adapt to marriage and parenthood."

Katy's pitying expression spoke volumes. "I made all the sacrifices. Your brother wasn't a giver."

"What would he have gained by taking Bethany?"

"Enough money to ease his separation anxiety," she said, finger-quoting the last words.

That couldn't be right. No man willingly gave up his child for cash.

Her head rested against the back cushion. "I don't think Jack wanted to be a father."

"Why did you leave?"

Her pale skin reddened in a way that made her embarrassment plain. She covered the details of how Jack never spent time with them. She spoke of the way he pushed to control her trust fund and later attempted to coerce her father into giving him money.

"He said he'd make sure they never saw either of us again. I told Jack I'd never agree to that. He called me stupid and a few other names before he left to go out with his friends. I took Bethany and left that night.

"He called my cell and my parents' home and tried to sweet-talk me into coming back. I refused. He got angry and said I'd be sorry. Then one night, Jack came to the restaurant where we were dining and threw his beer bottle at me. The gash required several stitches, and I had a slight concussion. My father filed for a restraining order. He told the judge Jack was unstable.

"I was given sole custody of Bethany, and Jack continued to communicate threats. It got so bad they threatened him with jail time if he violated the restraining order. Then Bethany was abducted."

"Given all that, why didn't the police take you seriously when you said Jack was involved?"

"He had an alibi. He brought a woman with him and made certain the police considered me a spurned wife out for revenge."

Another woman? Violence? Blackmail? Richie needed time to assimilate all she'd said. He twisted the top back on the bottle and got to his feet. "Guess I'll work on the bathroom floor."

"Richie."

Her pain-filled gaze bothered him.

"It's okay that you don't believe me," she said. "You loved him. I did, too. I like to think that there were times when he wasn't so self-absorbed that he loved us back."

His lack of fairness hit him like a two-by-four upside his head. What right did he have to judge? Sure, Jack was his brother, but he'd been Katy's husband, the father of her child, a daughter he hadn't told his mother existed. Why had Jack hidden that from them?

"I'm sorry Jack hurt you." Richie took a couple of steps forward and said, "And I'm even sorrier I've hurt you. In the future, I promise to judge you on your own merits."

She flashed him the barest hint of a smile. "That's going to be difficult for you. Just don't be so blinded by your love that you get hurt. I believed in Jack, too."

Her sad expression was his undoing. Richie turned and went inside, afraid he'd reach out to her if he lingered.

A seed of doubt flowered in his head. What Katy said made sense. If

Jack wanted out of his marriage, he wouldn't want their mom to know she had a grandchild. Nothing would have kept her away from Bethany once she learned the truth.

Jack knew they would expect him to seek joint custody and support his child. If they didn't know about the child, he could divorce Katy, keep his secret, and they would never know he'd left his daughter behind.

Richie found the thought sickening. He believed children were a blessing, a gift from God. He loved them. At times, the church youth spent more time with him than their parents. They confided the good and bad, and he listened and advised. He would have liked nothing more than to share Jesus with his niece.

He heard Katy enter the house. She came to stand outside the bathroom door. "I like this tile. If it were mine, I'd tile the entire cottage. Carpet isn't a good choice for the beach."

"Funny you should say that. Mr. Lennon e-mailed and suggested I ask you to help me pick out tile for the rest of the house."

Katy smiled. "It's the least I can do since they were kind enough to loan me the place for as long as I need."

～

Returning to the cleaning, Katy considered what Richie had told her. She didn't doubt Jack lied to his family. Hadn't he told her often enough that she and Bethany cramped his style? She wanted the white picket fence, and he wanted the life of pleasure and excesses.

After a while the scents of bleach, wet, and mildew burned her nostrils. She might pretend things were improved at the cottage, but it would be a long time before the odors completely dissipated.

Katy went in search of Richie. "I'm going out onto the beach."

"Why don't you go back to Aunt Lucille's? I'll be finishing up here soon myself."

"I want to sketch an idea before I lose it."

Outside, Katy settled in the sand and appreciated the sun-soaked warmth. Leaning over a sketch pad she'd taken from her car, she used the carpenter's pencil she'd found on the kitchen counter to capture her character. Lost in the creation, she jumped when Richie spoke.

"What are you drawing?" He stepped closer to get a better look.

"Prop ideas. I'm thinking of making them from plywood for use with my storytelling. If I put face and arm holes in some, the kids can stand behind and have their photos taken."

Katy drew a wide sweep with the pencil. "I've always wanted a business that caters to kids. Story hours, dress up, tea parties, that kind of thing. I thought of calling it Just Imagine."

"Sounds like fun."

The ocean breeze whipped her hair about her face. She shoved it aside. "I've thought about staying here—" Katy broke off. "I'll decide after I find Bethie."

"Mind if I watch?"

She noted his failure to comment about her missing child. "I don't want to take you away from your work."

"I'm finished for today." Richie dropped down next to her. "Maybe you can give me a few pointers for murals for the church. Where did you learn to draw?"

She worked quickly, sketching the unique fun creature she pulled from her head. "I've always loved art. Bethie already shows talent. You should see her work."

"I'd love to."

She looked at him. "I have a couple of her drawings at Lucille's. They help me feel connected."

Katy refined her character as Richie talked about their lack of budget for murals. She glanced at him. "You don't have church members who draw?"

"Most of us can barely draw a straight line with a ruler. Have you ever done a mural?"

"I did Bethany's nursery. A forest." Katy remembered the pleasure she'd found in creating that special place for her baby. "She had trees and bunnies and squirrels. When she started to walk, she went around the room patting the walls.

"Later, when I took her to the park, she chased after the squirrels as fast as her tiny legs would carry her," she concluded with a strained laugh. "She cried when they ran up into the trees."

Richie placed his arm about her shoulders and drew Katy close. A couple of minutes passed before they separated. Richie shifted, and Katy pulled the pad to her chest.

"Would you consider painting murals for the children's church? There's no pay, but we could provide the supplies. The teens could help."

Why not? It would help pass the time. "Sure. I'll sketch the scenes. The kids can paint them."

Richie smiled his pleasure. "But what if they don't have any artistic talent?"

"I'll do them like coloring book pages. Stay inside the lines—or maybe paint by number with a color chart. What type mural did you have in mind?"

"Bible-story scenes...Noah and the ark, David and Goliath, Adam and Eve in the garden, anything like that."

"You want them in panels or one big scene?"

"We'll take them any way we can get them," he said without hesitation.

⁓

Once she'd agreed to the project, Richie hadn't lost any time. He took her to see the area the next evening. He parked in his reserved spot and led her toward a side door. Katy paused to enjoy a meditation garden filled with gorgeous flowers, a fountain, and benches. She could enjoy spending time here.

Katy had no doubt the beautiful old church had housed generations of God's children in their hours of worship. She waited while he unlocked the door and followed him up the stairs. A long hallway with several classrooms off each side spanned the distance.

The stark white walls were the perfect artist's canvas. A thought struck her and she laughed.

"What's so funny?"

"Just thinking how Bethany loved to color on walls. When I told her she couldn't, she'd say, 'But Mommy, I have to make them bootiful.'"

He chuckled. "We have graffiti specialists here, too. These walls just got a fresh coat of paint."

She eyed him suspiciously. No way did she want to make an entire church congregation angry with her. "And you're positive they won't mind what we're planning to do to their paint job?"

Richie shook his head. "Not at all. Pastor Geoff got immediate approval when I told him you'd agreed to help. He's as excited about the project as I am."

"I thought maybe a progression of the different stories," she said, using the span of her arms to mark off the wall. When he looked surprised, she said, "Unless you only wanted one panel?"

"No. No," Richie said. "We'd love to see several characters represented. I just don't know that we'll be of much help to you."

Katy ignored his hesitancy. Everyone had a little artist in them. "We won't know unless we try. I'll help. I like working with kids."

"Me, too."

At least they had one thing in common. "Would you mind if I started tonight?"

Richie frowned with uncertainty. "Do you think you should? I just wanted you to see where you'd be working."

She pulled several pencils from her pocket. "I'm here. I have my tools." Katy tapped her forehead with her other hand and added, "And my creative genius."

He waved his arm in invitation. "Never let it be said that Richie Taylor stood in the way of creative genius."

She laughed. When Katy looked into his eyes, she saw a much different man than the brother she married. Richie might not be as handsome on the exterior, but his heart was the most beautiful she'd ever known. Why couldn't she have had someone like him to love her? She knew without a doubt that he would make a woman feel cherished. Katy shook her head. Where had that come from? No sense in daydreaming about what she could never have. "Do you have the long level I requested?"

"I'll be right back."

Richie brought his tool bag and the level. Using a tape measure, they divided the walls into an equal number of panels and drew lines with the long straight edge. Katy laid out her pencils on a nearby chair. Within the hour, Adam and Eve stood in the garden.

"They look so real," he declared in awe, reaching out and then pulling his hand back before he touched the pencil drawings.

"How many teens are there?"

"The number varies. In the summer, a lot of them show up in the afternoon and hang out. We plan some activities, do some impromptu Bible studies, and discuss their problems and concerns."

Katy added veins to a leaf. "Assign two teens to each panel, and plan a couple of special projects to involve the younger kids. You don't want them feeling left out."

Her neck and shoulders ached from the exertion. She rubbed her lower back and pushed against the wall. "Time to stop."

Realization dawned in Richie's eyes. "Do you have pain pills?"

Katy pulled ibuprofen from her pocket, and he brought her a cone of water from the water fountain at the end of the hall.

"I know I'm imposing, but I've always wanted a picture of Jesus with the children downstairs in the big room."

"Show me," she invited.

The open room held a stage and podium. Colorful industrial carpet covered the floor. She could visualize his audience lounging there during children's church services. Richie pointed to the wall behind the stage.

"Perfect place for a mural, don't you think?"

The sheen of purpose in his expression amused her. "Tell you what, finish the cottage and I'll finish your panels."

"You already know I'm going to finish the cottage," Richie objected before adding, "but the Lord will bless you for beautifying His house."

She laughed at his sudden attack of conscience. "God knows what I want."

Doubt changed his expression.

"Please don't say it," she said, turning away. Her shoulders heaved, her breath coming in shudders as she fought for emotional control.

He laid a hand on her shoulder. "I want her to be alive, too."

"I'd know if she were dead. I'd feel it here." Katy pounded her chest.

Even as the words left her lips, doubt took a foothold. What if she never found Bethany? Would she look at every child, hoping to find her little girl? Did she want to live if she never found her daughter?

"She's precious to Him, too," Richie agreed.

Chapter 6

They found Jack's car," Katy told Richie. "They're going to fingerprint and check it for evidence."

"What happens then?"

"They'll tow it to an impound lot."

"Did you and Jack only have the one car?"

"My SUV is at my parents' house. Jack had a fire-engine red Porsche," she said, a moue of disgust touching her mouth. "I cried when he brought it home, and he said I spoiled everything."

"You didn't think the car was appropriate for a family man?"

"The car was gorgeous, but he already had a nice car with no payments."

Her words transported Richie back in time to when his dad bought Jack's first car.

"It's an old man's tank." Anger had marred Jack's expression as he derided the older model vehicle his stepfather had found.

Richard Taylor stood his ground. "It's a perfectly good car for a young man learning how to drive."

"I know how to drive," Jack argued. "The guys will make fun of me if I drive that boat."

"I doubt that. You'll be the only one with a car."

"I don't want it." Jack threw the keys on the ground and stomped off. His dad pocketed them without comment.

In hindsight, Richie considered his half brother had always treated his dad with a lack of respect. *Dad won in the end*, he thought with a little smile. Jack had driven the old car for the remainder of his high school years and off to college.

Shaking off the memory, Richie turned to Katy. "You seem to be the practical one. How did you get together?"

"We met at a friend's party. Learned we attended the same college and talked the night away. I suppose I was in awe that such a handsome guy could be interested in me."

Her words raised a flag in his counselor mind. "What about Jack? Did he feel the same way?" He waved a hand. "Awed that a beautiful woman was interested in him?"

Katy's eyes widened at his compliment. "Jack had his choice of women. I never understood why he chose me."

"I'm sure he believed you were the right woman. Mom always told us we'd know." As he uttered the statement, Richie experienced regret that he hadn't met Katy first.

PEACE, BE STILL

"I felt that way about him. Then," Katy added softly, "somewhere between 'I do' and our fourth anniversary, a stranger replaced my husband. I couldn't allow that man to be part of our life. You can't begin to imagine what it was like," Katy whispered, her fingers whitening with the grip on her purse. "He never loved me in that special way you mentioned."

<hr>

The police agreed for her to see the vehicle. At the impound lot, Katy found the flashy red car had been traded for a smaller nondescript silver sedan. Yet another reason to believe Jack had been covering his tracks.

"So where's the Porsche?" Richie asked.

She walked around to the back of the vehicle. "I've never seen this car before."

Richie followed. He pointed to the local dealership sticker on the back. "Jack must have traded when he came to North Carolina."

"I imagine he needed cash." She turned to the impound lot employee. "Where was the warehouse?"

He double-checked the sheet. "Over on the edge of town."

"Probably close to where he was killed."

Richie leaned closer, looking into the backseat. "There's a bunch of dolls in there."

Katy looked inside. Barbies. Bethany wanted them, but Katy felt she was too young. Had she played with these? Held them in her hands?

"The tile place is just down the street."

"Okay," she agreed somewhat distractedly.

Richie looked at her before he started the vehicle. "You think he bought those for Bethany, don't you?"

"Why else would he have them in the car?"

"Maybe he planned to give them to her when she came home."

"Didn't you notice they weren't in their boxes? Someone played with those dolls."

A couple of hours later, Richie took Katy home. At Lucille's, Katy checked her messages, half hoping the police had called. She dialed Dina's office.

"Katy? Is everything okay?"

"They found Jack's car in an abandoned warehouse. He sold the Porsche. I'm still waiting to hear back on the fingerprints. I think he had Bethany with him."

"But I thought... You said the man who took her... You didn't know him."

"I didn't, but I believe he knew Jack." She told her sister about the two men.

"I can't believe you did something so stupid."

Katy had trouble believing it herself. "The police said they'd call once they verified the prints. I don't know how long it will take."

"I hope the news is good for your sake. Other than that, are you okay?"

"I'm working on murals for Richie's church."

"Jack's brother? Katy, do you think it's wise to involve yourself with his family?"

53

"Richie's nothing like Jack."

"Would you like me to come to North Carolina?" Dina asked.

While she'd love to see her sister and hear her opinion of the area, Katy said, "Let's wait until the cottage is finished." *And Bethany is found.*

~

The small prints in the car belonged to Bethany. They had matched them to the fingerprint identification card she provided to the LVPD. Katy dialed Richie's cell phone. She left a message.

He returned her call minutes later. After Katy shared her news, he said, "I'm sorry I doubted you."

Her need to rub his face in the truth evaporated. "At least we know she was with Jack. Where did he leave her, Richie?" Silence. "I thought you'd want to know. I'll let you get back to work."

"I did. Thanks for calling. I'm praying for you both."

"There will be a media release today. Detective Neumann has shared the information with the LVPD. You may want to tell your family. I imagine they will have a few questions for them."

"I've already spoken to the police. Told them we hadn't seen Jack in years and didn't know about Bethany until you shared the news."

"The LVPD was looking for Jack. I'm surprised there wasn't something on record that led them to you."

"Maybe the Wilmington police reported Jack as dead with no sign of a child. It would have been difficult for them to contact us with Dad's heart attack and then the storm. They might have called, but I didn't listen to my messages when I arrived home early Friday morning. They were erased when the power came back on." Katy heard someone talking in the background as Richie said, "I know I have to tell Mom, but it's going to cause her so much pain. I need to go. We'll talk later."

That afternoon, Katy was hard at work on the murals when Richie arrived at the church.

"We need to check with the dealership that sold Jack the car. See if he gave them an address. Did he have the title for the Porsche?"

She nodded. After Jack disappeared, Katy checked their safety deposit box to see what he'd taken with him. "He took the title, his passport, and some other papers."

"Was it just in his name?"

"Yes."

"Then he could trade it without problem."

"If we can tie the car to an address, maybe someone will know where Bethany is!" Katy exclaimed.

"An abandoned child would have been turned over to Child Protective Services," Richie said.

Why give her hope only to jerk it back? "Jack liked rich living. Though I imagine he stayed someplace where he could deal with cash. He wouldn't want to leave a paper trail. Why come back to where people knew you? It doesn't make sense."

"Jack didn't go where people knew him," Richie pointed out. "He came to an area he knew. Let's ride over to the dealership and introduce ourselves."

Katy hesitated. "Haven't the police already talked to them?"

"It can't hurt for us to ask a couple of questions. Maybe seeing you will remind them of something they didn't tell the police."

She suspected Richie had his own motivation, but his plan fostered more of the hope Katy needed so badly. After asking, they were directed to the salesman who conducted the trade. He confirmed Bethany had been with her father.

"She was very well behaved and quiet. He was a little rough on her when she asked for a snack. I gave her a pack of cookies I had in my desk drawer. She thanked me without any prompting from her dad."

Katy showed him the photo. "Is this the child?"

"Yeah." He smiled and nodded. "That's her. Real cutie."

Richie demanded, "Did Jack give you an address?"

The man looked suspicious. "We've already talked to the police. Who did you say you were?"

"I'm Richie Taylor. Jack was my brother. Katy was Jack's wife. The child is her daughter."

"What do you mean *was*?"

"Jack is dead," Katy said. "My daughter was kidnapped. The police have confirmed she was in Jack's car. She's still missing."

The man let out a shrill whistle. "They didn't mention that. Just asked if he was alone and what he'd said. Let me talk to my boss."

He returned with another man who introduced himself as the sales manager. "Tell them," he instructed the salesman.

The man seemed uncomfortable. "Mr. Sinclair told me you were dead. Said he and your little girl came home to North Carolina after they lost you. Hated to give up that sweet ride but needed the money."

"What address did he give for the paperwork?" Richie asked. They looked uncertain again.

"I can prove I'm Jack's wife." Katy pulled out her wallet and showed them her driver's license, their marriage license, and the family photo she carried.

Again, the sales manager nodded permission. The man gave them the address from their database.

"That's my address," Richie said with surprise.

"You say he's dead?" the manager asked.

Richie nodded. "Didn't you see the news about John Doe a few weeks back?"

"Can't say I did."

Katy spoke up. "Can you recall anything that might help us find Bethany?"

"Sorry," he said with a shake of his head. "She fell asleep after she ate the cookies. He took the keys, picked her up, and left."

"How did she look?"

His shoulders lifted. "Healthy enough. Just a little out of sorts. Like she needed a nap."

Katy glanced at Richie.

"We have the new tags. Couldn't get an answer on his phone. We've been leaving messages."

She wondered if Jack's phone had been in the car all this time.

Handing the men business cards, Richie said, "Give me a call if you think of anything else." Taking Katy's arm, he guided her from the showroom.

"Where is she?" she cried out once they were in the parking lot.

"They saw her on the twenty-eighth of June. Jack must have gone straight to the dealership when he arrived. Why do you think he waited until he got to Wilmington?"

"Maybe he didn't plan on trading cars. Maybe his partners in crime demanded more money than he had."

"Or his plans fell through."

Katy drew to a stop. Her forehead wrinkled with consternation as she asked, "You think he planned to borrow money from your parents?" Katy paused. "And he couldn't contact them because they were on vacation."

"So he traded the car to get his hands on cash," Richie offered thoughtfully. "It's possible. I'm sorry, Katy."

"You didn't know he was here. But where were they living? Why would he use your address?"

"I suppose he had to have an address for the paperwork. I just wish we knew the truth." He paused. "Do you want me to take you home?"

While she'd love nothing more than to curl up and cry, Katy knew it would serve no purpose. "The children are coming for story hour. I need to pick up my stuff and grab a burger before church."

They collected her duffel, called good-bye to Lucille, and visited a drive-through. At the church, Katy waited while Richie unlocked the door and turned on the lights.

"The kids should arrive soon. I'll show you the classroom so you can set up."

Katy had given the matter serious consideration before she volunteered. While church might not be her first choice for a test site, it definitely would show her how receptive the kids would be to her business ideas.

As always, tonight's experience would be bittersweet. Entertaining kids and not thinking about Bethany was impossible. This would be doubly hard considering what she had learned today.

"I've lost you."

She looked up to find Richie waiting outside a classroom door farther down the hall. Katy picked up her pace and mumbled, "Sorry."

"We never know how many kids will attend. I prayed for a good turnout."

"We'll have fun no matter how many we have."

Richie nodded. "I've made that my goal. Kids who love the Lord become adults who serve Him. I had my moments of rebellion, but God kept me on the right path. When I went off to college, I considered my options, and nothing appealed more than serving the Lord and working with children."

"Why not teaching?"

He frowned and shook his head. "Pumping education into unwilling minds wasn't for me. The Lord had another plan."

"You believe He has one for everybody?" she asked curiously.

"I do. He gave us freedom of choice. He knows the choices we'll make. God didn't direct the path of the man who took Bethany. The choice was that of man. God loves you, Katy. He's there for you. Seek His comfort."

The sound of children, yelling and screaming as they raced into the building, cut short their conversation.

"Big audience tonight," Richie said with a grin.

"I'd better get things pulled together."

Katy stepped into the classroom. "Richie?" she called, coming back into the hall. He paused on the stairs. "Is there a larger area? Something like the big room where the kids can sit on the carpeted floor?"

"The older kids meet there."

"Could we switch? Or join them for story hour?" She grinned. "I don't mind if they don't."

He waved his arm. "Follow me."

❧

Richie watched Katy. She was in her element, greeting the kids with a huge smile and asking their names. They admired the colorful name tags she stuck on their chests. When she sat on the edge of the stage, they settled, and she began the story of David and Goliath. Katy paused and pointed to a child, asking what he thought happened next.

The interaction took the Bible story to places Richie had never considered. Some responses were fact based and some were so imaginative he had to keep himself from laughing at their wild responses.

Even though her heart was breaking, she smiled often, giving a huge chunk of herself to these kids she didn't know. She delighted in their joy.

He wanted to delight in hers. Something had changed. Richie couldn't say exactly when his attitude toward her changed. His desire to escape had shifted subtly, and now he thought of Katy differently. Not as Jack's wife or Bethany's mother but as a beautiful woman he cared for more than a friend. He saw her as someone he wanted in his future.

If only he could give her Bethany back. Never see that sadness that filled her green eyes since he'd known her. In his heart, he knew she wasn't the woman Jack described to their mother. That woman had never existed.

He believed his brother had mistreated Katy. He wanted to right the wrongs Jack had inflicted but knew it wasn't something he could do. All he could do was love her and pray that one day she could be completely happy again. He intended to do his part. Richie inclined his head and beseeched God to help them find her daughter.

Chapter 7

Katy tugged the bedspread and smoothed the wrinkles. When the radio deejay announced an upcoming event date, she realized her precious baby girl would be three years old in less than a week.

After Bethany's birth, the role of mother took priority in Katy's life. Jack resented her spending so much time with the baby. She tried to make him understand Bethany needed her, but that only made things worse. She refused to allow his childish behavior to interfere with their bonding experience.

That bonding made this separation from her daughter even more difficult. How much longer could she hope for Bethany's survival? How long before she gave up?

She thought back to the moment the nurse placed her newborn daughter in her arms. Love different from any she'd ever known overwhelmed Katy as she fingered red-gold curls, counted tiny fingers and toes, and traced delicate features.

The responsibility had never been too much for her. Then, she anticipated seeing her child grow and develop into a beautiful young woman. Now, she feared Bethany would never celebrate her third birthday.

She pounded the decorative crocheted pillow with her fist, wishing she could pound Jack instead. Of all the things he'd taken from her, this was the most destructive.

Katy looked around in desperation. She needed to escape. Find something to occupy her mind. The cottage. Perhaps she could hasten things along there. Lucille was wonderful, but she wanted her privacy back. She needed to drop the pretense. To be able to scream, cry, and shout when the pain overcame her.

She drove to the Lennons' house. Inside, she found two gallons of primer. Richie had already taped protective paper to the newly installed tile floor. Katy poured paint into a tray and found comfort in blotting out the markings left from the storm. She looked forward to adding color.

When Richie showed up later that afternoon, he turned in a slow circle, taking in the walls. "You've made progress. All that's left is painting and outside work."

"I'm tired of being homeless."

"You aren't."

"I know. I don't mean to sound ungrateful. Lucille is wonderful, but I'm sure she'd like her home back, too."

"She loves having you there." Richie eyed her curiously. "What's the difference between her house and here?"

Staying with Lucille was like living with her family after Bethany disappeared. No responsibilities. No decisions. No expectations. "I just exist." He stared blankly and she rushed on. "It's like being a child again. Ever since I separated from Jack, I haven't been able to make one decision about my future. I'm stuck in limbo, just marking time until Bethany comes home."

"How will returning to the cottage change that?"

Frustrated, Katy said, "I don't know." That sounded lame, but how could she explain to him when she couldn't even explain to herself? "Maybe being here, doing my own chores, having to take care of myself will help me stop feeling lost."

"It's more involved than that, Katy. You have to allow yourself to grieve. Nothing will ever be right again until you do."

"How can I do that when I don't know what I'm grieving for?"

"You know," he said softly.

She loaded the roller in the paint tray and moved to the wall. "Bethany's here, Richie."

"How long has it been?"

He knew she could tell him to the date, hour, minute, and second. He only wanted her to confront the truth. She moved the roller along the wall. "Thirty-four days."

"Without her parents."

Katy shivered and said, "She's alive, Richie."

"I hope so for your sake," he told her. "I need to leave. The youth are helping man the homeless shelter tonight. You should come."

"I can't."

"Don't think you can handle a different perspective on being homeless?"

Katy didn't want to tell him. "You think it would make me a better person, don't you?"

"I didn't say that."

He hadn't. "I can't handle any angle tonight. I've overdone."

"What were you thinking?" Richie demanded, taking the roller from her hand.

"It's Bethany's birthday soon," Katy told him. "I thought keeping busy might help."

His mouth thinned with displeasure. "You can't keep doing this, Katy. You're at the beach. Think vacation. Allow yourself to relax."

"I do try, but it's impossible. I think about my child and get all knotted up inside. I hate this helplessness."

Katy turned toward the new french door. "Why can't life be like those waves out there? Just come and go routinely."

Richie rested his hands on her shoulders. "Life is exactly like those waves. Today they're coming and going without any great force, but they have the power to be menacing and destructive.

"The Bible tells of how the disciples feared their death while Jesus slept during a storm. They woke Him, asking how He could sleep when they were going to die. He raised a hand, said, 'Peace, be still,' and the storm quieted. It's a lesson, Katy. We need to trust in Him to quiet the storms of our lives."

When she'd recommitted to serve God always, Katy had reveled in their relationship. She'd studied His Word, taught her child, and witnessed to friends and family at every opportunity. Then Bethany disappeared, and she turned her back on Him. Katy knew He hadn't turned from her. She broke away. "Your kids are waiting, Richie."

"Let me help with the cleanup."

Katy shook her head. "It won't take long. I'll wrap the rollers in plastic bags and stick them in the fridge so they can be used tomorrow. Go on. I'll lock up here when I leave."

Richie hesitated. "I could do it faster."

She sighed heavily. "Go, Richie. I'm not totally helpless."

He gave in and walked away, holding up a hand in farewell.

After the door clicked shut, Katy busied herself with the cleanup. She appreciated Richie's attempt to help her understand. She wanted his friendship, but could he ever fully let go of what had happened between her and Jack? Katy hoped so. She'd love to have Richie in their future. If there was a future. *Stop it. You're going to find Bethany.*

If only. . . Katy stopped herself. She couldn't think of Richie like that. He was her brother-in-law. She shouldn't be. . .

He was everything Jack hadn't been. Everything she'd dreamed of finding in a man. There had been a change in their relationship since he accepted she'd told the truth. He'd been different, more caring. But then, why would he even consider a relationship with someone like her? This wasn't biblical times when a man married his brother's widow. Besides, they barely knew each other.

Back at Lucille's house, she rested for a while and helped with dinner. After they ate, Katy excused herself and went to bed. For the first time in days, she reached for the pain pills. Maybe they'd ease the nagging pain in her heart as well as the one in her body. Things generally looked better after a good night's rest. Streetlights filtered through the lacy white curtains, casting almost ghostly reflections as they billowed with the ocean breezes.

Her conversation with Richie kept coming to mind. Katy knew that she'd come very close to accepting Bethany couldn't be alive that afternoon. That frightened her. She couldn't give up hope. As long as there was no solid proof to the contrary, she had to believe her child wasn't gone.

Slowly the pill took effect, and she found herself relaxing against the crisp, clean linens.

"Katy, wake up," Lucille called, shaking her shoulder. "Richie's on the phone. He needs you at the shelter."

"Hmm." She tried to focus.

"Katy, Richie needs you."

Her eyes drifted closed.

Lucille shook her shoulder harder, repeating the request.

"Tomorrow," she mumbled.

"No. You have to go now. Here, let me help you."

Katy sat on the side of the bed. Lucille handed her the jeans she'd laid on the chair after dinner. Then she disappeared and returned with a cold, wet cloth.

"Wipe your face. Did you take pills?"

Katy nodded and fumbled her legs into the jeans.

The phone rang, and Aunt Lucille grabbed the extension.

"She took pain medication. I don't think she should drive."

Katy stared at Lucille through bleary eyes.

"What's going on, Richie?" Lucille wedged the phone beneath her chin and pushed Katy's hands out of the way to zip the hoodie over the pajama top.

"I can't wait."

"Wait for what?" Katy mumbled tiredly as Lucille hung up the phone.

Lucille handed Katy her sneakers. "Put those on and go downstairs. Richie's sending someone to drive you."

"What's he hoping to prove?" she mumbled. "He's right. I'm not homeless."

Lucille took her arm and guided her to the door. "You have to go, Katy."

They waited on the porch. A patrol car turned into the driveway and stopped.

"Ready, Mrs. Sinclair?" the police officer asked.

A police officer? Katy blinked. Richie had sent the law after her. If only she hadn't taken that pill. In the fuzzy recesses of her mind, Katy knew something was happening but couldn't focus on what.

"Here's your purse." Lucille pulled the strap up on Katy's shoulder. "You'll need your papers."

She didn't understand.

"Go with the officer, Katy."

Obediently, she followed him to the car. "Do you know what's going on?"

"I'll have you at the shelter in a few minutes."

The cool air from the vents made Katy more alert. Upon their arrival, she thanked him and went inside.

Richie waited by the entrance. He took her arm. "Are you okay?"

She rubbed her eyes and asked, "What's going on? I already said you're right. I'm not homeless. Why did you insist I come down here in the middle of the night?"

"Trust me, Katy." She held back and he implored, "Please, come with me."

He took her into a large room filled with people. As he led the way down the makeshift aisle through the center of the cots, she felt strong regret at her earlier mumbling. She didn't have a clue what it was like to be homeless. God had blessed her with nice homes and comfortable beds.

Richie pulled her over to the side, his arm about her shoulders as he said, "Take a look over there."

Confused, Katy shifted her gaze to where he pointed. When she would have stepped forward, Richie held her back. She fought to get past him.

"It's Bethany," Katy cried. "Let me go. They'll get away."

Heads turned in their direction, curious to see who was causing the commotion in the otherwise-quiet confines of the homeless shelter.

His hold tightened. "No one is leaving here tonight. They're watching the doors. You're sure it's her?"

"Oh yes," she said, staring at her Bethany. Less than ten feet separate them, and Katy looked at her through a mother's eyes.

The lethargy and reddened cheeks indicated illness. She'd lost weight. How long had she gone without nourishment? Bethany and her clothing were filthy, her red-gold hair stringy and matted. No matter how grungy, she was looking a miracle.

"Oh Richie, she's alive."

He hugged her tighter. "Just stay calm. I promise she's not going anywhere.

Chapter 8

Katy felt like a fanatical private collector desiring a priceless treasure just out of reach. She ached to hold Bethany, to assure herself the child wasn't a figment of her imagination, but Richie wouldn't let go.

A woman sat next to Bethany. Katy saw fear grow in her eyes as the officers came nearer. She groped for the child's hand, jerked her up, and started edging along the wall.

"Stop her!" Katy cried, terrified.

An officer stepped into their path, catching Bethany as she started to fall. He swung the child into his arms and laid her back on the cot. The other officer moved closer to the woman, asking questions. Based on her mutinous expression, Katy doubted he received any answers.

"It's okay," Richie soothed.

"Who is she? How did she know Jack?" Tired of waiting, she attempted to move away from Richie.

"Her name is Agnes." Richie held her arm. "Wait. Let the officers do their job."

His words hit her like a slap in the face. He sounded exactly like her father when Bethany first disappeared. She glared at Richie.

His expression grew serious. "Can't you see this is a miracle, Katy? Think about what's happened. Was it coincidence that Melody found Jack's obituary? That we met before the storm? That I'd come here tonight? I owe God a major apology for doubting He would bring her home to us." He looked over her shoulder. "Here comes the officer now."

She turned, searching for Bethany. "Is she okay?" Katy demanded, her tremulous voice betraying fear. *Please, God. Don't take her away again.*

"Mrs. Sinclair?" the officer asked.

"Yes, I'm Kaitlin Sinclair," she said, digging through her purse. She pulled out her wallet and handed him her driver's license and Bethie's birth certificate. "Bethany is my daughter. She was kidnapped."

He glanced at the license and returned it to her. "Yes ma'am. We have the information. We called an ambulance. You'll need to go to the hospital with her. They'll need your consent to treat her."

"Please let me see her now," Katy pleaded.

He led the way. Another officer questioned the woman a few feet away. Katy barely glanced at her as she knelt by the bed. "Bethie? Sweetheart, it's Mommy."

The child stirred but didn't open her eyes. Katy touched her forehead. "She's burning up." She looked at Richie. "We need to get her temperature down. Can you get me cold water and a cloth?"

"The ambulance will be here soon," the officer said.

"We have to get her fever down now." Katy didn't care how imperious her tone sounded. Bethany's temperature was dangerously high.

Richie went after the items. Katy took the cloth from him and smoothed it over Bethany's face. Flushed ivory skin emerged as the water darkened.

Upon their arrival, the EMTs took over, checking vitals and gathering information. In minutes, they had Bethany strapped on the gurney. Katy rushed out along with them, following their instructions when one told her to ride up front with the driver.

⁓

Richie followed. Bethany was alive. A little piece of Jack lived on in his child. Richie could hardly wait to tell his mother. She would be ecstatic.

Katy climbed into the passenger side of the ambulance while the attendants settled her child in the back.

"Why do you suppose she had Bethany?" Richie wondered aloud.

"I don't know. Oh Richie, she's so sick. Why hasn't anyone seen them before?"

"Someone has. They didn't know whom they were seeing. There's no telling where they've been living."

"Jack never bothered to find someone reliable to take care of her. Now do you understand what I've been trying to tell you?"

"He didn't go with the intention of dying."

The tensing of her jaw betrayed her frustration. "Jack let this happen," Katy insisted. "He didn't take care of her. He never did."

Richie didn't want to believe that about Jack. Seeing Bethany tonight had confused him. At first, he'd decided it couldn't be her, but returning doubt made him pull the photo from his wallet to confirm his suspicions. One glimpse and there was no denying she was the child in the picture.

"Ready?" the EMT asked when he climbed behind the wheel.

Katy nodded, turning to look into the back. "Is she okay?"

The attendant nodded. "We hooked up an IV."

"I'll see you at the hospital," Richie promised.

His gaze followed the flashing lights as the vehicle stopped in the driveway and then turned onto the street. He needed to be with Katy and Bethany.

Richie hurried back inside, intent on finding the other adult volunteers to explain that he needed to leave.

"Just go," his friend said, overjoyed for Richie and his family. "We've got this under control. Let us know how she's doing."

"I will," he promised and ran from the building.

At the hospital, he parked and hurried to the emergency area. "I'm here for Bethany Sinclair. She just came in by ambulance."

Richie glanced around. They were busy tonight. The sliding doors opened and closed with the ER comings and goings. There seemed to be no big rush, but people disappeared from the area regularly.

Finally, the nurse called his name and led him to the bed where Bethany slept, the IV dripping fluid into her tiny arm.

"How's her temperature?" He touched a hand to her forehead. It seemed cooler. "What's wrong with her? Why hasn't she woken?"

"The doctor will be here shortly," Katy said, never taking her gaze from the child. She sat with her arm threaded through the bed rails, touching Bethany. "Bethie honey, Mommy's here." The child shifted slightly but didn't open her eyes. "Sweetie, please wake up. I've missed you so much."

Moisture filled Richie's eyes. *Please, God. Make her well.*

A man entered the cubicle. "I'm Dr. Dietz."

Before he could continue, Katy released the same torrent of questions Richie had just asked her. "How is she? What's wrong with her? Is she going to be okay?"

"She's badly dehydrated and malnourished. I want X-rays to rule out pneumonia. Does she have asthma? Bronchitis?"

"Neither. She's always been a healthy child."

He reached to rub his neck. "We need to keep her here a few days. With treatment and nourishment, she'll recover. I can't speak to her mental state. No doubt she's been traumatized by everything that's happened."

"Can I hold her?"

The older man patted her shoulder kindly. "Let's get her admitted first. Once you're in a room, I'm sure it can be arranged."

He gave her shoulder another reassuring pat.

Time dragged as they waited for Bethany to be admitted. Richie accompanied them upstairs. Thankfully there wasn't another occupant in the semiprivate room.

Richie knew the nurse from church. "This is Bev Tyler," he told Katy. "You won't find a better nurse in Wilmington."

The woman laughed and said, "I'm sure there are those who would disagree."

She rolled in a laptop computer on a stand and started asking questions. Katy took Bethany's medical records from her bag.

A few minutes later the medical history was completed. "Thanks," Bev said. "We'll be checking her regularly. If there's anything you need, press this button." She indicated the NURSE CALL button.

"I will. Thank you."

Richie stood at the end of the bed, staring at Bethany in the dim light. "She's beautiful," he commented. "I can see she's Jack's daughter."

"Don't." Katy's voice thickened in her throat. "Please don't compare her to him."

"He's her father." The words slipped from him just as the sigh that followed. "Katy, I'm sorry for what's happened, but God in His goodness has brought Bethany home. Please put the past behind us."

"If God is so good and merciful, why would He allow this to happen to her?"

The controlled fury in her voice silenced him. Richie knew while Katy might be thankful for God's mercies, she would find it difficult to thank Him if she believed He permitted this to happen to her daughter.

"He sent someone to care for her."

"A bag lady? God sent a bag lady?"

"I'm thankful for that woman."

His words seemed to calm her. She gathered her hair in a bundle and dumped it down her back. "Me, too. What happened to her?"

"They let her go. She found Bethany wandering around the abandoned building, looking for her daddy."

"Why didn't she take her to the police?"

Richie hesitated. "I don't think she planned to give her up. She became very combative when they took Bethany away. Said she belonged to her."

He could see Katy found the thought too horrible to consider. She touched Bethany's red-gold hair. Each touch seemed to give her renewed strength.

"What did you call her? Agnes?"

"That's the name she gave when she signed in."

"I'd like to know where she is. I can never repay her, but I want to make her life easier."

"Money won't help Agnes."

"What can I do?"

"Pray for her. I'll see if we can keep in touch and maybe get her warm clothing and food for the winter."

"I'd like that."

"Will you stay here?"

She nodded.

"Then I'll ask Aunt Lucille to pack a bag. Anything special for Bethany?"

"Her favorite pajamas are underneath my pillow. I washed and dried them last week."

Richie allowed his gaze to drift back to his niece. "I'm calling my parents first thing in the morning. I'll be happy to call your family. I'm sure they'll be relieved."

"I'll call when Bethany is better."

His forehead grooved. "You'd allow them to grieve when you can alleviate their pain?"

"I need to focus on Bethany," she said almost defensively.

Disappointed, he said, "It's cruel."

"Why would you expect anything less of evil Katy?" Tears rolled down her face as the emotion of the past few hours overflowed.

Feeling guilty, Richie took a step forward. He took her in his arms, feeling her tense body relax slightly. "Katy, I'm sorry. Why don't you want to call them?"

She pulled away and wiped her eyes with her palms. The freckles stood out in her clean, pale face. "I need time to prepare for the fight."

He weighed her with a critical squint. "What fight?"

"The one that will occur when I tell my father we're not returning to Vegas."

Richie frowned. "I can understand he'd be disappointed, but a fight?"

"The dynamic makeup of our relationship is dominant male and rebellious female. When I don't do what my father wants, we argue."

"And everyone loses. Why do you force me to drag these things from you?"

"Tell your parents, Richie. Rejoice with them." Her attempted diversion failed.

"You know you put yourself in a bad light?"

Bethany stirred, and Katy waited until she calmed down. "I'm tired, Richie," she said so softly he strained to hear. "Tired of having my mistakes thrown into my face. I only want to see my child grow up healthy and happy. I need to concentrate my energies on getting her well. This miracle won't mean anything to my father once I tell him what I plan to do."

"But you can't do it alone," Richie objected, his hand resting on her shoulder.

"Bethany and I will get through this."

Awash with new determination, he said, "I'll stand behind you all the way if you'll allow me."

"I'm staying right here until I can take her home, and then I'm never letting her out of my sight again."

"Don't smother her, Katy. And don't forget your own injuries. I'm surprised you're still standing."

Adrenaline kept her going. Ever since she'd seen Bethany, Katy felt she could move mountains. "Why don't you go home?"

He ignored her hints that he leave. "I want to be here when she wakes."

"What about your youth? You left them at the shelter?"

He leaned against the wall. "They're supervised. I needed to be here." Richie glanced at his watch. "Why don't I get us some caffeine?"

"I'd love a soda."

Out in the waiting room, Richie sank into a chair. His behavior just now shamed him. He'd promised not to judge and had failed her. That troubled him. This entire situation made his human failings too obvious.

He bowed his head. "Blessed heavenly Father, please show me how to help her," he implored. "Forgive me for judging harshly and wrongly. Thank You for returning this precious child to her mother and for giving our family the opportunity to know her. Be with Katy as she makes decisions for the future. Help her family to open their minds to the knowledge that she's a strong, capable woman and give her the support she needs. Amen."

Jack had lied. Richie knew that as surely as he knew he'd sinned with his less-than-forgiving behavior. In his grief, he hadn't been interested in the truth.

Hearing her family had provided for so many of the young couple's needs made Jack's claims he couldn't please Katy ludicrous. Richie had never seen the personality Jack described to their mom.

The pay phone caught his eye. It was late, but he'd burst if he didn't tell someone. He unclipped his cell from his belt and dialed his sister's number. "Hey Luce," he called at her groggy greeting.

"Richie? Do you know how late it is? I just got Trey back down. You better hope you didn't wake him."

"At least he's too little to yell at me."

"You're such a child," his sister snapped. "Why are you calling? Has something happened?"

"Jack has a daughter."

"What did you say?" she demanded, her voice rising. He heard his brother-in-law ask a question and Lucy shush him.

"Jack has a daughter. I met her mother during the hurricane. I had no idea she was Jack's wife until the Lennons' cottage was damaged and I took her to Aunt Lucille's."

"You took a strange woman to Aunt Lucille's?"

"She's a friend of the Lennons'. She claimed Jack kidnapped their daughter and thought he had involved us. Bethany's nearly three. You should see her."

"I plan to."

Richie smiled at her comment. "Anyway, Bethany turned up at the shelter tonight with the homeless woman who found her wandering around looking for Jack. It's a miracle. She's been missing for more than a month. I've been certain the child was dead. The probability of her survival was impossible, but Katy insisted she wasn't dead. Said she'd know in her heart."

Lucy sniffed. "A mother would. Is Bethany okay?"

"She's sick enough to be in the hospital, but the doctor thinks she'll recover quickly. She's been asleep ever since they took her from the shelter."

"You should call Mom."

"I will. First thing tomorrow. You know she always thinks the worst about middle-of-the-night calls."

"Yes, but this is wonderful news. How long have you known Bethany existed?"

"Since after the hurricane."

"And you haven't said anything?"

"I believed she was dead," he defended. "You saw how Jack's death affected them. Knowing they'd lost a grandchild they'd never met would have done even more harm."

"Should I go over now and tell them?"

Her eagerness forced Richie to explain further. "No, but I want you to be there when I call."

"Why? You know Mom will jump on the first plane to Wilmington."

"She can't," Richie said reluctantly.

"You can't keep her from Jack's child."

"Katy's feeling very protective right now."

"That's understandable, but what does it have to do with Mom? She can see the child. Help with her care."

"Katy needs time. She has to deal with the emotional element of Bethany coming home. We don't know what she's been through since she was kidnapped. Mom has to stay put until I convince Katy we have the child's best interests at heart.

"Then there's the stuff Jack told Mom. Katy won't tolerate more prejudging from our family."

"I want to see Bethany."

"I'll scan photos and e-mail them to you. You can show Mom and Dad."

"Take one and send it now."

"Katy wouldn't want you to see Bethany like this. She's sick and dirty. Her hair is all chopped up. You have to help me with this, Lucy."

"I'll talk to Mom. Try to make her understand that she needs to be patient. Not too long, though."

"Not a minute longer than necessary," he promised.

"You know I'm not going to be able to go back to sleep now."

"Try. Trey will be demanding his next feeding soon. Pray for Bethany's recovery, that she won't remember the suffering she's endured. And thank God for this miracle He's given us."

"I will. Keep us informed on how she's doing."

"Sure thing. I need to call Aunt Lucille. She's probably sitting by the phone."

"Tell her we said hello. I'll be at Mom's by ten."

"We should know more by then."

He dialed his great-aunt's number. "We're at the hospital. Bethany's dehydrated and running a fever. They admitted her for treatment."

"How's Katy?"

"All over the place emotionally. Overjoyed to have her child back, blaming God because she's sick. She won't let Bethany out of her sight. Pray for her, Aunt Lucille."

"Oh honey, I will. That child has endured so much. I can't wait to see her precious daughter."

"I called Lucy. She's going to Mom and Dad's in the morning to be there when I tell them."

"This child will be the best medicine in the world for them both."

"I pray Katy accepts our family. I'd hate it if she wouldn't allow us to be a part of Bethany's life."

"I don't think that's her nature. She wants the best for her child."

"I'd better get back. Night, Aunt Lucille. Get some rest. You've had a stressful night."

"Give Katy my love. Tell her I'm thrilled for them both."

After getting sodas and snacks from the vending machines, Richie headed back to Bethany's room. Pausing in the shadow of the doorway, he listened as Katy whispered to her child.

How she must feel right now? How could he have doubted God's ability to make things right in a world gone crazy? "How's she doing?"

Katy whipped about. The low glow of the light above the bed illuminated her exhaustion, giving her a sickly pallor. "The fever spiked again."

He set the soda on the bedside table and slipped an arm about her shoulders. "The antibiotics will help."

She managed a wan smile. "Thank you for going to that shelter tonight."

"Thank God for sending me."

Katy's head moved in a silent nod.

"You should rest."

"I can't. Not now."

"Promise you'll let me help when you can't go any further?"

Her gaze shifted back to Bethany. "I lost her once. I won't risk it again."

"If you're afraid of my family, we wouldn't steal her away from you."

"That man is out there. What if he comes looking for her? What if Agnes decides she wants her back?"

"You can't watch her twenty-four seven, Katy. I want to help."

"I appreciate the offer, but I have to stay close. Bethany will be terrified when she wakes. I doubt she'll trust me. Who knows what Jack told her? What she's thinking right now? How can she trust any adult at this point?"

Richie believed Bethany would recover from the trauma much faster if her mother set a fearless example. "Bethany needs your love. Cuddle and reassure her. Provide the normalcy she's not had. You'll probably find she comes to you often for comfort. Gradually, she'll start venturing out on her own again. You said she was an outgoing child before?"

Katy nodded. "Never met a stranger."

"This is too personal for me to handle, but I know my colleagues would be willing to help."

"I plan to look into counseling."

"Don't just look, Katy. Start immediately, once Bethany gets past this illness. The goal must be to help her recover as soon as possible."

"I know that. I am not a bad mother."

"I never said you were."

"Just a bad wife?"

Richie recognized her combativeness as a protective shield. "I don't know what happened to Jack—and I never will—but I need to be part of my niece's life. My family needs to get to know Bethany as well."

"I don't think it's wise to introduce her to more strangers right now."

Richie felt torn. On one hand, he wanted what was best for the child, but he also wanted his mother to be happy. Seeing Jack's daughter would do that for her.

"Can Mom call? Jack's death devastated her. You know what it feels like to lose your child."

She stirred uncomfortably. "I can't handle her blaming me, too."

They had heaped a burden of gigantic proportions on Katy's tiny shoulders. "We all blame ourselves. We should have kept in touch with Jack. Maybe we could have seen this coming—done something to help."

"I lived with your brother, and I didn't see it until it was too late. Even after I left, I still hoped Jack loved us enough to change."

Bethany thrashed about, mumbling Agnes's name. Richie moved to the head of the bed, ready to assist.

"Bethie honey, it's Mommy," Katy called. "I love you, baby."

"Mommy?" she repeated. Her head moved from side to side.

"Open your eyes, Bethany," she called. "Look at Mommy. You're having a bad dream."

Dazed blue eyes fixed on Katy. Confusion made her voice tiny and weak. "Mommy?"

"Yes, darling," Katy whispered tearfully, taking the tiny hand into hers. "I'm here."

"Where you been, Mommy?"

She stroked the child's cheek. "Looking for you. You and Daddy played a very good game of hide-and-seek."

"I wanted to go home. Daddy said you didn't love me."

Katy pulled her against her chest and rocked gently. "I'll never stop loving you, Bethie."

There was no reply, and Katy laid the sleeping child back, hating to let go.

Richie helped settle Bethany against the pillow. "I called Aunt Lucille and my sister. Aunt Lucille is thrilled. Lucy is going over to Mom and Dad's in the morning to be there when I tell them. I'm asking Mom to give you time. I can't promise she will."

"Bethany and I need this, Richie."

"I know, and I'm doing my best to help you."

Chapter 9

As night slipped into early morning, Katy couldn't keep her heavy lids open. She slept lightly, waking as the hospital staff came and went. Richie left around five a.m., promising to return later.

At six, an aide brought in a kit for Bethany. She placed the pan and towels on the rolling table and laid a clean gown on the foot of the bed.

Katy stood and said, "I'll do it."

She bathed Bethany from head to toe, changing the water often. Katy wiped the cloth over her head, wishing she could wash her hair. Instead, she used her brush to work at a few of the knots.

Bethie's grimy nails struck a chord deep within Katy. Even when she played in their gardens, the child had never been so dirty. Rummaging in her purse for a manicure set, Katy clipped, cleaned, and filed the ragged nails.

Removing every trace of neglect couldn't heal the inner child. How had Bethany coped with being kidnapped, deserted by her father, and living with a homeless woman?

Time passed slowly. Growing more impatient, she wanted nothing more than to see her child's eyes open.

Katy forced herself to think about what she would do now that she had Bethany back. She'd considered remaining in the area but needed a plan before she went up against her father. They could live on Jack's social security, her trust fund, and the life insurance payout.

The one thing she'd done right. She'd paid the policy premiums when Jack decided he didn't need life insurance. He'd only shrugged when she said the insurance was for Bethany and it was wrong of him not to maintain the policy. He'd told her to pay it herself, and she had.

She could sell the house and her SUV. A smaller vehicle would work for them. Technically, she supposed the proceeds from the house and cars belonged to her parents, but they'd called them gifts.

In another three years, she'd have full access to her trust fund. Not that she planned to touch the money. She needed it for Bethany's college and their future. Once Bethany was in school, she'd find a job.

Her back throbbed. She thought of the bottles that sat on the nightstand back at Lucille's house. No, she couldn't take something that would knock her out. She'd have to suffer through. Katy rested her head against her arms on the side of the bed. She woke to a tiny hand patting her head. She sat up quickly and watched Bethie battle heavy lids.

"Mommy's here, darling. Wake up, Bethany." The eyelids lifted a fraction and then closed again. "Oh honey," Katy whispered, disappointed.

She glanced up when the door opened. Richie offered a smile. "How's our girl?"

"Still trying to wake."

He set the suitcase on a nearby footstool. "Aunt Lucille said to call if you need anything else."

The idea of a stranger sorting through her things didn't make her happy, but Katy accepted the necessity. "Please thank her for me."

He carried a tray with two cups of coffee and a paper bag. "I figured you could use this."

Accepting the coffee cup, she stirred in creamer and sugar and took a sip. Katy sighed in appreciation.

"Here's something else you might need," he said, fishing bottles from his pocket. "Has the doctor been in?"

She shook out a couple of ibuprofen and swallowed them with her coffee. "Not yet." Her gaze turned toward Bethany.

"She'll turn the corner soon. People are praying for her. I saw this stuffed dog in your room. Thought he might comfort her."

Katy hugged the worn dog to her chest. "Thank you. She loves him."

"I can stick around if you'd like to stretch your legs or catch a shower."

"Thanks, but I need to be here when she wakes."

"I'd like to stay for a while if that's okay?"

"You don't have to."

"I want to," he said earnestly. "Right now, there's not much I can do for Bethany other than take care of her mom. Think you could eat a sausage and egg biscuit?"

Katy laughed. "Definitely."

Bev came in to check the IV that had started to beep a few minutes earlier. "I see breakfast has arrived."

"I would have bought more if I'd known you'd be here," Richie told her.

She glanced at the wall clock. "I'm off in thirty minutes."

As Bev worked on Bethany, Richie passed Katy food and a napkin. "Shall we pray?"

She noted Bev bowed her head, too, as Richie gave thanks and petitioned God for Bethany's and Katy's full recovery.

Katy finished the biscuit, balled the napkin and wrapper, and stuffed them into the empty cup. "Will I be able to take her home to the cottage?"

"I don't think so."

Katy frowned.

"Home is wherever you are," Richie reminded. He pointed to Bethany. "She's all you need. Forget about the house. That's something I can do while you concentrate your efforts on getting Bethany and yourself well. Make her your focus, Katy."

"I wanted a place where Bethany could feel at home."

"You want to escape my family," Richie said glumly. "Katy, I'm sorry I've hurt you. Made you doubt my sincerity."

"I can't hate you for believing your brother."

"*Hate* is a strong word."

"It's a strong emotion. Every time you doubted me, I resented Jack even more. You can't know how often I defended him to my family and friends."

He reached for her arm when she would have turned away. "I'm sorry. Forgive me?"

"Yes. You're not your brother."

"Can we start over? I want to be your friend, and I definitely want to be involved in Bethany's life."

"I won't say no to that. It's important that she know her family. I wish you'd known her before," Katy said wistfully.

"I plan to make up for lost time."

"You'll make an excellent uncle," Katy said. Her gaze lingered on his face, seeing love in the blue gaze as he looked down at Bethany. "You should find the right woman and settle down. Have some kids of your own."

His head came up, his look strange as his gaze fixed on her.

"What is it? Do I have something stuck in my teeth?" she asked, reaching for her mouth.

"No," he said, sounding distracted.

⁓

The right woman. Richie swallowed hard. The strongest feeling he'd already found her washed over him. His brother's widow. What would his family think if they knew? He'd been drawn to Katy from the moment he saw her on the Lennons' deck. Then it had been a basic man/woman attraction, but as time had passed, he'd come to appreciate her in so many ways.

Katy's spirit appealed to him. No matter what he'd thrown her way, she'd remained strong and focused and held on when so many others doubted. Richie liked that about her. He wanted a fresh start, an opportunity to show Katy he could be the man she thought he was.

"Did I tell you the congregation is thrilled with the murals?" he asked suddenly, changing the subject.

"Wait until they're finished."

"You should see the kids checking them out."

"Budding artists?"

He nodded. "I've seen talent that I never dreamed existed. This has been an outlet for them."

"Maybe I can do art classes once Bethany is well." She looked at him. "Do you think my children's party business would work in this area?"

He perked up. "Tell me your idea again."

"A business called Just Imagine. Bethie and I have always loved playing dress up and having tea parties. I'd love to find a house with a couple of large rooms where I could offer tea parties or story hours. I could do it in people's homes, too. You think there's a market?"

"Parents are always looking for something special for children's parties. Would it pay enough to support you?"

She shrugged. "I don't even know what to charge."

"You should check with other entertainers. Get their prices. Once you get figures, you could work in expenses and a profit margin." He glanced at his watch. "Guess I'd better show my face at work," Richie said. "Need anything before I go?"

"I'll call if she wakes."

"What about lunch?"

"I can ask them to send up a meal. Thanks for everything, Richie."

After he left, an aide pushed a reclining chair into the room. "Pastor Taylor asked us to find you a more comfortable chair. He explained about your back. You should have told us."

Katy moved out of the way so the aide could wheel the chair next to the bed. "Taking care of Bethany is more important. Thank you."

She spent the hours resting and watching television. Katy approached near desperation as Bethany continued to sleep. She drifted off around 11:00 a.m. and woke with a start, only to find the nurse checking her patient. "Any improvement?"

"Her fever's down and she's breathing easier."

Katy rested her face in her hands. "Why doesn't she wake up?"

"Sleep is healing."

She sighed. "I know. I just want her to wake long enough to feel things are improving."

Sympathy flashed in the woman's kind eyes.

Later that afternoon, Katy realized there would never be a more glorious sight than Bethany's blue eyes. She forced back tears of joy as she leaned over the bed. "Hi, sweetie."

"Mommy?" Bethany said, sounding confused and frightened.

Katy smoothed her hair. "Yes, baby, Mommy's here."

⟳

Bethany was awake when Richie visited that evening. He watched the two of them together. Katy was a good mother—loving, aware, guiding. The trauma made Bethany needier, but Katy took it in stride, fighting her own emotions as she cuddled and comforted her sobbing child.

Bethany grabbed his heart from the moment they met. Katy held Bethany against her chest in the loose circle of her arms. "This is your uncle Richie. He's Daddy's brother."

"Daddy went away. Where he go, Mommy?"

Katy couldn't speak. Richie knelt beside them. "I'm really happy to meet you. I've never had a niece before." He tapped Bethany's nose and winked. She turned her face into her mother's shoulder.

She peeked out at him. Richie grinned. "Uncles love to spoil their favorite nieces."

"What's spoil?"

Katy looked to him to explain that one.

"Hmm, let me think," Richie said with exaggerated pretense. "You like candy, right?"

Bethany nodded.

"Well, uncles like to buy candy for their nieces."

"Mommy buys me candy. Is that spoiling?"

"Only if I give you too much," Katy said.

"Mommies sometimes say no when uncles say yes," Richie added.

Her head bobbed up and down. "I like spoiling."

He chuckled. "We're going to get along just fine, Miss Bethany."

Chapter 10

Katy added a generous portion of bubble bath to the bathwater. She undressed Bethany and helped her climb into the tub. The child played with the frothy suds, her giggles like music to Katy's ears.

After a while, she worked the no-tears shampoo Richie had brought through the tangled locks of Bethany's hair. A couple of washings later and a bit of cream rinse made it less snarled, but the jagged edges needed a cut. Hair that had once hung to her daughter's waist now hung at a jagged shoulder length.

Katy toweled Bethany dry and dressed her in fresh pajamas before calling to have her IV reconnected. She held her close as they settled in the chair by the bed. "Bethie, can you tell me what happened?"

"Agnes," the child said, stumbling over the name, "made me go with her. We slept outside. It was dark. People gived me money. Agnes said it was okay." Katy sucked in a deep breath.

Her child had begged for her very existence. How did she explain that people made decisions to live like that? Beyond charitable donations, no one in her family had ever so much as thought about the lifestyle Bethany lived in Agnes's care. How would they help her? "Did anyone hurt you?"

Bethany shook her head. "Agnes yelled at them."

Katy hugged her close. "Oh Bethie, Mommy's so sorry."

"Didn't you want me?"

Katy caught Bethany's face between her hands and kissed her forehead. "I always want you, precious. I nearly died when that man took you away."

"Mean man. We went on long car ride. Then Daddy came and said we were going on an ad–ad–venture. What's 'venture, Mommy?"

"It's doing something different and fun. Like when we went to the zoo and you petted the elephant. That was an adventure."

"I didn't like this 'venture." Her little face screwed up. "Daddy left me."

"Why did you leave the car?" Even though she asked, Katy knew it had been for the best. If Agnes hadn't found her. . . She shuddered, not wanting to consider the alternative.

"I wanted to go home. I had to tell Daddy. I couldn't find him," she said, her voice wobbly. "Agnes made me go. I said no, but her didn't listen."

Bethany's language skills had suffered in the past month. Katy rocked her gently, and when Bethany dozed off, she continued to hold her close. "I'll never let anyone take you away again," she whispered against her hair.

The doctor decided to release Bethany the next day. Katy shared the news when Richie arrived that night. He'd brought gifts as he did every visit, this time a silly stuffed monkey and a DVD player.

"These are for you." He handed Katy a tiny box of chocolates. "How are you feeling?"

"Relieved that Bethany can go home and afraid I won't be able to help my child understand everything that's happened to her."

"I talked with Glenda. She's agreed to counsel Bethany."

Richie obviously trusted her, but Katy knew nothing of the woman. This wasn't his choice or hers. Bethany had to like the counselor. "I don't know."

"Glenda's the best. We can help her, Katy. Please let us try."

Was there more to their relationship than co-workers? Katy wondered, finding she didn't like the idea. Dinner arrived, and she busied herself with making sure Bethany ate as much as possible.

"You're a hungry girl," he teased when Katy fed her the last of the dessert.

She nodded, her mouth ringed with chocolate pudding. As Katy shifted the tray out of the way, he used a paper napkin to wipe the child's mouth. "Aunt Lucille told me to get a list of Bethany's favorites. She's sending me grocery shopping."

They cleared the tray away, and Richie set up the portable DVD player so they could watch a popular children's movie. Katy enjoyed Bethany's laughter.

"You're spoiling her outrageously."

"Uncle's privilege."

"You'll bankrupt yourself."

"The player and movie are borrowed. And I can afford a stuffed monkey and box of candy."

Bethany reached out to her mother, and Katy picked her up. They cuddled on the reclining chair—Richie on the stool next to them—and watched the movie. He could see Bethany's giggles did Katy a world of good.

"She's out for the count."

Seeing her predicament, Richie lifted Bethany from Katy's chest and tucked her into bed. "What time do I pick you up?" he asked as she adjusted the over-the-bed lighting.

"We can't leave until the doctor signs the release."

"Give me a call. I'll be working at the cottage. I took a couple of days off."

Katy followed him to the door. "Thanks for everything, Richie. You've been wonderful."

His gaze lingered on her face. "My pleasure. See you in the morning."

~

After a restful night, the Sinclair females woke early. Katy bathed and dressed Bethany before packing the small suitcase. "Are you ready to go home?"

Her dog dropped to the bed. "To Grandfather and Grandmother's?"

Katy winced at the formal names. "I thought we'd stay here at the beach for a while. The bad storm damaged our house, so we'll be staying with Aunt Lucille."

A little crease marred the child's forehead. "Who Aunt Lucille, Mommy?"

"She's Uncle Richie's great-aunt."

Bethany dangled her legs over the side of the bed. "What's beach?"

"Just wait and see. You'll love it."

The door opened and Richie stepped in. He came around the bed and tapped Bethany on the nose. "You ladies ready to go home?"

"Not Grandfather and Grandmother's," Bethany told him. "Aunt Lucille's."

"That's right, precious. Aunt Lucille likes little girls. She gives them cookies."

"I like cookies," Bethany said with a satisfied nod.

"Me, too," Richie agreed. He glanced at Katy. "Have you signed the release papers?"

Katy zipped the bag shut. "All done. We just need to let them know you're here. They plan to give Bethie a special ride downstairs."

They waited while Richie went after the vehicle. Katy's gaze widened as he pulled up in a new black truck with a king cab. "Nice vehicle."

"Thanks. I've never owned anything new. Figured it was time."

She grinned. "No wonder you weren't worried about the monkey and candy."

He opened the back door and swung Bethany into the top-quality car seat.

"Did you buy this, too?"

Richie nodded. "I want her to be safe when she's riding with me."

"I'll sit in back with her."

He went around and opened the opposite rear door so she could climb inside. As he loaded the suitcase and other items from Bethany's hospital stay, Katy considered what Richie had said.

How was it possible to be excited that he planned to spend time with them and at the same time be fearful of what that meant? Katy had strong feelings for Richie. She knew the symptoms. When he was away, she wondered where he was and what he was doing. Her heart beat a little faster at the sight of him. She looked forward to their chats and learning everything about him.

But then the little devil of doubt raised his head and mumbled that he was only using her to get to Bethany. No. This was Richie. Not Jack. She refused to accept that he would ever do anything to hurt either of them.

The movement of the vehicle soon had Bethany nodding. She fought sleep, but when her head tipped against the side of the car seat, Katy settled her more comfortably.

"She tires quickly," Richie said, catching her eye in the rearview mirror.

"The doctor says she'll soon be her old self."

"Physically, maybe. What have you told her about Jack?"

"For now, I've told her he's gone. I'll explain what happened when I think she's old enough to understand. I wish I could take Bethany to the cottage. I'm afraid getting used to two new places will be unsettling for her."

"She'll like Aunt Lucille's house. When we were kids, it was our favorite place to go."

"It's a wonderful house." Katy fingered a lock of Bethany's red-gold hair. She'd arranged for a stylist to come to the hospital. Everyone said the shorter cut would be good for summer. "How's the mural coming along?"

"The kids are working hard to get it done." He sounded so pleased.

"I didn't mean to abandon them."

"They know. They're praying for you and Bethany."

The thought of strangers caring so much made it difficult to speak. "Maybe I'll take her to meet them."

"They'd love that." Richie parked in the driveway. "Want me to carry her inside?"

Katy busied herself unhooking the seat belt. "I've got her."

"I don't plan to run off with her, Katy," he insisted, his impatience resurfacing. "I only wanted to give your back a break."

She felt the flush run across her cheeks. "If you'll carry her, I'll grab the bag and get the door," she offered penitently.

"Leave the bag. I'll bring it in after we get her settled."

Richie settled Bethany against his shoulder. She opened heavy eyes, looked at him, and then laid her head against his chest. Katy hurried to open the door. "Lucille?" she called. "We're here."

The woman bustled into the room, trying to get a glimpse of Bethany. "I thought we'd put her in the room next to yours. There's a connecting door."

"We'll share my room. I don't want her alone in a strange place."

Lucille followed them into the bedroom and trailed arthritic fingers across Bethany's cheek after Richie laid her on the bed. "Our little miracle. She's so beautiful, Katy."

She nodded, swiping at her eyes as she slipped Bethany's shoes off. Katy pulled the sheet over her.

"Your sister called," Lucille said. "I told her you were at the hospital with Bethany. She seemed surprised. I hope I didn't say anything I shouldn't have."

"Not at all." Katy pushed Bethie's socks into the sneakers and set them on the floor. It had been easy to make excuses not to call, and while others might think her mean-spirited, she'd done what she needed to do.

Cliff Dennison would swoop down, and before she knew what happened, they would be back in Vegas living with her parents until they found the man they felt she should marry.

Her parents had their own ideas for her future. If Bethany had not been found, in time she would have been expected to marry someone they deemed appropriate and accept her social responsibilities. Any man they approved would be out to make a name for himself and his wife expected to concentrate all her efforts on helping make him a success. They'd live in the perfect house and maybe produce a perfect child when the timing was right. Or maybe it would be decided she shouldn't have more children because of her heartbreak over Bethany.

Their perfect man wouldn't know the godly traits she needed in a husband. Neither of them would really have time for that perfect home and family. Growing up, she'd heard a million excuses, reasons why her father's work was more important than scheduled family events. The things hadn't replaced a close relationship with her dad. They only increased Katy's longings for a normal family life. She'd set about creating that home but quickly learned she'd chosen the wrong man.

Katy needed a man who would put God first in his marriage and his life. A man who made sure his family knew they were loved and appreciated. A man who provided for their needs and gave with his heart. A man like Richie.

She shook her head to free herself from this thought. Richie was on her mind entirely too much lately. She even cared about what he thought when she considered her decisions for the future.

The only thing she knew for sure was that she couldn't give in to her father's dictates or Bethany would never know the life Katy wanted for her. Her daughter needed an opportunity to pursue the plans God had for her.

Now that Bethany was better, Katy felt stronger. Joy and fear battled within her. The feeling of loss receded with the joy of finding her child, but she feared the role of single parent. Could she do a good job without the support of her family?

"What's her favorite meal?" Lucille asked.

"Chicken tenders, french fries, and chocolate milkshakes."

"Let's make that our celebration lunch. You're looking pale. Richie says you haven't slept much."

"I needed to be there when she woke."

Lucille nodded. "Bethany needs you more now than ever. Sleep as long as you need. I'm here to help out."

"Thanks, Lucille."

The door closed, and Katy reached for her cell phone. After the initial answer, she waited for their butler to summon her mother or father to the phone. She jumped when her father's gruff voice came over the line.

"It's about time, Kaitlin."

"Hello, Dad."

"Dina tells me my granddaughter is alive."

"Yes sir. They released her from the hospital today."

"Why didn't you call?"

Resentment welled up in Katy. Had it even occurred to him that she'd been at the hospital with her sick child? Before she could help herself, the words came out. "I wasn't sure you cared."

Several moments of silence punctuated the connection. "We both said things we regret, Kaitlin."

Katy regretted nothing. If she hadn't followed her instincts and come to North Carolina, she would never have found Bethany. In fact, she would have eventually accepted their fatalism and lost her daughter forever. She didn't even want to consider the life her innocent child would have endured living among the homeless.

"Where has she been since Jack's death?"

"With a homeless woman named Agnes."

"A homeless. . ." She winced when he cursed. "Why?"

"From what we can ascertain, Jack hid Bethany in an abandoned warehouse. She was looking for her daddy when the woman found her." Katy didn't share the probability that they wouldn't have gotten Bethany back if not for the miracle of her coming to the shelter.

"It's shameful Jack did this to her. He got exactly what he deserved."

"No one deserves to be murdered."

"They do when they put themselves in jeopardy. When are you coming home?" The blunt question demanded an answer.

Katy pushed away her dread. She had to tell him. Sucking in a deep breath, she released it and said, "Mr. Lennon has offered me use of the cottage for as long as I need. I plan to take him up on his offer."

"But Dina said the cottage was damaged."

"It's nearly repaired. Bethany and I need time alone to focus on what's happened."

"She's three, Kaitlin. She probably doesn't remember what she had for dinner last night."

Her father didn't believe in coddling children. Maybe if Bethany had taken after him, the incident could be easily forgotten, but like her mother, Bethany suffered from emotional hurts.

"What about your life here? Your home? Your family and friends? How do you plan to support yourself? Or do you think you can continue to live off your trust fund allowance?"

She noted the chill in his tone as he released the torrent of questions. "I'd like to sell the house."

"That's a good idea. You can live with us."

"That's not what I have in mind," Katy began, her confidence increasing as she continued. "You and Mother have done far too much already. It's time I took responsibility for my life and my child."

"Think about this, Kaitlin. Do you know what you're doing?"

She'd never been more certain about anything in her life. "I'm becoming the parent my child deserves."

"I'll tell your mother Bethany is fine."

"Not fine," Katy said. "We can't begin to know the ways this has affected her. Right now, all that's important is that she be happy. I'm willing to give up everything to give her that."

"I see."

Katy didn't think he did. "I'll stay in touch. Let you know how things are going."

"Give Bethany a kiss for us."

She turned off the cell phone. Would it kill him to offer her a bit of encouragement? Her father could solve any number of problems with his checkbook, but she needed reassurance, confirmation they believed in her, and she'd never get that from Cliff Dennison.

She called Dina. Her sister's tone when she asked about Bethany bothered Katy. She was hurt.

"She's sleeping. We just got home from the hospital."

"You should join her," Dina said. "You're exhausted. I can hear it in your voice."

"I will. I'm sorry I didn't call. It's been crazy."

"I know, Katy. You were so totally focused on Bethany that you didn't think your family might like to know she was alive. I don't imagine you've let her out of your sight since she was found."

Was Dina criticizing her? "I called Dad. He's not happy with me. I told him I plan to stay here for a while longer. I think the different environment will be good for Bethany."

"Trust your instincts. They got you what you wanted."

"Don't be like this, Dina. I'm sorry."

Dina sighed. "I'm sorry, too. It hurt to hear the news from a stranger. Now go to bed, Katy. We'll talk later."

She cut off the phone and went to answer the knock on the bedroom door.

"Everything okay?" Richie asked.

"I just spoke with my father and Dina."

"I'm sure they were delighted with your news."

She yawned. "Not all of it."

"They'll come around. I'm going to the cottage. You have my number. Call if you need anything."

"Thanks, Richie."

After he left, Katy fell into a deep sleep and woke to find Bethany playing with her dolls in the corner of the room. A small glass and plate indicated she'd had her snack. Katy knelt on the floor and reached to touch her face. "Did you have a good nap?"

Bethany nodded and continued to dress her doll.

"Are you hungry? Aunt Lucille said she'd make chicken tenders and french fries."

Bethany nodded again.

"Cat got your tongue?" Katy teased.

The tip of her tongue peeped out between Bethany's lips.

Katy smiled. "Oh. . .so you don't want to talk to Mommy. Is that it?"

She shook her head. "Mommy sleep! Do not wake!"

The child's stern tone and waving finger shocked Katy. Who had berated her little girl to make her speak like this? She pulled her close and said, "You

83

wake Mommy anytime you want, Bethie. I won't be angry."

They ate lunch and enjoyed a peaceful afternoon. Bethany played and napped again while Katy handled a few chores. That night her daughter slept close to her on the double bed.

The next morning, Katy lay watching her, and when Bethany's eyes opened, she smiled brightly. "Morning, sweetness."

The little girl returned her smile and opened her arms. Katy hugged her tight. "Let's get you dressed. What would you like for breakfast?"

Bethany named a favorite cereal. Katy doubted Lucille had any in the house. "How about I make you cheese toast and we'll go shopping later?"

The child was amiable, and they went downstairs to find Aunt Lucille and Richie drinking coffee in the kitchen.

"Mommy, look," she cried, running to the table.

Katy noted the cereal box on the tabletop along with a bowl and glass of milk.

"My favorite niece and I like the same kind of cereal," Richie told her.

When had they discussed cereals? She had rarely been out of Bethany's presence. Oh well, Bethany would have her favorite breakfast. "Thank Uncle Richie."

The child offered him a shy smile.

"Can I have a hug?"

Richie opened his arms wide, and Bethany moved into his embrace. Their connection surprised Katy.

"So what's the plan for today?"

"We're going shopping," Bethany told him.

"I planned to take her to the grocery store for cereal. I didn't realize you'd already bought a box."

"It was on the list. So now we can play on the beach instead."

"What's beach, Uncle Richie?"

"You don't know what a beach is?" he asked with mock surprise. "Well, young lady, we have to fix that right now." He glanced at Katy. "Does she have a swimsuit?"

"She does. Miss Bethany swims like a fish." Katy had been hopeful when she packed the suit.

"Okay." Richie rubbed his hands together enthusiastically. "I'll take my sand toys, and we can build a castle after we play in the water. Let's finish our cereal. We have an adventure to plan."

Bethany's eyes grew wide and fearful and tears bubbled over.

Richie looked confused. "What did I say?"

"Her dad called their trip an adventure," Katy explained. "She didn't like it."

"I see." He came over and knelt before the little girl. "Bethany, I promise I'd never do anything to hurt you." The child wasn't convinced. "I know you're going to like the beach, but if you don't, tell Mommy or me, and we'll bring you home right away. Okay?"

Bethany's tiny smile met his, and Katy realized why he'd looked so familiar that first night. They both shared Jack's smile.

He stood and held out a hand to Bethie. "Let's raid Aunt Lucille's fridge. I know she has juice boxes. Cookies are in the big jar on the counter. How does that sound for a beach picnic?"

She nodded approval.

Richie swung her up into a big hug. He kissed her forehead. "I love you."

"Do you love my mommy?"

Katy sputtered the coffee she'd just sipped. She grabbed a paper towel to clean up the mess. "Sorry."

Richie looked at her and grinned. "Yeah, Bethany, I love your mommy, too. You're my girls."

⁓

The day was better than Richie could have imagined. He'd packed the cooler and changed into board shorts while Katy and Bethany changed. Katy wore a one-piece swimsuit with a cover-up while Bethany wore a one-piece with a favorite cartoon character on the front. Richie knew he'd never forget Bethany's expression when she got her first look at the ocean. After piling their gear on the sand, they captured Bethany's tiny hands and led her to the water.

At first, she tried to dodge the waves and then grew braver with each incoming surge. Soon she pulled her hands from theirs, dancing about and giggling when the water washed away the sand about her feet.

After a while, they went to work on their sand castle. Their group increased when kids from church showed up, and their royal kingdom soon filled a goodly portion of the area.

Richie jogged over when he spotted Bethany lying on the beach towel. "Is she okay?"

"Tired."

"You want to go home?" he asked the little girl.

She shook her head against the rolled towel that served as her pillow.

Richie looked back to Katy. "If she falls asleep, I'll carry her back to the house."

Katy smiled at him.

"Happy?"

"Oh yes. Right now, the past seems like nothing more than a bad dream."

"There will be good and bad times," he cautioned. "But we're going to pray that God keeps the bad at a minimum and gives our sweet girl peace."

"Let's play in the water, Mommy."

Unable to deny her anything, Katy said, "For a few minutes."

Bethany jumped up and chased after the seagull that landed nearby, her hair sparkling in the sunlight. Katy chuckled and said, "Guess she's not as tired as I thought."

Chapter 11

As predicted, Bethany loved the beach, and they spent hours playing in the water, building sand castles, hunting shells, and chasing seagulls. Despite the sunscreen Katy slathered on them both, her daughter turned berry brown while Katy's paler skin suffered through burn and peel sessions.

Things were not all rosy. Every day featured periods of laughter and smiles or tantrums and tears. Bethany's inconsistent behavior and not knowing which personality to expect kept Katy on edge. Bethany's withdrawals hurt the most.

Then Cynthia Taylor called. Their polite and somewhat stilted conversation erupted when Katy refused to put Bethany on the phone.

"She's all I have left of Jack," her mother-in-law declared. "I'll contact my lawyer. Grandparents have rights, too."

"I'm not saying you can't see her, Mrs. Taylor. Bethany needs time to adjust. She's very fragile. Ask Richie if you don't believe me."

Obviously, she had. When Richie called to say Glenda had an 11:00 a.m. appointment open, Katy wondered if his mother had shared her threat with her son.

She told him she needed to talk to Bethany about the session, and later Katy wished she'd kept the reason for the trip to herself.

"No, Mommy. I don't want to." Bethany's screams reverberated throughout the room.

Katy knelt before her on the floor. "It will be good for you, honey."

"No!" She shoved her mother. Katy caught her balance just in time to avoid tumbling backward.

Bethany's defiant behavior made Katy think they both needed a time-out. "Play here in our room."

The little girl went to the corner and settled among her toys. Katy took her cell into the hallway. After leaving a message on Richie's pager, she sat in the window seat to await his call. The tiny ormolu clock on a nearby shelf read nine fifteen.

"Bethany doesn't want to go," she told him a few minutes later. "I've always been honest with her. I can't betray that trust. Particularly not now."

"You could tell her you're visiting me."

"I wouldn't feel right about deceiving her," Katy said.

"No deceit. I'll be here. Tell Bethany she's coming to see where Uncle Richie works. I really want her to talk to Glenda. She can help get her past this, Katy."

Katy wished she felt that way. "I'm beginning to think nothing will ever be the same."

"Prayer helps. Turn your burden over to God."

"God doesn't always answer our prayers, Richie."

"You can't shoulder this load alone. You need Him."

"What I need is for my daughter to be normal again."

"Then bring her to visit me."

In the bedroom, Bethany played with her stuffed dog and monkey.

Katy missed the old Bethany. This clingy, quiet child was far from her independent motormouth. Her father had once said Bethany could talk the ears off an elephant. More than anything, Katy wanted Richie to see that child. "We're going to visit Uncle Richie."

Bethany shook her head. "I'm playing."

"We can play later."

"Wanna play now."

"I thought we'd take Uncle Richie out to eat at your favorite place. Spend some time in the play area." Katy shrugged and walked over to sit in the armchair. "Guess we'll stay home."

Okay, so she wasn't above bribing her child. Bethany loved the play area, but fast food wasn't something Katy allowed often.

Bethany bounded to her feet. Her daughter had never been so agreeable. Wearing the clothes Katy picked out, Bethany chattered all the way to the office. She caught Katy's hand when they walked toward the entrance. Butterflies twirled and danced in Katy's stomach. She stopped at the desk and gave the receptionist their names. "We're here to see Richie Taylor."

"I'll let him know you've arrived."

Katy pulled Bethany into her lap and handed her a book. She turned a couple of pages before asking, "Now, Mommy?"

"Just a few minutes longer," Katy promised.

When Richie came into the room, Bethany darted to him. By the time Katy joined them, she'd told him about their lunch plans.

"She did, did she?" Richie said, glancing at Katy with a knowing smile. "I'd love to go, but first I want to introduce you to my friends."

Bethany slipped her hand in his and reached back for her mother's.

It was the only way I could think of to get her here, she mouthed over the child's head.

He nodded and glanced down when Bethany tugged his hand. "Hurry."

Richie laughed and swung her into his arms. He stopped at the desk and made the introductions. They moved down the hallway, stopping in offices along the way. When they reached the end office, he said, "Bethany, this is my very good friend Ms. Glenda. Glenda, this is Katy and Bethany Sinclair."

Pushing back her surprise, Katy greeted the middle-aged woman with a nod of her head. For some reason, she'd thought Glenda would be younger, closer to Richie's age. A time or two, when he referred to his boss in glowing terms, Katy found herself envious of their relationship and the things they had in common. Of course she and Richie had common interests, too. Bethany and the cottage restoration.

"We're going to lunch," Bethany announced.

Her excitement reminded Katy of the old Bethany. An ember of hope stirred.

Glenda came around her desk. "But I wanted to visit with you," she said, sounding disappointed.

Bethany turned her head away, and Katy's spark of hope burned out.

"Can I speak to you in the hall?" Richie said to his boss. He handed Bethany over to Katy. They returned a couple of minutes later. "Glenda's hungry, too. Do you think she could go to lunch with us?"

Bethany peeped out long enough to nod. Richie carried her out to Katy's car. He waited while she buckled Bethany in. She shut the door and turned to him.

"Glenda agrees it's best to keep this informal. I hope you don't mind that I invited her along."

Her gaze shifted to the child in the car and back. "I want what's best for Bethany. I'm sorry you have to leave the office."

Richie touched her arm gently. "Actually, it's a good idea. This way we can see her in a happy, relaxed environment, doing what she enjoys."

Could it be Richie had actually given her the tiniest bit of credit? Katy wondered as she started the car and headed for the fast-food restaurant.

The outing proved very little beyond Bethany's new aversion to strangers. No matter what Richie said or did to encourage her repartee with Glenda, the child shied away from the woman and responded only to him.

Soon she ran off to the play area. The adults watched from a nearby table.

"She's exhibiting signs of withdrawal. Has she always been this shy, Mrs. Sinclair?"

"Please call me Katy. The best word to describe Bethany before would have been *precocious*. She never met a stranger and at times was too determined for her own good."

"And now?"

"She doesn't sleep well, won't let me out of her sight for more than a few minutes, and strangers scare her to death."

"Are you being overprotective? Perhaps not encouraging exploration?" Glenda asked.

Katy glanced at Richie, wondering if he'd fostered this idea. "I'm as over-protective as any mother who lost her child and feared she might be dead can be. I'm not pushing Bethany to explore. I'm too afraid of what could happen."

"But why be afraid?" Glenda asked. "Your husband is no longer in the picture."

"There are too many unknowns. The reason Jack came here. The woman who found Bethany. The men who chased me."

"Chased?" Glenda repeated, confused as she glanced at Richie.

Katy nodded. "When I showed them Jack's and Bethany's pictures, they demanded money. I ran and they chased me. Busted my car window. They were gone when the police went out."

"She went alone to the neighborhood where they found Jack," Richie explained. "She's convinced these men knew my brother."

Angered by Richie's observation, Katy snapped, "I'm right here. And I'm more than convinced. The first man told the second I had a photo of his old friend Jack. Then he demanded the money Jack owed him."

"That certainly explains your feelings, but what about experiences where you're guaranteed she's safe from harm?"

Katy saw danger everywhere. "We were buying ice cream when she was taken. I won't put either of us in that situation again."

"That's not a healthy attitude, Katy."

Hadn't this woman heard anything she said? Her only hope of protecting Bethany was to outthink the bad people. Friend or foe, she would not give anyone ready access to her innocent child again. "Healthy or not, it's going to be a long time before I'm comfortable enough to let go. A very long time."

"Mommy, look," Bethany called from the slide.

She waved and smiled, hiding the fear that welled up inside her. Would she ever feel safe again? Katy doubted it was possible.

Katy thought about the visit on the way home. Richie seemed to think this Glenda woman could reach Bethany, but she didn't agree. Bethany seemed to want nothing to do with her. She hoped Richie's admiration for his boss wouldn't blind him to that truth. Back at Lucille's, she checked her voice mail and found she'd missed a call from her father. After Bethany went down for her nap, Katy returned his call.

"The agent thinks the house will sell quicker if you pack up the clutter and paint over the mural," he said without as much as a hello. Her father hated her kid-friendly decorating style. "Would it help if I hired a painter and mover?"

She was tempted to let them pack up everything and put it in storage. At least until she felt more secure about their future. But change meant she needed to rid herself of excess baggage. "No. I need to sort through everything. I'll come home for a few days."

"Where did you say you're staying?"

"Lucille Miller, Jack's step great-aunt, invited us to stay at her house."

"I'd think you'd want to steer clear of that family."

"They're Bethany's family. Her uncle Richie has been extremely helpful. In fact. . ."

"Probably sees dollar signs like his brother did."

Katy snorted. She'd never known a less-materialistic person. "Richie is a Christian counselor and youth minister."

"He can't be all that good with a brother like Jack."

Just as Richie judged her, her father judged Jack's family based on his experience with Jack. "Richie and Lucille have been nothing but kind."

"Blamed you for Jack's shortcomings, I bet."

She would not allow her father to undermine her relationship with Richie.

"He doesn't understand why Jack changed either."

"I don't think he changed. Good riddance, I say."

"I can't change the past, and I wouldn't want to because if I'd never met Jack, I wouldn't have Bethany."

"She's the only good thing that came from your marriage."

At least they agreed on one thing.

"Would you like for me to have my secretary make your flight arrangements? She can e-mail you the specifics."

Katy thought of the money it would save her but also considered she would be beholden to her father yet again. "No. I'll let you know when we'll be arriving."

Dread filled Katy four days later when they boarded a plane destined for Las Vegas. This wouldn't be easy, but it had to be done. Beside her, Bethany sat preoccupied with her book bag filled with the toys and books she didn't want to leave behind. Katy didn't know how she'd gotten the stuffed dog and monkey into the bag.

Once in Vegas, they caught a cab to her parents' house. Katy could hardly quell her disappointment at their unemotional welcome. She'd brought the grandchild they thought was dead to visit them. What was it that kept them from wanting to hug Bethany close and never let go? Within minutes, her child was relegated to the kitchen for a snack so the adults could talk in the drawing room. Their action only served to reinforce Katy's belief that she'd made the right decision for Bethany and herself.

"Will you stay here at the house?" her mother asked as she poured tea.

Katy accepted the cup. "Probably easier to work from home. There's a lot to be done before we leave again."

Rachelle Dennison's head shot up. "You don't plan to stay for a while?"

"I don't want to interrupt Bethany's counseling sessions." The little white lie slipped out easily. Not a lie, Katy justified. There would be sessions when they returned to North Carolina.

"What's going on, Kaitlin?" her father demanded.

"She went through a very traumatic situation. Counseling will help her."

"There are specialists here."

"Bethany is responding to her uncle. He's a nice guy."

"You're too gullible for your own good."

She felt an instant's squeezing hurt. "You think I'm gullible because I trust people not to hurt me?"

He got the point. "Water under the bridge."

If only it were that simple. Her father had done his part to rob her of her naiveté. Never again would she be the same trusting daughter or wife.

Rachelle Dennison set her cup back on the saucer. "Your father and I think you should sell the house and move back in with us. Now that Jack's out of the picture, we can put the past behind us and move on."

"We're going back to North Carolina."

"When are you going to get this foolishness out of your head?" her father demanded.

"It isn't foolish," Katy denied.

"You're moving across the country alone to stay at the beach. What about the support of your family?"

Support. Control. The words meant different things but not to her father.

"We'll stay in touch. You could visit. Wrightsville Beach and Wilmington are beautiful areas."

"How will you support yourself?"

"I plan to start a children's party business."

"That won't support you and Bethany."

"Then I'll find a job. Mr. Lennon offered me the cottage through the winter. I'm going to sell the car, house, and most of the furniture. Bethany and I will make new memories."

"There are bad memories there, too."

She refused to let him change her mind. "Yes, but Bethie loves the beach. And her uncle Richie."

"How can you associate with Jack's family?" he demanded with something akin to disgust in his tone.

"Richie is nothing like Jack."

"If you say so. That man did a world of harm."

"And he's dead. I can't bring Bethany's father back, but I can do everything possible to make her happy."

"I'd think you'd welcome the support of your family. You certainly depended on us in the past."

How like her mother to point that out. "Too much so. I do appreciate everything you've done for us, but it's time I stop letting others direct my path."

Her cell phone rang. Katy pulled it from her bag and saw it was Richie. "Excuse me."

"Hi, Katy. I called to see how things are going."

Had he really? Or had he called to see if she planned to run away? She pushed aside her doubts. "We're fine. How are you? And Lucille?"

"We're okay. Started your packing yet?"

"Hold on. I need to check on Bethany." As she walked from the drawing room, Katy said, "I start work on the house tomorrow. We're visiting my parents right now."

"How's Bethany adapting?"

"So far so good. No meltdowns on the plane or here."

"I miss her. And you, too. When are you coming home?"

Home. What a wonderful word. "Probably by the end of the week."

"That's great. I have some good news for you, too. The house is finished."

"Oh Richie, thank you."

"I thought you'd like to know. The murals are finished, too. They're wonderful, Katy."

"I can't wait to see them. I know the kids did a great job."

"Thanks to you."

"We made a good team."

"I'll let you get back to your visit. Promise to call if you need anything?"

"Thanks for checking on us, Richie."

She peeked into the kitchen to find Bethany sitting at the table with cereal and milk. As she returned to the drawing room, Katy couldn't help but think of Lucille's big, comfortable house. Its beachy comfort radiated welcome to all who entered while this house shut people out with its cold formality.

Katy had made her home a cozy abode for the people she loved. A place where feet on the coffee table weren't an issue, baskets of toys weren't an eyesore, and a child's artwork was more valuable than that of a master artist.

She refused to live life at a distance. Never saying "I love you" to her child. Living in a showplace instead of a home.

"That was Richie," she told her parents. "He wanted to know how Bethany is handling things."

The look her parents shared spelled out their thoughts on the matter. But there was a more important matter at hand. The two of them argued their viewpoint for what seemed like hours. Once they accepted they couldn't change her mind, her father left for a golf game and her mother retired to her room with one of her sick headaches, leaving them free to leave.

Katy packed up the items they'd left at her parents' and took the SUV keys. After loading their stuff, she retrieved Bethany from the kitchen and they left for home.

They stopped for groceries and a few packing boxes. In the backseat, Bethany sang along with a video while Katy attempted to organize her plans for the week. She wanted to get the job done fast and get out of there as soon as possible. She would donate some things to charity but needed to find a consignment shop for Jack's expensive clothing. She might get more for her furniture if she found an auction company.

Katy hit the garage door opener and parked inside. She feared what she might find. Jack had lived there for the month following their separation. He never cleaned up after himself, and she thought the place might be a pigsty.

The house was clean. Her father had probably had his secretary make the arrangements after they discussed putting the house on the market.

Dina showed up after work. Kevin was working late. She joined them for a soup and sandwich dinner and played with Bethany until the child fell asleep. When Katy carried her into the master bedroom, Dina followed. She waited as Dina folded back the covers and laid Bethany on the bed. She tucked her in and turned the lamp off. Then they moved over to the bedroom's sitting area.

"Did Dad send you to talk sense into me?"

Her sister grinned. "He's worried about you and Bethany. He loves you. We all do. We don't want you so far away."

"I need this, Dina. We love the beach."

"Then move to California. Not across the country."

Katy returned to her sorting. She tossed a pile of mismatched socks into the trash bag. Jack's underwear and T-shirts followed.

Dina watched her closely. "What aren't you telling us, Katy?"

"Richie. . ."

"Jack's brother?"

"Half brother," she corrected. "Bethie is responding to him. He can help her."

"Stay away from those people, Katy. Isn't it enough Jack nearly ruined our life?"

"What's important is that Bethany and I make a fresh start. We can do that in North Carolina."

"You can do that here."

"No, I can't," Katy cried, dropping onto the armchair. She tried and failed to catch the tumble of clothes her movement dislodged. Katy left them on the floor. She sighed and lifted a tray of expensive cuff links from the small table. Would Kevin be interested in these?"

Dina ignored the tray. "This is important to you?"

Katy nodded and rested the tray in her lap. "I want to start a business. Do the things Bethie enjoys for other kids."

Dina placed a hand on hers and squeezed. "Then you should do it. Just take care, Katy. Don't put yourself or Bethie at risk again. If you need help, call us. Kevin and I want to be there for you and Bethany."

She hugged her sister close. "Thanks for understanding. Now about these cuff links."

"Sell them," Dina said. "Neither Kevin nor I want anything to remind us of Jack."

Chapter 12

Katy led Bethany out of the house. She looked adorable in the denim jumper and print shirt. Her mom looked adorable, too. Richie stifled the thought. He'd missed them.

"How are my girls today? You're looking mighty pretty."

Bethany turned her head against her mother and wrapped an arm about a slender leg. "Tell Uncle Richie thank you," Katy prompted.

The child nodded but didn't speak.

"I think that's what's known as a nonverbal response," Katy said with a smile. "Let's drive my car."

"Are you enjoying the cottage?" He had helped them move their things in the day before.

"Oh yes," Katy said. "We miss Lucille, but we're enjoying having the place to ourselves."

Richie swung Bethany up in his arms and asked, "Did Mommy tell you where we're going today?"

Bethany's head bobbed up and down. "School. I've never been to school before. Mommy said I'm too little."

"Children of all ages attend Sunday school."

"Do they ride a bus?"

"Some do. Others come in cars with their families."

Bethany's attention shifted to the new topic. "Mommy, where's Daddy?" she asked, interrupting Richie's description.

He watched Katy's eyes close briefly. She drew a deep breath and said, "Daddy's gone away, Bethany."

"I miss Daddy," she announced. "When's he coming home?"

"He's not coming back, honey."

"But I want Daddy to come home," she whined.

"He can't, Bethany," Richie said. "Daddy's gone to be with Jesus."

He could see from Katy's expression that she didn't want him saying that to Bethany. What did she expect him to do? Let the child worry about her missing father? Richie couldn't do that.

"In heaven?" Bethany asked.

Richie's brows rose at his niece's question. She obviously understood more than he thought.

"She's attended church," Katy said softly. "And she's lost pets that went to heaven. Uncle Richie wants to tell you about the children's activities at his church, Bethany."

"Do they have tea parties and dress up?"

"They've had story hours since your mommy came to visit."

"I like stories and parties."

Like her mother, his niece knew what she liked. "We study about Jesus."

"What's study?"

"She asks a lot of questions for one so small."

Katy stopped for the light. "There's a lot to learn in life. I don't discourage her, even though there are times when the questions become wearisome."

He nodded and looked back at Bethany. "You go to Sunday school to learn about God and His Son, Jesus."

She nodded her head. "I know about Jesus. Are we there yet?"

He chuckled at her response. "Soon."

Bethany started talking to her dog, putting an end to the conversation.

"Mom's eager to meet Bethany. They'd like me to bring her to Charlotte."

"No one is taking my child anywhere. It's not open to negotiation."

Richie understood, but Katy's disregard for his mother bothered him. He'd witnessed her devastation at the loss of her son. "She's their granddaughter. Mom needs this, Katy."

She glared, speaking between clenched teeth. "Then have her come here."

"Dad can't travel. They expect you to come, too."

"And no doubt be as welcome as ants at a picnic," Katy commented. "I'm sure they think I'm an awful person. I never contacted them or offered to bring their grandchild to meet them. I didn't want it to be that way. I dreamed of having a great relationship with Jack's family."

Two fat droplets trailed down her face, and Richie fought back the urge to wipe them away.

"They don't know you like I do, Katy. Just give them a chance to love you."

"How is that possible? There's too much water under the bridge. Jack made sure of that. I had to look bad for him to look good."

"I think maybe Jack never learned respect for the true treasures in life. Love for the Lord, the love of a good woman, the blessings of beautiful children, and a good job." Money was the evil that drove his brother to throw away every opportunity to live the good life. "Though they've never met her, my family adores Bethany. We thank God daily for bringing her back to us." Katy found a place and parked in the church lot. "And for caring for her."

The emotion-filled comment brought his gaze to her. "Do you believe that, Katy?"

"I want to, Richie," she said, resting her hand against her heart. "I want to feel God's love and peace surround me again. Now that Bethany's home, I pray it's possible."

"Don't blame God," Richie said. "Jack took Bethany to serve his own purpose and ended up paying a pretty hefty cost."

"He took Bethany to hurt me. To punish me for daring to reject him." She grabbed her purse and busied herself finding a package of mints. The keys jangled as she dropped them inside. A few seconds later, Katy added, "I had to free

Bethany and myself from his destructive ways. I won't forgive him for what he did to our child." She opened the door and paused just before stepping out. "I want Bethany to have a relationship with your family, but it's not going to be easy."

She climbed from the car and opened the back door to unhook Bethany's seat belt.

"Katy?"

She glanced at him.

"I'm sorry. What you've seen. . .it's not my nature."

"Mine either, Richie. All my life, I've endeavored to be a likable individual who never hurt anyone. Marrying Jack cast me in the role of villain, and it's not a good fit." She smiled sadly. "I'll never again be the woman who existed before he came into my life."

"God can free you of the pain you're experiencing."

"I hope so, Richie. You'd better go inside. I'll bring Bethany."

Katy sat cross-legged on the carpeted floor with Bethany leaning by her side. Another child around the same age as her daughter joined them. Holly talked nonstop, not seeming to care that she got no reply from Bethany. Then she offered to share her book, and they chattered until the teacher called for their attention.

Moving to the sidelines, Katy smiled encouragement and hoped Bethany would enjoy herself. Richie was right about this being a good place for her to make friends.

After the story ended, she dreaded Bethany's response to the question-and-answer session, but her child had no questions for the teacher. Other children raised their hands, but Bethany withdrew when the teacher assumed her position of authority.

She needed to ask Richie about that. Thinking of him brought a resurgence of the strange emotions she experienced when she was with him. Comfort and discomfort rivaled each other at the strangest times. Like this morning when he'd brought up visiting his parents. She wanted to go to Charlotte for his sake but didn't know what to expect from his family.

Katy knew Richie would do everything possible to smooth the way between her and his family. He'd put himself right in the middle and defend her with shoulders that seemed broad enough to carry the weight of the world.

The probability of more criticism from Jack's relatives didn't sit well with her. Glumly, Katy considered she had to do this for Bethany's sake. But she wasn't the guilty party. She wouldn't let them blame her for Jack's actions.

After Sunday school, the children assembled for children's church. They sang and listened to Richie's sermon before church dismissed. Holly remained at Bethany's side.

"Looks like she's made a friend," Richie said as the two girls chased each other around the churchyard. "Holly's a great kid."

Katy and Bethany treated him to lunch, and then they headed for home.

Her thoughts went back to Richie's request. How much longer could she put him off? He only wanted to introduce Bethany to his family. That wasn't a bad thing.

Katy's cell phone rang just as they arrived at the cottage.

"Mrs. Sinclair, this is Detective Neumann. I called to let you know we picked up the man you identified. We questioned him, but he denies any knowledge of Jack Sinclair."

"What about the other man?"

"No sign of him. I told the suspect he'd been identified from a mug shot, but he claims to have been confused with someone else."

He's the confused one. "Will I need to file charges?"

"There's not much hope he's going to get off on the other charges. We plan to put him away for a very long time."

"What about his friend?"

"There's no indication that he's still around."

"Thanks for letting me know. I've decided to take Bethany to visit the Taylors. I'll have my cell if anything comes up."

And just like that, her decision was made.

Chapter 13

We thought we would go out to dinner tonight," Cynthia told Katy. "If you think it's okay?"

"Why don't we order pizza?" Richie suggested. "Bethany's tired from the trip, and a restaurant would be another strange place. Let her get used to us first."

His mother grimaced. "I should have thought of that."

Richie slipped his arm about her shoulders. "Just follow Bethany's lead."

As if in total agreement, Trey clapped his hands together and chortled. They all chuckled. The senior Taylors were babysitting their grandson while his parents attended a business function. "He's such a darling baby," Cynthia said proudly. "Smiles all the time."

"Bethany did, too," Katy said, touching Bethie's shoulder reassuringly when she moved closer. Doubt flickered across their faces as they took in the fearful child hugging her mother's leg. Their reaction irritated Katy. None of them had known Bethany before Jack made her afraid.

Richie swung Bethany up. "That's right. Bethany laughs all the time, don't you?"

He tickled her stomach. The child giggled and the adults smiled.

"I put you and Bethany in a room together. Richie said she'd feel more comfortable with you nearby."

As would I, Katy thought. She needed to feel there was someone on her side.

"Let me show you to your room," Cynthia said, leading the way down the hall. "Richie, you'll have to bunk on the sofa in the den."

"No," Katy protested. "Bethany and I can go to a hotel."

"This room has an en suite bathroom. You two ladies need your privacy much more than Richie."

"Gee Mom, why don't I just pitch a tent in the yard?"

Cynthia glared at him.

He held up his hand. "Teasing. Katy and Bethany do need the bedroom."

His mother opened the door to a spacious guest suite. Richie swung their suitcase onto the king-size bed.

"Really, it's no trouble for us to go to a hotel. We can spend the days here with the family," Katy said.

Richie met her gaze and shook his head. "Why don't you settle in and rest for a while? Dinner around seven, Mom?"

She nodded. "Is there anything else you need? Extra pillows? Blankets?"

Resigned, Katy said, "This is fine."

After they left, she unpacked, placing toiletries in the bathroom and clothes in the dresser. All the while, she watched Bethany explore the room. A basket of toys enticed the child, but instead of diving in, she just stood and looked. Katy went over and pulled a stuffed kitten from the basket. "Isn't he cute? Your grandparents put him here for you."

"Me?"

The insecurity in Bethany's voice made it difficult for Katy to equate her child to this timid little girl. She lifted the toy to her ear. "What's that? You want to take a nap with Bethany?"

She felt encouraged when Bethany hugged the stuffed toy and waited for her mother to lift her onto the high bed. Katy lay down next to her and covered them with a light throw.

That evening, she bathed Bethie and debated dressing her for comfort or style. Comfort won out. Katy picked up the canvas bag of items she'd brought along to show the Taylors.

They found Richie and his mother seated at the round table just off the kitchen drinking coffee and talking. Cynthia jumped up and busied herself placing items on the table. She went to the refrigerator and opened it. "Milk?"

Katy nodded, and Cynthia filled a child-size cup with a built-in straw. The cartoon characters on the side intrigued Bethany. Cynthia knelt beside her chair. "We're so glad you came to visit us. Your aunt Lucy wants to take you and your cousin to the park tomorrow."

A tiny frown marred the child's delicate features.

"She doesn't know what a cousin is," Katy explained. "Remember Auntie Dina, Bethany? Lucy is your aunt, too. Her baby boy is your cousin. Remember Trey?"

Bethany nodded.

"Trey is named for his daddy," Cynthia told her granddaughter.

The child absorbed this information and asked the dreaded question. "Mommy, where's Daddy?"

Katy's eyes drifted shut. This wasn't something she wanted to discuss in front of Jack's mother. "Daddy's gone away, Bethany."

"Where he go? He left me." Hurt filled the blue eyes.

Cynthia's hand flew to her mouth, similar pain filling the matching blue gaze.

Katy hugged Bethany close. "Daddy couldn't take you."

"When's he coming back?"

She glanced at Richie. His sympathetic expression encouraged her to change the subject. "Eat your cookie."

Bethany took a couple of small bites and wrapped the rest in a napkin.

Katy had been furious the first time she witnessed her child hoarding food. "Eat it all, sweetie," she prompted, laying the napkin open on the tabletop.

"I made them just for you," Cynthia said. "Would you like ice cream in your milk?"

Bethany looked up at her mother. "Is she spoiling me, Mommy?"

Richie chuckled and touched the child's cheek. "Miss Bethany likes being spoiled."

"And her grammy likes spoiling her." Cynthia glanced at Katy. "Is there anything. . ."

Richard Taylor came to stand in the doorway. "Don't overwhelm the child, Cyn."

"I'm trying not to, Richard."

Katy noted she was none too happy with her spouse's comment. "Did you thank your grandparents for the toys?" she prompted. Katy decided she would become quite adroit at subject-changing before this visit ended.

Bethany dropped her head. In the past, she'd hugged and showed so much enthusiasm for gifts. Katy's tears overflowed before she could stop them.

"Will you call us Grammy and Gramps?"

"It may take her awhile to understand. My parents insist she call them Grandfather and Grandmother. I told them she was just a child, but they felt it was proper."

"We just want her to be comfortable."

"Another cookie, Grammy?"

All eyes focused on Bethany.

"Oh yes, darling."

Bethany's comfort became the focus of the visit.

The pizza arrived, and Cynthia slid a slice on a plate for Bethany. The child pointed to the pepperoni and whined, "Don't like that."

Cynthia looked miserable. "I should have ordered a cheese pizza. Can I fix her something else?"

Katy pulled pepperoni from the pizza and popped it into her mouth. "There. It's okay now, isn't it, Bethany?"

She nodded and started to eat. For a while, the conversation was a series of nods in response to their questions. "Talk to them," Katy prompted.

She tugged a photo book from the bag and laid it on the table. "Let's show Grammy what you looked like as a baby."

Cynthia jumped up and washed her hands. "May I?"

Katy nodded. Cynthia pulled a chair between her husband and Bethany and turned the pages. "Oh you were so beautiful," she cooed. "Look Richard, Jack's holding her in this one." Cynthia lingered over the shot of her son with his daughter.

"This book is for you," Katy said. "I always have her picture taken on her birthday so there are three eight-by-ten photos as well. I plan to have her third-birthday photo taken on the beach."

Cynthia hugged the album to her chest. "Thank you for this."

Noting Bethany had tired of the adult conversation, Katy provided her with paper and a small box of crayons. The child set to work, the tip of her tongue appearing between her teeth as she concentrated on her art.

"She's very talented," Katy said, passing around some of her child's artwork.

"She gets that from her mother," Richie commented, his warm smile encompassing her. "You should see the murals Katy drew for the church. They're fantastic."

She blushed and continued to share the information from her bag with his family.

Bethany's finished picture was of the beach with the sun and a sand castle. She handed it to her grandmother. "For you."

"This is wonderful," Cynthia enthused. "I'm going to put it right here on the fridge so we can see it all the time. I miss the beach."

When Bethany's eyes drooped, Cynthia said, "Looks like our girl is ready for bed. Why don't you tuck her in and come back? I left the baby monitor on the nightstand."

"I'll hold her. She'll be frightened if she wakes alone in a strange place."

"You can lay her on the sofa." She produced a pillow and lightweight throw.

Katy watched Cynthia watch her granddaughter, the longing in her expression plain to see.

"She has her father's features. I could show you."

The last thing Katy wanted to see was Jack's baby pictures. "No need. I've seen the similarities."

"What happened to my son?"

The question put an end to their polite dance.

"Mom," Richie called in warning.

Her piercing blue gaze showed as much determination as Katy had ever seen in Jack. "I need to know, Richie."

"Are you prepared for the truth?"

Her jaw clamped tight. "Jack married Kaitlin, and we know nothing of their life together. They didn't even tell us they had a daughter."

"I believed Jack had told you," Katy said.

When she was born, Jack passed around cigars and called Bethany his little princess. At home, he barely touched his daughter, much less handled any of her care. The only time he showed an interest in Bethany was when he hoped to impress Katy's parents. Those were the times he ordered Katy to dress the baby in something fancy and took them to visit. In their presence, he never let Bethie out of his arms, unaware her parents believed a baby's place was in the nursery with her nanny.

Katy had tried to accept that her parents didn't show their love for her as other kids' parents showed theirs. Her children would never experience the same feelings. She planned to be a stay-at-home mom. Katy forced the issue by quitting her job when Bethany was born. She'd enjoyed her work and it paid well, but she had new plans for her future. While Katy struggled with the long hours her job required and never having time to spend with her husband,

Jack never complained until she resigned. He resented losing her income and repeatedly said Bethany would be okay in day care. Katy had no intention of working twelve-hour days and stealing moments for her baby.

"Why so secretive? I know Jack wasn't ashamed of his family," Cynthia said.

"I'm not ashamed of mine either," Katy said, responding to Cynthia's implication. She told his mother what Jack had said about their elopement. "He never said you wanted to talk to me, so I thought you were still upset."

"I wasn't upset. You were never home when Jack called."

"I never knew when he called you. I wanted to meet his family. He put me off."

"Why?"

"Who knows why Jack did the things he did?"

"Why was he in Wilmington?" Richard asked.

She didn't share her suspicions with them. "We were separated. I'd returned to my parents' home. He disappeared after Bethany was kidnapped."

Cynthia's gaze pinned Katy in place. She felt the burn of emotion in her throat. She didn't want the Taylors to think she was a crybaby. In fact, she'd spent too much of her life in tears because of Jack. "He changed."

"This is serious, Mom," Richie warned. "What we've learned is very upsetting."

"I have to know."

"Tell her," he said.

Katy told the story of how she'd met Jack, the things he'd done, and concluded with how he'd taken Bethany. "When I first met him, I felt wonderfully blessed. Then after we married, he couldn't keep a job and partied with his friends every night.

"He stayed home while I worked full-time. Every time I asked when he was going to find work, Jack produced money, and we lived off that until it ran out. Only later did I discover he had borrowed from everyone with no intention of paying the money back."

"You asked too much of him," Cynthia protested. "He told me you belittled him in front of your parents. Said they treated him like a lower-class citizen. He never should have married. . ."

Her comment trailed off, but the lies stabbed at Katy.

"Mom! I didn't bring Katy here to be insulted."

She flashed him a sad smile. "I never expected more of Jack than to be a good husband, father, and provider. As for how my parents treated him, I told him they were too involved in our lives. They gave us the house we lived in. Even paid for the cars we drove and the clothes Jack wore. But everything came with a price. I pleaded with him to break free, but he wouldn't."

"I'm sure he felt he had to maintain your previous lifestyle," Cynthia offered coldly.

"I never asked that of him," Katy denied. "Jack knew I would receive my trust fund when I turned thirty. He tried to get access. Thank God he never managed, or Bethany and I would be destitute."

"My son wasn't like that."

"Your son kidnapped my child," she said, feeling her facial muscles tighten with the strain. "Maybe I was wrong to deny his rights, but I couldn't allow him to harm Bethany."

"He wouldn't have harmed her," Cynthia defended.

"He left her alone and got himself killed," Katy declared bitterly. Bethany whimpered and stirred. Katy smoothed a hand over her hair. "Shush. It's okay, sweetie."

Silence reigned until Bethany drifted off again. "He wasn't a fit father," Katy said. "On the few times he kept her, he left her with strangers when he went out every night. He wouldn't bathe or feed her. When the courts awarded me sole custody, he warned me I'd be sorry.

"Jack went out of his way to make me miserable. After Bethany was kidnapped, he showed up with his female alibi and made me look foolish before the police. Then he disappeared, too. I know how it feels to be afraid for your child's life.

"Everyone insisted Bethany was dead. I refused to accept that but had no idea where she could be until she showed up at the shelter with a homeless woman who did not intend to give her up.

"Jack never wanted to be a husband or father. And when I saw him for who he truly was, he took the one thing he knew I valued most. He let me believe she was dead. He wanted to make me suffer because for once I chose to put our needs before his. He was a toxic human being, and the world is a better place without him."

Bethany whimpered and Katy rose to her feet. Her soft voice trembled with fury as she said, "Think what you will of me, but I will never forgive Jack Sinclair for what he did to my child." She lifted her daughter from the sofa and carried her from the room.

❧

"Katy!" Richie called, taking a step to follow. Realizing it wasn't a good time, he whirled to confront his mother. "Why did you do that?"

"Jack told me all about her."

Richie cradled his forehead in his hand for several seconds. Katy would never forgive him. He'd promised to take care of her and look what happened.

"Jack lied, Mom."

Horrified, Cynthia demanded, "How can you say that? She's the reason. . ."

"No, Mom," he interrupted. "She's not. I wouldn't blame Katy if she took Bethany and left tonight."

"That man she described was not my son," she said, her voice breaking with a sob.

Richie hugged his mother close. "I admit to doubting her story, too, but we've all turned a blind eye when it comes to Jack."

"He's your brother."

"I loved him, but evidently our love wasn't enough. Just as the love of his wife and child failed to satisfy him."

"How can you be sure she's telling the truth?"

Richie pulled back and looked her straight in the eye. "I just know. Besides, they found Bethany's fingerprints in his car. Mom, Jack had her. He told the police he wasn't involved, but he left her alone in an abandoned warehouse and got himself killed." Richie couldn't tell her he believed Jack had no intention of telling them he had a daughter.

Teary-eyed, Cynthia whispered, "How could he have changed so much?"

Richard came to stand by his wife. "It's too late for Jack, Cyn. We have to think about Bethany. Jack put her through more than any child should ever experience."

"We owe Katy an apology," Richie said.

Cynthia looked at him. "What's going on, Richie? Why are you so concerned about Kaitlin?"

"I care about her. A great deal."

"What do you mean *care*? She's your brother's wife."

"My dead brother's widow," he corrected. "Jack never treasured Katy. He took her love, her money, and her child. He demeaned her with words and actions no decent woman deserves."

"What are you saying?" The words came out like a demand.

"I love her, Mom. I don't plan to lose her or Bethany ever again. I'm going to make her smile."

His father nodded. "You're making a big promise, son."

Richie agreed as he walked out of the room. He needed to check on Katy. No matter how long it took, he planned to keep his promise to her. No doubt she was sick of his family.

Tapping on the bedroom door, he called, "Katy? Can we talk?"

The door cracked open a few inches, her red eyes an obvious sign of her distress.

Panic made him feel sick. "I'm sorry."

She shrugged, pretending it didn't matter. Richie knew it did. Katy cared what others thought of her, but she also knew the impossibility of changing someone's first impression. Particularly when someone they loved and trusted had already greatly influenced their opinion.

"It's not the first time I've heard this."

Shamed, Richie asked, "Do you want to go home?"

"I want Bethany to know her family," she said, her voice hoarse with frustration.

"No more accusations, Katy. I promise."

"Don't make promises you can't keep, Richie. Your mother is grieving Jack's loss and not likely to change her mind about me."

He struggled with the need to defend his family. "We only want to understand."

"And you never will," Katy said. "Maybe he didn't change. Maybe Jack used his looks and charisma to get what he wanted." Her breath came in shudders. "I feel I've been let down by everyone I love."

Richie didn't want her to feel that way. He pushed the door open wider and pulled Katy into his arms. He rubbed her back and murmured, "I'm sorry."

Though she struggled to hold it in, soon great heaving sobs racked her tiny frame.

Richie regretted the role he'd played in that pain. She'd come here and sacrificed her pride for her child. Katy would pretend not to care about the accusations and humiliation out of love for Bethany. Because she wanted her child to be loved by her family, she'd let them attack and fight back, but she'd hang in there for the sake of her daughter.

"It's going to be okay," he said.

She wrapped her arms about his waist and rested her head against his chest. "Do you really think so?"

"Yes." No one would ever hurt Katy again.

Chapter 14

They spent three days with the Taylors before Dina called to tell Katy their father had gone in for emergency surgery.

"Can you take us to the airport? My father's in the hospital," she told Richie. "I need to catch the first flight out."

He touched her arm gently. "Katy, calm down. I'll make arrangements for our flights and explain to my parents while you pack."

She stared up at him. "You don't need. . ."

"I'm not about to let you go off on your own when you're this upset."

"But your job."

"I'll tell them I need a few more days. Now go pack."

Upon arriving in Las Vegas, they went directly to the hospital. Cliff Dennison was in recovery. Dina hugged her sister and niece and shook Richie's hand.

"He's okay," she said, reassuring Katy. "He complained of chest pains, and they determined he had a couple of blocked arteries and put in stents. He didn't have a heart attack."

When Katy slumped slightly, Richie slipped an arm about her waist for support.

"Come sit down. Mom's in with him now."

Dina introduced Richie to her husband, and they waited until their mother returned to the waiting area. She greeted Katy and Bethany with a kiss on the cheek and offered him a limp handshake.

"How is he?" Katy asked.

"He's resting. The nurse thinks they'll put him in a room."

Meeting her family told Richie a lot about Katy. Their already-strained relationship had suffered as a result of the emotional stress of Bethany's abduction. It was obvious to him that Katy wanted to please them but couldn't.

He felt Katy's pain when she tried to talk to her mother, only to have the woman accuse her of adding to her father's stress with her poor choices.

It seemed her parents believed she used her decisions to punish them, but Richie didn't feel that had ever been her intention. His own perception of Katy was that of a decent, honest, loving woman who got a raw deal from the man she trusted with her heart.

Their mother refused to leave the hospital but insisted Katy take Bethany to their house. Katy didn't want to leave. She called Melody, and her friend came for a visit and declared she would take Bethany home with her. Richie could see Katy's struggle, but she eventually gave in.

"She'll enjoy seeing J. J. And I promise not to let her out of my sight for one second," Melody added.

Katy watched them disappear down the hall, Bethany's hand in Melody's. "She'll be fine," Richie reassured.

When they moved Cliff Dennison into a private room, Richie went in with Katy, and despite his illness, her father didn't bother to hide his disdain for him, Jack, or Katy's plans. Richie recognized the Dennisons as the type who required people about them to conform to their mold.

"So it takes me being at death's door to get you back here."

Katy paled. "Please don't talk like that."

"It's a wonder I didn't die. All this stress and aggravation."

"The doctor says you'll feel better now," Katy said.

"He doesn't know what I have to put up with," Cliff Dennison growled impatiently. "Where's my granddaughter?"

"With Melody Lennon-Gerald."

"I'm surprised you agreed to that."

Richie slipped his hand over hers and squeezed gently. He admired Katy's refusal to argue with her father. After a while, she said, "Mom wants to come back in."

The doctor released Cliff Dennison at the end of the week. Richie held himself back several times as he listened to the man belittle Katy.

"You don't know anything about operating a business," he roared when Katy said she planned to return to North Carolina.

"Daddy, you need to calm down," Dina said finally. "Katy just wants to try something new with her life."

"Then let her try it here."

Her older sister obviously knew how to handle their father. "Maybe she will," Dina said. "Once she and Bethany have their beach experience, they might decide to come home. Now you need to rest. Is there anything you need before we go?"

Over dinner that night, Katy demanded, "Why does he keep doing this to me?"

"You know what he's like," Dina said. "You either play by his rules or accept the consequences."

Richie watched the interplay between the two sisters. "I'm a huge disappointment to him and Mother."

Dina frowned. "No you're not."

"I am. I've never done anything that pleased them. Now he's sick. How can I go off and leave him like this?"

"Do you feel you've made a bad choice?" Dina asked.

"No. I believe this is the best thing for Bethany and myself right now."

Dina's husband, Kevin, surprised them all when he said, "Then you should follow your heart. Spend this time helping your daughter get past the loss of her father. You heard the doctor. Your father will be better than before."

"Kev's right," Dina agreed. "Now stop worrying and eat your dinner."

They visited with her father a number of times over the next few days. Richie watched Katy's emotional state go back and forth as she struggled with what she needed to do as opposed to what she wanted to do.

Things worsened when Katy announced they were flying back to North Carolina the following day. On their way to the airport, they stopped to say good-bye. She left her parents angry and frustrated because she refused to remain in Las Vegas.

She cried all the way to the airport. Richie tried to comfort her. Katy opened up and told him the only way she could ever hope to make her own decisions would be to put miles between herself and her parents.

He supposed it was different for men and women. His parents expected him to live his own life and respected him enough not to interfere. Well, other than the times his mother offered strong advice in regard to finding a wife and producing grandchildren.

Richie suspected Katy married Jack to escape her father's control. Unfortunately, the marriage had taken her backward in her parents' estimation, not forward.

Once at the airport, they visited a couple of shops and waited for their flight. Onboard, she grew even more silent. Richie felt fairly certain her thoughts were on their departure from the Dennison home. He sent up prayers for her comfort.

Richie passed the empty cups and napkins to the flight attendant and glanced down to find Bethany engrossed in the book they'd picked out at the airport bookstore. The colorful pictures held her attention for now. He'd have to read it to her later.

Katy thumbed through a magazine, dropping it into her lap when she turned to stare out the window.

He looked down when Bethany's head dropped against his arm. Katy lifted the armrest and tucked her child closer. Richie suspected she needed the comfort right now. "You okay?" he asked softly.

She nodded. "I can't wait to get home. I miss the beach."

He grinned and teased, "Even rainy days are better at the beach."

Her slight smile belied her preoccupation. "Do you think he's okay?"

Richie knew she meant her father. "The doctor wouldn't have released him otherwise."

"He wants us to come home, but I can't. I love my parents, but I don't want them telling me how to raise my child."

"Have you considered it's a parent's role to advise?"

"Normal parents, maybe. My father believes to control is to advise. If I follow his orders, do everything he suggests, they'll be happy, and Bethany will become just like them."

"No. She'll become like you."

Katy snorted. "Then she'll feel as miserable and out of place as I've always felt."

"Did you tell them you weren't happy?"

"I tried, but they didn't listen. I won't allow the pattern to continue. My child will know she's loved."

Though Katy had covered all the angles on her business plan, her father had no interest in her artsy career choice. "He's concerned the business won't support you and Bethany."

Katy shrugged. "We'll get by. And if necessary, I'll find a different job. I have an art degree. Maybe when Bethany starts school, I'll consider what I'm going to do, but for now, I have to be there for my child. That plan hasn't changed since the day she was born."

"You like being a stay-at-home mom?"

"It's all I ever wanted. Jack and I talked about more children, but then he. . ." She stopped speaking.

Richie touched her hand. "You're a young woman, Katy. There can be another love. More children. A happier life for you and Bethany."

"How can either of us ever trust again?"

"God will lessen the pain, Katy. And He can deliver someone worthy of your trust."

She played with a lock of Bethany's hair. "You know, out of all the reasons I hate Jack, making me doubt God is right up there on the list."

"You have to let go of the hate."

Emotion burned in the green gaze. "Jack tore down everything I worked so hard to build. The solid foundation of the marriage I wanted, a happy childhood for my daughter, the respect of my parents."

"You think they lost respect because of Jack's behavior?"

"In their eyes, choosing Jack confirmed my inability to make the right choices."

Troubled, Richie shook his head. "How could you have known, Katy? Loving unwisely doesn't make you wrong. You upheld your vows."

"Did I? I let them convince me to leave."

"You need to forgive yourself, too. Every person makes good and bad decisions. The lesson is to get on with your life. Put the harm Jack's done in the past. Don't allow him to control your future."

"I can't," she cried softly. "I loved him and he used that love to hurt me."

"Love hurts sometimes."

~

Streaks of lightning flashed through the sky. She pulled the window panel closed, finding it almost symbolic that they'd flown into the storm just outside Charlotte.

Katy knew God frowned on her lack of compassion, but it was becoming more and more impossible to turn the other cheek. Just that morning her father had struck out at her, saying she'd be back because she was incapable of handling her own life. His harsh words made the need to prove him wrong even stronger.

Self-doubt made her wonder if he were right. Could she provide a good life for her daughter? Katy believed God gave her the chance to prove herself by bringing Bethie home. And maybe one day she could find a bit of forgiveness for Jack—but not now.

Despite the weather, the plane touched down on time, and they began the process of gathering their belongings to deplane. Katy grasped Bethany's hand firmly in hers as she collected their bags. The child whined, but Katy refused to let go.

"Here, let me get those," Richie said, grabbing the suitcases from the carousel. Their luggage had increased as they traveled, each family giving Bethany clothes and toys. He hefted his smaller duffel to the floor.

"Let's get a cart. We'll shift it outside, and I'll get the truck and pick you and Bethany up."

"If you stay with Bethie, I can go."

"I'll do it. Princess here is tired and grumpy. I don't want her screaming for her mommy. Someone might beat me over the head with their umbrella." Sudden realization dawned. She trusted him with her child. "I'm sorry. I shouldn't have said that."

Katy shrugged. "I wish there were more people out there who wouldn't hesitate to protect a child in trouble."

A few minutes later, Richie ushered them into the truck and placed their luggage in the backseat of the twin cab.

"At least nothing will blow away," he said, closing the door and climbing behind the wheel.

"Might be a blessing if half of it did," Katy said, her droll humor making him laugh. "I don't know where we'll put it. Did you plan to stop by and see your parents?"

"We need to hit the road so we can get home before too late. I'll call them later."

More than four hours later, Katy was so happy to see the cottage. The storm had slowed their travel. Immediately upon entering the house, Bethany ran off to her room.

Richie carried the heavy suitcases into their bedrooms. "I put them on the bed for you. Guess I'll head for home."

They walked out onto the deck. He paused and said, "Thanks for going with me."

She smiled. "And thank you for going with me."

They stood facing each other for several seconds before he reached out and touched her cheek. "I love you and Bethie. I want you to be happy. Think about what I said?"

"I do. I have." Katy felt the despair welling up inside her as she considered the size of the mountain she needed to overcome. "Do you think I want to hate anyone?"

"I think you're a beautiful woman blessed with a beautiful spirit. Don't let Jack or anyone else destroy that."

Richie leaned forward and kissed her. His hands were gentle as he stroked her cheeks and gazed deep into her eyes. "Nice," he said, smiling before he turned and walked down the steps. He paused to lift his hand in farewell.

Very nice, she agreed, waving good-bye to him.

Chapter 15

He kissed her. The gentleness of his callused hands against her face and the soft kiss made the experience very enjoyable. And he'd used the word *love*. He had to feel something, too. No one kissed a relative or friend like that.

After she settled Bethany in bed and put away a few of the items they brought back with them, Katy allowed herself to think about what Richie had said. *"A beautiful woman blessed with a beautiful spirit."* No one had ever complimented her in that way.

But there had been warning in his words. Did she let others dampen her spirit when she refused to forgive them? She loved her family, and it had been difficult to leave them behind. Still, Katy knew that once her parents entangled her and Bethany in their loving arms, they would never again be free. One mistake per person, and she'd already made hers.

No. That wasn't true. She could have another chance at happiness. With Richie.

She touched her lips. So unexpected, the softness of his kiss lingered. What would life be like with a man like Richie? God-fearing, dependable. Jack's half brother. Though slightly diluted, they shared the same blood. Would Jack's nature surface in his brother?

Katy knew it wouldn't. They were different in all the ways that counted. Richie was a giver. He truly loved God and put Him first in his life. He was a man to be admired, a man to whom she felt a strong pull.

But was it too soon? Why couldn't she put the past behind her and move on? Jack was dead. She'd have to deal with the repercussions long term, including the damage to her own self-esteem. He had beaten her down with his criticisms. She needed rebuilding just as much as Bethany did.

She'd lived with Jack's cruelty ever since Bethany was born. At times she believed he hated her for the choices she'd made, but she stood by her right to choose to be a stay-at-home mother. He hadn't been fair to her. All she wanted from life was someone who loved and supported her. Was it too much to ask?

Katy took the magnetic grocery pad from the fridge door and sat at the table. She listed the things that needed doing.

She planned to ask Richie to counsel his niece. Katy believed he could talk her through the situation better than his co-workers could. He was involved, but he didn't know Bethany all that well. They could become better acquainted as he helped her work through the experience.

Katy definitely planned to take Bethany to church. And to work on her own relationship with God. She'd turned her back on Him and needed to seek forgiveness for her hostility. In her heart, she knew none of this had ever been God's intention. He'd taken care of Bethany and brought her home.

She needed to order more flyers and business cards. And research the best way to distribute the information. She jotted a note on the pad. Maybe even run some ads in the freebie magazines and newspapers.

Meanwhile, she would gather items from thrift shops and yard sales to prepare for the onslaught of customers. Katy chuckled. If only she could plan on that. The economy was so tight right now that she would need to price her services reasonably if she hoped to get any business at all. People were looking at their spending, and while they wanted memorable events for their children, affordable was important.

Over the next few days, her life had purpose. She took Bethany yard-saling on Saturday, and they came home with quite a few treasures. On Sunday, they attended church and spent the afternoon playing on the beach. Richie showed up and agreed to do what he could to help Bethany. He understood Katy's reasoning and said they would see how it worked.

As they walked, Bethany slipped her tiny hands in theirs and laughed joyously when they swung her over the waves. Richie had plans for the evening so Katy took Bethany to visit Lucille. They stayed for dinner. Exhausted from her day, Bethany fell asleep in Katy's arms as they rocked on the deck.

They talked about the visit to the Taylors and the situation with her family. She told Lucille what Richie had said. "How do I forgive Jack?"

"Give it to God," Lucille said. "Don't empower Jack to turn you into a bitter, angry woman."

Katy knew she was right. What purpose had her anger served? She'd alienated loved ones and made others think she was a mental case.

"I'm trying, Lucille. The pastor spoke from the book of Mark this morning. When he told how Jesus calmed the tempest, it reminded me of something Richie said about the ocean. I asked why life couldn't be as calm as those waters, and he said life was exactly like those waves. At times calm but at others stormy."

"Good analogy. You survived the storm."

Katy smiled with the realization. "I did. Even if she doesn't like me, Cynthia will tolerate me because she wants a relationship with Bethany."

"She'll more than tolerate you. In her heart, Cynthia knew the real Jack. She may be in denial, but the time is coming when she'll ask your forgiveness."

Katy shifted Bethany and wiggled fingers that had fallen asleep. "I could have been a better daughter-in-law. If I'd worked at the relationship, maybe they could have helped when things got tough."

"Stop blaming yourself for everything," Lucille chided. "Richard called this afternoon. He's concerned for Cynthia but agrees that we need to put the past behind us. I put in a good word for you."

Katy smiled. "Thanks. I know she's grieving, but it was difficult to hear some of the things she said."

"It will get easier over time." Lucille reached for the fan on the table and swung it back and forth a few times. "So what are you planning now that you're back home?"

Katy told her about her idea. "I need to find a place with room to hold the events."

"I have a couple of big rooms on the ground floor that open out onto the side porch. You could use those."

"I couldn't do that," she protested. "Having children around would destroy your peace."

"Bethany has been a breath of fresh air. I think I'd enjoy having youngsters around. Let's pray over it," Lucille suggested.

Katy broached the subject with Richie when he came over the next afternoon for his session with Bethany.

"What do you think?"

He nodded thoughtfully. "It would probably work."

"But don't you think it would be upsetting for Lucille?"

"I think she gets lonely."

"It's tempting," Katy admitted. "What are you planning with Bethany today?"

"I thought maybe a tea party."

Her eyes widened. "You're kidding."

He shrugged. "She likes parties. I can observe her happy and see if she'll open up."

"It's always been our thing," Katy said softly, not sure how her daughter would react to a man at a tea party. "Her dad never participated."

"You can attend, but you can't play a leadership role. I have to hear what Bethany has to say."

Katy shook her head. "If I'm there and she says something that bothers me, I'll jump in and ask questions. Just promise you'll share the outcome with me."

They worked together, assembling the small table with little china teacups and peanut butter and jelly sandwiches cut into quarters with the crusts removed. While Richie placed cookies on a plate, Katy filled the small teapot with milk.

"No tea?" he asked quizzically.

Katy grinned. "It's white tea when it comes from a teapot."

"And when it comes from a glass?"

"Milk."

He chuckled. "Woman, there are Southern mothers who give their toddlers tea in their bottles."

"I may have to adjust my tea party beverage, but my daughter needs milk."

Katy told Bethany she'd be working on the deck and left them settling in at the table. She found it difficult to concentrate on the brochure.

Nearly an hour later, they came outside. Bethany bounded out the door and picked up a ball. She ran toward the steps then paused, waiting for Richie.

He looked at Katy. "Let's go for a walk."

She tossed her sketchbook inside and locked up the house. As they walked, Richie slipped his hand around hers. Bethany darted here and there, examining shells and the tiny crabs that scuttled into holes when she came near.

"How did it go?"

Richie smiled and said, "She's very precise on how things are done."

"It's a good time to teach etiquette and manners."

"Mommy-and-me time," he said with a nod. "She said her daddy didn't like tea parties."

"Jack didn't have a lot of patience with her. She's very imaginative, and he didn't like that either. Especially when she behaved like a child, became whiny, loud, or overly active. He would yell at her."

He nodded. "I asked her about the day at the ice cream shop. She got quiet and wouldn't say anything."

Katy nodded. "She did the same when I asked. I think it frightens her to remember."

"What if we took her for an ice cream now? She didn't eat a lot, so she might be hungry."

"I don't know," Katy said uncomfortably. She located Bethany wandering a few yards ahead of them.

"If she opens up, we can address the things that are bothering her."

Katy shook her head. "Not tonight."

"Then let's go after dinner one night soon. Maybe we can grill hot dogs and then go for ice cream."

Bethany ran back to show them the shells she'd found. Katy slid them into the pail she carried and considered what they were about to do.

Please God, don't let this be another storm.

～

Richie arrived on the day of their cookout to find the area underneath the house filled with boxes and furniture. Katy stood amid the jumble.

He looked around. "What is all this stuff?"

"The items I thought we couldn't live without. I boxed them when I went to Vegas, and Dina made arrangements to have them shipped. I just hope whoever buys the house will want the rest of the furniture. I should have gotten rid of more, but I couldn't." While the memories for some items were bittersweet, she couldn't just toss them out. One day her daughter would want to know more about her father.

"You need storage. A couple at church has rental units. Want me to take a truckload over?"

"Yes, please."

When some items proved too heavy for him alone, Richie asked a neighbor to give him a hand. Soon the men had the bulk of the furniture secured on the back of the truck.

"Wilbur said he'd go with me to unload. We'll cook the hot dogs when I get back."

After dinner, they went to the ice cream shop. Once in line, Bethany edged closer, and Katy lifted her into her arms. They waited for their turn at the order window.

"What's wrong, Bethie? Don't you want ice cream?" Richie asked.

The child glanced at the crowd and buried her face into her mother's shoulder.

"She's trembling," Katy whispered.

Richie's hand smoothed along the little girl's back. "It's okay, Bethie. Mommy and I won't let anything bad happen to you."

"Man," she muttered.

The customers surrounding them were an assortment of men, women, and children.

"No one here wants to hurt you," Katy told her.

"Man," she said again.

"Let's go," Katy told Richie. "I don't want her having nightmares."

She placed Bethany in her car seat. Richie sat in the back talking to Bethany as Katy drove them home.

"Why are you afraid, Bethie?" Richie asked softly.

"Man."

"We won't let anyone hurt you, sweetie," he said.

"Mean man."

At least she'd expounded on her fear. Then Katy frowned as she braked for the red light and barricade that meant the bridge was about to open. She looked over the seat and asked, "Did you see someone who looked like the man?"

Bethany nodded in the darkness.

"Sometimes people look similar, but they aren't the same," Richie said.

"Mean man," Bethie repeated.

"Okay sweetie, it's just us now. We're going home. You're okay."

Richie stuck around for a while, moving some of the boxes upstairs while Katy bathed Bethany. He asked if he could do bedtime prayers and Katy agreed. Afterward, she tucked Bethany in and turned on the night-light before turning off her lamp. They went into the living room.

"I think she saw someone who reminded her of the man who grabbed her," he said.

"I hope not. I can't help but think that man who chased me was the same man. I haven't seen him since, but he could be around. He was scary."

"I'm sure he's long gone. Any response to the business cards?"

They had posted cards on grocery store bulletin boards and a few other places around town.

"A few calls. One lady said she'd call back tomorrow with a head count to get a final price."

"Want me to pray for your business?"

"Sure," Katy said, slipping her hand into his. It felt so comfortable, so right as he squeezed gently and beseeched God to give her success in business and life.

"Thanks, Richie."

He gazed at her for several seconds. "You're welcome. Thanks for supper tonight."

"It was nothing."

"Food is always better when shared with others. Katy. . ." He trailed off and leaned forward, cupping her face ever so gently, and then he kissed her.

She didn't pull away, just kissed him back. "What would you say if I asked you out?"

The blue eyes didn't shift from her face, questioning and speaking volumes as he waited for her response.

"What did you have in mind?"

"We can go anywhere you want. We'll take Bethie, too. I want to spend time with you both."

Katy eyed him speculatively. "To get to know us as brother-in-law and uncle, or do you have another motive?"

"I do have an agenda," he admitted with a grin. "Does that bother you?" She shook her head. "You think we can put the past behind us and look forward to the future?"

"I'm willing to try if you are."

He touched her cheek gently. "Oh, I'm definitely willing. Need any more help with the boxes before I go?"

She glanced over to where he'd stacked them neatly in the corners. "I have to go through them and take out what we need before I move them to the unit. But not tonight. I didn't sleep well last night, and I think I'll have an early night, too."

"Okay, I'm out of here. I'll talk to you tomorrow. Be thinking about where you want to go on our date."

They held hands as they walked to the door, and he brushed her cheek with his lips and said good night.

Chapter 16

Richie couldn't believe Katy had agreed to a date. Letting himself into the house, he dug around in the fridge. He crunched on a dill pickle and decided he really needed to go shopping.

His gaze touched on the note that he'd scribbled on his calendar. He'd told Katy he'd be over tomorrow for a session with Bethany, but now he could see he had a conflicting appointment. He needed to let her know.

The phone rang until her answering machine picked up. Maybe she was in the shower. He waited a few minutes and tried again. Still no answer.

Feeling uneasy, Richie let himself out of the house. He'd stroll down the beach and tell her tonight. He didn't want to risk her missing the message and them sitting around waiting on him.

From what he could see, all the lights were off with the exception of the living room. She had said she was tired. Maybe she fell asleep on the sofa.

Still, a niggling doubt made Richie take care as he walked up beside the house. A strange older-model car sat in the driveway. Through the window, he saw the shadow of a tall man. Where was Katy? Who was this man?

Climbing the stairs, Richie knocked. He heard voices, and there was a delay before the door opened.

"Hey, I called and got your voice mail. I need to reschedule Bethany's session tomorrow. I forgot I had an appointment."

"It's okay." Her voice wavered despite her effort to sound normal. The green eyes were wide with fright.

"I'll talk to you tomorrow, then," Richie said, trying to communicate that he knew something was amiss. She all but closed the door in his face.

He went down the steps, aware of being watched through the crack in the curtains. He walked under the house and around to the beach side.

What was happening here? An overwhelming urge to pray for their safety gripped him. He stopped and dropped to his knees in the sand.

"Dear God, enfold them in Your loving arms and keep them safe. Let Katy and Bethany feel Your protection against the prevailing evil. Show me what You would have me do."

Almost as if led, he rose and moved stealthily toward the deck. He avoided the stairs and climbed the section near Bethany's bedroom. The window was open a crack. "Thank You, God," he whispered.

With the aid of the night-light, he saw his niece sitting on the floor by the bed, hugging her dog while holding the cordless phone to her ear.

"Bethie, it's Uncle Richie," he called softly. "Come to the window. Be really quiet," he whispered, hoping she could hear the words over the banging of his heart.

He pulled a penknife from his pocket and stripped away the screen, praying the window wouldn't make any noise as he pushed it upward.

Holding a finger to his lips, he motioned Bethany forward. Her tone was unnaturally soft as she murmured into the phone and brought it with her. Richie took the receiver and listened, surprised to hear a 911 operator on the line.

He pulled the child through the window and hugged her, retaining his hold. Carrying Bethany away from the house, he prayed he wouldn't lose the signal.

"This is Richie Taylor." He recited the address. "I've removed my niece from the house, but Kaitlin Sinclair, my sister-in-law, is in the living room. I saw one man's shadow earlier, but he hid when I knocked on the door. Katy was frightened when she answered the door."

The operator told him she'd dispatched officers. He turned the phone off and tossed it onto the lounge chair.

Richie swung Bethany onto his back and climbed down the decking. "Sweetie, I know you're afraid, but I need your help."

Bethany tightened her death grip about his neck. "Want Mommy. Bad man."

"Me, too," Richie agreed. "First, we need to keep you safe."

The child sniffed, and Richie wanted to charge inside and do harm to the man. Never in his life had he felt this way toward another human being. "It's okay, sweetie," he said, thankful he knew the lay of the land. He walked around the house, avoiding the security lights. A dog barked and he paused.

"Are you okay, Bethany? Did he try to hurt you?"

"Want Mommy." She popped her thumb into her mouth.

Richie wanted Katy, too. He loved her. And God willing, he intended to share his life with her and Bethany.

A light flashed on next door when Wilbur opened the door for the dogs to go out. Richie jogged over, and the barking dogs brought the neighbor farther outside. He quickly explained the situation and passed Bethany over the fence.

"Take care of her. I'm going back for Katy."

"Richie, wait," Wilbur said. "Let the police—"

"I can't," he told the man.

~

Katy had experienced this overwhelming fear only one other time in her life. When the police said Bethany wasn't with Jack, she'd wanted to die. Now she probably would.

Lord, she called silently, *I know there's no reason for You to listen to me now. Please help us. Keep my precious baby girl safe. Forgive me for trying to control my own life.*

When someone knocked on the door earlier, Katy assumed Richie had forgotten something and pulled the door open without thought. She immediately recognized the man she'd encountered in her search. He held a gun on her and shouldered his way into the house.

"Bet you thought I wouldn't find you," he said, his menacing tone almost gleeful.

She backed up against the wall. "What do you want?"

"Jackie's money."

"Jack didn't have any money."

"But you do. I want the kid. Jack had big ideas. Kept saying you'd give everything for that girl."

The pounding in her ears increased. *Lord, don't let me faint,* Katy beseeched. The man lied. Jack wouldn't do that to his own child.

"Where's the kid?"

"She's asleep. Leave her alone. I'll give you money. I can write you a check."

He laughed, a string of foul language emitting from his lips. "Yeah, I'm that stupid. That paper would be useless before I got out the door."

"No, I wouldn't do that," Katy said, shaking her head. "I have some cash."

"Lady, we ain't talking pocket change here. Your old man promised us a few grand apiece."

"Us?"

"My friend got hisself arrested. Guess I'll take his share, too."

"Jack promised you money before you killed him?"

He muttered a curse. "We didn't kill him. The idiot got himself killed."

Katy frowned. "The police thought he was involved in a drug deal."

Menacing laughter emitted from the man. "Your old man wouldn't touch the stuff. Had his own scam going. He came around to discuss the plan."

"What plan?"

"I told you, lady. We was going to collect a ransom for the kid. He said you'd pay anything for her."

"You'll go to prison for kidnapping."

"I'll be so far away with the loot they'll never find me. Pay up or there's gonna be two more bodies for the police to make assumptions about."

"They'll find you," Katy told him.

He shrugged. "I'm no fool. I know how to cover my tracks."

"How did you meet Jack?"

"Me and my buddy ran across your old man in Vegas. He was drunk and poured out this sad story about how his old lady ran home to her rich daddy. He wanted to hurt you bad. Make you pay for dumping him. Said you owed him for putting up with you for all those years. Kept saying the only thing you cared about was the kid. He couldn't get over that we was from his old hometown."

"And you bonded," Katy murmured, not bothering to hide her sarcasm.

"Yeah we did. Jack picked up the tab that night and the rest of the time we were in Vegas. We drank and partied, and he asked a lot of questions."

"When was this?"

"You ask too many questions."

Katy indicated the gun. "You're the one in control."

"We finalized the deal a couple of days before the kid was grabbed. Borrowed that SUV and got everything ready. Jack thought we'd snatch her from the yard, but then you decided to go to the mall. Saw you when you went into that ice cream shop."

Having her suspicions confirmed didn't give Katy any satisfaction. Just sadness made worse by fear. How could she have loved a man who could do this to her and his child?

"I figure the kid's worth a fortune. Maybe you, too."

"Please. I'll give you money. Just leave Bethany alone. She's been through too much already."

"I don't plan to harm her as long as things go my way."

"You don't want to spend the rest of your life in prison," Katy argued.

"No more than you want to die tonight. Words like *prison* upset me. Now shut up so I can think."

Katy sank back in the chair, fear pulling at her. He outweighed her by a good hundred pounds. What could she do to stop him?

"We ain't got all night."

"What do you expect me to do? At best, I can only get a few hundred from the ATM." Katy remembered the money Richie had placed in a safety deposit box. "I can get more when the bank opens tomorrow."

"Get the kid. I can't hang out here until that boyfriend of yours comes back."

"Please. Think about this."

"Lady, I've thought about it for weeks. I want the money."

"Jack lied to you. There isn't any money."

"You think I'm stupid. I checked you out. Your daddy, too."

Katy doubted her father would pay one cent of ransom money.

"Get the kid," he growled. "Now."

His threatening tone put wings to her feet. Katy raced toward the kitchen, trying to put a bit of distance between them. If she could lock the door, she could call the police from Bethany's bedroom. Not much of a plan but it was all she had. He fired the gun. She ducked and screamed.

Please God. Please God. Forgive me for ever doubting You. Protect us.

A glimmer of light from the deck cast a shadow, and Katy's heart jumped into her throat. Did he have someone waiting outside?

The shadow shifted, and the door opened onto the deck.

"Run, Katy. Bethie's safe."

Never had there been a sweeter sound than that of Richie's voice.

She dashed forward, her captor on her heels. Richie slammed the door in his face, grabbed her hand, and ran around the side of the house and down the steps.

The man came onto the deck, swearing and calling out in the darkness.

"Help's on the way. Bethie called the police," Richie quietly informed Katy.

"Good girl," Katy whispered in reply.

They slipped into a dark corner underneath the cottage and stood silently.

"You might as well come out," the man yelled into the night. "I know where you live. I won't give up. You'll never get away from me." He started down the stairs, and Katy moved closer to Richie.

There was a grunt, and they knew he'd met the police before the officers informed him of their presence.

Katy turned into Richie's arms and broke into tears. "I was so afraid."

"I know, sweetheart. It's over. You're safe. Bethany's safe."

"How can I thank you?"

Richie hugged her more tightly. "Thank God. He was in charge the entire time. Let's go get Bethany."

After a late-night visit to the police department, they went to Richie's home. Bethany slept nearby on the sofa.

"Where are we going, Richie? We can't go back to the Lennons' cottage."

"Aunt Lucille's. She's missed you and Bethany. You'll be safe there. The guy's in jail."

"But he knows people. He'll send someone to finish the job. Bethany must have seen him when we went for ice cream."

Richie nodded. "I never dreamed this would happen. I just thought maybe Bethany would open up and talk. I can't believe I thought she was confused."

"He said Jack was angry because I'd gone home to my parents."

"I heard," he whispered, burying his face in her hair. "It gets worse every time something new comes out. Kidnapping your own child to scam money is worse than being killed in a drug deal." He hugged her close. "We'll get through this, Katy. Together."

Epilogue

Two years later

"You'll be a good girl for Grammy and Gramps, won't you?" Katy asked as she attempted to braid Bethie's long hair. Her daughter wiggled in the chair, making her task impossible. Katy paused as another pain hit.

"They're here. Let's go," Richie called impatiently, holding her bag in his hand. "Mom can finish that."

Katy kissed Bethany's cheek. "I love you, baby."

"Love you, Mommy."

Cynthia and Richard Taylor rushed inside, breathless and anxious. "Are you okay?"

She smiled at her two-time mother-in-law. "I'm fine."

"We have to go now," Richie declared.

Katy studied her anxious husband, noting his pallor and understanding his need for haste.

"Go on," Cynthia said. "We'll see you at the hospital."

Katy made her way to the car, pausing when Richie raced around to toss her case in the backseat and settle her in the passenger seat. She secured her seat belt.

"Okay?" he asked, grabbing her hand.

"Breathe, Richie. We've got time."

"You're the one who needs to practice breathing."

He attempted to back around his father's vehicle, stomping on the brake when he came too close.

Katy thought it best not to comment on his driving. She pressed a hand against her stomach, thinking of all that had transpired since that fearful night so long ago.

The courts had found Jack's partner in crime guilty and sentenced him to prison. His friend sang like a bird when he learned his buddy planned to keep all the money for himself.

Richie's counseling background had helped them come a long way in achieving a healthy relationship. He'd been agreeable to Katy's intention to take their time, and their friendship evolved to courtship and commitment to a partnership they knew would last. When he asked her to marry him, she said yes without hesitation. Their wedding had been a simple affair on the beach, just the three of them and their families. Melody and Dina had been her attendants, and Richard Taylor had been his son's best man. Katy had worn white—a beautiful V-necked sleeveless lace dress with a puddle train. Richie and his dad wore tuxedos. Everyone went barefoot. Bethany had been in her element as she dropped flower petals along the beach. Afterward, Melody and Dina had held a reception for them at the beach cottage.

Her party business was doing well. She'd booked successful events and garnered a good number of word-of-mouth referrals that kept her busy. Lucille's house had been the perfect place for those who desired a locale, and the senior citizen enjoyed the parties as much as Katy and Bethany.

Sadly, they lost their great-aunt two months earlier. Katy grieved as she would have for her own family. Lucille had become a good friend and had been so happy when she and Richie married. The old woman looked forward to holding Richie's son or daughter in her arms. Instead, she joined her precious Maria in heaven.

Lucille left her house to Richie and Katy. Both felt honored to share the love-filled environment and planned to carry on the tradition of the Taylor family, living at the beach for many years to come.

Bethany had never fully revealed what had transpired with the kidnapping. In the end, they determined the missing bits and pieces didn't matter and gave the child all the love she could handle. They gave thanks as she became more like her old self.

She'd grown close to her grandparents, and the senior Taylors had come back to the beach when Richie told them Katy was expecting. She'd grown more comfortable in allowing them to take Bethany on outings. They were very good about letting her know their schedule.

They'd even made progress in their relationship with her family. Katy's dad finally admitted Richie was nothing like his brother when they clashed over his effort to give them money. Richie returned the check with a polite thank-you.

"We're here," Richie said, pulling up in front of the ER and running around to help her.

Katy struggled to her feet, pausing when another pain struck. He talked her through the breathing they'd learned in class and settled her in the wheelchair.

Hours later, she looked into the beaming face of her husband as he studied his newborn son.

"I have to call Dina."

"I already did," Richie said. "Sent photos, too. Aren't you proud of me?" Katy kissed him. "She e-mailed to say she'll be here tomorrow. She's bringing Aaron."

Dina's son was almost ten months old. Katy had gone to be with her for the birth. Dina had taken a three-month maternity leave and decided to reduce her workload so she could spend more time with the baby.

They had talked a lot, and Dina admitted she was thankful Katy followed her heart and hadn't let them convince her to give up hope. Katy told Dina she believed Bethany would have been lost to them forever if she hadn't come to North Carolina. The miracle of Bethany's return had helped Dina and Kevin accept they needed God in their life.

They now attended Katy's former church, and Dina and Melody had become good friends as well. Dina and Katy prayed their parents would one day accept the Lord.

Katy touched her son's cheek. "So what do you think? Can the family handle another Trey?"

Richie shook his head. "He needs his own name."

"He needs his daddy's name," Katy said firmly. "Richard Samuel Taylor III. Rick or Sam. Your choice."

"Let's give it more thought," he suggested.

He likes the idea, Katy thought, loving his tender expression as he gazed at his son.

The Taylors arrived with Bethany. Captivated by her new baby brother, the little girl climbed into a chair and demanded to hold him. Richie knelt by her side, helping support the baby as Cynthia snapped photos. Katy knew total contentment.

"What do you think, Bethie?" she asked. "Does he look like a Sam or Rick to you?"

Bethany hugged the baby closer and giggled before she recited from the Dr. Seuss books she loved so much. "Sam I am."

Cynthia smiled and moved to take a turn at holding her new grandson. She eyed him closely and said, "He looks like a Sam to me, too."

"Okay, you win. Sam he is. Though I'm sure that will soon become Sammy," Richie said.

Katy giggled at his pessimism and her joy overflowed. Richie came to stand next to the bed. "Hey, no tears," he said and wiped them away.

"Happy tears," she whispered. "I'm so thankful to God for all He's given us."

"He knows, honey."

Richie kissed her. Katy grasped his hand and held on. Thanks to him, she'd learned to trust God to quiet the storms in her life. And in return, He'd sent her the man she could trust to always protect her heart.

WITH NOT A SPOKEN WORD

Dedication

To Jesus Christ—the one protector we can always depend on.
To Mary, Tammy, JoAnne, Rachel, and Margie—
thanks for helping me make my stories work.

Chapter 1

Arianna Kent sat on a deck perched on the side of a mountain and thought about living high in the sky. Unlike her parents' Gold Coast penthouse with its sky-top terraces and incredible vistas of the lake and the Chicago skyline, this place seemed more like a tree house.

Surrounded by thick forests of trees to her right and left, scenic Lake Hiwassee stretched out before her as far as the eye could see. In the distance, other houses looked down from their high perches with long flights of stairs leading down to the lake. Though the day was early, the August sun made itself felt as it sparkled off the silvery gray water. She pushed away the remnants of her breakfast and shifted her gaze to the floating dock where Simon played. He knelt too close to the edge, and she wanted to call out to him to take care but remained silent, frustrated by her inability to speak the words of warning that churned inside her head.

How could she protect her younger brother when she couldn't even warn him of danger? Maybe she should turn his care over to someone else until she got her voice back. She grimaced at the thought.

Ari wasn't about to abandon Simon when he needed her most. He'd spent far too much of his young life being cared for by someone other than his family. She also needed to get past the self-pity. She wasn't alone. Elsewhere on the property, Tom Brown, her father's longtime chauffeur and now their self-appointed security guard, patrolled the area with a dedication that couldn't be bought. He had worked around the clock, determined to keep them safe.

Their elderly nanny, Dora Etheridge, had stepped up to the role of parent pro tem out of love for the charges she often referred to as her babies.

Still, with her inability to speak, Nana's age, and only Tom providing security, there was no way they could hope to protect Simon from every threat that might arise. And while Gary Bishop of Bishop Security insisted they were secure here in this Murphy, North Carolina, safe house, Arianna found it impossible to feel safe anywhere.

As a Christian, Ari believed God would care for them, but her human side had brought her here. She willingly accepted this safe haven in hopes of overcoming her sudden disability but couldn't relinquish the anxiety and terror that kept her awake at night or the overwhelming dread that never went away.

They hadn't wanted to leave their home and lives behind, but their emotional response to the idea that they were not safe in Chicago gave them sufficient motivation to run away.

They'd flown into the Western Carolina Regional Airport on Tuesday, picked up the SUV Gary arranged, loaded their belongings inside, and took off for the address Tom had been given. As he followed the GPS instructions that led them along the rural roads to the Bear Paw community, Ari couldn't begin to imagine where they were going. At best she considered they would be staying in a log cabin in the middle of nowhere.

The gorgeous home was indeed a type of log cabin, but its open design and ample interior space had been a pleasant surprise. The gated community gave her a degree of comfort; so did the fact that the two houses, one for them and the other for security, were located in a paved clearing at the end of their own street, the surrounding wooded area too overgrown to be easily negotiated. The area seemed isolated but wasn't. People surrounded them in the mountaintop houses situated throughout the wooded area, and yet each home had its own private access from the paved streets that wound throughout the community.

The spectacular view appealed to her senses, and the house provided them with the privacy they required. Ari needed to believe that no one would find them here.

She stood and moved to the railing. Simon glanced up and yelled for her to come on down. Ari shook her head. She held up both hands and gestured toward herself, hoping he would understand her sign language. Simon took a couple of steps toward the center of the dock, and Ari flashed him a big smile and a thumbs-up.

She returned to the table. Her staff meeting would begin soon. Ari signed on to her laptop and then jotted a few thoughts on a legal pad in preparation for the long-distance event. The Chicago Hotel Kent would continue to function in her absence. Its guests would come and go, hopefully happy and content with their stays, unaware the grieving manager conducted business from a deck hundreds of miles away in the Great Smoky Mountains.

That didn't make it any easier to accept that she couldn't be there, doing the work she enjoyed and living the life she'd created for herself. Never the type to sit around wasting time, Ari hated feeling useless. There was so much more she could be doing in Chicago, but for now she had to be content here. Simon's life could depend on her doing the right thing.

From the corner of her eye, movement and a flash of color on the hill alongside the house caught Ari's attention. She jerked around and spotted a man strolling down the pathway.

Stranger alert.

Arianna fumbled around on the table until she located one of the many whistles they owned underneath her napkin. They had rehearsed this plan numerous times, never expecting to carry it out. She sucked in a deep breath and issued the shrill warning that quickly brought Simon to his feet.

The seven-year-old stood there looking like David coming up against Goliath. Ari considered his options, wondering if he could make it to the stairs before the intruder came too close.

Where was Tom? Had this man overpowered him elsewhere on the property? Ari ran to the door and banged on the glass. Nana hurried over. She pointed, and the woman picked up the phone. Ari started down the stairs, praying God would deliver them safely from this man.

Noting the commotion, the stranger drew to a halt. He lifted his hands and yelled, "I'm with Bishop Security! My name is Mitchell Ellis." He pulled a badge from his pocket and flung it in Simon's direction.

The child took a few steps forward, not taking his eyes off the intruder as he bent to pick it up. He edged back toward safety before he checked it out. "It's a Bishop badge," Simon called to his sister.

The breath rushed from Ari, and she grabbed hold of the stair railing to support herself as her knees weakened. Why hadn't she thought of that earlier? Gary had planned to send another man to help Tom as soon as he could make the arrangements. She hadn't expected him to arrive without some type of advance warning.

Where was Tom? Why hadn't he alerted them to the man's arrival? Surely the guardhouse had notified him.

Nana stepped out on the deck and announced, "Tom says it's the Bishop guy."

At the same time, the man named Mitchell shouted up to her. "I spoke with Tom Brown. Told him I would introduce myself. I thought Gary had told you I'd be arriving this afternoon."

"You can come on up," Simon invited as he returned the badge.

The two of them moved toward the stairs. Simon laughed at something the man said. Ari returned to the deck and sat down at the table, fearful her legs would give way.

The climb to the deck took longer for the man. He paused to draw in several deep breaths before he managed, "I am sorry, Ms. Kent. I saw Simon on the dock and thought I'd introduce myself. I should have realized you were on high alert."

"Mitch said it's a good thing you didn't have a gun or he'd probably be dead," Simon told her.

Ari forced a smile. He probably meant it as a joke, but considering how threatened she'd felt, "shoot first, ask questions later" might have been her initial reaction.

"You okay, Ari?" Simon asked, grabbing her hand.

She forced another smile, determined to hide her inner agitation from them. Her gaze came back to Mitchell Ellis. This man looked nothing like she expected. Most of the Bishop men blended into the background, but this was not a man who faded into obscurity.

Ari found herself acutely conscious of his tall, muscular physique. He wore the expensive clothing with the air of a man who knew he looked good. Not that there was anything wrong with that. She found his aristocratic facial features, olive complexion, and perfectly cut dark brown hair to be very attractive as well. His eyes were the same shade of brown as her favorite dark chocolate. He reached out to shake her hand, and she noted his hand was that of an executive, the clean nails buffed to a shine. She estimated him to be in his midthirties.

Stop being so critical, she chided. So the man took care of himself. There was nothing wrong with being well groomed and immaculately turned out when meeting a new client.

Arianna focused on Simon's chatter. Her heart thudded in an uneven rhythm that matched her breathing. Though she believed Mitchell Ellis meant them no harm, the reality lingered in her thoughts.

And the episode pointed out one more chink in their security system. She hadn't been able to reach Tom, and where would Simon have gone if the man had been a predator?

His options—a long flight of stairs, the heavily wooded area, and the lake—weren't really possibilities. A grown man could have easily overcome the child in any of those places. She needed to contact Gary Bishop. Maybe even insist on full-time armed bodyguards to protect Simon when he played outside the house.

Her computer screen caught her attention, reminding Ari that a conference room of managers waited for her to join the meeting. She pointed to the laptop and turned her attention to the business at hand.

Stupid! Stupid! Stupid! Mitchell Ellis berated himself. Brother-in-law or not, Gary would tell him to get lost fast if he pulled another stunt like this.

What had he been thinking? He should have known better than to come up at any point other than the front door. They were afraid and had every right to feel threatened by a stranger strolling casually down the hillside.

But he'd become so used to walking along the path to the dock during his vacations that it never occurred to him that it wasn't a good idea. He'd been considered a decent security man in his day. Had the years of medical school and working with patients dulled his edge? Anyone with Security 101 knew you didn't scare a client like that.

Awareness flowed to life within him when he caught Arianna Kent watching him. Earlier when he'd looked up and seen her beautiful face in distress, Mitch wished he could rewind and approach them correctly. Her reserved smile and the way she hurriedly shifted her green gaze back to the computer screen gave him pause. Surely this beauty wasn't shy.

When Gary had approached him regarding the use of his two somewhat secluded Murphy mountain homes in the gated community of Bear Paw, he insisted they could easily hide the Kents there.

Today's security breach showed a hole in his theory. Mitch had witnessed their fright as they considered what to do. Simon had nowhere to run and Arianna had no way to help him, untenable situations for them both.

"Come on, Mitch," Simon said as he opened the door off the deck. "I'll introduce you to Nana while Ari has her meeting. She'll give us something cold to drink. You think it's always this mad hot here?"

"It is summer."

Mitch glanced back at the young woman he'd rarely seen in the Chicago social columns. Petite and slim, she wore white shorts and a royal-blue sleeveless top. She'd pulled her white-blond hair up into a loose chignon with little tendrils framing her ivory-skinned heart-shaped face. Fragile. The one word summed her up perfectly.

From the rumors, Arianna Kent had gone off to college and found God. Some socialites snickered because she preferred church to parties, but Mitch hoped Arianna's decision gave her great joy. Especially at a time like this when she had experienced so much pain.

"You coming?" Simon asked.

Arianna looked up again, this time her gaze bolder and more confident when their eyes met. He smiled, tossed a wave in her direction, and said, "Right behind you."

⟿

Ari felt his gaze on her and assumed he was analyzing her reaction to his sudden shocking appearance. She doubted he wanted to get into trouble with the new boss on his first day.

The computer chimed as her staff indicated their presence in the room. Ari laughed at their aliases. Captain Cook. Big Money. Broom Hilda. They were truly getting into the intrigue.

Shannon Crown, aka Princess and Ari's assistant general manager, had already sent the agenda and daily operation update that morning.

Ari couldn't imagine a more dedicated employee. Her friend's exceptional work ethic inspired Ari. Having Shannon there was as good as being there in person. They had met in college when Shannon became her roomie and later led her to Christ.

After graduation, Ari suggested her friend come to Chicago and talk to her father about a job. Shannon had worked her way through college part-time in a hotel sales office. Within months of starting work at Hotel Kent, her impressive sales ability garnered Charles Kent's attention, and he offered her the position of sales manager. Ari had found Shannon's guilt over receiving a management position humorous.

"I should be working my way up with you," she insisted.

Charles Kent believed Ari needed to learn the business from the ground up, and her first job assignment was as a front desk clerk.

"No way," Ari denied. "I was born into a family of hoteliers and you have more experience than me."

From his corporate office, her father knew exactly how Ari performed. Determined to prove herself, Arianna mastered each aspect of operations in a very short time. No one could refer to her as the spoiled child of the owner. She worked shoulder to shoulder with the other employees. Within a year, her father put Arianna in charge.

Ari had managed the hotel for three years now, maintaining the high level of operation that resulted in award-winning recognition. She asked nothing of her staff she wasn't willing to give and received their dedication in return.

Time to get their meeting under way. Ari typed, *Good morning*.

At her request, Gary had directed his IT people to set up a private chat room on the Bishop Security site so they could communicate using a question-and-answer session.

Old-fashioned, considering the technology used by most businesses, but no one knew where they were and Ari planned to keep it that way. She had an air card that was not traceable to her or the company, a disposable phone well stocked with minutes, and no video cams. No reason since no one needed to see her mute persona on a screen.

In turn, each manager reported on their respective area of operation, covering the problems and plans for sales, food and beverage, front desk operations, housekeeping, and accounting. They discussed the situations every hotel dealt with in the course of providing quality services to their guests and even the unique things that at times baffled them all. They reviewed upcoming events and ways to increase their revenue in a difficult economic time. Fortunately for them, the hotel chain was popular with tourists and businesspeople.

Almost an hour later, Ari concluded the meeting, thanking each of them for their efforts on her behalf. Several additional messages appeared, asking if she and Simon were doing okay. Teary-eyed, she assured them they were doing as well as could be expected.

Grief was a strange thing. She would be fine, and then a random memory triggered the pain and she cried for hours. Losing her parents naturally would have been difficult enough, but finding them murdered was at times more than she could bear.

Her cell beeped and Ari found a text message from Gary Bishop. One of her conditions for hiring his firm had been that she be able to contact him at any time, day or night. She paid his firm very well to guarantee every aspect of their safety and didn't feel this was an unrealistic request.

She read, Here's a photo of the new guy. Mitchell Ellis will be a great addition to your security team.

A little late, Ari thought. She typed a response. Thanks, Gary. He arrived unexpectedly over an hour ago. Will discuss the drama that occurred in greater detail after reviewing the incident with Mr. Ellis. Probability we may need to take further security precautions.

Gary immediately texted that he would be waiting to hear back from her.

Ari closed the lid on the laptop, leaving it on the table. There was other work, but it could wait. Digging around on the cluttered tabletop, she found the white dry-erase board and a marker. Yet another of the outdated tools she used for communication these days.

Chapter 2

Inside, Mitch and Simon were seated at the table drinking soda. Ari pulled out a chair. She scribbled busily on the whiteboard, hoping he could read her writing. *"Gary sent a photo. Told him you'd already arrived with ensuing drama."*

Looking sheepish, Mitch said, "Sorry, Ms. Kent."

"Call me Ari. It concerns me that you slipped up on us like that," she wrote. *"If I hadn't seen the movement, you could have gotten to Simon rather quickly. How do you recommend we avoid that in the future?"*

The wait was prolonged as he drank from the glass and considered his response. Ari thought of the question as a test. Wrong answer, he failed and she would send him packing no matter how confident Gary felt.

Mitch lowered the glass to the table, taking even longer to center it on the coaster. "We've been talking." He waved his hand to indicate Simon and himself. "Simon understands that he needs to think about where he is at all times and where he can go if a stranger appears."

"He says if there are no options, I shouldn't be there," Simon piped up. "I won't be able to leave the house."

Mitch spoke with quiet emphasis, glancing at the boy as he spoke. "I'm fairly certain most people who come to visit wouldn't come down that steep slope."

"We don't have visitors," Simon muttered.

His comment gave Ari pause. Not that she claimed to be an expert on seven-year-old boys, but she did understand that he missed his home and friends as much as she did. Ari wanted this to be over for both their sakes.

"Someone with the intent to kill might very well choose that route," Ari wrote. She angled the board about so that Mitch could read what she'd written.

He shrugged and said, "I doubt they'd exert themselves to that extent."

Ari considered his unspoken implication. Anyone could use a rifle to pick them off like bugs on a leaf. There were too many perfect hiding places among the hills and trees.

Mitch continued, "I've been thinking and plan to make recommendations to Gary. We could install a screen to block access, but I think our best course of action is to place alarms that give you adequate time to react."

Ari considered both ideas. While the screen would keep them from view when they were down near the water, it would also keep them from being seen by the occupants of the security house.

"Why can't we go home?" Simon asked.

She wiped the board clean and wrote, *"You know why."*

"I could look out for you and Nana," Simon said. "There's nothing to do here."

Ari stared into his green eyes—their father's eyes. She wanted to tousle his blond hair and tell him everything would be okay, but she couldn't make that promise. She had to protect him even if he came to hate her for doing so. She loved Simon far too much to ever allow something bad to happen to him.

Besides, she'd seen to it that he had plenty to keep him busy. They had turned the entire lower level into a game room complete with television, game console, pinball machine, piles of his favorite books, trading cards, action figures, not to mention board games, boxes of science projects, and Legos.

"Do you understand why you're here, Simon?" Mitch asked.

Idly pushing his glass around on the table, he nodded. "Why can't they find the people who killed Mom and Dad? It's been forever."

Ari understood that a week could seem like a long time to a seven-year-old.

"The police are doing everything they can," Mitch said. "Gary has been in touch with the Chicago PD and says they are under a lot of pressure to solve the case."

"I hope they do it soon," Simon said, his vexation evident. "I want to go home."

"There's more to this than finding the killer," Mitch said. "Your sister has suffered a traumatic shock and needs this time to recover."

The boy stood and threw an arm around her shoulders. "I'm sorry, Ari."

She kissed his cheek and mouthed, *Love you, Simon.*

"Love you back. Can I go play?"

Ari nodded.

"See you, Mitch." He ran off down the stairs.

Ari wrote, *"Please don't make him feel guilty over what's happened to me. The situation is bad enough without that. He's entitled to feel restless. I've ripped him away from everything he's ever known and brought him to the middle of nowhere."*

Determination highlighted his handsome features. "He needs to understand you're doing this for him. It might make him think twice before taking a chance that could cost him his life."

His comment surprised her. She'd expected him to say, "Yes ma'am," and go on with business, not challenge her. She cleaned the board and wrote, *"He's a child. Our responsibility is to protect him. What about an armed guard?"*

Mitch shook his head. "I don't care for guns around children. Bad things happen when weapons are in the mix. We can find less dangerous ways to protect you both." His gaze focused directly on her. "I apologize for frightening you unnecessarily. Your response was excellent. Whistles, air horns, anything that makes noise can be an excellent deterrent."

An image of them tooting noisemakers as they ran away from the killer immediately came to mind. It seemed almost too silly to imagine, but Ari agreed that guns could be hazardous.

She scribbled on the board and held it up. *"Why didn't Gary come with you?"*

Mitch grimaced and said, "He's tied up in the city. I told him I could handle the introduction on my own. He gave me an overview of the case and instructions on how to handle the job. It's a very private area. The guard at the gate isn't going to tell anyone you're here, nor will he allow anyone access. The dense woods surrounding the house will also provide a level of protection. Not many people would brave those hilly woods to get to this point."

"Not many people would access a penthouse apartment either," she wrote.

He nodded agreement, his expressive face showing his sympathy. Few Chicagoans had missed the report of the Kents' murder. Every major news outlet to the national level had covered the story. The hoteliers had been well known throughout the United States. One of few remaining family-owned chains, the Kent Hotels were popular.

"After we finish here, I plan to walk the perimeter. Then I'll talk with Gary. Is there anything else you need me to do now that I've arrived?"

Ari shook her head.

Nana placed a salad plate with fruit and baked chicken on the table before her and commanded, "Eat."

Ari glanced at her watch and saw that the morning had disappeared and it was indeed lunchtime. Her appetite had been almost nonexistent since the night her parents were killed. Nana seemed equally determined that she would not fade away in her grief.

The woman served Mitch and placed a basket of croissants and yeast rolls along with honey butter on the table. She walked over to the stairs and called Simon. He bounded into the room and took his place at the dining table. Nana set a club sandwich and fries before him. She brought her fruit salad over and sat down.

"Let's join hands and say grace," she said, reaching out to Ari and Simon. Simon reached for Mitch's hand. Nana thanked the Lord for His provisions and for Mitch's presence to help keep them safe.

One positive of this place was the lack of formality, Ari thought as she forked a piece of apple into her mouth. At the penthouse, Nana would have taken her meal in the kitchen or nursery. Ari liked sharing the table with her.

Ari sneaked one of Simon's fries.

"Hey," he cried, moving his plate out of reach.

She grinned and poked him playfully.

Simon giggled and blocked her attempts to snag more with his small body.

"If you want fries, Ari, there's more on the counter."

Ari retrieved the plate, pausing to take the ketchup bottle from the fridge. She slid the plate in Mitch's direction.

He took one and popped it into his mouth. "French fries are hard to resist."

"I'd have made more, but we're out of potatoes," Nana said. "I need to take a trip into Murphy."

"Is it something I can do for you?" Mitch asked with a pleasant smile.

"Groceries."

"Give me a list and I'll have them picked up."

Good luck with that one, Ari thought. Ever since she'd taken on the self-appointed role of cook here in the mountains, Nana hadn't trusted her shopping to anyone.

"No thank you. I prefer to choose my own meat and produce."

"Then one of us will take you. I'm covering the day shift, but Tom can drive you later this afternoon after he wakes."

Ari grabbed her marker and wrote, *"Let's all go. I wouldn't mind getting away from here for a bit."*

Mitch frowned. "That could be dangerous. It's difficult to protect three people in a public place."

"We look out for each other," Nana said. "Ari and Simon have been in my care ever since they were born. I'm not about to let anyone harm either of them."

"When did you want to go?"

"In the morning will be fine. Today is nearly over."

Ari nearly laughed at Nana's timekeeping. It was noon, not midnight. The phone next to her plate beeped.

"Please turn that off," Nana ordered. "Can't have a decent meal without some kind of technology interrupting."

Ari slid the phone around to read the e-mail. She felt the oncoming tears and hurriedly wrote, *"Excuse me,"* on the whiteboard.

❧

"What happened? Is something wrong?" Mitch asked when she disappeared into the bedroom off the left of the main room.

Nana reached for the phone and read the message. She frowned and laid it back on the tabletop. "I'd better check on her."

Mitch looked at Simon, who didn't appear the least concerned by the drama. He continued to work his way through the french fries as if nothing had happened. He glanced toward the door where the women had disappeared, not sure what he should do. He looked back at Simon and found the boy watching him as he ate. "Have you been fishing since you arrived?"

Simon used a paper napkin to clean his fingers. "I don't know how."

"Not much to it," Mitch said. "Stick some bait on the hook and wait for the fish to decide he wants a snack."

Simon frowned. "What's fun about that?"

Mitch chuckled. "It's the challenge. Man against nature. You fish to catch the big one that makes all your friends jealous. Then you mount that fish and hang it on the wall. They have to catch a bigger fish.

"And then you need to learn how to tell fish tales about the one that got away." He indicated how men usually measured their catch.

"Take me fishing and I'll catch one this big." Simon jumped up and threw both arms open wide.

Mitch laughed at the boy's antics. "Well buddy, you've got that part down. You really know how to exaggerate."

Simon's childish laughter filled the room. The women returned just as Simon jumped up. Nana told him to sit down and finish his meal.

"Ari received a reminder to check on the reservations for tomorrow night. She'd planned a surprise party for her dad's birthday," Nana explained softly as they sat down.

Mitch grimaced in sympathy. He could see Ari had been crying and wondered if his presence had been her reason for returning to the dining table. Perhaps he should make himself scarce.

"Can Mitch take me fishing?"

Too late, Mitch thought as he noted the way Ari's attention moved from the salad she rearranged to the boy and then to him. He'd have to stay and answer any questions she might have.

"He says it's real easy."

She reached for her whiteboard. *"We'll discuss this later."*

"Please, Ari."

She tapped the message on the board with her marker.

"Okay," he mumbled and turned his attention back to his lunch.

"I have fishing gear at the house," Mitch said. "I'd make sure he's safe."

Her gaze fixed on him as she tapped the dry-erase board a second time.

She wiped the board and wrote, *"Shannon said she sent you a couple of new games. We'll pick them up when we go into town."*

"Okay," Simon declared almost happily.

They finished their lunch in silence. Mitch was the first to speak.

"I need to get to work. Simon, would you mind showing me around downstairs? Thanks for lunch," Mitch told Nana. "It was delicious."

Chapter 3

Ari lay in her bed, listening to the house settle for the night. Simon and Nana slept, but she remained wide-awake, considering everything that had transpired that day. She'd refused the prescription the doctor offered, not wanting to medicate herself to the point that she might not be aware if something happened outside the house.

She tossed and turned until the sheet tangled hopelessly with her long cotton nightgown around her legs. Fighting free of the covers, Ari slid off the bed and padded barefoot to the door. Silence. Nana slept in the bedroom on the opposite side of the open kitchen, dining, and living room area. Simon slept on the sofa bed in the sunroom. He couldn't understand why he couldn't sleep in one of the two downstairs bedrooms, but Ari wanted him where she could get to him quickly.

She pulled on a sweater to protect herself against the night chill and slipped through the house and out the french door onto the deck. Ari chose a rocker at the end near her bedroom, not wanting to disturb Simon's sleep. She felt the cool dampness of the dew as she sat down and pulled her feet up onto the curved seat, jerking the flowing cotton gown over her legs.

Should she have said yes to Simon's pleas to go fishing with Mitchell Ellis? Her brother had wrapped her around his tiny fingers almost from birth, and Ari knew he wasn't about to stop now. She hadn't wanted to disappoint the child but needed to get to know Mitchell Ellis better before trusting him completely with Simon. She knew nothing more than what Gary had shared, and while his confidence should have been sufficient to calm her nerves, it wasn't.

Once her eyes adjusted to the darkness, Ari appreciated the solitude. Peaceful. No twenty-four hours of people or traffic here. A new moon and very few stars in the sky tonight. In the distance she could see lights in homes where others remained awake. While she appreciated the sense of isolation the area generated, Ari knew there were people in the homes sprinkled throughout the mountain forest.

Every little sound, mostly scrambling wildlife and birds, drew Ari's focus. At times she imagined footsteps and froze until she decided it must be her imagination. Occasional breezes soughed through the trees, rustling leaves. The air smelled fresh and clean.

She took her phone from her pocket and checked her e-mail, seeing the reminder message that had appeared that day. Her father's birthday—the first of those she'd never celebrate with him. He would have been fifty-two. Much too young to die.

Ari read the e-mails through teary eyes, mostly invitations for charity fund-raisers. Didn't they understand that she was grieving? She wanted to blast them for their insensitivity. Instead she instructed Shannon to send the standard message. As long as things remained like this, there would be rare public appearances—no parties, no social engagements, and no church.

She closed her eyes to the nightmare image that filled her head every time she recalled that night.

"Call the police. My parents are dead." Gus, the doorman at her parents' home, heard her last spoken words.

She and Simon had spent their Saturday at a church function. Then she'd taken him and his friends out for pizza and a movie afterward, and it was around 11:00 p.m. when they arrived back at the penthouse. Ari promised to pick him up for church the next morning and sent him off to prepare for bed. She paused by her parents' bedroom door, intending to wish them a good night. The television volume seemed unusually loud, and Ari thought maybe they hadn't heard when there was no response to her knock.

She turned the knob and stuck her head around the open door. Inside, the bedside lamps glowed brightly, highlighting the carnage that had been wrought. Her parents lay still on the bed, their lifeblood seeping from their multiple stab wounds. Recalling the vast amount of bright red against the white bed linens still made her shiver. Ari knew without doubt that they were dead. No one could have survived such a vicious attack.

The screams came from deep down inside as she charged back into the hallway. Simon came running, asking what was wrong. Some part of her registered that he couldn't witness the nightmare in that room. She grabbed the boy and shoved him toward the private elevator they had arrived in minutes before.

"Ari, I'm wearing my pajamas," Simon objected, looking at his sister like she'd lost her mind.

She registered the superhero on his shirt and said, "We have to get out of here. Now."

In the lobby they ran to the desk. She spoke those final words in a state of disbelief, realizing too late that she shouldn't have said them in front of the child.

Simon's eyes widened, questioning her. "Ari?"

She nodded and Simon's pitiful wail broke her heart. She dropped to her knees and pulled him close, rocking him as they sobbed together. She wanted to comfort him, but the words would not come. The doorman guided them to a nearby sofa before notifying the police.

"Did someone really hurt Mom and Dad? Ari?" Simon looked at her questioningly. "You're scaring me. Why won't you say something?"

The question was a stab in her own heart. She worked her mouth, but nothing came out. Simon's cries started up again. She pulled her cell phone from her purse and typed, *"Can't talk. Call Nana."* She located the number and handed him the phone.

Their nanny had the night off. Her family was in town, and she planned to stay over at the hotel with her sister. Ari had made the arrangements herself.

"Nana," Simon said, his voice wobbly with emotion, "something's wrong with Ari. She can't talk. She told Gus Mom and Dad are dead." He paused to listen. "Okay."

He shoved the phone at Ari. "Nana wants to talk to you." She listened as the woman said she'd be right there.

"Ms. Kent? Are you okay? Can I do anything to help?"

She looked at Gus and shook her head. He had worked as a doorman since she was a child.

The image from the bedroom played over and over again in her head. Simon clung to her and Ari held on tight, her gaze moving around the lobby, fearful the killer or killers might have stuck around to finish the job.

The police arrived and the detective flashed his badge. "Can you tell us what happened?"

"She can't talk." Simon started to cry again. Ari pulled him into her lap.

A kindly female officer knelt by Ari's side, talking softly. "Is there anyone you'd like to call?"

"We called our Nana," Simon said with a mighty sniff.

"Okay. What's her name?"

The male detective produced a pen and paper. "We need you to share what happened."

As Ari wrote quickly, describing the scene she'd discovered upstairs in her parents' bedroom, the lobby filled with police and curious tenants.

"Is there somewhere private they can go?" the detective asked, and the doorman led them to a small office.

"So you saw nothing?" the female officer asked.

Ari opened her mouth and still no words came out. "You need to go to the hospital," the woman said.

Ari wrote her family doctor's name and *"No hospital,"* underscoring the words three times.

Minutes later Nana arrived and convinced them to let her see the Kents. Both were in need of comfort and they sat on each side of the elderly woman.

The night stretched on into the predawn as the police worked the scene of the double homicide. The crime scene investigators arrived around the same time as Dr. Dwayne Graves.

His insistence that Ari go to the hospital so they could run tests met her refusal. She wrote that she was fine, but Dr. Graves insisted she was in shock.

Ari and Simon sat on the sofa while the crime scene techs fingerprinted them. She hugged him close as his tiny body trembled with sobs.

"When can they leave?" Nana asked the officer.

"Is there someplace safe they can go?"

"My place," Ari scribbled on the pad of paper.

Nana shook her head. "Not without protection." She called Tom Brown.

He arrived within minutes and was brought into the office.

Keeping his voice low, Tom said, "We can't risk them getting to you or Simon. We need more security."

"We can put a car out front," the detective said.

They all agreed that would work for now.

On the way to her place, she texted Gary Bishop on the private cell number he'd given her. She'd met him a couple of times at the hotel when someone had hired him for security and felt comfortable with Bishop Security.

He arrived at the townhouse minutes after they did. After hearing what had happened, Gary immediately suggested they consider leaving Chicago for a while. Ari wouldn't feel safe in either of the family's Aspen and Greece vacation homes. Too many people knew of their existence. Gary promised to find them a place where they could feel secure.

The investigation and memorial service had delayed their departure, but Gary had carried through on his promise and now he'd sent someone to help keep them safe. Mitchell Ellis filled her head. Something about him didn't fit her image of a security man. Granted, her heart had beat a little faster after his arrival, but Ari couldn't say whether it was the man or her reaction to him that scared her nearly senseless.

❧

Late that night, Mitch patrolled the property and stayed out of range of the security lights, not wanting to frighten the family with the burst of bright lights Tom had warned him about. His was the only human presence in the area. Night-vision goggles enabled him to find his way without a flashlight.

Mitch had flown out of Chicago early that morning. Last weekend, his plan had been to work through his patient load and start his three-week vacation here in the mountains on Friday. Then Gary had called about using the two properties as safe houses for the Kents.

"I promised to find her a safe haven."

Mitch pointed out that the gated community with a guard had a good amount of traffic and wasn't totally private.

"Yeah, but the houses are blocked under your name, and providing extra security would make the situation workable. Ari's so freaked out right now that it's playing havoc with her condition."

Gary went on to share his concerns about putting them out there with a stranger and how glad he was that Tom Brown intended to go with or without his permission. He went on to outline Tom's experience.

"You'd have been foolish to refuse his help," Mitch observed.

This wasn't the first time he'd heard Arianna Kent's name. Dwayne Graves had called on Sunday afternoon for a consult. Mitch was no expert, but he had studied conversion disorder and knew that the affected part of the body had symbolic meaning whereby the conflict was converted into a physical symptom, which in Ari's case was her inability to talk. He'd told Dwayne to give it time.

Mitch knew what he had to do. He could see to it personally that Arianna Kent got the privacy and time she needed. When he volunteered to work security during his vacation, Gary was surprised but not about to say no to the perfect solution to his dilemma. Though Gary explained the Kents were willing to pay expenses, he would have offered his houses free of charge.

Mitch felt a strange mixture of sympathy and empathy for them. He knew about having your parents ripped from you. He particularly wanted them to feel safe during this time of grief. And while he looked out for them, he could see Arianna Kent's condition for himself.

Earlier that afternoon Mitch had called Gary to discuss the panic his arrival had caused.

"Since our client can afford it, we'll put technology to work for us," Gary said without hesitation. "I want them to feel safe. Are you okay with us adding a perimeter alarm on the driveway with a computer connection so we can see who is out there? And extending the alarm on the hill around the base of the house to include the stairs and the dock?"

"Do you think there's any chance they were followed? That someone could know where they are?"

"We're operating in the dark here. The police are no closer to learning who killed the Kents than they were on Saturday."

Mitch doodled on the notepad lying on the table. "So we protect them by land and by sea?"

"Right. I'll check into having alerts sent to your cell phones."

"Ari suggested an armed guard for Simon while he's outside playing. I don't like the idea."

"What brought that up?" Suspicion tinged Gary's question.

Mitch hesitated and then admitted, "My surprise appearance and subsequent discussion regarding them being aware of their surroundings. Things evolved when I said I didn't think anyone coming after them would bother to walk down the hill."

"Mitch, I didn't send you there to frighten my client more." He'd heard that same displeased huff of agitation when his brother-in-law was upset with his wife.

"She came up with the shooter idea on her own," Mitch defended.

Gary sighed again. "They probably shouldn't be out in the open during the day."

"You can't keep them locked up inside," Mitch protested. "That's no life for anyone."

"I know. But Ari has stressed that I should spare no expense in protecting the boy. I have to do what I think best."

"Only Simon?" Why would she put her brother's safety before her own? Certainly she realized Simon needed her.

"He seems to be her focus. I believe she's afraid they will come after him because he wasn't at the penthouse with their parents."

"Or could be they waited until they were certain he wasn't at home," Mitch offered.

"I told her that, too. Right now, she's too afraid to think rationally," Gary said. Mitch could hear a phone ringing in the background. "I'll get the ball rolling with the alarms. Have them overnighted. See if Tom can do the installation. I don't want to call attention to their presence by bringing in an alarm company. Gotta go."

Strange he'd mind someone seeing the alarms installed but not the attention they'd bring to their location if they went off. Oh well, maybe the surrounding mountains would make it difficult to pinpoint where the sound was coming from. And the sirens would give them time to handle the situation before it got out of control.

A flash of green light caught his attention, jerking Mitch fully back to his patrol. His heart rate picked up. Someone was on the deck. He focused and saw Ari Kent sitting in the rocker. What was she doing out there this time of the night?

"It's Mitch," he called softly as he started to climb the stairs. Ari rose and came to stand by the rail.

"You're up late." Breathless from the steep climb, Mitch propped his arms on the rail next to her. He obviously needed to spend less time in his office chair and more time at the gym.

She typed into her phone and held it up for him to see.

"Can't sleep?" Mitch read aloud. "Is something bothering you? I've checked the area and there's no one out there."

Ari shrugged and pointed toward the house.

Mitch didn't want her to leave. "Don't go. Stay a few minutes. Just to talk."

Her phone acted like a night-light, and he caught her mocking look. "Okay, so I talk and you listen."

Ari returned to the rocker and sat down. Mitch settled in the chair next to hers.

She typed and turned her phone in his direction. *"Why are you working? I thought Tom had night shift."*

"Tom needs the rest."

More silence. This one-sided conversation took a great deal of work, Mitch decided. He looked out onto the valley. "This place is great. So peaceful."

From the first time his real estate agent brought him out to take a look, he'd been hooked by the privacy. He'd been looking for an investment and the two properties were perfect. A Realtor handled the leasing to tourists who wanted houses while visiting the mountains. And when life in Chicago got to be too much, he headed for the mountains and de-stressed.

But Ari didn't know these houses were his property. And Mitch knew Ari wouldn't like it if she knew the truth about him. He doubted a real-life psychiatrist would fit her idea of a security guard. "Gary ordered the alarms. Hopefully they won't scare you even worse if they go off."

She nodded and used her thumbs to type quickly into the phone. He marveled at her ability. His hunt-and-peck method took forever. Soon she held the phone for him to read.

"Whatever it takes. I'm afraid enough for both of us. I don't want Simon to suffer. But you're right about him being more aware. Neither of us gave any thought to the danger.

"Simon's not happy about being here," Ari typed. "What do you remember about being seven?"

"Not much," Mitch admitted. "Kids and the world have changed so much that my childhood experiences would be far different than Simon's."

"The only experiences I have with boys his age are those from school, and that's been more years than I care to count."

Mitch smiled and said, "Not that many."

"I'm 27."

He'd guessed right. "Simon's pretty young for all that's been dumped on him lately," Mitch agreed. "But he appears to be taking it all in stride."

"He doesn't understand why this happened any more than I do."

"But you're here for him, and that's the most important thing. I really would like to take him fishing," Mitch said, broaching the subject again.

She typed, *"Maybe later."*

"You're smart not to trust me yet," he said, hoping to soothe her reservations about him. "I had the feeling earlier today that you would have come over that deck to take me out. You were aware of what was going on and focused on how to handle the situation Simon was in. That makes my job easier. I don't want him to be afraid, but he needs to keep his wits about him until the killer is found. My job is to keep you safe."

They sat in comfortable silence until he heard the soft sound of her breathing and realized she'd fallen asleep. Mitch opened the door and came back to gently lift Ari into his arms. He carried her inside and paused by the sofa. Deciding she'd be more comfortable in her bed, Mitch carried her into the master bedroom and laid her on the bed, pulling a blanket over her. He hoped she'd sleep away the remainder of the night as he removed the phone from her hand and turned it off, placing it on the nightstand.

Chapter 4

Y ou're making my job too easy," Tom told Mitch over breakfast the next morning. "You took over all day yesterday, and now you want to take the family into Murphy today. Sure you won't fall asleep at the wheel?"

Mitch's first impression of the man had been of a dedicated soldier. Tom was older, his graying hair clipped in a neat military cut. He stood at medium height and was solidly built with a muscled chest and shoulders. A Texan, he wasn't the type to waste words and looked as if he could hold his own in a fight.

"I grabbed a couple of hours after you got up this morning," Mitch said. "I need to see how these outings work. Besides, the alarms should arrive today, and Gary said to ask if you'd do the install."

Tom nodded. "I told Gary Bishop he might as well take advantage of my experience. Former Navy Seal. Had a tough time when I left the service and Mr. Kent took a chance on me." He paused to butter another slice of toast. "I'm gonna find out what happened that night. Charles Kent was more than my boss. He was my friend."

Impressed by the man's loyalty, Mitch nodded. "Have you taken the three of them into Murphy before?"

"We stopped when we first arrived."

"I told Ari I didn't think it was a good idea."

Tom sighed. "Give it up. No matter how scared Ari might be, she won't allow Dora to go alone. That girl has a massive protector instinct when it comes to Simon and Dora."

"Dora?"

"The kids call her Nana, but her name is Dora Etheridge. She came to work for the Kents when Ari was born. Retired when Ari was sent off to boarding school, and then the Kents brought her back when Simon was born."

Mitch filed away the tidbit of information. His assessment of Dora Etheridge was the grandmotherly type. Her little more than five-foot frame was slightly stooped with her advanced years. Mitch suspected she was closer to seventy than sixty. She wore her salt-and-pepper hair in a tightly permed short cut and had a no-nonsense personality that he appreciated. She certainly didn't mind telling the Kents what she thought. "They wouldn't recognize the nanny."

"Not the same. Consider them a package deal. Where one goes, they all go."

"Do you think both of us should accompany them into Murphy?"

"It would call even more attention to them if we did. You'll find they're very cautious and look out for each other."

"What about other people? Do they pay attention?"

"Well," Tom said, his Texan drawl becoming more obvious, "Ari is a beautiful woman, and I've seen some admiring looks cast in her direction even when she tries to downplay her appearance."

Mitch didn't doubt that. Blond and beautiful made her most men's type. He certainly wasn't immune to her appearance. "How does she do that?"

"You'll see." Tom chuckled. "This trip could take a while. Dora likes to take time with her shopping. You may be going to more than one place. All purchases go on a Bishop credit card."

Mitch went to refill his coffee mug. He held up the pot and Tom shook his head.

He turned a wooden chair about and straddled it before taking a drink from his mug. "What's your gut telling you about the murders?"

Tom looked him straight in the eye and said, "Inside job. Place has private elevator access straight into the entrance and off the kitchen. Somebody had to let them into the penthouse."

Mitch caught the inference and wondered if Tom knew something the others didn't. "Them? You're thinking more than one?"

"Can't say for certain. The Kents could have been asleep or drugged."

"Gary said they had a party that night?"

Tom nodded. "A few close friends and business acquaintances. Their friends and that lawyer, Todd Langan, and his date, Ann Radnor. She worked for Mr. Kent in the past."

More names to file away. "Anyone else?" Mitch prompted.

"The other two couples were longtime acquaintances. Neither of them had anything to do with this."

"The lawyer?"

Tom frowned. "Hard to say. He's the pushy type. But Mr. K shoved back when required. He would have me leave the window open when I drove them around so I could hear him give Langan fits over his legal advice."

"Why did Mr. Kent keep him around?"

"I asked him the same thing. He said Langan was a capable attorney, except for the times he was too pretentious for his own good."

Mitch considered that for a moment. "You think maybe Langan did something stupid?"

Tom shook his head. "Nah. Langan was out to impress the boss. Not kill him. Too bad Dora wasn't around that night."

"She might have been killed as well. I'm thinking the murderer planned things so everyone but the Kents would be out of the house."

Tom frowned. "That means they would have been aware of everyone's schedule."

"Possibly even someone they considered a friend. But what was their motive? Did they rob the Kents?"

"A few things were taken. Nothing worth killing anyone over."

Not much Mitch hadn't heard before. Did Langan resent the way Charles Kent had treated him? And he'd like to know more about this Ann woman. And who had the Kents trusted with their schedules? "Do you believe they intended to kill Ari and Simon as well?"

Tom crossed his arms and leaned back in the dining chair. "I plan to see to it that they don't get a chance."

Mitch nodded agreement. "I talked to Simon about being more aware yesterday." He described how he'd almost walked up on the child before Ari blew the whistle. "He was looking for a place to hide. That's why we're adding the alarms."

"Figured as much."

⁓

Over at the other house, Ari drank coffee and ate a pastry as she read news on the Internet.

Behind her, withered hands opened and closed cabinet doors as Nana checked her grocery list, making noise as she pushed aside and rearranged items.

A can thudded on the hardwood floor, and Ari nearly jumped out of her chair.

"Sorry."

Ari retrieved the can and set it on the table. She was strung tighter than a fiddle with new strings. Was it because of the planned trip into Murphy? She wasn't about to let Nana go grocery shopping unassisted. The task would go quicker if she was there to help.

Nana brought her list over to the table. "Do you need any personal items?"

Ari shook her head.

"Better get dressed. Mitch will be here in a few minutes. I'll call Simon."

Mitch? How long did he think he could go without sleep?

When she'd awakened in her own bed that morning, Ari had been more than a little aware that she hadn't gotten there on her own. Why hadn't he left her in the rocker? She'd have made her way back to her room eventually.

As Nana predicted, Mitch arrived a few minutes later. Ari was dressed and Simon was downstairs changing into clean clothes.

She wrote on the whiteboard. *"Are you up to this? You didn't sleep last night."*

His smile was wide, his teeth strikingly white against his olive-toned skin. "I'm good. Tom's an early riser so I managed a couple of hours' sleep before breakfast. He said Simon was down at the dock alone. Simon shouldn't be wandering about like that. We have to know where he is and what he's doing at all times. I'll talk to him."

⁓

One look and Mitch understood what Tom meant by downplaying her looks. Ari wore very little makeup and her hair was braided down her back. Shades covered her eyes, and the capri pants and loose T-shirt didn't call attention to her body. Not many women her age could make themselves look younger, but

Ari had managed to do exactly that.

The drive went pretty much as expected. The women opted to sit in the back of the SUV, leaving shotgun for Simon.

The boy rattled on for most of the trip. Mitch multitasked, driving, keeping up with the conversation, and paying close attention to what was going on around them. He wasn't used to children's chatter and was thankful when Nana suggested Simon give their ears a break. The child played games on his phone for the rest of the trip.

Mitch pulled into the parking lot at the tourism center. "Anyone mind if we stop here?"

Simon looked up and asked curiously, "Where are we?"

Mitch killed the engine and opened his door. "Tourism center. Thought we might pick up some information on the area."

Nana chose to remain in the vehicle, but Ari and Simon joined him and plucked brochures from the covered board outside the building. Mitch found a couple of things that interested him.

"Anyone want to go inside for more information?" Mitch asked.

Both shook their heads, and they all returned to the vehicle. He drove on into town.

Mitch followed them into the store, taking note of their surroundings. He pushed the cart and told Simon to stay in front. The women walked together off to his right side. When a couple of guys focused their attention on Arianna, she moved closer to Mitch, taking his hand in hers. The men moved on and she let go, flashing him a smile as she did so.

Mitch noted that Ari walked faster in public, frequently glancing over her shoulder to see if anyone followed. He didn't doubt the not knowing who to trust gave her a feeling of overwhelming paranoia. For a couple of moments, he wondered why she'd put herself through this, but then he knew. Ari refused to give up completely. For Simon and Nana's sake, she would do everything she could to keep life as normal as possible. Even though there was absolutely nothing normal about their situation.

He saw Simon type into his phone and Arianna type something back. He appreciated that they used technology to communicate but thought how tiresome it must be not to be able to talk normally. When Simon and Nana spoke to each other, Mitch noted they didn't call each other by name. At times, Arianna e-mailed Simon, who in turn relayed the message to Nana. Too bad they didn't know sign language.

Simon lingered by an arrangement of rods and reels near the sports section of the store. "Are these the kind you use to fish?"

Mitch nodded. "I have several at the house. I'll loan you one and you can fish off the pier, if your sister is okay with that."

His questioning gaze turned in Arianna's direction.

She laughed, shaking her head at Mitch's determination to teach Simon how to fish. Ari texted her brother.

"Yes," came out like a hiss as he pumped his arm and his small face split wide with a grin.

She reached out and smoothed his wild hair.

"Ari says I can have one. Help me pick it out."

Mitch glanced at her and said, "There's plenty at the house."

She typed, *"Let him have his own. Maybe he'll become a great angler."*

They paused at the display while he removed a basic rod and reel he felt would work well for Simon. "We can buy bait at the marina."

"And then I'll catch one this big," Simon declared, throwing his arms open wide.

"Maybe." Mitch suspected the boy would be surprised by the size of his first fish. "I think you can fish on my license. I'll check to be sure. You know, there's more to this than fishing. You have to learn the angler's creed. And always eat what you catch."

"Speaking of eating, let's get this shopping done," Nana said.

The group followed the older woman up and down the aisles, retrieving the items she called out from her list. Soon the groceries were paid for and loaded in the back of the SUV. Simon's new fishing pole had been relegated to the back when Nana said he'd poke out someone's eye if he kept it in front with him.

Mitch liked the older woman's practical mind-set. She said what she felt and the Kents respected her. Back at the house, he helped carry the groceries inside. Arianna sent Nana off to rest while she unpacked the bags and put the items away. Simon took his new rod and reel down to his playroom. Mitch cautioned him not to remove it from the package until they could assemble it together.

"Did you rest okay last night?" Mitch asked, shifting some of the canned goods into the pantry cabinet.

Ari blushed and nodded.

Mitch halted next to her. "You're embarrassed that I carried you to bed?"

She nodded.

"I couldn't leave you out there in the night air, and I thought you'd be more comfortable in your bed than on the sofa." Mitch emptied and folded the last bag. "Nothing to feel ashamed about. I'd better find Tom and see if those alarms arrived."

Ari mouthed, *Thank you.*

⌘

After finishing in the kitchen, Arianna took her Bible out to the deck. One of her resolutions had been to read through the Bible in a year again, and despite all that had happened, she'd managed to stay on target with her reading. God had granted her a great deal of peace and knowledge in these daily sessions.

She missed her church. It had been a key part of her life ever since she gave her life to Christ. And now when she felt she needed it most, she couldn't attend.

Dear Lord, she prayed silently, *please be with me as I struggle to overcome this fear and regain my voice. Guide the police in their search for my parents' murderers and give us strength to deal with the outcome. Shield us from harm.*

And bless me in the reading of Your Word and give me a clear understanding of what I read.

Ari's biggest regret was not being able to share her love for the Lord with her parents. They didn't tell her she was crazy for making the decision, but they weren't interested in hearing about what had changed her. She'd witnessed to them at every opportunity but hadn't touched their hearts with her message.

When she'd gone off to boarding school, Ari doubted her parents suffered from empty nest syndrome. She hadn't wanted to go, but they felt the experience would polish her and prepare her for college. Though she'd missed her parents and Nana, she had survived.

Her first year of college was all-consuming, and Ari relished each new experience. She lived in one of the dorms, made her own decisions, chose her own friends, and dated when she wanted.

Her roommate was a believer and invited Ari to attend church with her. Shannon never gave up, repeating the invitation every time she left for church until the night Ari said yes.

By Christmas of her sophomore year, Ari had accepted Christ as her Savior. His love was more than sufficient and she'd stopped thinking about the must-do activities of college and focused on her must-do list for Christian life.

Ari came home for winter break to find her parents traveling overseas. She could have joined them but chose to spend the holidays in Chicago. As usual, the house was beautifully decorated and there were gifts under the tree. Ari had thought maybe they planned to have a party for the New Year.

When Ari called to ask if Nana had time for a visit, she encouraged her former charge to come immediately. Ari stayed with Nana through Christmas. Nana was pleased to hear that Ari had given her life to Christ. Her parents had not returned by the time she returned to school after the New Year.

By spring break, Simon was nearly a month old and Dora Etheridge was living with the Kent family. Ari hugged Nana and asked, "Why didn't you tell me you were coming back?"

"Didn't know myself until a few days ago."

She handed Simon over and Ari cuddled her tiny baby brother close to her chest. She went in search of her mother. "Why didn't you tell me?"

Michelle Kent wore a designer suit and expensive shoes, not a hair out of place and her makeup flawless as she thumbed through a fashion magazine. She looked nothing like a woman who had recently become a mother at the age of forty-four. "We missed you at Christmas."

"But we talked and you never said a word."

"We weren't sure about the outcome."

Concerned that her mother's pregnancy had been risky, Ari said, "You should have told me. I could have come home."

Tiny lines creased her mother's forehead. "You have your own life now, Arianna."

Her arms tightened protectively around the tiny bundle swathed in a soft knitted blue shawl that Ari knew had to be Nana's work. She nuzzled his cheek, loving the sweet baby smell of him. "He has Daddy's hair and eyes."

"Ari, do take him back to Nana," her mother exclaimed suddenly. "You'll throw him off schedule."

"But Mom. . ."

"Take the baby back to Nana," she repeated sternly. "I don't want him upset. He already cries enough as it is."

Ari looked up and demanded, "Why does he cry?"

"The pediatrician said his formula didn't agree with him. You never had problems like that."

"Poor baby," Ari cooed. "Did that nasty old formula make you sick?"

"It's been changed and he's doing better. Take him back to Nana."

Reluctantly she returned Simon to the perfectly decorated nursery. She kissed his cheek one last time and started to place him in the wooden cradle.

Nana sat in a rocker next to a fireplace that burned merrily as her fingers moved the knitting needles in perfect precision. "Babies need love."

"But Mom says I'll disrupt his schedule," she repeated, feeling confused by her nanny's contradictory message.

Nana indicated the bottle in the warmer and the second rocker. She continued to knit as Ari fed Simon for the first time. After a while, she followed Nana's instructions and burped him. Eventually he slept. Ari snuggled him closer and set the bottle on the table. She was in love with this little guy. She looked at her long-ago caregiver. "Did Mom have a difficult time with the birth?"

Nana shrugged. "Couldn't say. They called me after Simon was born."

Twenty years before, Michelle Kent had lured the older, well-established nanny away from another family when Ari was born. After ten years of caring for her sole charge, Nana retired at the age of fifty-two. She'd gone to live outside Chicago near her family. Ari remained in touch with the woman she loved like a grandmother. Nana was sixty-two when the Kents called her back into service.

"I told your mother I'm too old, but she pleaded with me to come back. Said they would hire extra help if I needed someone."

Ari looked down at the bundle in her arms. "I can't believe they didn't tell me." Had her mother been so overwhelmed by the news that she hadn't known what to say? They should consider themselves blessed. Sure, her mom was older, but she was in good physical condition. And she had given Charles Kent the son he'd always wanted.

Ari knew that about her father. More than anything in life, he'd wanted a son. She knew he must be thrilled beyond words. In a way, her inability to measure up hurt, and yet she found it difficult to harbor a grudge against her baby brother.

Yet strangely enough Charles Kent seemed equally distant from Simon. Ari knew her parents weren't typical parental examples. Simon's childhood experience was similar to her own. Their parents had left it to Nana to provide their children with unending love.

Simon's arrival changed her world. Ari returned to college but looked forward to the times she could be home with Simon and Nana. She loved him and there was nothing she wouldn't do for him. That included keeping him safe now.

After graduation, at a time in her life when she could have gone anywhere and tried anything, Ari knew she had to come home. Her parents left the majority of Simon's care to Nana, and Ari wanted to take some of the stress of caring for the active little boy off the woman.

Her off-work hours were dedicated to church and her brother. Thankfully her parents hadn't objected to her taking Simon to church, and Ari was glad the child enjoyed himself enough to want to go back. Now she could only hope their parents had listened when she spoke to them of Jesus.

The click of the door opening snapped her back to the present. Mitch stepped outside.

"Just wanted to let you know the alarms are connected. No more worries that anyone will slip up on you and Simon. Tom says they'll make a lot of noise, so be prepared."

Better to frighten people than for us to die, Ari thought.

"The fingerprint door lock on the lower floor is in place as well. We'll need to get everyone registered." He pointed to her cell. "I noticed you use your phone to communicate," Mitch said. "Would you like to learn sign language? I'd be happy to show you the alphabet and a few phrases that might help simplify your communication."

Ari shook her head negatively. To her, learning sign language showed acceptance of the situation. She would never accept that her voice wouldn't return.

"Let me know if you change your mind. Oh, here's the mail we picked up."

All mail was forwarded to a post office box for Bishop Security, which in turn had it delivered to a post office box in Murphy for pickup.

Ari thanked Mitch and watched as he disappeared from sight before she flipped through the correspondence looking for anything of importance. Most items had already been forwarded via e-mail. There were sympathy and memorial donation cards from friends and acquaintances and one envelope from the attorney.

A frown creased her forehead as she slit open the envelope from Todd Langan. She read through the papers, breathing a relieved sigh when she found they were copies of a follow-up report on another hotel the chain was considering.

No doubt Todd Langan wasn't happy that he had to communicate with her through the security company. She knew the brief handwritten note instructing her to contact him as soon as possible for the reading of the will had been his reason for this snail mail.

Since Todd hadn't been involved in the writing of her parents' will, Ari wasn't sure why he thought he would have anything to do with the probate.

While she knew it had to be done, Ari needed time. Her parents were barely in their graves. Day-to-day operation of the business had not stopped. Her father had always kept competent people in place to assure the business continued as usual in his absence, and Ari knew it wouldn't stop in hers either.

Her knitting lay in the basket at her feet, and she reached for the soft baby blanket. It was a gift for her sales manager, who expected her first child around Christmas. Most days her frustrations eased as she worked the yellow yarn into the design. The soothing quality of the activity took over and occupied her hands if not her mind.

But not today. She couldn't concentrate. This wasn't what she needed to be doing. She should be in Chicago, running her hotel and doing the things she enjoyed in life. She should be visiting her parents and sharing God's love for them. Not hiding in the mountains grieving their loss. Frustrated, Ari stabbed the needles into the ball of yarn and shoved it back into the basket.

Maybe she should see the specialists as Dr. Graves suggested. No. She had to help herself. She needed to try harder.

Ari considered her changed attitude since the loss of her parents and her voice. Always a strong-willed woman, she now felt defenseless, the fight drained from her. Nothing else mattered but keeping Simon safe. Seeking escape from her thoughts, she rose from the chair and went in search of her brother.

She found the child in one of the lower-floor bathrooms—his laboratory, as he called the room. Simon often bolted here when he tired of female companionship. He messed around with weird concoctions for hours, his intelligent young mind eagerly absorbing every drop of knowledge. He routinely requested more equipment and books when he mastered what he already had.

At his age, she'd barely been reading, but he was reading a couple of grades above his age level. She handed over the games that Shannon had sent, and he laid them on the countertop.

"Hey Ari, watch this," he said, adding a mint to a diet soda bottle. The soda shot up like a geyser from the bottle. "Cool, huh?"

She nodded. Luckily for him, he'd thought to place his experiment in the shower stall. Ari gestured upstairs and made the motion of eating.

"A few more minutes," he begged, his green gaze pleading in a manner that melted the best of intentions. Maybe she should allow Mitch to take the boy fishing. He needed companionship.

Ari relented, holding up ten fingers. She gestured upstairs with her thumb, making it clear that she expected him to be washed up and at the table in exactly that amount of time.

After dinner at the other house, Tom said, "Think I'll catch a nap before my shift."

Mitch nodded. "I'll do a walk-around." He turned off the dock and perimeter alarms, leaving the driveway alarm activated during his prowl.

His thoughts turned to what Ari was doing. They were out on the deck, playing something on a boom box. What was it? Mitch paused, listening as different voices read aloud. He walked a few steps farther and sat down on the bottom step.

"I like this," Simon said, his childish voice eager and enthusiastic.

Mitch wished Ari could respond. He wanted nothing more than to hear her speak. He fantasized about her voice, imagining it to be soft and sweet.

More than anything he wanted an opportunity to get to know her better and share the truth about himself with her. She was a special woman. Would she be willing to think of him as more than a security guard?

He was a doctor with good standing in the medical community. More than suitable for her. But then, he didn't feel Ari worried about things like that.

The changing voices in the work being read caught his attention and Mitch agreed with Simon. It was interesting—the reading as dramatic as any theater.

The Bible, Mitch realized. Actors read from the book of Exodus when Moses led the children of Israel from Egypt. Sound effects, including horses whinnying, chariots moving, and the sea receding, gave even more realism to the reading.

"Sweet," Simon exclaimed at the conclusion. "Can we listen to more?"

Mitch could imagine Ari's smile of pleasure. He heard footsteps on the deck and shot up from the steps, not wanting to get caught eavesdropping. Simon came to the railing.

"Mitch, hey," he said, waving at him. "Come on up."

He made his way up the stairs with a rapidity that astonished him. Eagerness to see Ari? He'd noticed how often she was in his thoughts. No other woman had ever managed to occupy his mind like that.

He and Simon knuckle bumped and he smiled at Ari. An easy smile played at the corners of her mouth. Their eyes met and held for several seconds before she broke away.

"What are you two up to on this fine evening?"

"Listening to an audio Bible. It's cool. You should come and listen, too," Simon invited. "We went to Bible study at home. Ari likes to discuss the Bible. She teaches the three-year-olds' class at church."

Mitch looked at her. She shrugged.

"I bet you're good with them." An overwhelming sadness filled her expression. "Miss them?"

She nodded.

"She likes doing fun things with them. Sometimes I help, don't I, Ari?"

His sister nodded. "She says I'm a big help. I like it, too. At least they don't cry a lot like the real little babies."

"Hey champ, that's their way of communicating. Did you know that parents can tell whether they're sick or hungry or need a diaper change by the way they cry?"

"No kidding?"

Mitch could see the suggestion intrigued the boy. "No kidding. Guess I'd better get back out there and finish my walk-around. Tom's on tonight," he said to Ari, wondering if she would miss their midnight chat as much as he would.

Simon bounded to his feet. "Can I come with you?"

Mitch glanced at Ari. "I've already checked most of the area, so it'll be a stroll down to the dock and back up the hill."

She nodded and the two of them left as she picked up the box of CDs and went inside.

Chapter 5

The next morning dawned dismally gray. The mountains hid behind a layer of fog and storm clouds, giving the area an entirely different atmosphere. Ari supposed it was one of the reasons they were called the Smoky Mountains. She glanced at the clock and realized the outer dimness made her room dark. She crawled from the bed, still tired after only four hours' sleep. No Mitch to keep her company last night. She'd heard Tom making his rounds, but he hadn't come up the stairs to find her on the deck.

China rattled in the kitchen. Nana was already up and at work. Ari fought back her natural concern for the elderly woman.

Ari insisted they could cope for themselves so that she could get more rest, but Nana pshawed the idea, reassuring her she wasn't old enough to take life that easy. Ari disagreed. Sixty-nine was plenty old enough. Maybe she should check into hiring someone to prepare meals while they were here.

She dragged herself to the bathroom. Quickly braiding her long hair, she tucked it underneath the shower cap and stepped beneath the spray. The cold water did the trick. Ari felt wide-awake as she stepped out and toweled herself. Slipping on a short white toweling robe, she went to her room and dressed in jean shorts and a cool cotton top. She moved around the bedroom, making the bed and putting her clothes in the hamper, chores she knew Nana would do if she didn't.

"Morning, Ari," Nana called with a smile, setting a plate of bacon and eggs on the table. "You're later than usual this morning."

Ari glanced at her watch. A few minutes after eight. Late? Only Nana would think that. Bowing her head, she said a silent prayer before picking up the fork. Thunder rumbled as she took her first bite.

She pulled a whiteboard over to her and wrote, *"Where is Simon?"*

"Last I saw of him, he had that fishing pole and was headed for the dock. He needs to come inside."

Simon needed to stop disappearing like this. Had Mitch talked to him yet? Exasperated that he had gone outside with a storm brewing, Ari wiped her mouth and dropped the napkin on the table. The boy might be smart, but he wouldn't come in because of something as trivial as a thunderstorm. Ari slid her feet into a pair of sneakers.

Once outside, she quickened her step, hoping to find Simon and get back inside before it got any worse. Jagged streaks of lightning lit the dark sky. Thunder rolled ominously and the winds gusted.

From the deck, she looked down at the dock and panicked when she didn't see him anywhere. Had Simon gone in on the lower floor? Then she spotted the rod and reel lying at the base of the stairs. Something had happened. Ari knew how fastidious Simon was with his things. He'd never leave the new fishing gear lying around like that.

She raced down the steep stairs, frantically surveying the surrounding area. The lot around the house had been cleared except for the low undergrowth along the hillside. The forest picked up where the lot ended.

At the bottom, Ari raced back and forth across the cleared area near the water. No sign of Simon. Ari jumped onto the dock to get a better view. The deafening wail of the alarm started about the same time as the torrential downpour that soaked her hair and clothing in seconds. She shivered, closing her eyes when a lightning strike seemed too close for comfort. She'd hated storms since the age of six when she'd gotten lost in the park.

Where were Mitch and Tom? Why weren't they here? Terrified, she started up the pathway, her shoes filling with the water that channeled down the hill. Where was Simon? Had he been kidnapped? Taken by an intruder? Ari began to shake as the fearful images filled her thoughts.

⸻

At the first sound of the alarm, Mitch shot out of the other house, jerking on his raincoat as he ran. He saw Ari working her way up the hill, soaking wet and obviously frightened. What had happened? He ran to where she stood and clutched her shoulders. "What's wrong?" He shouted to be heard over the storm and the sirens.

Her green eyes glittered with fear, stark and vivid, as she gestured toward the dock. *Simon,* she mouthed frantically. Her hand measured a distance from the ground.

Another lightning strike. Mitch grabbed Ari's hand and tugged, yelling again, "Come on. Let's get out of the storm."

She gasped, all but panting in terror as she struggled against him. She mouthed Simon's name again.

"Simon?" He looked around. "Where is he?"

She raised her hands, palms out, shaking her head in desperation. Ari struggled to break free to continue her search. She started to run off, slipped in the mud, and fell.

Mitch lifted her to her feet and looked her in the eyes. "Ari, go inside. I'll call Tom." She struggled against him, tears intermingling with raindrops. "Stop fighting me," he ordered, tightening his hold. "Look at me." She lifted her gaze to his. "We'll find Simon. No one has been in the area. You set the alarm off when you came down to the dock. Now go upstairs before you get hurt. I'll find him."

Worry was plain on her face as she took a step toward the house. "Go," he repeated.

Mitch kept glancing her way to make sure she was moving as he viewed the area. He ran and slid down the hill, toward the dock, thankful when Tom killed the piercing sirens. He could barely think with all that noise ringing in his ears.

Rain poured from the black skies as thunder boomed and brilliant flashes of lightning helped to light his way. He saw Ari's tiny footprints in the mud. She'd already checked these areas. He began to trek back and forth across the lot, pulling back the low vegetation that could hide a small boy.

He glanced up and saw Ari and Nana standing on the deck. The agony on their faces nearly did him in. Mitch neared the edge of the wooded area and heard something strange. Almost like something or someone crying.

"Simon?" he yelled. "Is that you, buddy? Talk to me. Where are you?"

"Mitch."

The weak cry was music to his ears. He cupped his hands around his mouth and yelled up to them. "He's here." He watched as Ari turned into Nana's open arms and allowed the woman to comfort her.

"Mitch?"

"I'm here, buddy." He jerked the ground cover out of the way and spotted Simon crumpled in a rocky depression.

Blood flowed from a gash on Simon's forehead. Mitch quickly assessed the situation. The cut would require a couple of stitches.

"What happened?"

Simon groaned, his face wet with rain and tears. "Tripped on a rock. Hit my head. Hurts," he whispered.

"Does anything else hurt?"

"My leg."

A quick examination told him Simon had broken his right fibula. Mitch debated taking time to find a brace but decided they needed to get out of this storm. "I'm going to carry you back to the house."

"I can. . ."

Simon trailed off, his face blanching white when Mitch lifted him from the ground. He watched the boy's face, seeing the tears that trailed along his cheeks. "Hang on, buddy. I'll have you there in a minute."

Mitch entered the house through the lower door. He cradled Simon against his body and leaned to place his finger on the lock and hit the handle. "We're downstairs," he bellowed once they were inside.

Carrying Simon into the nearest bedroom, Mitch settled him on the bed, jerking the covers over his small wet body. Ari and Tom ran into the room.

"Get me some towels," Mitch demanded.

Tom ran into the bathroom and returned with a big stack of clean towels. Mitch wrapped one around Simon's shoulders and used another to dry his hair. Another stemmed the flow of blood from his forehead.

"We need dry clothes," he said. "Better make it loose shorts. His leg is broken."

He saw Ari take a deep breath and go white. She had seen the blood. He pushed her down onto the end of the bed.

"Put your head between your knees," Mitch directed, his firm hands pushing her head forward. She hung suspended for several minutes. "Better?" he asked when she tried to sit up.

She nodded.

"Good. He needs to have that leg set. What's your doctor's name?" Mitch didn't let on that he already knew the Kents' doctor. "We'll call and see if he knows of an orthopedic in the area willing to set Simon's leg in his office."

"I'll do it," Tom said as he handed over the dry clothing. "You need to change, too."

"Later." He used one of the towels to swipe at his hair and face. Mitch caught Ari's uncertain expression and suggested, "Why don't you help Nana make cocoa? Hot and sweet. It will help warm him up." After she'd gone, Mitch looked at Tom and said, "We need something to splint his leg."

"There were some lengths of heavy cardboard on the packaging for the alarms. I stuck it down in the basement for recycling. We can use that and some duct tape," Tom said. "Bone come through?"

Mitch shook his head. "Clean break. We can put it back in place."

Tom grimaced and glanced down at Simon. The boy lay with his eyes closed. "Think he can handle it?"

"Probably better than trying to get him to the doctor like it is."

"I'll get the material and make that call. And get you a dry shirt."

Mitch toweled Simon and dressed him in dry clothes. He pulled the comforter over the wet place on the bed and covered Simon with a dry blanket. He held the cup of cocoa Ari handed him as Simon sipped and blew. "Still cold?"

"I'm good."

Mitch admired Simon's effort to put on a good front as the boy shivered against his chest. Mitch hitched the blanket up around his shoulders. "What were you doing out there?"

"Nothing."

Mitch knew from the slightly defensive edge in his voice that Simon was lying. "I saw the fishing pole," he said. "It's out there in the rain."

Simon looked guilty. "You've been busy. I thought maybe you'd have time to help me today."

Mitch smiled. He'd once been an impatient boy himself. He'd become pretty anxious a few times when an adult promised him something and seemed in no hurry to carry through.

He rubbed the towel over Simon's head again. "It's okay. They're made to withstand water."

Tom returned with the supplies.

"Simon, this is going to hurt, but it'll be easier for you if we set the leg now. Think you can handle it?"

The boy nodded. Mitch looked at Ari. "What about you?" She nodded. "Sit here next to him and hold his hand."

Simon's skin turned whiter as he fought the pain of setting the bone, but he only cried out once.

"Good job," Mitch comforted with a pat on the arm. "We're going to splint your leg and then we'll take you to the doctor."

After it was over and Simon lay back, Mitch said, "I need to change my shirt. Don't let him move too much."

Mitch pulled his golf shirt over his head as he walked into the big room and used the towel around his neck to dry his hair.

He heard a gasp and turned around to see Ari standing behind him. She covered her mouth with her hand.

She'd seen the scars. "I nearly died in a fire when I was thirteen."

Ari's eyes drifted closed. Mitch took a step forward, preparing to catch her if she fell. She touched her forehead.

Thankful she'd chosen not to dwell on his own injuries, Mitch said, "He banged his head when he fell. Head wounds bleed a lot."

She mouthed, *Thank you,* and went back to Simon.

Mitch went upstairs and took the cup Nana handed him. He walked over to the glass wall. The storm had blown over. Rain pattered lightly on the deck, an occasional distant streak of lightning flashing in the sky. Thunder rumbled far off.

The idea that Ari's fear might have triggered the return of her voice niggled at him. Why hadn't the words come when she tried to tell him Simon was missing? What would it take to bring back her voice?

Mitch considered how bad the storm had been. Ari never should have gone off like that. Why hadn't she blown her whistle? Done something to alert them? They wouldn't have known she was out there in the storm if she hadn't set off the alarm. She could have hurt herself badly while running around on that hill. He needed her to understand that the purpose of having security was to depend on them to take care of things. Time to lay out a few ground rules for both of them.

◆

"Hi, Ari," Simon said sleepily.

She smiled and touched his cheek. Ari longed to throw her arms around his small frame but contented herself with sitting on the edge of the bed next to him.

"I messed up, didn't I?"

Ari nodded and wished she could tell him no harm done. Instead he would have to deal with the inconvenience this break was going to cause. For weeks to come his world would become even more limited.

"Mitch and Tom did a neat job on my leg," he said, flinging back the covers to show her. "Tom got this cardboard from a package. It's really hard and folded in a V. They taped it like a box." He tapped the cardboard with his fist.

Tom came into the room, waving a piece of paper, Mitch right behind him. "Dr. Graves says this guy is willing to set Simon's leg and keep quiet. He has X-ray equipment in his office and will do it after hours. We're supposed to be there at six."

"Can Simon wait that long?" Nana asked as she stepped into the room.

Mitch smiled reassuringly at her. "We've done what we can to make him

160

comfortable. He's tough. Barely cried out when we set his leg."

Nana frowned. "How did you do that?"

"I've seen it done," Mitch said, hoping she would accept his answer.

"I'm going with you," Ari jotted onto a piece of paper on the nightstand.

"You'll have to. You're Simon's guardian." He glanced at Tom. "Let's get blankets and pillows and make a bed in the SUV for Simon."

"Stay with them," Tom said. "I'll handle it."

Ari touched the white gauze taped to Simon's forehead.

"How are you feeling, buddy? Dizzy? Light-headed?"

Ari was thankful when Mitch asked the questions she needed answered.

"Okay."

"Ready to get that leg casted?"

Simon looked apprehensive.

Mitch's hand came to rest on Simon's shoulder. "The worst is over. You'll soon be up and about on your crutches. I broke my leg when I was about your age and it healed as good as new."

"I scared Ari."

Mitch nodded. "Yeah, she thought you were out there playing Ben Franklin in that storm. Told her you didn't have a kite," he teased. "Didn't anyone tell you not to stand under trees when it's lightning?"

"I couldn't get up. My head and leg hurt real bad. I was cold and wet. I yelled, but the storm was too loud."

He patted Simon's shoulder. "I know, buddy."

Ari sat there, a silent onlooker as Mitch reassured the child. He was good with Simon. Mitch always seemed to know the right thing to say. Ari noted a little color had come back to Simon's cheeks.

"He's all boy," Mitch said to Ari. "I can't tell you how many broken bones I had."

Simon never had any until she brought him here to keep him safe, Ari thought. She knew better than to blame herself. It could have happened to anyone. Didn't the child have enough problems? He'd be miserable being stuck inside.

"I'm sorry, Ari," he said sleepily.

She wrote him a note. *"I'm OK if you're OK."*

"I'm good," he said. "I went down that hill like a rubber ball. Except I don't bounce."

His giggle brought a smile to her face. Everything would be fine.

Chapter 6

The doctor hadn't asked questions beyond those related to Simon's injuries. He x-rayed the leg and casted it in the denim-colored fiberglass Simon chose when Mitch suggested he might want to choose something a little less obvious than fluorescent orange. He even stitched up the cut on the boy's forehead and gave them the go-ahead to take him home. Mitch paid for his services with a Bishop credit card.

Back at the house, they ate a late supper and Ari suggested Simon take her room or sleep in the second bed in Nana's room.

"No. I want to sleep in my room," Simon said, sounding tired and whiny.

"Ari and Nana have to monitor you overnight," Mitch said.

Simon didn't say anything.

Ari looked at Mitch from her place behind the sofa and shook her head.

"Okay buddy, sunroom it is."

Simon nodded.

Earlier the boy had insisted he could make it into the house on his own with the new crutches. The steps had proven to be too much for him. After Simon was settled comfortably on the sofa bed with his favorite book, Mitch said good night and left.

❧

Around ten, while doing his perimeter search, Mitch called Dwayne Graves. "Sorry it's so late, but I thought you'd like an update. It was a clean break. The doctor handled the situation himself."

"Know him from medical school. He's a good guy. How's Ari?"

"She calmed down once the doctor told her Simon would probably be back to normal within a month."

"I wondered if she spoke."

Mitch had his own thoughts on the matter. Given her reaction, he was almost surprised that she hadn't expressed herself verbally. "There was a time there when I thought I'd have two patients. She nearly passed out when she saw the blood from the head wound. Probably experienced a flashback of her parents' bedroom."

"Poor kids. Have you told her yet?"

"No," Mitch said. "I'm working security, Dwayne."

"Why would it matter?"

"You know why. Once the truth comes out, everything changes. Let me do my bit to keep them safe. I'm qualified."

"Okay, Mitch. I trust you to do what's right."

What was right? He might have started this out of some sort of sympathy, but facing an unknown enemy together made them friends. Would Ari be upset when she learned the truth about his real profession?

"Thanks for letting me know about Ari and Simon. Take care of them."

"I'm trying. They're pretty determined."

Dwayne chuckled. "Man, you're preaching to the choir. Thanks for calling."

Mitch turned off the phone and tucked it into his pocket. Ari's reaction to Simon's injury had been pretty strong. Had the shock made things worse rather than better? Had fear pushed her ability to speak even further away? Maybe he should find a specialist—someone experienced with conversion disorder who could tell him what to expect.

Their fear really bothered him. As far as he was concerned, Ari and Simon had received a raw deal. Neither of them deserved this horror that pervaded their lives. And he would do everything possible to make sure they weren't hurt again.

Mitch found Arianna Kent intriguing. Over the years, he'd met a number of spoiled wealthy women, some socially and others in the course of his work. Ari was nothing like them. Despite her fears, she exuded a peace he found fascinating. Was it her focus on God that carried her through the tough times? He sure would like to know. Maybe he should ask.

Mitch let himself into the house and found Ari dozing on the sofa. He'd noticed she wasn't on the deck when he checked the area earlier. He should have known she'd remain close to Simon.

He went into the sunroom and gently shook Simon awake.

"How's your head, buddy?"

"Hurts."

Mitch went through the questions, waiting for Simon's groggy replies. "You want something for your head?"

"I'm okay."

He patted his shoulder and said, "Go back to sleep. I'll check on you again later."

He adjusted the pile of pillows underneath Simon's leg and made sure his covers were in place before going back into the other room.

He bumped against a stack of books and they fell over. Ari jumped to her feet.

"Sorry." He bent down to pick them up.

She sat down on the sofa, reaching for her whiteboard. *"Is he okay?"*

"He's got a bit of a headache, but that's to be expected. I took him through the doctor's checklist and he passed with flying colors."

She relaxed a little. *"Figures I'd fall asleep the night I need to be alert."*

He'd gotten into the habit of joining her for a midnight rendezvous each night he was on duty. They talked until Ari decided she could sleep.

"Why don't you go to bed? I'll check in with him every hour or so."

"I'll stay in case he needs me."

"He's already asleep."

"I feel so inadequate," she wrote on the board.

163

Tears started to trickle along her cheeks.

Mitch sat down next to her. "Come here," he whispered, pulling her into his arms. "You're not, Ari," he crooned as he held her close. "Simon's lucky to have you."

Her arms tightened around him as they sat there silently. Neither attempted to break free. The tears flowed and she trembled in his hold. Had she allowed herself to cry like this since her parents' death? Like most men, Mitch wasn't comfortable with tears, but he knew their healing power.

After a while, she started to sniff. He pulled tissues from the box on the table and placed them in her hand.

They separated. She dabbed at her face and reached for the board. *"He's hurt, Mitch. I should have done a better job of protecting him."*

His brown gaze met hers as he said, "He's a boy, Ari. You can't watch him every minute. You're lucky he hasn't broken something long before now."

He'd taken more than a few forays into dangerous territories and knew the risks Simon faced as a curious child.

"Don't beat yourself up about this. It's not your fault. None of what's happened to you is your fault."

"It's going to make the situation even harder for him and everyone else."

"We'll manage. In a day or so, Simon will be on the mend doing all the things he did before. You'll see. That cast won't hold him back."

She managed a tiny smile and scribbled, *"Thanks for letting me cry on your shoulder."*

He took her hand. "It's yours anytime you need. I know you're trying to be strong for Simon, but it is okay to show your emotions. You've suffered a grievous loss that has affected you in a big way. You have a right to feel afraid. Have you considered keeping a journal? It would be a good way to get those feelings out that you can't share normally. Do it for yourself."

"God already hears most of my concerns," she wrote. *"The mental dialogue with Him helps."*

"I've been meaning to ask you about that. Is the peace you exude a result of your relationship with God?"

Ari brushed an errant curl out of her face. *"I don't feel I'm exuding peace."*

"Probably because of the fear. Maybe I feel at peace when I'm around you."

"I'd like to believe that people see God in my every action," she wrote. *"At times like this when I know how strong God is, I feel extremely weak."*

"You don't always have to be in control, Ari. I promise no one will consider you a total wreck if you shed a few tears or show your fears. Those who know the truth will share those emotions."

"Thanks, Mitch. How do you always know what to say?"

He didn't tell her that years of education and professional experience guided his efforts to advise others, and he hoped he said the right things to give them comfort.

Instead he squeezed her hand. "It's been so crazy around here today that

I forgot to tell you Gary called this morning. He plans to come Sunday afternoon. He wants to bring Jennifer and Will with him."

"Why is he coming?"

"Said he wants to see things for himself and determine if any improvements can be made. Did I tell you Jennifer is my sister?"

Ari shook her head.

"Jen and Gary met back when I first worked for Bishop."

She looked puzzled.

"I've recently started working for them again," Mitch explained, not adding that it was a volunteer job.

Ari wrote, *"Nana would like to celebrate her birthday in Asheville with her sister. She wants to leave on Sunday if you don't think it's a problem. I'd like either you or Tom to escort her."*

"I'll talk to Tom. I'd like to stick around here, but if he doesn't agree, I'll go. We can celebrate her birthday Saturday night. Maybe grill out so she doesn't have any reason to be in the kitchen."

"I ordered a cake."

"Sounds good." He needed to get back to work. "How are the nerves?"

She shrugged.

"This is why Simon needs to check in with us before he goes wandering. It could have been more of a life-and-death situation if that head injury had been worse."

"I hate restricting him even more," Ari wrote.

"As his guardian, you'll have to establish rules. I'm sure your parents did."

Her skin paled.

"I'm sorry," Mitch said.

"My parents didn't supervise Simon. That's Nana's job. She coordinates his schedule. Tom drives him around."

"Did your parents spend time with Simon?"

"Not as much as he would have liked. Daddy was at the office and Mom had her social activities. They did try to have family dinners with us on Sunday nights."

At least Simon had that much, though Mitch doubted their Sunday night experiences were like the dinners he'd had with his family. They were required to be at the table at seven sharp every night. No excuses. They were expected to do their homework before dinner. Once at the table, they discussed their days and then after dinner sometimes watched television together or had movie nights or played games.

He appreciated the sacrifice his parents made for him and Jen. No doubt they were exhausted after their long days. His dad had been a pharmacist and his mom a nurse in a doctor's office.

"I tried to take some of the load off Nana whenever possible. Simon entertains himself a lot. After I came home I made a point of coming over a couple of nights each week to eat dinner with him. Afterward we snuggled and watched movies or I read to him." She stopped writing and smiled. *"He used to read with me.*

I thought he was a genius. I didn't realize he'd memorized his favorite books. I tucked him in and said his bedtime prayers with him. He was such a sweet little guy. Still is, but he's changing."

"Growing up on you?"

She nodded. *"I know it's going to happen, but it scares me. I don't know anything about boys."*

"Nothing?" Mitch teased.

She fiddled with the marker cap, popping it on and off the pen. *"Dating isn't the same as raising a male child."*

"Don't most women think of men as overgrown little boys?" he asked with a grin.

"Some guys act that way."

Mitch couldn't deny that even he acted like a child at times. "You could get your dates involved in activities with Simon."

"Doesn't work. Most aren't looking for a big sister/little brother combo to date. They want to lose the kid or pawn him off on someone else."

Mitch hadn't considered that. "What do you do?"

"Lose the guy as quickly as possible. Simon's important to me and I'm looking for a take me, take my brother kind of man."

Mitch didn't find that unrealistic. When he found the right woman, he hoped to be as close to her family as he was to Jen. "You'll find the man who accepts Simon as part of your life and doesn't think of him as a straggler. Want some advice?"

Her expression indicated she did.

"Take everything one day at a time. And remember change is necessary for him to become a well-adjusted adult. Whether he slides through puberty without angst or he struggles along the way, remind yourself that it will pass."

"Thanks, Mitch, but days like today make it difficult to believe I can handle the responsibility."

"Oh, I suspect you'll come through with flying colors, Arianna Kent. You strike me as the kind of woman who could mother a dozen children without losing control."

She seemed surprised by his comment. *"Maybe if I never get my voice back. I imagine kids would love a mom who can't yell at them when they do wrong."*

He chuckled. "You're going to get your voice back."

She looked down at her lap when she wrote, *"I worry about finding someone who loves me and not the money. If our parents were alive, the inheritance would be far into the future and I could feel more confident."*

Mitch touched her hand and a little charge shot through him.

"What do you do in your spare time when you're at home?"

"Church. Spending time with Simon. Shopping with my girlfriends. You?"

"I'm a big sports fan. I read. And I like to cook."

Her eyes widened.

"I'll have to prepare one of my specialties for you sometime."

"I'd love that."

A big yawn escaped and Ari covered her mouth.

"You should try to get some sleep. It's late and you must be exhausted. I'll check Simon when I do my next walk-around, and I promise to wake you if anything changes."

She nodded and placed the whiteboard and her book on the coffee table. "Night, Ari."

She waved at Mitch as she lifted her legs onto the sofa and pulled the throw over her.

Back at the other house, Mitch found Tom watching television, his arm wrapped around a bowl of popcorn. "Things okay over there?"

He dropped into the leather armchair. "Ari's not sleeping well. I can't determine if she's protecting her family or suffering from insomnia."

"Probably nightmares. The situation was pretty grim and I'd be willing to bet her need to protect Simon has a lot to do with it. She's always looked out for him."

Mitch considered that.

"Tell me about Simon. You worked for the Kents when he was born?"

"Not much to tell. Michelle Kent went away in early December, came home with the baby in early March and turned him over to Dora. I don't think she wanted another child. Never spent much time with the little guy.

"But then, she's never struck me as the motherly type. She didn't spend a lot of time with Ari either. Hired Dora and then sent Ari off to boarding school after she retired the nanny. Why are you asking about Simon?"

Mitch shrugged. "Ari's made a few comments about their parents that made me wonder."

"The Kents were always on the go. Ari and Simon are blessed to have Dora. She loves them."

Mitch nodded agreement. "Gary's coming in on Sunday for a few days. He's bringing his wife and son. You okay with them staying here?"

Tom shrugged. "Fine with me. The entire downstairs is open. That should give them plenty of privacy."

Mitch wasn't sure how his sister would react to living with a stranger.

Tom stuffed a handful of popcorn into his mouth and offered the bowl to Mitch.

He shook his head. "Ari says Dora wants to go to Asheville on Sunday to meet her sister and celebrate her birthday. Ari wants one of us to escort her. Means a few days in the lap of luxury. I'd like to stay here with my family, but I'll go if you want."

Tom was silent. After a while, he said, "No. Being your family is coming in, I'll go."

"Thanks, Tom. I promise to keep close watch over Ari and Simon. I told Ari we'd have a cookout on Saturday for Nana's birthday. She's ordered the cake."

"Sounds good. I wield a mean spatula."

"I'm not so bad myself." They watched TV for a while. Mitch looked at his watch. Time to make the rounds again. "I think I'll check on Simon."

"I'm going to finish this movie and see if I can sleep. We've been working such crazy hours that I can't get myself on a normal schedule."

Mitch found the two Kents much as he'd left them. Ari's hair had come loose and curled around her face. Unable to help himself, he brushed back one of the curls and stared at her for a few minutes. She was so beautiful. He picked up the throw that had fallen to the floor and spread it over her. She sighed and shifted on the sofa.

Simon sleepily mumbled his way through the questions, and Mitch left him to his rest before going out to walk the grounds.

The birthday party proved to be fun. As Mitch had said, Simon rebounded and could maneuver himself around the house with a little assistance. The headaches had ceased, and Ari felt comfortable with his recovery.

The two men turned the grilling of the burgers and hot dogs into a competition. When asked to choose the best, Nana declared it a tie and gave each an extra big piece of the birthday cake that had arrived by special delivery that morning.

Ari and Simon's gift was the hotel stay at the Inn on Biltmore Estate along with passes for the Biltmore house and garden for the three of them. There was also a spa day at the Grove Park Inn for the sisters.

"What about you, Tom? Would you like a spa day?" Ari wrote on her whiteboard.

He shook his head. "No ma'am. I'll drop the ladies off and find something to occupy my time until they finish."

"Ellie will be beside herself," Nana commented. She held up the envelope and eyed Ari. "You know this is way too much."

Ari shook her head and mouthed, *Love you.*

Nana stood and opened her arms. "I love you, too."

Late the next morning they waved Nana and Tom off on their journey. They would return late Thursday afternoon.

"Take care of her," Ari wrote on her board, showing the message to Tom. She had added instructions to have fun for both of them.

Nana looked Mitch straight in the eye. "You take care of my babies."

Tom nodded in agreement.

Mitch smiled and promised he would.

Chapter 7

You already know Gary. This is my sister, Jennifer, and my nephew, William." Mitch lifted the boy from Jen's arms. "Will, meet Ari and Simon."

The baby laughed and waved his arms when Simon made faces at him.

"Hey Will," Simon called. He hopped around behind Mitch with as much agility as anyone sporting a cast could muster, holding on to Mitch's back as he played hide-and-seek with the baby. Will wiggled against his uncle's shoulder, trying to find his new playmate. Simon popped up from the other side and the baby cackled with glee.

Ari rested her hands on Simon's shoulders and shook her head when he glanced up at her.

"It's okay," Mitch said. "Will thinks Simon is great."

Simon grinned broadly.

"I hope you'll come over and play with him this week," Jen invited. "He can't even walk yet and wears me out some days. Heaven help me when he gets older."

"I can't walk good either," Simon said, showing off his casted leg.

"Does it hurt?" Jennifer asked, sounding sympathetic to his plight.

"Itches a lot."

She grimaced. "Yeah, they do. I broke my arm and it itched like crazy."

Gary indicated he wanted to talk to Mitch, so Jennifer took her son from her brother.

The two men strolled over to the edge of the pavement, looking down over the hill.

"Careful. The trip wire is right there and it's active."

"You'll need to show us where they are so we don't set them off."

He glanced back to where the others stood, Jen talking with Simon and Ari listening and watching baby Will with longing in her eyes. Did Ari want children? There was so much he wanted to know about her. Hard to believe he'd known her for less than a week. "I'll turn them off and we can do it now if you want."

Gary nodded agreement. "I'll show Jen later."

Mitch took care of the system. "Any progress on the case?" he asked as they strolled down the hill.

"They're following leads but nothing yet. Charles and Michelle Kent have powerful friends. They won't let their murders go unsolved. They're also angry over what's happened to Ari and her feeling the need to be in seclusion. The detective says there have been several offers of secure estates with armed guards. Luxury homes."

"Did you tell her?"

Gary nodded. "She says they're fine here. Ari's comfortable with you and Tom. Did you tell her?"

Mitch shook his head. "No. I don't need to muddy up the water with facts."

"Why are you here, Mitch?" Gary asked curiously. "You've never volunteered to assist before."

"Maybe I wanted to be sure nothing happens to my rentals."

Gary shook his head. "You have something on your mind, and I'd like to know what it is."

Mitch glanced at Ari and back to Gary. "I was coming anyway. You know it's all good, don't you? I won't let you down. Nothing is going to happen to them."

"Yeah, I believe that, but I'd still like to know what you're thinking."

Gary wasn't going to let this drop. Mitch supposed his brother-in-law's purpose was twofold—business and personal. "When you first told me how frightened they were, I felt this overwhelming need to do something. Now that I've gotten to know Ari, I find her to be an intriguing, fascinating woman. I wish we'd met outside the current situation."

"The police have talked with everyone from the party. No one recalls seeing anyone who didn't belong."

"Someone does," Mitch said. "Either the killer had help or they need to look for someone with superb climbing skills."

"The last waitstaff to leave has been pinpointed as a person of interest, though the doorman recalls seeing him leave within five minutes of the others."

Gary had made some good connections with the local police over the years and often garnered information when others couldn't.

"Too obvious," Mitch said dismissively.

"I thought so, too. Did you know that lawyer, Langan, lives in the same building as the Kents?"

Mitch's head shot up. He hadn't known.

"Definitely not the penthouse suite, but I suspect he's living above his means. The prices on those places are steep."

"Does the doorman recall any strangers in the building that night?"

"He told the police strangers come and go all the time visiting the tenants."

"Don't they sign in?"

"They call and clear visitors with the residents."

"He also said it appeared Langan and Radnor were arguing when they left that night."

"Wonder what that was about."

"No one knows."

"The answer is right there in our face," Mitch said, instinct telling him all was not as it seemed. "I think Simon being with Ari probably saved his life."

"Me, too," Gary agreed. "Let's finish up here. Jennifer wants to grill out for dinner. Think Ari and Simon would like to join us?"

"I'll ask. She might feel they're intruding and say no."

"We'll have to convince her she's not."

                ~

While the men grilled pork chops out on the deck, Ari helped prepare side dishes for the meal. Jennifer insisted they call her Jen.

Ari missed her girlfriends, seeing them at church, getting together to talk or shop. Jen was a great deal of fun and Will was the sweetest baby. She loved his cherubic grins. Simon enjoyed the baby, too. Only thing was his age difference placed him in the role of protector.

After dinner, they all sat around the great room. Simon sat on the floor, his casted leg stretched out to the side as he played with Will on the rug. The cast drew the baby's attention more than the toys Simon offered him.

When her son became fussy, Jen picked him up and announced, "Bedtime for you, little man. I'll be back as soon as I tuck him in."

Simon tried to get up but couldn't. Mitch got up to assist and swung the boy to his feet.

"Will's neat," Simon said as he leaned against the sofa arm and stretched out his leg.

"We like him," Gary agreed. "You want to watch a movie?"

"I checked out the titles already. I've seen all the ones Ari will let me watch."

"We could play games," Jen suggested as she returned to the room. "Thanks, Simon, for helping with Will. He's so tired he could barely keep his eyes open."

Ari smiled at her brother.

"Let's play charades," Mitch suggested. "Ari, Simon, and I will be a team against you and Gary."

Ari frowned and shook her head. She hated charades.

"Oh come on. It'll be fun," Jen said.

Simon and Mitch put their heads together to come up with clues while Gary and Jen came up with theirs.

"Let her go first," Simon said, pointing to his sister.

Ari pulled a clue from the opposite team's bowl and stared at it for a few moments. One thing was for certain: she wouldn't blurt out the answer. She cupped a hand behind her ear.

"Sounds like," Simon called out. Ari nodded and held up three fingers. Then she made the sign of a movie camera.

"It's a movie," Simon told Mitch.

Ari held up two fingers.

"Second word?"

She pointed out the window toward the lake, stretching her arms outward.

Then she moved her arms like she was swimming.

"Swimming," Simon shouted.

She shook her head.

"Water," the boy guessed. Another shake of Ari's head.

"Lake," Mitch called.

Ari smiled and pointed at him, nodding. She held up three fingers.

"Third word?"

Ari held out her arms and looked around the room. Simon and Mitch looked at each other. Ari touched the walls and then the floor.

"House," Simon shouted.

"Something Lake House," Mitch called. "*The Lake House*."

Ari did a happy dance.

"I told you that clue was too easy," Jen told Gary.

"You never know. Sometimes the most obvious clue is the hardest."

They played until Simon fell asleep on the sofa.

"Come on, buddy," Mitch said, swinging the boy up in his arms for the trip home. "Time for bed. See you guys later."

Ari waved good night and followed Mitch outside. After Simon had been tucked in, Mitch joined Ari for a cup of cocoa. They sat next to each other at the kitchen island.

"Missing Nana?" Mitch asked.

Ari nodded before taking a sip from her mug. She pulled a whiteboard over and wrote, *"She texted me that they arrived safely. I hope they have fun."*

"I'm sure they will." They sat in comfortable silence. Mitch considered this was the way it was with old friends. They didn't need to talk to enjoy each other's company, though he couldn't think of anything he'd like more than to hear her voice. "Ari, tell me about Ann Radnor. When did she work for your father?"

She wrote, *"Years ago. She attends our church. Helps out in Simon's classroom. I've gotten to know her there."*

"What does she look like?"

Ari scribbled, *"Around 5'9", 32 years old. Long dark hair and blue eyes. Why do you ask?"*

"Just wondered. She was at your parents' dinner party."

"She's engaged to Todd Langan."

Mitch read the last comment and thought about how everything linked to the man he wanted to know more about. Why did the doorman think they were arguing? And if they were, why?

"Jen wants to visit the Fields of the Woods Bible Park while she's here, and Gary and I would like to rent a boat and go fishing. Of course our plans depend on whether you and Simon want to come along. If not, we'll hang out here at the house."

"Simon's leg?" Ari wrote on the board.

"I think we can make provisions to get around that. And you might appreciate having others to help entertain him. He'll probably get out of sorts when he can't do what he wants."

Ari shrugged. *"If he's up to it, we'll join your family."*

"Great." Mitch stood. "I'm off to do my walkabout. Call if you need me."

"Come for breakfast," Ari wrote on the whiteboard.

"I'd love to."

Mitch let himself out the downstairs door, whistling softly as he walked the area. He was so glad Jen liked Ari and Simon. He had hoped that would be the case. Of course, his sister was one of those people who never met a stranger and fell into friendships easily.

He thought of Gary's revelation regarding Langan living in the Kents' building. So many things he'd heard seemed to click, but there wasn't a connection that he knew of. Mitch walked down to the dock.

He was standing there when Raquel Wilson came to mind. She had been his patient for nearly six years. Mitch feared her unrelenting anger toward the man who had wronged her would destroy her if she didn't put the situation in the past and move on. Why was he thinking about her now?

Their last session strengthened his feeling that she would never heal emotionally. Tears flowed nonstop as she talked about the man's mistreatment of her. Mitch understood that she would feel wronged. But she hadn't been an innocent. She wasn't so young and naive that she didn't know the price of getting involved with a married man.

He still had no idea who the man was. For six years she had spoken of her experiences without naming one person. While he'd restrained his curiosity when it came to this mystery man, Mitch believed Raquel still loved the man.

Two years before, Raquel hadn't exhibited the excitement of most newly engaged women. She hadn't shared her fiancé's name, set a wedding date, or attempted to show off the large diamond engagement ring Mitch noticed her wearing. He feared for the marriage. At best, he thought she might be settling.

Chapter 8

Ari let Mitch in when he arrived early the next morning. He offered to help Simon shower and dress while she worked in the kitchen, putting together their breakfast. After helping Simon settle in his chair, Mitch walked over to the kitchen.

"Anything I can do to help?"

She pointed to the plates of bacon and eggs. Ari picked up the plate of toast and paused to remove a pitcher of orange juice from the fridge. The honey butter and jam were on the table. After Simon said grace, they began to eat.

"We were thinking of renting a pontoon boat and going fishing today." Mitch shook out his napkin and placed it in his lap. "You interested or would you prefer to hang out here?"

Ari wasn't sure about spending the day with them but could see the longing in Simon's expression and gave in to his pleas. She had dressed in shorts and a sleeveless top and slid her feet into a pair of backless sneakers.

Mitch cleaned the kitchen while she made preparations for their outing. After rubbing sunscreen on her arms and face, she packed a carryall with the items they would need, including her whiteboard and marker. A safari straw hat would shield her face from the sun. She handed Simon a baseball cap and sunshades and put on her own sunglasses. She added snack items and indicated she was ready to go. Simon moved in front of her, swinging along on his crutches.

They met the Bishops at the vehicle and drove over to the marina. The men quickly made the arrangements to rent the boat and bought bait. They filled a large cooler with ice for their catch and another smaller one with ice, sodas, and water. Gary asked someone from the marina to help them rig a shade canopy to protect the baby from the late August sun's strong rays.

Jen stepped onto the pontoon boat and settled herself and Will underneath the canopy. Mitch carried Simon on board and sat him up front before going back to help Gary with the rest of their gear.

Ari chose a seat near Jen. She rooted around in her bag and tossed Simon the tube of sunscreen. He rubbed it onto his face, arms, and one bare leg and then lobbed it back.

She offered it to Jen, who read the label and smeared some over Will's exposed body. "Thanks for reminding me. I was going to pick up a tube and forgot."

Ari pointed to Jen's arms, indicating she should use the sunscreen as well. When Mitch stepped onto the boat, Ari offered him the tube. He wore shorts, a worn T-shirt, and an old fishing hat, lures of all kinds hanging from the brim.

"Thanks." He grinned and flipped open the cap, rubbing the lotion onto his face and arms. With his darker complexion she doubted he'd burn as easily as her and Simon with their fair skin. She nodded toward Gary, and Mitch passed the tube on.

"Okay, now that everyone is properly protected," Mitch said with a teasing glance in Ari's direction, "I think we're ready to cast off."

He expertly slid the boat from the berth and moved out into the open water, going slowly through the wake. Ari noted the ease with which he handled the boat. He'd done this before.

Ari truly appreciated Mitch. Handsome, kind, and considerate were major adjectives that described him in her book. Plus he always seemed to know what to say to comfort her when she felt depressed.

She remembered the way he'd comforted her after Simon's accident and blushed slightly. Ari liked the feeling of being in his arms, and the soothing timbre of his voice was something she could listen to forever.

"So what do you think of my big brother?"

There was a definite twinkle in Jen's brown gaze when she shot her brother a cheeky grin. Ari pulled out her board and a marker. *"He's been a great help to Simon and me."*

"That's good. Generally he makes a pest of himself." Mitch made a face at Jen, and she retaliated by sticking out her tongue. Her expression changed to one of sadness. "Actually, I'm thankful he's here for you both. I know it's a difficult time. I'm praying."

Ari mouthed, *Thank you.*

"Mitch tells me you're a believer, too." She settled her son in her lap and leaned back in the seat. "I don't know how people make it through without Jesus to lean on in times like this. I was ten when we lost our parents in a fire. Mitch was thirteen. He got burned in the fire and was in the hospital for a long time. We went to stay with Mom's sister. I love Aunt Sandy, but she wasn't Mom or Dad. She didn't know our special things. It was hard, and I cried myself to sleep for weeks."

Ari had witnessed the scars left behind by the fire. Mitch said he nearly died but hadn't mentioned his parents. Why hadn't he told her? Surely he understood what she'd been feeling. He'd been the older sibling, too.

She understood the sudden loss of all you held near and dear. While families often seemed to take each other for granted, losing key members changed everything. "Don't get me wrong. I know we were blessed to have a place to go and someone who loved us. Aunt Sandy is like a grandmother to Will. He adores her." Jen's gaze filled with love as she glanced down at the baby in her lap. "She keeps him while I work." Jen noted Ari's interest and said, "I help Gary at the office for a few hours each day."

"She's quite the detective." From his seat at the front of the boat, Gary shared a private smile with his wife. His right eye closed in a playful wink. "My sweet, sweet computer expert. Need a background check or a missing person found, call Jen."

The look of love that passed between husband and wife gave Ari a bitter-sweet feeling. Would she ever find that special person who looked at her with that much love? She hoped so.

"That's how we met." Jen's gaze rested on her husband. "Mitch worked for Gary's dad and asked if they had something part-time for me."

Mitch thumped Gary's shoulder. "And you fell right into trouble's open arms."

"Hey, watch it." Gary took a step back to catch his balance.

Jen chuckled. "Aunt Sandy worried about me spending too much time on the computer. Gary taught me how to put it to good use. If it's out there, I can find it."

"Maybe the police can hire you to find out who killed our mom and dad."

Four sets of adult eyes rested on the child's forlorn expression. *If only it were that easy,* Ari thought.

Mitch patted Simon's shoulder.

"I'm sure they're looking as hard as they can," Jen told Simon.

"The police won't stop looking until they find them," Gary added.

Unconvinced, Simon shrugged.

Ari's phone beeped. She mouthed, *Excuse me,* and clicked on the e-mail to find a message forwarded by Shannon. She scowled as she read through yet another of Todd Langan's demanding e-mails.

"Something wrong?" Jen asked.

Ari shook her head. She wasn't about to ruin everyone's day with her problems. Her gaze drifted to where Simon sat at the wheel listening as Mitch showed him how to drive the boat.

The child's frequent questioning glances in Mitch's direction showed his eagerness to please. Mitch rewarded him with a big grin and another pat on the shoulder. Simon beamed with happiness.

Ari considered how different their father had been. Charles Kent wasn't the type to heap compliments on anyone's head. If you performed well, it was no more and no less than he expected. Fail and suffer his wrath. She knew. She'd failed a time or two.

He hadn't kicked her out of the family, but he'd treated her exactly like his other employees. She had reprimand letters in her personnel file to prove she'd let him down. It occurred to Ari that she should do away with them now that she was the boss. No, they would remain to serve as a reminder not to let herself or her parents down in the future.

What would Simon's adult relationship with his father have been like? Would he have been more understanding of his son? More tolerant? Or tougher?

Ari guessed their father would have demanded more of Simon. Even at a young age, the boy had more activities than most kids. Dad probably thought Simon would carry on the family business. She knew her father believed she would marry, have children, and lose interest, but Ari loved her work and intended to find a way to merge business and family in a mutually satisfactory way.

As they moved farther onto the lake, Ari noted the shadows cast by the trees that surrounded the large expanse of water. She felt hopelessly lost in the vastness of the lake.

Mitch pointed up the hill. "There's your house."

That caught Ari's attention. How had he found his way here? She was hopeless when it came to navigating. Even Chicago where she had lived most of her life.

Mitch turned the boat in a wide swath and headed back out into the lake. After a while, he shut down the engine and allowed the boat to float.

"Are we going to fish now?" Simon asked, his voice filled with childish excitement.

"Yep." Mitch settled the boy in a seat near the bow and pulled a cooler over to serve as a leg prop. He added an extra life jacket as a cushion. "Comfortable?"

Simon nodded. Mitch had come over the day before and they'd assembled the spinning rod. Now he demonstrated how it worked.

"You take care of your rods, and they'll serve you forever. I have some my dad owned. He took me fishing when I was your age. Those were some of the best times of my life."

The boy's eyes widened. "Really, your dad took you?"

Ari paid close attention to their exchange, hoping Mitch wouldn't make promises he wouldn't keep.

"He did. We went on father-son fishing trips a couple of times a year. He taught me everything his dad taught him."

"Will you teach me what your dad taught you?"

"You bet."

"The rods and Daddy's fishing boat were in a building behind our house," Jen told Ari as they witnessed the exchange between the man and boy. "Aunt Sandy had to sell the boat, but she kept the rods for Mitch."

"I'm sure he treasures them," Ari wrote.

Jen nodded. "One day Mitch and Gary will use them to teach Will like they're doing for Simon now." A tear leaked out and ran along her smooth cheek. "I'm glad he has this little piece of our dad to hold on to. Something he can pass on to his son. I wish he could find someone and settle down. Though I don't know how he'll ever meet anyone. He works way too many hours."

Ari considered Mitch's interaction with Simon. He'd make a good father. A good husband for that matter. Obviously a hard worker and dedicated to taking care of his security company assignments, he'd be a good provider. It surprised her that he hadn't been snapped up long before now.

Mitch reached into the box he'd picked up at the marina and demonstrated for Simon the technique of baiting the hook. "You can do this next time."

She couldn't look.

The boat floated on the currents. Everyone talked softly. Ari felt like a very minute part of a much bigger world.

"I've got something," Simon yelled, jarring the peacefulness.

"Let's see."

Mitch stood behind the boy's shoulder and directed, reaching out to net his catch. Simon's fish was a striped bass about ten inches long.

"Wicked," he declared in a long, breathless cry. "Ari, look. I caught a fish."

She smiled. Jen snapped a picture of him holding his first catch. Gary offered his hand in a high five.

Mitch slid the fish into the cooler and reached for the bait container. Ari closed her eyes again as Simon worked it onto the hook without doing harm to himself. Once more Mitch demonstrated how to cast the line back into the water.

"Come on, Gare," Mitch said with a grin. "We can't let this newbie out-fish us."

Simon swept out his arms, the pole clutched in one hand. "This big," he said with a pleased giggle.

"You'd better hold on with both hands in case that monster comes looking for you," Mitch said.

Jen spread a blanket on the bottom of the boat and slipped down to play with Will. Ari had missed most of this stage with Simon and found it intriguing. The baby turned and twisted in all directions, rolling from his back to his stomach.

Occasionally he sat up without his mother's support. He inched across the blanket to the toys out of his reach and reached for those she dangled. Will babbled as he moved his toys from one hand to the other and looked at his mom when she called his name. When he started to cry, she slipped a pacifier into his mouth.

Jen was a good mother, Ari thought. Caring and capable, her love for her child obvious in the way she handled him. He grinned as he stood on tiptoes and bounced in her lap.

When Ari held out her arms, Will jumped at her.

"Hold on tight," Jen told her. "He's a wiggly one."

Ari considered that she could communicate on the baby's level. Would the others understand her cries if she reverted to the alarms of infancy?

She lifted his shirt and blew a raspberry against his soft stomach. Will laughed and reared back in her arms.

Mitch glanced over at them and said, "Check out Will over there hanging out with the pretty girls."

"Yeah, my boy's quite the ladies' man," Gary said with fatherly pride.

"Not so hard to get attention at that age," Mitch said.

"Don't be a hater," Jen called.

Mitch laughed and said, "Okay, so Will and I need to talk. Maybe he can give his old uncle a few tips."

Everyone laughed. Maybe Will could give her some tips, Ari thought wryly.

They fished on. The sun moved in the sky. Half a dozen catches later, Jen wiped away the fine beads of sweat clinging to her forehead and said, "It's time to cruise for a bit. It's hot sitting in one place."

Mitch dropped a largemouth bass into the cooler. "Okay. We have enough fish for dinner anyway. Simon, looks like you have the biggest catch of the day."

"I do?"

Mitch nodded. "Now you get to learn how to clean a fish."

"You mean like give it a bath?"

"No, like take off the scales and gut it. Get it ready to cook and eat."

Simon grimaced and cried, "Ewww."

"It's not so bad. Remember what I told you. We eat what we catch. You'll be glad once they're cooked. Fish have all sorts of health benefits. They are great brain food."

"You should eat—" Jen began.

"Don't say it," Mitch warned, pointing a finger at her.

Her slow grin indicated he was no threat to her. "A whale."

"You'll pay for that. What do you think, Simon? Should I toss her overboard?"

"No, Mitch. Will would be sad without his mom."

"Okay, Jen, thank Simon for your reprieve."

She took a couple of steps forward and kissed Simon's cheek before she thumped Mitch's head.

"Ouch. You bully. Go sit down before I change my mind." He nudged Simon and said, "We get to use knives."

"Ari won't let me have a knife."

He frowned. "Yeah, I suppose you are a little young for that. We'll try you on the scaler. I'll show you how it's done. Then when you're older and go camping, you'll be able to prepare and cook your catch."

Jen passed around sodas and snacks to everyone. They ate and stayed out on the water for another hour before calling it a day. Back at the marina, they cleaned off the boat and headed for their vehicle.

At home, Jen took Will inside for a nap. Mitch, Gary, and Simon made quick work of cleaning the fish and put them in the fridge.

"We'll fry these," Mitch said. "I need to make a grocery run. Gary will be here."

Ari had showered and changed into clean clothes. Her wet hair hung down her back. She held up the whiteboard. *We'll ride with you.*

He glanced at Gary and shrugged. Gary went home, and Mitch helped Simon shower after wrapping his leg in a plastic trash bag and securing it with tape. After Simon was dressed, they accompanied Mitch over to the other house to wait while he did the same.

"Simon could hang out with us at the pool," Jen said. "He could stick one leg in the water."

Simon thumped his cast. "I can't swim or do nothing with this stupid thing."

Mitch came into the room, dressed in worn jeans and a T-shirt bearing the Bishop Security logo.

"They make waterproof cast protectors. We need to find a medical supply store. Get you one for the shower, too. Easier than rigging plastic bags and tape."

Simon's eyes widened. "Really? They make those?" He turned to look at her. "Hey Ari, can we find one? Please?"

She glanced at Mitch.

"Let's check the phone book," he said. "If they don't have them locally, we'll get one overnighted. Think you can wait another day, Simon?"

He nodded enthusiastically. "If it means I can go swimming again before the end of the summer."

Mitch called around and found the item in Murphy. Simon decided to stay with the Bishops. Ari went with Mitch. At the store, they decided on a couple of cast protectors and paid for them with the company card.

"You never know what they'll come up with next," the salesclerk said as she dropped the items and receipt into a bag.

"This is going to make one little boy very happy." He glanced at Ari and they shared a smile.

After a trip to the grocery store for fresh cabbage, cornmeal for hush puppies, batter mix, and a couple of other items, they picked up the mail. Mitch drove toward home as Ari reviewed the correspondence that had been forwarded.

"Something wrong?" Mitch asked when she glanced at him.

Ari didn't know what to make of the letter. Back at the house, she handed the sheet of stationery to Mitch and watched as he read the personal note from a board member's wife.

"Ari dear," Eileen Reynolds wrote. *"I've returned home from Paris and must tell you I'm very troubled by all that's happened to your family in my absence. If there is anything I can do to assist you, please let me know. Perhaps it is wise to put someone in an acting managerial role until you get your voice back. You poor thing. This is so terrible."*

He handed it back. "What does she mean by put someone in an acting role? Has anyone said anything to you about doing that? What's going on?"

Ari shrugged and reached for her whiteboard. *"First I've heard of it."*

"Mind if I share this with Gary?"

She shook her head.

~

"Something's going on in Chicago," Mitch told Gary as they fried up the fish that evening.

He had planned an old-fashioned fish fry for dinner. The coleslaw was made and chilling in the fridge, and he would start dropping the hush puppies in hot oil shortly. "Ari got this letter from a board member's wife." He handed it over.

Gary read and demanded, "What does she mean about assigning someone in an acting managerial role? Ari's not having any problems managing things from here."

"Someone's up to no good. Think the husband knows the wife spilled the beans?"

"I doubt it," Gary said. "She probably doesn't even realize it's a covert operation."

"I'd like to know who they're proposing for the takeover."

Gary appeared thoughtful. "We need to find out. How's Ari taking the news?"

"She's as confused as we are."

"I'll make some calls in the morning."

Mitch doubted Ari would wait that long to learn what was going on.

Inside, Ari sat at the dining table with her laptop, reading Shannon's comment over and over.

SCrown: *I did hear a rumor the board plans to put an acting chief executive officer in place until you're able to resume your full-time duties. I wanted verification before I told you. There's been so much garbage regarding the company floating around.*

Ari stared at the screen. No doubt the board was worried, but they had even less to lose in all this than she and Simon did. Why wouldn't they attempt to contact her with their concerns? All they had to do was send an e-mail to the hotel. Todd Langan should have told her in one of his many e-mails.

AKent: *Any idea who's involved?*

SCrown: *I've heard Todd Langan's name mentioned in connection to Kent more than once. I've taken to recording his calls. He's threatening me. I've been meaning to forward his last one.*

AKent: *I will be at the next board meeting. Eileen Reynolds sent a note in that last batch of mail. I don't think her husband intended for her to share the news, but apparently what you've heard is true. They're up to something and I want to know what it is.*

SCrown: *What do you need to be able to communicate in the boardroom?*

AKent: *Laptop, projector, and screen.*

SCrown: *I'll make sure they're available. When will you arrive? Will you stay at your townhouse?*

AKent: *No. Book two rooms with connecting doors and another single room across the hall. Put the rooms in Gary Bishop's name.*

SCrown: *I'll handle it myself.*

AKent: *Thanks, Shannon.*

Ari printed the screen and signed off the IM program.

A few seconds later, the forwarded voice message clicked onto her phone. She turned up the volume to listen.

"This is Todd Langan. I need to speak to Arianna Kent immediately."

"I'm sorry, Mr. Langan, but as I've told you many times, Ms. Kent is unavailable."

"Where is she?" he demanded. "She needs to be here. The police would be more productive if she were present, pushing them to investigate. The board needs to know what she plans to do. This is ridiculous. I am her lawyer."

His gruff, angry tone infuriated Ari.

Shannon's voice came over the phone. "Ari will be in touch when she's ready. Meanwhile, I'm sure the police are doing everything they can. And surely the board understands how traumatic this is for her and Simon?"

He snorted. "I don't think you're forwarding my messages to Ms. Kent. In fact, I plan to discuss your attitude with her."

"You do that, Mr. Langan. Have a nice day."

Ari laughed, cheering silently when Shannon hung up on the man. She didn't need this sneak representing her. Sure, she'd been out of contact, but there was no reason for him to attempt a coup. It was time she showed Mr. Langan who was in charge.

She turned to the laptop and typed a memo to Erik George, the law firm's senior partner, requesting a private meeting early Thursday morning to discuss replacing Todd Langan as counsel for Kent Enterprises. She also requested his presence at the next board meeting.

A thought occurred and Ari texted another message to Shannon. PLEASE NOTIFY ALL SENIOR STAFF THAT MY PRESENCE IS TO BE KEPT UNDER WRAPS. I DON'T WANT THE PRESS OR ANYONE ELSE KNOWING I'M IN CHICAGO.

WHAT WILL YOU WEAR?

Clothes. She hadn't planned that far yet. There certainly weren't any power suits in her wardrobe here.

PLEASE RUN BY MY APARTMENT AND PICK UP MY BLACK SILK AND THE NEW NAVY SUIT. IT'S STILL IN THE GARMENT BAG. CHOOSE SOME BLOUSES

AND BRING MY FERRAGAMO PUMPS. THANKS, SHANNON.

I'M PRAYING, ARI.

PLEASE KEEP IT UP. KNOWING THAT GOD'S LOVE SURROUNDS ME MAKES LIFE BEARABLE RIGHT NOW.

Ari turned off the computer and walked out onto the deck.

Mitch glanced up. "Gary and I were discussing the note. He'll do some follow-up tomorrow morning."

"No need," Ari wrote on the whiteboard. *"I've verified that there is a rumor and suspect something is planned for the next board meeting. I need to be there."*

Gary nodded. "Let's meet after dinner to discuss the particulars."

Not hungry, Ari managed a few bites of the tasty fish before putting down her fork. Simon's enthusiasm over his role of provider in the meal was obvious. Afterward Ari helped clean up and load the dishwasher. Jen took Will and went downstairs with Simon to check out the playroom.

"You want to meet in here or on the deck?" Mitch asked.

She pointed toward the living room.

They settled on the sofa and armchairs. Ari held her whiteboard and marker.

Gary took a pad of paper and pen from his shirt pocket. "You want the same amount of security you have here or more?"

She wrote on the board and held it up for him to read. *"Nana and Simon will remain in North Carolina with Tom. You and Mitch will travel with me."*

"That's good," Gary said. "We can keep a closer watch on you without worrying about them. Jen plans to stay here while we're gone. She'll help Nana with Simon. I can bring in more people if you feel the need."

"Tell her to come here and stay. Nana will enjoy spoiling your son rotten," Ari wrote, grinning as she held up the board again for Gary to read. She swiped it clean with her palm and jotted the plans for their hotel stay.

Gary whistled. "If you're ever in need of a job, let me know. I need people as thorough as you in my business."

She swiped again and wrote, *"Let's see what happens at the board meeting. If they divest me of my job, I may take you up on the offer. Oh, there's more."*

Ari took out her phone and played the call for them.

"You think Langan's behind this?" Mitch asked.

She wrote, *"I do. I've contacted Erik George and requested a private meeting Thursday morning to discuss removing Langan as counsel for the company. I have no idea what Todd Langan's agenda is, but he's not going to succeed."*

"When is the board meeting?"

She scribbled on the board and flipped it up for them to view. *"Next Thursday at 10 a.m. Before then, I want to meet with staff and the attorney and familiarize myself with everything that's happened since Daddy's death. I want to leave late Monday afternoon so we don't arrive in Chicago too early. Shannon will notify the hotel management staff of my presence but it will not be made public."*

"I'll make the flight arrangements," Gary said.

Chapter 9

Later that night, Ari rocked on the balcony, her thoughts on the future and what their parents' deaths meant to her and Simon. The most difficult thing for her was knowing they wouldn't be there when she needed them most. Her dad would have known what to do. The board would never try something like this with him. Ari knew she had to take a stand now if she hoped to maintain control in the future.

The changes she'd made in her life since college had been difficult for everyone to understand, particularly her parents. They couldn't comprehend why church was more important than the other activities they felt she should be enjoying at her age. Nor had she been interested in the men they often sent her way.

Ari knew her beliefs would have a major impact on her management role within the company. Already she prayed continuously over the operation of her one hotel, and she could see herself praying around the clock with the added corporate responsibilities.

She had to do what was right. And her promise to God was to do it in a Christian way. Still, the information she'd learned today made her angry. They had no right. She and Simon had lost so much. And to know members of the board questioned her ability hurt.

Ari knew economic changes made investors more cautious, but she also knew without doubt that not one detail in the day-to-day operations had been left unhandled.

Even though Charles Kent was no longer with them, his legacy was a system that assured business as usual in his absence. Not one man or woman he'd chosen would willingly allow a negative to reflect badly on them or the company.

Having her in the chair behind the desk or at the table in the boardroom was not going to change anything. She would continue to depend on their staff. She had not remained idle here in the mountains. Ari communicated with corporate staff on a daily basis. She'd also read and responded to every document she'd been sent. Every member of her staff could testify that she'd been hands-on even at a distance.

Ari considered what returning to Chicago and the requirements of the job would mean to her and Simon. No matter how demanding the situation, she had to be certain he knew she was there for him when he needed her.

"You okay?" Mitch's greeting was a husky whisper.

So lost in thought she hadn't heard him climbing the stairs, Ari let out a little scream. He had pulled on a navy windbreaker since dinner, making him nearly invisible in the dark. She took the phone from her lap and typed, *"Have I done the right thing by staying away?"*

"Why would you ask that?"

She typed, *"Ann Radnor e-mailed that the church is praying for us and wants me to contact her and let her know we're okay. I don't even know her that well."*

"Isn't she Langan's fiancée?"

Ari nodded.

"You think she's trying to get in touch with you for Langan?"

Ari nodded again.

"These people can't even begin to understand what you're going through, and for them to try to pressure you now is wrong."

"What if my presence would make the police work harder?"

Mitch read and shook his head. "Gary already told you the police are under a great deal of pressure. I think it's safe to say you have sufficient representation in Chicago to keep the police on the case. But even without the pressure, they want to find this person as much as you want them found. If you were there, they would have to protect you and Simon."

She considered what he'd said and accepted it was true.

"You aren't worried about this trip, are you?" he asked.

Ari picked up her phone and typed, *"Trying to think things through."*

"And finding it harder because you're feeling betrayed?"

Jesus and Judas. Ari knew her situation didn't begin to compare, but she did feel wronged. Her fingers moved on the keyboard. *"Why can't they give me time?"*

The light from the phone illuminated her sad expression before she turned it in his direction.

"Someone has gotten into their heads and convinced them they can't afford to delay. No doubt they're receiving the same amount of information, but they let their doubts force them to take action because there's not a Kent behind the big desk."

Mitch sat down next to her and took her hand in his. Ari welcomed the comfort of his touch and the familiarity of their midnight routine. Her inability to speak didn't seem to matter.

"Your hand is cold," Mitch said, raising it to his lips. The warmth of his breath against her skin felt nice. He kissed her hand.

She drank in the comfort of his nearness, wishing for more.

"My guess is they're as afraid of what's going to happen as you are," he said with quiet emphasis.

"Different reasons perhaps, but this nightmare affected them in different ways. For one thing, you can be sure they're considering their own security in a world gone crazy. A couple they trusted and liked is dead and their murderer is out there on the streets.

"Who knows, maybe they consider it a kindness to lift the burden from your shoulders. They probably don't realize they're doing you a great injustice and causing you unnecessary pain with their actions."

"You should be a counselor," Ari typed.

He moved restlessly, releasing her hand. "What's your biggest concern? What you fear could happen to you and Simon? Or what will happen with the company?"

"Simon," Ari wrote.

"Don't worry. Gary and I will be there making sure you're safe. Tom and Jen will be here looking after Simon and Nana. And while Jen might look like an innocent, my sister has her own pistol and can outshoot the trainers at the range."

Ari could see Jen taking on the bad guys. She smiled. *"I'm not worried,"* she typed. *"God is in control. I've asked Him to cast a net of safety over us all."*

"The police are going to find this person, Ari. Sooner or later, someone will slip up, and when they do, they'll be caught."

They sat in silence, studying the huge moon hanging over the water. It was almost as bright as daylight out here.

"Jen wants to go to the Fields of the Wood Bible Park tomorrow. You okay with that?"

Ari nodded. She'd read about it in the brochure she'd picked up at the tourism center and decided it would be an interesting place to visit. The sudden wail of the alarm made the hairs on her arms stand at attention.

Mitch jumped into action. "Get inside. Now. Lock the door."

Ari froze. His no-nonsense tone made her heart pound in rhythm with the loud bleat. When she didn't move, he opened the door and pushed her inside.

~

The need to protect her overwhelmed Mitch. He pressed the TALK button on the phone, calling Gary. "I'm on the deck at the other house. Someone set off the alarm. Looks like a boat down at the dock."

Gary's clipped tone ordered, "Stay with Ari and Simon. I'll check it out."

In the distance, Mitch heard voices, saw the three men who had climbed out of their boat. Their voices carried in the night air as an argument ensued.

"You idiot. This isn't our dock."

"Looks like our dock," the man muttered.

"You said you knew where you were going."

A couple of minutes later, the alarm stopped and Mitch spotted the flash-light as Gary jogged down the hill. He'd break his leg if he didn't slow down.

He shouted, "You're trespassing on private property."

"Hey man," one guy objected, holding up his hands and taking a step back on the dock. He nearly fell over the edge. The others grabbed him. "We got lost. Came in at the wrong inlet."

"Then I'd suggest you move this party along before we call the police."

"Police? Hey man, no foul. We were having fun."

"Probably best to have your fun during daylight hours without the aid of alcohol. Deep water in this lake. No one would ever find you if you fell overboard."

"What do you mean by that?" another man slurred.

Mitch took a step forward on the deck, feeling as Simon must have felt that first day. There was no way he could get down there in time if these men jumped Gary. Did he have his gun?

"No foul, man," Gary countered somewhat sarcastically. "You've obviously had too much to drink to find your way home."

"Don't antagonize them, Gary," Mitch mumbled under his breath.

"We're good. We're right around there," the man said, pointing in the opposite direction. Then he frowned and turned to point the other way. "Or maybe there."

He noted Gary kept a good distance between himself and the men.

"I suggest you get back in the boat and get out of here now."

They started to move away. One of them stopped and demanded, "Hey, who's staying up there? Must be someone important to have these noisemakers."

"No one you'd know," Gary said. "You should get out of here before my partner summons the police. He's armed. My wife is on the other deck and she's an even better shot."

They all but jumped from the dock into the boat.

The motor started up after a few tries and they rode off into the vastness of Lake Hiwassee.

"All clear," Gary said into the radio. "Idiots got lost on the lake. Thought they were on their dock. I'll watch for a while to make sure they don't double back, and I'll reset the alarms. Might be wise to notify the guardhouse before they call the police."

"Will do."

Mitch dialed the guardhouse and explained what had happened.

"Thanks," the man told him. "Maybe I should give the fish and game people a call. We don't need those idiots out there frightening people."

"Might be a good idea for their safety as well," Mitch agreed as he opened the door and stepped inside.

Ari huddled on the sofa, Simon hugged close to her. His crutches rested against the chair arm. Mitch knelt before them. He touched Simon's arm. "You okay, buddy?"

The child appeared anxious. "Who was it? Why did they come on our dock?"

"They were lost. Gary's watching to make sure they're gone. Think you can go back to sleep?"

Simon snuggled closer to Ari. "Maybe I'll stay here on the couch for a while."

"Okay. You want something to drink? I make pretty good cocoa."

Simon nodded. Mitch looked at Ari. "What about you?"

She followed him to the kitchen. They took out milk and a bottle of chocolate syrup and heated the milk on the stove.

"Not the traditional recipe," Mitch said as he stirred to keep the milk from scorching. "But it will do for tonight. That alarm scared ten years off my life."

Ari reached for a whiteboard and wrote, *Mine, too.*

She produced a bag of marshmallows and floated two in each cup. They took their mugs into the living room and sipped the hot chocolate, the warmth helping to chase away the anxiety.

Several minutes later, Simon struggled to keep his eyes open.

"Think you can sleep now?" Mitch asked.

The boy nodded and reached for his crutches.

When Ari stood to help Simon, Mitch caught her hand and squeezed reassuringly. "I won't let anything happen to either of you."

Ari smiled her thanks.

The radio chirped. "All clear," Gary said. "They're still fumbling around out there. Probably try every inlet between here and Murphy."

"They may get a visitor. You think they'll return?"

"Maybe out of curiosity, but with any luck, they'll forget their way back. They know about the alarms now. I'm headed back up to the house. Jen and Will are probably already asleep."

"I thought she was on the deck," Mitch said.

Gary laughed. "Messing with their heads."

Mitch chuckled. He followed Ari and Simon into the sunroom and helped Simon settle on the sofa bed.

He shifted in the bed and winced. "My leg hurts tonight. Can I have something for the pain?"

Ari nodded and left the room.

"Are those guys really gone, Mitch?"

He nodded. "Gary says they're out there on the lake trying to find their way home. How bad is your leg?"

Simon shrugged. "Cast feels really tight."

Mitch turned back the cover and probed his foot and upper thigh. "Your leg is swelling. Let's prop it a little higher." He stacked two more pillows under the casted leg. "Comfortable?"

Simon nodded.

Mitch sat on the side of the bed. "You did really well for your first time fishing. We'll have to go out again soon."

Simon grinned with pleasure. "I like fishing. When you first told me about it, it didn't sound like fun, but it was."

"Told you." Mitch grinned and patted his shoulder.

Ari returned with the medication and water, and Mitch left them alone. After a while, she came back into the living room and curled up on the leather sofa, wrapping herself in a chenille throw. The silence stretched on for several minutes. "What's on your mind?" he asked finally.

She shrugged, looking despondent.

"Everything's okay. They were drunk and lost."

She reached for the whiteboard. *"No. It's not. I'm sick of scurrying off to hide."*

"Sometimes it's wise to be afraid."

After a derisive look, she wrote furiously, *"Not if I'm afraid of my own shadow. Tonight a group of innocent strangers put me in a panic. I let the fear break through my shield of faith. I became afraid and ran for my life. I didn't trust God and now I can't stop running."*

Mitch thought about trusting God. Ari had done what she had to do. She'd moved herself out of harm's way. Surely this was God's plan to keep her safe. "This other situation has you on edge. I wish I knew what that lawyer thinks he's doing."

The near fury in his tone flabbergasted her.

Ari swiped the board clean and wrote, *"Nothing makes sense."*

"You're tired. Go to bed. Try to sleep. You'll feel better in the morning."

She shook her head and wrote, *"I can't live like this, Mitch. I have to take back control of my life."*

"You will. Meanwhile, I'm here, Ari. Keeping watch over you and Simon. Sleep, and then tomorrow you can concentrate on this situation with the board."

She nodded.

Mitch secured the house and went outside to start his patrol.

"Sleep well, sweetheart," he whispered a few minutes later when her bedroom light flashed off.

Mitch thought of Ari's comment about his being a good counselor. He knew he should tell her the truth, but for now, it was more important to keep her safe. He didn't even realize what he was doing when he prayed the remainder of the night would pass in silence and that God would give Ari comfort. She surely needed it now.

Chapter 10

Ari let Mitch in when he arrived around nine thirty the following morning. Simon sat at the table eating a bowl of cereal.

"Good morning. Figured you wouldn't mind sleeping in. You up to sightseeing today?" he asked cheerfully.

Ari picked up the whiteboard and scribbled, *"What about those men? Will they come back?"*

Mitch kept his voice low as he said, "The alarms worked, Ari, and they'll continue to work. Did you sleep at all last night?"

She shrugged and he knew she hadn't. She scribbled on the whiteboard and held it up. "Probably as much as you."

"Gary covered me for a few hours this morning. Would you feel safer somewhere else?"

Ari shook her head. *"I have to take a stand or I'll be running for the rest of my life. I have to trust God to take care of us."*

"We'll make sure you're safe," Mitch said.

"He will, you know. He's already blessed us with you, Gary, and Tom," Ari wrote.

Mitch felt uncomfortable with the idea that she saw him as some kind of guardian angel sent by God. He was just a man and not always proud of his actions.

"Are you too tired for Fields of the Wood today?"

She shook her head.

"Okay then, let's go. It'll do you good to have something else to occupy your mind for a while."

The day was overcast.

"Rain?" Jen asked when they gathered at the SUV.

"We've had beautiful weather up until now," Mitch said, leaving her to draw her own conclusions.

Jen punched his arm. "There's no rain cloud over my head."

"Grab your raincoat and let's go. You won't melt."

Gary greeted Ari and Simon. "You doing okay after that scare last night? Mitch said you're worried. Don't be. I doubt they could find their way back."

"I thought I was going to have to come downstairs to help you," Mitch said.

"If they'd intended harm, I'd have been toast by the time you made it down those stairs. You need a zip line off that deck. Or an elevator.

"That's why I live in the city," Gary continued. "I'm a big fan of elevators."

"He wants to put one in our house," Jen said. "I told him he's crazy. It's two floors. Between the remote and an elevator, he'd never get any exercise."

"I get plenty of exercise," Gary objected.

"Yeah, to and from the elevator in your office building," Jen teased. "One of these days you're going to get stuck in one, and then we'll see how you feel about them."

Fields of the Wood Bible Park was down the road from where they were staying. Mitch drove, and when he passed through the white archway, they were all pleasantly surprised. Earlier Mitch had asked Jen to help him cheer up Ari and Simon. She'd appointed herself tour guide for the trip and brought along the information she'd printed off. His sister never went anywhere without a computer and collected electronics like most women collected jewelry.

"Says the park was built in 1945 by the Church of God of Prophecy and there's over two hundred acres," Jen read from her papers.

"Those are the world's largest Ten Commandments. Three hundred feet wide with five-foot-tall letters and three hundred fifty steps between the tablets."

Everyone looked toward the display featured on the mountainside. Mitch let out an impressed whistle. Simon followed suit.

Gary groaned. "More steps."

Her husband's reaction prompted Jen to add, "And you can climb up inside the Bible at the top."

Mitch parked and everyone but Will climbed out of the vehicle. The baby slept peacefully in his car seat. Ari motioned for them to pose and lifted her phone to snap a photo with the backdrop of God's laws spelled out on the grassy hillside.

Mitch pointed to the right. "There's the service road. If you three want to climb up Ten Commandment Mountain, Simon, Will, and I can meet you up top."

"I'm willing if you are," Jen told Ari.

"Hey, wait a minute—that means I have to walk with you," Gary said. He eyed his brother-in-law suspiciously. "I'm onto you, buddy."

Mitch's innocent and slightly offended expression didn't fool anyone as he said, "Your wife thinks you need exercise, and I offered to babysit your son."

Gary gave Mitch the evil eye. "Okay, ladies," he said, offering them his arms, "shall we go for a stroll?"

Jen and Ari shared a smile as they stepped forward. Mitch didn't fool anyone with his plan. He'd never intended to climb the mountain.

The feeling of oneness with God returned as Ari read the commandments.

Jen appeared at her elbow. "This place is wonderful. I feel that way every time I come here. Can you believe the detail? Someone spent a lot of time getting it right."

Every time? Ari wondered how often the Bishops visited the area. Maybe they knew the owner of the houses. Gary had come up with the safe houses relatively quickly.

Ari agreed with Jen. She wouldn't mind coming back. If only she coul[d] voice her feelings. She was overwhelmed by the love and dedication that ha[d] created this wonderful site.

Jen and Gary moved on ahead, reading the commandments aloud as the[y] climbed.

She glanced up and saw Mitch and Simon off to the side of the thirty-by-fifty-foot Bible at the top.

~

Simon left the vehicle and made his way over to the seating area at the top o[f] the hill. There weren't any sightseers that day. Mitch parked the SUV nearb[y] and glanced at Will dozing in his car seat. He rolled down the window in case he woke and walked over to look down the hill. The others looked small i[n] the distance.

"Something else, isn't it?" he commented, glancing back at Simon.

"Yeah."

"Want me to take some photos for you?"

Simon handed him the phone and Mitch snapped pictures of the others climbing toward them.

"You okay, buddy?" he asked when he noticed Simon's sad expression.

"Just thinking about my mom and dad."

Mitch placed a hand on Simon's shoulder. "Good memories, I hope?"

The boy bravely fought back tears. "Why did they have to die like that, Mitch? Who would do something so mean? Mom and Dad never hurt anyone."

Mitch could have told him there was a lot of depravity out there, but Simon was too young for that. "Some things can't be explained."

"I know," he agreed glumly. "If Mom and Dad had gone to church with us that day, they'd still be alive."

Mitch shrugged. "You can't be sure of that, Simon. Your parents didn't deserve to be killed any more than you and Ari deserved to lose them."

Simon sniffed. "And Ari didn't deserve to lose her voice. Do you think she'll ever talk again, Mitch?"

"I do. One day she'll break free of whatever is holding her back and she'll be normal again." He bent to retrieve something shiny in the gravel. Mitch flipped the dime in Simon's direction and the boy caught it. "Until then, she's still the sister you've always known. She loves you. A lot. It's okay to miss your parents, Simon. Okay to talk about them when you're sad. Okay to share your good memories. And your anger for what this person has done to your family."

Simon's brow creased with worry. "I don't want to upset Ari."

Mitch recognized that attitude from when he and Jen lost their parents. He hadn't wanted to upset his sister either. But Jen had been a kid. Ari was an adult. "I'm sure Ari would love to hear what you have to say. Right now she's trapped in a world where she can't voice her pain but she's suffering, too. Could be something you say will make her feel better."

Mitch sat down next to Simon and laid a comforting arm around his shoulders.

"What am I going to do, Mitch?" the boy asked. "Who's going to take care of me?"

"Ari," Mitch said without hesitation. "Are you afraid she doesn't want you? She's been appointed as your guardian."

"But she has a job. Like Daddy."

"Her job won't stand in the way of her taking care of you, Simon. She worries that she might not be a good parent, but I think she'll be the best. Sometimes she might be weird, but you need to remember that she wants to keep you safe when she doesn't allow you do something you really want to do."

"Like fishing?"

"Exactly. Though I think the fishing had more to do with me than you. She didn't know me well enough to trust me when I first offered."

"I think she'll let me go again. I liked fishing yesterday."

Mitch smiled at the boy. He wanted to tell him there would be times when he wanted to talk to his mom or dad about something and it would hurt because they weren't there. That there would be times when a boy needed his dad, and he might not feel comfortable talking to his sister. But Ari would be there to help him through the stages of grief, and they would survive the nightmare of their loss.

Will's screams reverberated throughout the area. Mitch rushed to remove him from the car seat.

"Hey buddy, take it down a few decibels," he encouraged as he jiggled the baby. He glanced at Simon and said, "Kid's got a powerful set of lungs on him."

Simon nodded, poking his fingers into his ears.

Mitch carried his nephew over to the hilltop and pointed. "There's your mom."

The baby cried harder, and Jen picked up her pace as she neared the halfway point.

He called, "Take your time. He's fine." Mitch carried his nephew over to the seating area. "Look Will, here's your old buddy Simon."

"Hey Will," Simon said, holding his hands over his face and playing a modified peekaboo that occupied the baby's attention for a few minutes. Mitch popped a pacifier into the baby's mouth when he thought he might start to cry again.

The others cleared the top as the sky turned darker and the clouds that had threatened all morning spilled heavy raindrops.

"Looks like this visit may be a rain out," Mitch said, gathering the baby and handing Simon his crutches.

They piled into the SUV, shaking off the water.

"I knew it would rain," Gary mumbled. "Always does when we commune with nature. Do we wait to see if it stops or go back to the house?"

"Let's ride for a few minutes," Jen suggested, playing with Will as she fastened him into his car seat.

Mitch backed the SUV out of the parking space and drove along the unpaved path. They passed a marker.

Paper rattled and Jen said, "That's the One Fold, One Shepherd marker. It's meant to symbolize God's perfect plan for Christian unity. He'll be our Shepherd and we'll be His flock."

Mitch followed the sign when the road split and pointed to the flags. "What's this, Jen?"

"All Nations Cross. The world's largest cross of its kind. We're on All Nations Mountain. The flags represent every nation of the world."

"There's the United States," Simon declared.

Mitch punched his shoulder playfully. "Good job, buddy."

Simon grinned.

Mitch drove until the road dead-ended. "What's this?"

"I'm not sure," Jen said. There were engraved markers and concrete steps.

Mitch turned around and drove back down the hill. The rain seemed determined to linger. He parked at the gift shop. "Anyone need a bathroom break? Something to eat? They have a grill inside."

"Come on, Ari," Jen said. "We'll visit the ladies' room and the gift shop."

The men opted to wait in the car.

There was a duck pond off to the side. "Look Will, ducks," Gary said, trying to divert his son's attention from his missing mother. "Hope she doesn't buy out the place."

Mitch grinned. His sister did like to shop. "Simon and I were talking about some of the other stuff there is to do around here. There's a canopy tour outside Bryson City, but the minimum age is ten."

"I doubt Ari would go along with that anyway," Gary said. "He's already broken his leg. No need to break his neck, too."

"Oh, come on, Gary, they have state-of-the-art equipment on those rides."

"Not for me."

"There's the Great Smoky Mountains Railroad out of Bryson City. And Chimney Rock."

"Seen Chimney Rock and Lake Lure," Gary said. "There's a real curvy road up through the mountains to get you there. Except for that fast ride up in the twenty-six-story elevator, it's pretty much all climbing."

Mitch started to laugh. "Have you noticed everything seems to come back to taking an elevator or walking?"

"Yeah," Gary pronounced glumly.

The women came out of the gift shop, each carrying a small bag.

"Souvenirs," Jen announced as she tucked hers inside her purse. "I think this trip's a bust. Lady inside said the front will probably hang around the rest of the day."

"Home it is," Mitch said.

As they drove through the park, Jen pointed out the replica of Mount

Calvary, the baptismal pool, the tomb, and the Bethlehem Star. "That tower is seventy-five feet tall. And that's the Arise, Shine marker. It commemorates the church's fulfillment of the prophecy recorded in Isaiah 60:1. Those are the Psalms of Praise, and that entrance takes you up through Prayer Mountain. That's where the road dead-ends," Jen said. "Three hundred and twenty steps to the top, Gary."

Everyone laughed.

"And no elevator," Jen teased. "Too bad it started to rain. I think I might have wanted you to see that with me."

Gary grinned. "God truly does answer prayers."

The rain fell steadily as they drove along the road leading back to the house.

"Let's ride down to the end of the road and see the Tennessee Valley Authority setup," Gary said.

They parked and looked out over the water with the shadowy mountains in the background.

"Definitely a study in grays," Jen said.

"It's too depressing," Gary said. "Let's go home."

Back at the houses, they said their good-byes and went their separate ways. Mitch helped Simon into the house. "What did we plan for lunch?" he asked.

Ari opened the freezer and glanced at the packages of frozen meat.

"We could drive into Murphy for fast food," Mitch suggested.

She shook her head and took packages of sliced meat and cheese from the fridge and assembled sandwiches. She added dill pickles and potato chips, and they sat at the kitchen island. Before they ate, Ari bowed her head and Simon said grace.

"You make a tasty sandwich," Mitch said after swallowing his first huge bite. "What are we going to do this afternoon?"

"There's a Monopoly game downstairs," Simon said. "We could play."

"Sounds good. What about you, Ari?"

He chuckled when she waved her hands in a "bring it on" gesture.

⁓

Ari was glad when Nana and Tom returned home safely. Although Ari had been tied up with business when they first arrived home, she now sat with the woman in the living room, listening as she talked about their trip.

"Here's the picture they took of us." Nana handed over a portfolio holding a photo of her with her sister with a picture of Biltmore on the opposite side. "You really need to see this place. It's the largest private residence in America. The guide said George Vanderbilt and his mom visited and he was going to build a small house and then decided to construct something that suited the mountains. It's about as big as a mountain."

The woman chattered on.

"All of it was done without public funds. They even had the first forestry program. With all those rooms, guess they needed it to keep the home fires burning." She chuckled at her own joke.

Ari loved Nana's enthusiasm and the way she shared random facts. She'd obviously enjoyed her time at Biltmore.

"How was the spa day?"

"I'm not one for all that pampering, but Ellie loved it."

"I hope you enjoyed your birthday," Ari wrote.

"I did. Tom took us out to dinner. Ellie is quite taken with him. Told her she's too old for him. What did you do while we were gone?"

Ari wrote about the guys fishing on the lake and how they had visited Fields of the Wood Bible Park.

"We'll have to come back," Nana said. "Everyone says we have to see the mountains in the fall to truly appreciate them."

"I have to go to Chicago," Ari wrote on the whiteboard. *"Something is happening and I need to sort it out."*

"I'll get our things packed."

She shook her head. *"Mitch and Gary are going with me. I need you to stay here with Simon. Jen and Will are going to stay, so I told her to come and stay with you. They can use my room. Tom's going to be over at the other house."*

"If that's what you want."

"I'd love to take you and Simon home," Ari wrote, *"But we aren't safe there."*

Nana nodded agreement. "Take care of yourself, Ari. Don't take any chances."

"I don't plan to."

Chapter 11

Gary made arrangements for the private plane that flew them into O'Hare. From there they took a rental vehicle to the hotel. Gary went for their room keys while Ari waited with Mitch in the vehicle.

"Okay?" he asked, looking back at her from the driver's seat.

She wondered if he realized how often he asked her that. She wasn't okay. This was her hotel. She should be able to walk in the front door with her head held high, not be forced to sneak in through the service elevator.

He reached over the seat and took her hand in his, giving it a gentle squeeze. "We're going to figure out who's behind this."

Ari wished she could voice all her concerns. It would take entirely too long to write down everything that floated around in her head at that particular moment.

Gary returned to the vehicle to escort Ari to the service elevator where Shannon waited. "Mitch needs to run some errands. I'll stay with you while he's gone. Then he can stay with you later while I check in at my office."

Mitch removed his and Ari's suitcases from the trunk. Shannon held the elevator door, and once they were inside, her friend hugged her.

"It's so good to see you. Is Simon okay? How's his leg? I'm sorry," Shannon exclaimed with a little laugh after releasing the barrage of questions. "I've been so worried for you both."

"We're taking good care of them," Gary offered. The elevator stopped on the tenth floor.

Shannon smiled and said, "I know you are. Now, what do we do first?"

"Lunch would be good," Gary said, glancing at Ari, who nodded agreement.

"Let's go to your room, and I'll have the chef send up a meal. The managers are aware you're in the building, but we haven't told the rest of the staff."

Shannon unlocked the door. "If anyone catches on to you being here, we'll tell them you're doing an undercover quality check."

Ari laughed at the woman's grin.

After lunch, she reviewed hotel operations with Shannon and then took a nap. Gary told her he'd be across the hall. Mitch tapped on the door a few hours later to let her know he was back.

That evening he came over to call the house in North Carolina on the speakerphone so Ari could check in and hear how things were going in her absence.

"Jen and I are playing video games," Simon told them. "She's good."

Mitch chuckled. "Watch her, Simon. She cheats."

"I do not," Jen yelled in mock offense.

Ari and Mitch left the hotel early the next day. He looked very handsome in the dark suit. She could tell from the cut and fit of the material that it was expensive. She wondered if that had been his errand. She hoped he hadn't bought a suit for her sake.

They entered the Kent corporate office building via Charles Kent's private elevator and met with her father's assistant, Shirley O'Brien. The woman hugged her and said how sorry she was and how she missed Mr. Kent.

Ari managed to nod and smile sadly at the woman.

"I've placed all the documents you requested on your father's desk. Are you going to be able to work in there?"

Ari would rather have been anywhere else, but she had to do this. Not because her father expected it of her, but rather because she demanded it of herself.

"I'm Mitchell Ellis, Mrs. O'Brien. Either Gary Bishop or myself will be with Ms. Kent here in the office and the boardroom."

She noted the way the woman gave him the once-over and the little nod of approval she offered in return.

"I'll be here at my desk. Let me know if there's anything you need. Anything at all."

"Thank you." Mitch took Ari's arm and walked over to the big carved wooden door to her father's office. He turned the knob and Ari stepped inside. Nowhere else on earth would she find a place where his presence was more obvious. The penthouse was her mother's domain. This office was her father's.

The room smelled of expensive leather and his favorite cologne. The walls reflected his love of art. Ari paused as she touched the large leather chair behind the desk. He'd joked about the chair when it first came in, saying it was more comfortable than any sofa he'd ever sat on. Now it would be her chair.

Moisture filled her eyes and she dabbed carefully at her eyelashes, hoping not to smudge her mascara. She'd probably find out if it held up to the waterproof claim before the day was over.

"You okay?" Mitch asked.

She flashed him a smile and shrugged, drawing in a deep breath before she rolled out the chair and plunked down.

Ari didn't feel much older than when she was a child and waited for her father to complete his work. She leaned forward and pulled the first folder from the pile. She had a lot of material to cover before the board meeting.

She studied the agenda outlining what would be covered. Other folders contained financial documents, contracts, and plans for future expansion. Ari feared she'd never finish in time.

Mitch sat on the sofa by the door, first reading the paper he'd brought along and then a paperback. They followed the same format on Wednesday.

Thursday morning at eight, the phone buzzed. When Ari answered, Mrs. O'Brien informed her that Erik George of Kearns, George, and Howe had arrived for their meeting.

Mitch stood and opened the door, gesturing the man inside. Erik George nodded at him before advancing in her direction, his hand outstretched. "Ari, so good to have you back in Chicago. Hope you're doing well?"

She smiled graciously and indicated the chair on the opposite side of the desk.

"Thank you for the update on Todd Langan's activity. We had no idea he has been harassing you. I apologize."

Ari glanced at Mitch. They had debated whether the firm's partners had any idea of Todd's efforts on their behalf.

"I regret the situation that has brought us together but assure you it's a temporary setback at best. Understandable given your experience. No reason the company can't continue to operate."

She reached for the whiteboard and wrote, *"Todd Langan seems extremely eager to have my parents' will read. Do you know why?"*

"Todd can be overzealous at times. Perhaps he felt he needed the information to advise you properly. Whatever the case, I have a copy of the will here and plan to make you aware of the facts before the meeting."

He reached for his briefcase and Mitch moved closer to Ari, ready to offer the support she might need.

Erik George set the case on the other visitor chair and pulled out the legal document. Flipping the first page, he said, "Other than a few minor bequests, your parents left the majority of their estate to you."

Stunned, Ari touched her chest.

He nodded. "After Simon was born, your father asked me to draw up papers giving your mother control of 51 percent of their company shares. They own 60 percent of the company shares. At the time I assumed it had to do with Michelle giving him a son. Later, when the wills were drafted, your mother left her shares to you. Your father split his shares equally between you and Simon. They also designated you as Simon's legal guardian in the event something happened to them. I assume you're willing to assume that responsibility?"

"Without doubt," she wrote in dark print, two exclamation points at the end.

He nodded. "You control your parents' shares plus the additional shares you were given when you joined the firm."

Ari didn't understand her mother's blatant show of favoritism. Why had they not inherited equally? Did it have something to do with Simon being a minor? Was there another stipulation regarding his coming of age? Still, that didn't mean he wasn't entitled to a fair division of the shares.

"I must also tell you that your mother stipulated that the 51 percent go to charity if you challenge the will. She does say that she feels you are more than capable of carrying on their legacy and believes you will do what is best for Kent Enterprises."

She looked at Mitch.

Erik George continued, "There are a few more items we need to cover before we go to the boardroom today. I have no doubt you'll be appointed CEO. I also plan to apprise Todd and the board that he no longer serves as counsel for the firm."

"Security?" Mitch requested.

"I doubt Todd will cause trouble. While he may not be happy, he should leave the room without causing a scene."

Mitch glanced at Ari and she nodded.

"Don't say anything until he reveals his plan."

"Pardon?" Erik looked taken aback by his comment.

Mitch glanced at Ari and back at the lawyer. "We need to know Langan's intent. We suspect he's behind this plan. Who has been proposed to take on the role of CEO until Ari is deemed competent?"

Erik looked uncomfortable. "Ann Radnor."

"Langan's fiancée? What qualifies her?" Mitch asked.

"I learned what I know from talking to the board members who support Ari. This woman has no experience beyond the brief time she worked as Charles Kent's assistant several years ago. A fact that has made these board members question Todd's intent." The lawyer glanced at his watch. "I suggest we run over the agenda and put together a plan of attack."

The three of them sat talking, Ari writing notes on the whiteboard.

The attorney gave a quick overview of the plan. "Is that correct?"

Ari nodded.

Erik George pushed up the french cuff of his shirt and looked at his watch. "It's almost ten. Are we ready for the boardroom?"

Ari retreated to her father's executive washroom. She emerged a few minutes later, her hair twisted into a neat chignon at the base of her neck and her makeup and lipstick refreshed. She slipped her arms into the sleeves of the black silk suit coat Mitch held and smoothed it into place. The high heels pushed her up to his shoulder height.

"Ready?" he asked.

She drew in a deep breath and nodded.

Mitch gave her arm a gentle squeeze and led the way through the double doors. Ari strode into the room and took a seat at the head of the table. Mitch went to stand behind her next to Gary, who had opted to meet them in the boardroom.

Ari focused on Todd Langan. While he appeared pleased to see her present, she noted the suspicion in his eyes. Had he expected that he could carry off this upheaval and leave her in the dark? At least Todd would realize she was as much in the know away from her company as in the office.

The meeting began. She noted that Ann Radnor was not in the boardroom. The underlying anger she felt toward the two of them gave her the impetus she needed to attack the situation. They would not take her company away from her.

Ari brushed moist hands along the expensive suit skirt and lifted her hands to the laptop keyboard. A projector displayed the computer screen on the far wall.

I APOLOGIZE FOR THIS UNUSUAL FORM OF COMMUNICATION, BUT AS MOST OF YOU ARE AWARE, I AM UNABLE TO SPEAK. I HAVE BEEN DIAGNOSED AS SUFFERING FROM CONVERSION DISORDER. MY DOCTOR, DWAYNE GRAVES, IS PRESENT AND WILL ANSWER ANY QUESTIONS YOU MAY HAVE.

The board members listened avidly as the doctor outlined the specifics of her condition. "I assure you Ms. Kent is 100 percent capable of carrying on with her duties. Her ability to speak could return as quickly as it left. The shock of finding. . . Well, we can imagine how traumatizing the experience was for her."

Cedric Reynolds spoke up. "I'm sorry for all she's been through, but I'm concerned about how her problems will affect the company."

Ari eyed him and began to type furiously.

NO ONE HERE HAS MORE TO LOSE THAN SIMON AND MYSELF. WHILE I UNDERSTAND YOUR CONCERNS, I ASSURE YOU MY CONDITION DOES NOT STAND IN THE WAY OF DOING MY JOB. YOU'VE SEEN THE FIGURES ON THE HOTEL KENT CHICAGO. MY TEAM INCREASED THE PROFITS THERE BY NEARLY 25 PERCENT IN THREE YEARS. I CAN ASSURE YOU MY GOAL IS TO DO THE SAME FOR THE ENTIRE KENT ORGANIZATION.

AND IF, FOR WHATEVER REASON, I FIND I CANNOT PERFORM MY DUTIES, I'LL BE THE FIRST TO RECOMMEND HIRING A CEO.

She sounded like a pageant winner, Ari thought as the words appeared on the screen.

"How can a mute conduct business?"

All heads swiveled in Todd's direction. Several people appeared shocked by his outburst.

Erik George stood from his place in the back of the room. "I don't believe Ms. Kent's ability to perform her job is in question, Todd. Everyone here is aware of Ari's history with the company. She possesses an MBA from a prestigious university, and she trained with her father to step into the role."

"Sir, I didn't mean to imply—"

Erik George continued, "After speaking with Ms. Kent this morning, I can assure you she is in no way deficient in her ability to perform her duties. And as I have informed her today, she is the beneficiary of the majority of her parents' shares, and as young Simon's guardian, she controls his shares as well. She also has the shares she was given when she joined the company."

"She can't talk. How does she expect to represent the company?" Reynolds asked.

Ari looked from him to Todd. Here were her troublemakers. If she remembered correctly, Reynolds's small number of shares had come to him via an elderly aunt.

"Ms. Kent can hear, and if you'll address your concerns to her, I'm sure she'll respond," Mitch ground out. "She was, and still is, in fear for her life. Coming here today could very well put her in jeopardy."

Ari stared at Mitch. What had set him off?

"You're all so worried about your bank accounts that you can't find a bit of sympathy in your hearts for two innocents robbed of their parents. I hope none of you ever have to confront the same devil Ari's living with right now."

Angry, quiet mumbling started among the board.

"How dare you," Cedric Reynolds said, rising to his feet. "What gives you the right to judge our actions?"

Mitch stood tall and spoke confidently. "I can tell you without reservation that Arianna Kent's inability to speak has nothing to do with her ability to run this organization. And if this board takes action because of her condition, it will be a blatant case of discrimination."

"Get out," Reynolds ordered, pointing to the door.

"Gentlemen," Dwayne Graves called, "Dr. Ellis is as upset by what he's witnessed here today as I am. Despite any misgivings you may have, Ms. Kent's inability to speak in no way compromises her competency to operate her parents' company."

Ari looked from one man to the other. Dr. Ellis? No. This was Mitchell Ellis. He worked for Bishop Security.

Voices raised as each member tried to outtalk the other.

Finally, Erik George called out, "Ladies. Gentlemen. Please. Let's keep this to the business at hand. Out of fairness to the Kent family, my recommendation is that you give Ms. Kent time to prepare a plan showing how she proposes to conduct business until such a time as her voice returns.

"And effective immediately, Todd Langan will no longer serve as counsel for Kent Enterprises. Per Ms. Kent's request, I have assumed the role as of today."

As Erik had predicted, Todd charged from the room. Stunned by the revelations of the boardroom, Ari texted Gary to get her out of there. He stepped forward to escort her. She refused to look at Mitch as she walked past.

⌒

Mitch tried to push past the press of board members leaving the room. It was the voice that caught his attention. A voice he'd heard weekly for years now. He looked for and found the woman.

A tall, dark-haired woman clung to Ari's arm. Gary stepped forward to remove her hand and blocked Mitch's view.

"Where is Simon? How is he?" the woman demanded almost frantically. Ari pulled herself free.

"Please, Ari. Listen to me," she pleaded. "I can help you. I know how your

202

father did business. Right now you're upset with me and with Todd, but we want to help."

Ari walked away and the woman called, "You forced us to do this. You wouldn't return Todd's calls. He had to do what was best for the company. For Simon."

The crowd cleared and Mitch looked straight into the woman's eyes. "Raquel? What are you doing here?" he demanded.

She lowered her head slightly, averting her gaze. "My name is Ann Radnor."

Who was she trying to fool? He'd know her anywhere. This woman was Raquel Wilson.

Chapter 12

I *want you to take me back to Simon."*

Mitch read the message Ari had written to Gary on the whiteboard and knew he'd messed up big-time. He should have told her the truth before going into the boardroom.

"You'll have to return to Murphy with Mitch or wait until I can take you," Gary told her. "Something has come up and I can't leave now. He has your best interests at heart, Ari. You can't deny that he performed his duties admirably."

She didn't write a reply to that. The chilling blast of anger in her green gaze spoke of her feelings of betrayal.

"I'll go alone."

"No, you won't," Mitch declared. "You're safe with me. Once we arrive back in Murphy, I'll stay until Gary sends a replacement. Then I'll get out of your life forever."

Ari burst into tears and ran into the bathroom. Mitch felt like a total jerk.

Later that day, they traveled to O'Hare in a helicopter to avoid the crush of media that had hounded her ever since learning of her presence at the board meeting. Settling in the luxurious private plane, they waited while the crew performed their flight check.

"Please let me explain," Mitch pleaded.

Ari turned to stare out the window.

She wouldn't listen. Hadn't listened to a word he'd said since his explosion in the boardroom. He'd known the truth would come out. And he couldn't talk his way around what he had done.

"This is why I didn't tell you. I knew how you'd react. You think I'm here in the capacity of psychiatrist, but I'm not. I wanted to protect you and Simon."

Thin lines creased between her brows.

"When Gary asked to use the houses. . ."

Her head jerked up to look at him.

"Yes, the houses belong to me," he admitted. "I frequently visit the mountains and was scheduled for a three-week vacation when I volunteered to help. When Dwayne told me what happened, I was overcome by this need to help you and Simon to feel safe. I had to help.

"I did help," Mitch declared. "I lost sleep to take care of you in every way I could. I've been your friend. I can't deny that your condition interests me because I want you to recover."

Ari stood and took a seat as far away from him as possible. The rest of the journey passed in silence. As they neared the mountains, lightning flashes in the dark night indicated a storm. Mitch noted the way she closed the window

204

shade and then her eyes as it came nearer.

At the airport, they deplaned in a downpour. Ari waited in the car as Mitch collected their luggage. His clothes were soaked when he climbed into the driver's seat.

The heavy rain made the trip even longer. Sharp jagged slashes of lightning and booming peals of thunder surrounded them, and Ari withdrew even deeper within herself. Mitch had to pull over a couple of times when visibility got so bad he couldn't see to drive.

He made a few more aborted attempts to explain before giving up. She wasn't willing to listen. In her eyes, he was no better than Langan and Radnor. A Judas who had infiltrated her home and pretended to care about her.

It wasn't a pretense. He did care for her. A great deal.

"I never intended to hurt you," he said as he turned into the Bear Paw entrance and rolled to a stop at the guardhouse.

"Welcome back," the security guard said.

They both glanced up when a nearby lightning strike seemed a bit too close for comfort.

"Thanks. Nasty weather."

"Definitely," the man agreed. "Take care going to the houses. There have been reports of washouts from a couple of homeowners."

"We'll keep our eyes open."

Mitch powered up the window and drove forward. "Please understand, Ari. It was never my intention to keep this from you indefinitely. You had enough going on in your life. You didn't need more to worry about then or now. You have a major task ahead of you in the next month. Let me help."

Mitch turned onto their road. Silence reigned. He glanced over at her. "Please. . ."

Before he could continue, the vehicle tipped off the side of the mountain.

"Ari! Hold on!" he yelled as they slid sideways, banging against tree after tree like a pinball machine until one tree refused to let them pass. Mitch's head hit the window with a sickening thud, causing the glass to spiderweb. He groaned as the side air bag covered him. Blackness filled his world and he knew no more.

～

Blood spilled from Mitch's head. Too much blood. Ari closed her eyes against the horrible image, fighting back waves of nausea and encroaching darkness.

She drew in several deep breaths. She had to get help. Terror spurred her into action. Ari searched for an out. The window. She tried the control. It wouldn't work. A tool. She needed something to break the glass.

Then she could climb out and go for help. She pulled open the glove compartment, her hand closing around a flashlight. The metal tube would serve her purpose, Ari thought as she attempted to maneuver herself around to strike the glass.

The pressure of the seat belt cut into her as she hung from the passenger side of the vehicle. If she released the latch, she'd tumble onto Mitch and cause him even greater injury.

As she raised the flashlight, the communication service in the vehicle came to life. "Mr. Ellis, we have a report this vehicle has been involved in an accident. Are you okay?" the representative called.

Answer her, Mitch, Ari willed silently. *She's asking you a question.* He didn't stir. Ari didn't know how many minutes had passed without his regaining consciousness.

No, he definitely wasn't okay. Mitch was in trouble. She had to do something. She had to help him. Now. Ari opened her mouth, so afraid she'd fail this man who meant so much to them.

"Please," she began, her voice quavering and unfamiliar after so long. She gained volume as she said, "Mr. Ellis is badly injured. We slipped off the side of the mountain. A tree is all that's keeping us from tumbling farther."

"Can you verify the address of where you are?"

She knew the name of the neighborhood but not the street. Ari fumbled around in her coat pocket and pulled out her phone, thankful she hadn't put it in her purse. "Hold on." She dialed the house and demanded, "What's the address here?"

"Ari? Is that you?" Nana demanded suspiciously.

"Nana, yes. I need the address. Mitch is injured. I'm trying to get help."

Tom came on the line and gave her their location. "I'm coming down."

She recited the address to the woman at the communications center.

"We'll notify the police."

"Ari?" Tom called on the phone. "Are you hurt?"

"No, but Mitch slammed his head against the window. There's lots of blood."

"Did the window break?"

"No. It cracked. He's been unconscious for several minutes."

"I'm coming. Hang on. We'll get help."

She knew he didn't mean the "hang on" part literally, but that was exactly what she was doing. "Please be all right," she prayed as she looked down on Mitch's still form. Minutes seemed like hours as they passed with no immediate sign of help.

Finally, a raincoat-clad Tom and Jen ran toward the vehicle, their flashlights bobbing in the darkness. Rain sluiced down the front window, distorting Ari's vision.

Tom grabbed the door handle. He banged on the side and shouted for her to unlock the door. Ari fumbled around and tried to grab the knob but couldn't get her fingers around the rounded top. It was too low in the opening. She pushed the shoulder harness down and left the seat belt in place.

The first movement rocked the vehicle slightly. She tried again without as much momentum. It took several tries to reach the remote hanging from the ignition, but she finally managed to grab hold and push the button for the door lock.

Tom pulled the door up. Jen grabbed and held on so that it wouldn't slam back on Ari.

"Can you shove your legs over the side?"

"No," Ari said. "If I release the seat belt, I'll fall on Mitch."

"Give me your hand," Tom said. "I'll hold you when you release the latch."

"It won't work."

Siren wails could be heard in the distance.

Tom pulled himself up on the side of the vehicle and called to Mitch. No response. The vehicle shifted slightly.

"Be careful," Ari warned. "That tree is all that's keeping us from falling."

The ambulance pulled up, keeping its distance from the gaping asphalt above them. The attendants came running only to realize they couldn't do anything until the vehicle was moved. The wrecker and police officer arrived at the same time.

The wrecker driver took several precious minutes to connect the cables, and then with a slow movement, the vehicle came back onto the road. Tom helped Ari from the vehicle. She stood on wobbly legs, very aware of how frightened she'd been.

"Are you okay?" Jen asked, supporting Ari with an arm around her waist.

"I'm fine."

Her gaze turned to the other side of the vehicle, where the ambulance attendants used equipment to force open the jammed door. They checked Mitch's vitals, supported his neck with a brace, and carefully transferred him to the stretcher. Once loaded with the patient, the vehicle reversed down the street and Ari nearly collapsed from exhaustion.

Jen pointed to the hole and asked, "How are we going to get past that to get to the hospital?"

"I'll take you," the officer said.

"Thank you. I'm Jennifer Bishop, Mitch Ellis's sister. This is Arianna Kent. She needs to be checked as well. She was in the vehicle with my brother."

Ari shook her head, indicating she was fine.

"Relax," Jen instructed, her arm around Ari's shoulders as she hugged her close.

Ari found this to be an impossible task. She was soaking wet. The officer cranked up the heat. She couldn't be still and fidgeted nervously in the backseat of the police car. How could she have treated Mitch like that? Was he okay?

The officer took them to the Murphy Medical Center. Jen led her inside and one of the nurses brought a warm blanket. Ari wrapped it tightly about herself, welcoming the comfort. She shivered uncontrollably.

"Drink this," Jen said, handing her a cup of hot coffee.

Ari warmed her hands slightly before taking a gulp.

"Careful," Jen warned, too late as Ari felt the stinging burn to her tongue.

"The doctor is with Mr. Ellis in the examining room," the nurse told them.

"Thank you." After the woman left, Jen turned to Ari. "When did you get your voice back?"

"When that communication service representative asked Mitch if he was okay, I knew I had to get help for him. I was so afraid."

"He's going to be fine, Ari."

She looked into Jen's eyes and saw hope. Here she was being comforted when this woman needed comfort. Her brother lay battered and bleeding in the exam room.

"I'm sorry, Jen. I'm so selfish."

A smile touched her face. "It's not your fault the road caved in."

"It's my fault he wasn't paying attention," Ari offered sadly. "We had a fight. Mitch didn't tell me he was a psychiatrist. He knew I believed he worked security for Gary. He said he wanted to protect us."

"Then that was his intent. Mitch isn't the type to play games, Ari. When Gary asked to use the houses, he told him he was scheduled for a vacation. Gary was surprised when Mitch offered to help out, but he was also concerned about sending you to North Carolina with people he didn't know."

"Then why?"

"Mitch has his reasons. He always does."

Ari mulled that over as they waited. What reason could he possibly have had? He hadn't known them. Hadn't known their parents. Why would he give up his vacation to work security?

The ER doctor came to talk with them. "Mrs. Bishop, I'm Doctor Stokes. Mr. Ellis has a two-inch laceration at his hairline which we will staple closed. He hasn't regained consciousness yet. So we're running tests and monitoring his brain activity."

Ari looked at the man through a haze. Mitch had to be all right. She could see his face, his beautiful face, and couldn't help but feel it was all her fault. If he hadn't been trying to convince her of his innocence, he would have paid more attention to his driving. Ari felt herself falling.

Ari's eyes fluttered open. She lay on a stretcher with the doctor looking down at her. "What happened?"

"You fainted. How do you feel?" the doctor asked.

"I'm okay."

"Rest for a while," he said, pulling a sheet over Ari's body. "We'll see how you feel and decide if you should be admitted."

He looked at Jen. "Stay with her. I'll let you know as soon as I have more information about your brother."

The doctor left, and Jen pulled a chair over next to the bed. She reached for Ari's hand and soothed her with the same gentle murmuring she used with Will. "It's going to be okay," she whispered. "Mitch will be fine. I know he will."

"Pray for him," Ari said.

"Yes," Jen agreed. "Let's pray now."

They bowed their heads and Jen said, "Blessed Father, we come to You seeking Your protection for our loved one. You know what's going on with Mitch right now and we pray that You heal him with Your powerful touch. Touch his heart and remind him that he's still Your child."

"Is Mitch a believer?" Ari asked softly.

"Our parents took us to church when we were kids. He accepted Christ when he was eleven. Then our parents died and he stopped going to church.

"Aunt Sandy said he needed time. It was pretty bad. He was burned trying to rescue Mom and Dad. The investigator said they had already been overcome by smoke when he went in. He nearly died."

"I've seen his scars," she said softly. "They looked so painful."

"It was bad, but he survived."

Mitch understood loss. He had been so young. Only thirteen.

"What happened?"

"Old house. Faulty wiring. Their bedroom was on the opposite end of the house from ours. Mitch got me outside before going back in for our parents."

"Didn't anyone try to stop him?"

"It was in the wee hours of the morning. The house was fully engulfed by the time the fire department arrived. Two neighbors rescued Mitch. He hadn't made it beyond the living room when the smoke fumes overcame him. I feared he would die then.

"But he recovered and we went to live with Aunt Sandy. She's our mom's sister. Never married. Taking on two adolescents couldn't have been easy for her, but she didn't hesitate. You're like her. Simon's blessed to have you."

"I hope I'm up to the task."

"Love is all Simon needs. Give him that and the rest will come naturally. Not to say you won't experience some rocky paths along the way, but love will make it right for you both in the end."

"Why didn't Mitch tell me about what happened to him?"

Jen shrugged. "He doesn't talk about it often. He's a good man, Ari. Mitch used his pain and suffering to help others overcome theirs. He's good at listening and asking the right questions. It's his gift. Now, you should rest."

Ari closed her eyes. Why had Mitch never spoken of his parents' deaths? Maybe it had been too soon. They'd known each other for such a short time.

Still, he'd hurt her with his secret identity. Hearing Dwayne Graves call him Dr. Ellis had come as a great shock on top of so many others. It had been more than she could handle. She wanted to trust him with all her heart but didn't know how she could.

⌒

"Ari," Mitch called, holding out his hand to her. He couldn't disguise his joy at seeing her. It was her first visit since he'd awakened. He'd been so afraid she wouldn't come. She looked so good he wanted to hug her.

She kept her distance, and the hospital bed seemed more like a prison than a place of healing. His head hurt, the lump beneath the white bandage tender and large.

His sister had told him how Ari had spoken to summon help for him.

"Jen says the doctor says you're doing better," Ari said.

He sucked in a breath at the low, honeyed sound. Exactly as he'd imagined all those times when he'd longed to hear her speak. Soft-spoken and delightful, as pleasing as he'd dreamed it would be. Their time without a spoken word seemed so long ago. He longed to hear more.

"Your voice," Mitch said. "Jen told me. You sound exactly as I thought you would."

She seemed uncomfortable with his comments.

"I'm glad to have my voice back," Ari said finally, maintaining her distance.

"Please, Ari," he beseeched, trying to sit up in the bed. "I know you're angry. You have a right to be. I don't have any excuse. I do know Dwayne and I talked, but at no point did he ask me to do a consultation. In fact, when I offered, he said you would refuse.

"I didn't take the security job to check you out. Though I have to admit I was curious. I am a doctor after all. And you have to admit your situation merited consideration.

"But as I told you, the houses belong to me. I knew the area. I worked security back when I was in college. I honestly wanted to protect you and Simon. I wanted you to have the time you needed to recuperate."

"Maybe it goes back to losing your parents?" she suggested. "Jen told me what happened. Why didn't you ever tell me about them? I thought we were friends."

"We were—we are. I didn't want to add to your grief. You were already struggling with what had happened to you. I didn't want you feeling sorry for me about something that happened so many years ago."

"Knowing you'd been there and understood would have been reassuring. The loss of your parents was as tragic and senseless as that of my parents."

"I failed, Ari. I let them die in that fire."

"Not your fault," she said with a shake of her head. "It was one of those terrible things that happen and we can't explain why."

"It's been a driving force in my life. I've been told my need to help others stems from that night."

"Probably," she answered him thickly. Her lashes dropped to hide her hurt. "I trusted you, Mitch. Told you things I never told anyone else. Do you understand why I feel betrayed?"

Mitch nodded. He stopped and grimaced with the pain. One glimpse of her hurt expression and he felt worse than Judas.

"I won't tell your secrets. I'm a doctor. I deal with patient confidentiality all the time."

Frustrated by his comment, she uttered, "I am not your patient. Don't you understand? I never wanted to be your patient."

"You weren't," he insisted. "We're friends. More than friends. I care about you and Simon. My initial decision may have been made out of sympathy, but I did what I needed to do to keep you safe."

Ari didn't understand. "Why?"

Her entire being seemed filled with waiting. What did she want to hear from him?

"Because I had to," Mitch admitted. "I felt the attraction the moment I laid eyes on you, and it's strengthened as we've gotten to know each other better. I want your parents' killers found so you can put this behind you."

She struggled to speak. Mitch knew the misery of that night remained with her.

"I can't put it behind me. It's there, haunting me every step of the way. Making me question why God would let something like this happen."

"You can," Mitch insisted, resting his throbbing head against the pillows as he spoke. "In time, the pain will fade. Your grief has been so much worse because you couldn't share your feelings.

"Now you can talk it out with Simon and Nana. You can't change what happened. Finding out who did this is not going to bring them back. In fact, the discovery will more than likely provide you with someone to hate. And I know that's something you don't want to do.

"I questioned God, too," Mitch admitted. "My parents were God-fearing Christians. We were in church every time the doors opened. To have them burn to death didn't make sense."

"Do you go to church, Mitch?"

"Now and then. Usually Christmas and Easter with the family."

"Do you believe?"

Do I? The conscious decisions he'd made over the years not to serve the Lord or attend church had nothing to do with his belief that Jesus Christ died for his sins. "Yes. In all the years since their death, I've kept myself too busy to spare time for God, but I do believe. Now I've witnessed your love for Him and accepted the only person I'm hurting is me. Instead of reaching out and accepting the love He offered, I pushed Him away and pretended it didn't matter.

"You exude a peace that I know comes from your faith. That's why I believe you'll get past this anger at me."

"I've been praying," she admitted.

"Maybe in time," Mitch said softly. "Once life gets back to normal, you'll be busy taking care of Simon and dealing with your work as CEO of Kent Enterprises. I know you'll do a great job. And now that you have your voice back, I doubt the board will be as anxious. Look out for Langan. He's behind that effort in the boardroom. And that woman, the one you call Ann. Watch her as well."

"But he's been removed from the position. There's no reason for him to contact the board."

Suspicions of what Langan might try tugged at Mitch's consciousness. He knew it had something to do with Raquel Wilson, aka Ann Radnor. And unless he was way off base, Charles Kent.

"Watch out for them, Ari."

She nodded. "I will."

"And hopefully you'll find it in your heart to forgive me. I'm going to be praying, too. I live in Chicago. My practice is on the lower floor of my house. Maybe one day we can get together for lunch to discuss this situation?"

She stared at him, and Mitch wished he knew what she was thinking. For so long he'd longed to hear her speak. He wanted to hear more. His injury was so worth the outcome.

"Thanks for all you've done for us, Mitch," she said with a frightening finality. She took a step forward and leaned to kiss his cheek. "I'll pray for your swift recovery. Good-bye."

"Not good-bye," he whispered as she walked out the door. Not as long as he had breath in him to convince her differently.

Mitch spent the intervening hours thinking of Ari. The pain of his head was nothing compared to that of his heart.

"I couldn't stop her," Gary told Mitch when he called a few hours later. "After you talked, she went back to the house, packed up the family, and requested transport back to Chicago. I'm here at the townhouse with her now."

Mitch's heavy sigh made his head hurt worse. "Is she okay? Still talking?"

"Not a lot, but she is talking. Mostly planning how she's going to handle things now that she's back at home. Funny how she broke loose like that to save your sorry self."

Mitch wished Gary's insinuation were true. He'd love nothing more than having Ari right here next to him, soothing his brow and encouraging him to come home soon. "More likely terror galvanized her into action. We were hanging off the side of a mountain with one lone tree keeping us from possibly rolling to our deaths."

"Maybe the tumble was worth it," Gary suggested.

Despite the pounding headache, Mitch decided Gary was right.

"Jen had me bring Will back to Chicago. She's staying there with you until you're released."

Mitch smiled at his little sister's penchant for organizing everyone's life. "I'll send her home. I'm coming back to Chicago as soon as they release me."

"Any word on when that will be?"

"Another day or two. Look after Ari, Gary. She's vulnerable and she's going to be called upon to make decisions she might not be ready to make."

"Ari says she's done with hiding."

"Did she terminate your contract?" Mitch demanded, suddenly fearful that she'd separated herself from Bishop Security because of him.

"No. I've got four men assigned. And Tom's sticking to her like glue."

"I wish we knew the motivation behind the killings."

"Yeah, it would have been nice if they had left a signed confession providing us with all the specifics."

"You know what I mean."

"I know Arianna Kent is a beautiful young woman who will come across more than her fair share of people willing to relieve her of her money. She will develop her scam antennae very quickly."

Mitch suspected his actions had aided in that development. Her reaction to the things he'd been privy to as her friend troubled him. It probably bothered her that he'd been present at the reading of the will. And the other things she'd shared in the comfort of their late-night confidences, such as her concerns over becoming Simon's guardian and taking over the company.

Mitch would never tell anyone what she'd said. It was between the two of them, and that's where it would stay.

"If you talk to Jen before I do, tell her to come see me. I'll talk her into going home."

"I don't think you'll be successful. It's okay, Mitch. After that lick on your head, you probably need a traveling companion. Aunt Sandy will help look after Will."

"He'll miss his mom."

"So hurry up and get out of there and come home."

"The plan is to spend the least possible amount of time in this place. With any luck they'll throw me out soon."

"Getting thrown out is not an option," Gary commented. "You need to stay as long as they feel is necessary. And don't worry about Ari. I plan to be with her every step of the way. She trusts very few people right now, and that's a good thing. She's making plans for her move to the corporate offices. Shannon Crown will take over as GM at the hotel."

He frowned. Ari loved her hotel.

"She's definitely got a huge load resting on those tiny shoulders, but we have to give her credit for taking it on," Gary said. "She wants me to set up a safe area for Simon. She plans to move the occupant out of the office next to hers, remove the existing door, and install a door into her office. She's already got carpenters working on that. I suspect she'll look into hiring a tutor once school starts back."

"What about Dora?"

"Ari is sending her to visit family. She plans to personally vet my man before allowing him to accompany Dora. She's paying for him to stay until they find the killer."

"I'm surprised Dora agreed."

"She won't go without argument. I think Ari considered sending Simon with her but decided it was too much on the woman."

"Probably needs to keep him near anyway," Mitch said. "They have lots to discuss now that Ari has her voice back. They can support and reassure each other through all this."

"I have to run. I'm sure you'll see Jen soon."

"Thanks, Gary."

Half an hour later Jen breezed into his hospital room. She kissed his cheek and placed his shaving kit on the table. "I brought clean pajamas and a robe," she said. "And your slippers. How are you feeling? Head still hurting?"

"I want you to go home. Will needs you more than I do."

Jen sniffed. "Will doesn't have a major gash on his head or a concussion. You need to let me take care of you. Gary can handle our son."

Mitch smiled at his sister. She loved opportunities to tell her older brother what was best for him.

"I need a favor," he said. "Some highly confidential research."

That got her attention. "What kind?"

"The kind you'll need to do in Chicago. You can't tell anyone, but I suspect Michelle Kent isn't Simon's birth mother."

She frowned. "Ari says he's her brother."

"There's something weird about the situation." He shared how Simon had come into Ari's life.

"She came home for spring break and learned she had a brother?" Jen asked.

He nodded slowly, afraid any movement would set off the pounding headache that had begun to ease.

"Tom said Michelle Kent went away in early December and returned home with Simon in early March."

Jen shrugged. "Maybe she went someplace less stressful for the birth."

"But why leave her entire inheritance to Ari? If you had two children, would you favor one over the other? She even stipulated the money would go to charity if Ari tried to change the will. Charles Kent split his equitably."

His sister's expression changed with her sudden curiosity. "That is strange. I can see Ari acting as Simon's guardian and looking out for his interests, but you'd think his mother would have left him equal shares."

"So will you nose around and see what you can find? And keep it to yourself?"

"How will Ari feel if she finds out what we're doing?"

Mitch rubbed his neck. "She's already upset with me, but my gut says there's something going on. I feel as though I'm assembling a puzzle with missing pieces."

"So maybe you have more names you'd like me to research? Confidentially, that is."

He considered this. "Will you tell Gary?"

"He's my husband," she reminded.

"And you should never keep secrets that could harm your relationship. I promise to ask for help when I reach a point where I can't do anything else on my own."

"You're okay with me sharing your Michelle Kent theory?"

Mitch nodded. "So long as he keeps it to himself."

Chapter 13

Another week passed before Mitch returned to Chicago. After his hospital release, he made arrangements for another place to stay while he contacted companies to repair the damaged roadway.

"Your patients are getting restless," his service told him when he called to let them know he needed a few more days.

"Tell them I was in an accident."

"Raquel Wilson has called several times since you were last in Chicago. Said she must see you right away."

Mitch had a good idea the woman intended to conduct her own fact-finding mission. No doubt she wanted to know about his association with the Kents. "Share what I told you, and if she calls again let her know I'll contact her when I return."

He really wanted to know more about the Ann Radnor persona. Most people who used aliases were up to no good. Was that the case with Ann?

Per doctor's orders, Mitch spent a good portion of each day resting, which for him meant thinking. Today he'd rented the pontoon boat for a fishing trip. As he fished, he thought of Simon's enjoyment of his first time and wished he and Ari were here with him now.

He thought of Ari and Simon often, wondering about their lives in Chicago. Mitch knew from conversations with Gary that they were being careful. He hoped they were happy.

The beautiful summer day was meant for communing with nature. There wasn't a cloud in the sky, and he hadn't seen anyone else on the lake. His phone rang.

"Hey big brother, whatcha doing?"

Jennifer. He should have known. She had checked on him several times a day since his release from the hospital. "I'm out on Lake Hiwassee, thinking about all the fish you scared away when the phone rang."

She laughed. "Ah, too bad for you but good for the fish."

"Yeah, they're safe for another day. What's up?"

"Thought I'd check in with the results of my research."

"Is it what I thought? Wait, we'd better not discuss this on my cell. Can you call me on a landline in a couple of hours?"

"Sure. I'm on my way to Aunt Sandy's to pick up Will."

"Tell her hello and give him a kiss for me."

"Will do. Talk soon."

Mitch quickly reeled in his line and prepared to head home. Back at the house, he answered the phone on the first ring a couple of hours later. "So what did you find out?"

"I checked the will and verified Michelle Kent left everything to Ari," she said. "That includes the penthouse, which was in Michelle's name, and all her jewelry, which is substantial. Plus she has a large investment portfolio that originated from her parents. The Kents did not have joint accounts. If Ari is her only child, it stands to reason that she would be her sole beneficiary. But how did Simon enter the picture?"

"You didn't find anything?"

"His birth certificate lists the Kents as his parents. If he's adopted, it could have been a private adoption."

"Where does the birth certificate say he was born?"

He could hear the click of computer keys. "Chicago."

"But Michelle Kent wasn't in Chicago when he was born. Jen, what if Charles Kent is his real father?"

"Are you thinking Charles Kent had an affair?"

"Erik George told Ari her father insisted on the stock division in her mother's favor after Simon was born. There had to be a reason he would do that."

"It's possible the birth mother signed over her rights to him. Mitch, what do you know about this?"

He could almost hear her mind working.

"Ari doesn't doubt that he's her brother."

"He could be her adopted brother. Or her half brother."

"If this has something to do with what happened to the Kents, you should go to the police."

"That's the problem. I'm speculating. Besides, I'm sure they've already checked out everything I've come up with. Not to mention, my theory involves a patient. I could be sued."

Jen grunted and said, "There's no way Charles Kent ever planned to leave his wife. Not after giving her controlling interest. I agree that it must have been a good faith gesture."

"Should we continue to look?"

"Oh definitely. I checked the newspaper archives for anything around the time Simon was born. Michelle Kent went missing from the social register sometime around early December and returned to Chicago in early March with a birth announcement."

That matched what Ari had shared. "You have time to add another name to your list?"

"Sure. Let me have it."

"Todd Langan."

"What am I searching for?"

"Anything on his association with the Kents and Ann Radnor."

"What do I tell Gary?"

"That your brother is the curious sort."

She laughed at the tongue-in-cheek reply. "He already knows that about you."

"Send me a bill for your time."

"This one's on the house."

"Thanks, Jen. I'm flying out tomorrow. Should be home midafternoon."

"How's your head?"

"Still aches now and again. Otherwise I'm fine."

"Well, take care and see you soon. Love you."

"Love you, too."

Mitch pondered what Jen had told him.

Ari and Simon had been in his thoughts all afternoon. Once he returned to Chicago, he planned to double his efforts to gain Ari's forgiveness.

Deciding there was no need to wait, he dialed the number she'd given him. Busy. He looked at the other contacts. Simon's number was right underneath. Mitch hit the CALL button. The boy answered right away.

"Hello, Simon."

"Mitch? Are you okay? Ari said you hurt your head when you slid off that mountain. Man, that hole was big. Why didn't you see it?"

"Dark and rainy night. I'm doing better. I still have headaches like you did."

"Isn't it awesome that Ari got her voice back and could help you?"

While Mitch considered that the accident had been the impetus for shocking her back into speech mode, he felt thankful she hadn't been injured. "Totally. Have you talked about your parents since she got her voice back?"

"Yeah. You were right. She feels the same way I do but couldn't tell anyone."

"Keep talking to her, Simon," Mitch encouraged. "I went fishing today. Wished you were there with me."

"Cool. Did you catch the big one?"

"Not even a minnow. I suspect those big fish decided it wasn't worth showing their gills because you weren't around to catch them."

The boy chortled with laughter.

"How are you doing, Simon? Everything okay now that you're back in Chicago?"

"I want to go home, but Ari says the police won't let us. She makes me go to the office with her. Won't let me go to my friends' houses. They have to come here."

"Hang in there, buddy. Is Ari around?"

"She's on her cell phone."

"Will you tell her I called? Ask her to call me?"

"Sure. What's your number?"

She already had his number and hadn't used it in the days she'd been gone. Mitch recited his cell number to the boy. "Call me anytime you like, Simon. I want to stay in touch with you and Ari. I consider you friends. Look after her, buddy. And yourself."

"I will, Mitch."

After dinner, he cleaned the kitchen and went to pack. He'd get to bed early. Ari hadn't returned his call and Mitch doubted she would. He'd hoped she might have had a change of heart and would be willing to talk.

Had he been fair to involve Simon like that? Why hadn't he told her the truth? Because he'd known her response would have been more immediate. She would have sent him away on that first day. Those nights on the deck never would have happened because she wouldn't have bared her soul to a psychiatrist.

Why couldn't she accept that he was a flesh-and-blood man prone to mistakes? Sure, the medical degree was part of who he was, but not all. He wouldn't give up hope. Couldn't. Mitch had to believe that one day she would find forgiveness for him in her heart.

After he showered and climbed into bed, Mitch allowed his thoughts to center on the God of Ari's life.

His faith had died with his parents. Jen had been completely different. She attended church with their aunt. His sister derived a great deal of comfort from her love of God and had shared that with him frequently over the years.

He listened out of politeness but doubted God could do anything for him personally. When Jen said she prayed for him, Mitch decided it was something she needed to do. But for some reason the idea of prayer didn't seem as alien since he'd witnessed Ari's love for the Lord. He'd searched for something ever since his parents' death. Maybe now was the time for him to find it in a relationship with God.

Mitch lay against the pillow, propping his hands behind his head as he pondered what he needed to do.

"Jesus," he said finally, "I don't know the right way to do this. I don't even know if You're listening. I sure could use Your help. Ari is angry with me. She's entitled, but please help her accept I never intended to hurt her. And Lord God, guide me. It's been too many years since I accepted You as my Savior. Years when I didn't serve You or follow my faith. Help me find my way back to You now. Please take care of Ari and Simon. Aid the police in locating their parents' killer and give them peace. Take care of my family and keep them safe. Amen."

⁓

"That was Mitch. He wants you to call him at this number," Simon said, handing over the scrap of paper he'd scribbled on.

She nodded, wishing Simon would share more of their conversation. Why had Mitch called? What did he think they had to discuss? She'd ended their relationship at the hospital in Murphy.

Pain filled her at the thought. She liked Mitch. She had trusted him, made him privy to information about her life and business. He'd broken her heart with his lies.

"When, God, when will this stop?"

As a Christian, Ari knew she wasn't protected from attack. She also knew that she had someone to turn to in times when she felt most in need of help.

She could accept that Mitch wanted to help Gary, but she couldn't deal with his hiding the truth from her. He had talked to Dwayne Graves. Mitch knew about her condition. Ari didn't want to be psychoanalyzed by anyone, particularly not by a man to whom she felt a strong attraction.

Mitch had to know how she'd feel, but he'd hidden the truth. Perhaps he felt it best, but it wasn't his call. He should have told her. Let her decide.

She and Shannon had discussed the situation yesterday at lunch. She had asked her friend to pray with her.

"You already admitted you like him. So he messed up. It's not like he tried to do something really bad to you."

"He lied. You know how I feel about that."

"No, he didn't," Shannon said. "He chose to hold back a fact that he knew would make you send him away."

"That's worse than lying. It's deceit."

"Not everyone can live up to your standards, Ari. You couldn't afford to send him away. You needed him. Have you considered that maybe it was a chance he wasn't willing to take? That he felt so strongly about being near you that he was willing to risk making you angry?"

"Maybe that wouldn't have happened if he'd told me from the beginning."

Shannon shook her head at Ari's response. "Now who's lying? He didn't tell you because he knew how you'd react."

"How could he know, Shannon? He didn't know me. He assumed I was like everyone else."

"And he wasn't wrong. Did you not behave exactly as he expected?"

To her annoyance, she felt a blush spread over her cheeks. Shannon was her friend. Why was she defending Mitch? "Why is it wrong for me to expect truth from the people I associate with?" she demanded.

"Sometimes it's best to keep things to yourself until you have a better understanding of the situation."

"Is that what you do, Shannon?"

"If you mean would I keep something that might hurt you a secret, I have to admit it's possible."

She stared.

Shannon went on. "I'd pray over the situation. Seek God's guidance and then do what I felt led to do. And anything I do would be out of love for you and with the best of intentions. There's more to trust than you think. Sometimes you have to trust a person to stand by you and do what they feel needs to be done.

"And whether you want to admit it or not, you owe Mitchell Ellis a debt you can never repay. Your feelings for him pushed you to cry out for help that night. You had to save him because no matter what he'd done, you cared. And you still care. That's why you're avoiding him."

Shannon made sense. Ari had trusted him. Hadn't he been there for her? Done his best to help her overcome her fears? Like Tom, Mitch had lost sleep to see that they were safe. He'd even provided her a safe haven to hole up in until she was able to move on. Until the accident that gave her voice back. And then she'd run away again.

She might say she wanted her life back, but she was still acting like a coward.

Chapter 14

R aquel, come in," Mitch said as she entered his office. "Good to see you." Even though he had resumed seeing patients a couple of days after returning to Chicago, this was her first appointment since his return.

"You, too, Dr. Ellis. Your service told me about your accident. I hope you're okay."

The hairline scar was barely noticeable.

"Yes," he said, more out of politeness than anything else. "I'm doing fine now. Have a seat and we'll get started. How have you been, Raquel?"

She took a seat on the sofa. "Not so good."

Mitch wondered how long they were going to dance around the truth of their last meeting. "What's wrong?"

"This situation with Ari. She won't talk to me."

Two things hit him at once. Raquel had used a name in their session. Ari's name. And she'd said Ari wouldn't have anything to do with her.

That's my girl, Mitch thought, happy to hear Ari had listened to his advice and steered clear of this woman.

Raquel continued to talk. "I wanted to be there for her and Simon, but they disappeared and no one knew where they went. Now she's had Todd removed from his position. He's devastated. He worked so hard to gain his position in the firm. But then, you already knew that. Why were you at the meeting with Ari? I didn't know you knew each other."

Mitch glanced at the folder in his lap. "Why did you call yourself Ann Radnor?"

"Why were you at the meeting?" Raquel repeated.

"I attended at Ms. Kent's request." Mitch could see that the round-about response frustrated Raquel. "Does it bother you that she got upset over Langan's plan for Ann Radnor to take over her job?"

She didn't acknowledge the use of her alias.

"He said she asked for his help."

Not likely, Mitch thought. Evidently Mr. Langan hadn't shared his failure to make contact with Arianna. "Why wouldn't you think your action would cause her further upset at a dreadful time in her life?"

Raquel's expression turned defensive. "We wanted to help. She stopped talking and disappeared without a word. Todd said. . .Ari asked for help. I never would have agreed otherwise."

"She didn't."

Raquel became more agitated after Mitch's denial. She stood and walked the room. "I'm not so sure I should continue seeing you."

Mitch strove to appear concerned. Given what she'd done to Ari, he wasn't so sure he wanted to see her either. He forced himself to remain calm. He needed to hear what she had to say. "Why did you call yourself Ann Radnor?"

Raquel didn't answer.

"Did you attend the Kents' dinner party with your fiancé?"

"Yes," she snapped.

In their last session, she'd raged over the mistreatment she'd received at a party. "Is Charles Kent the man you've talked about all these years, Raquel? Or should I call you Ann?"

"I didn't want it to become common knowledge that I was seeing a shrink. My name is Raquel Ann Radnor. Ann is more suitable for business. Wilson is my mother's maiden name."

"Our sessions are confidential. I would never share your true identity."

"I can't be certain of that, can I, Dr. Ellis?" She turned around and eyed him for several seconds.

"You can," Mitch said with a shrug. "You said you're troubled by the Kent situation. Do you want to discuss those feelings?"

"Of course I'm troubled that someone I knew and respected was senselessly murdered. It's wrong on so many levels. And I resent being considered a suspect. I had nothing to do with their deaths."

"Are you grieving for Charles Kent, Raquel?"

"I'm thrilled Ari has her voice back. Were you working with her?"

Mitch eyed her but didn't respond.

"You are. What made her voice return?"

More shock, Mitch thought, recalling that night on the mountain. "It happens that way."

"I've called, but she refuses to take my calls."

Mine, too, Mitch thought glumly. "You don't think she's entitled to feel angry after that furtive attempt to take over her company?"

"She shouldn't be upset because we wanted to help her. I heard Ari has been appointed Simon's guardian and has complete control of her parents' shares."

Mitch watched the play of emotions on her face.

"If that's true, they should appoint someone to look after Simon's interests."

"Why would you say that?"

"He needs someone to protect him."

"Ari loves her brother. She'll make sure he never wants for anything."

Her face whitened.

"Simon has a nanny, Raquel. I recall a session where you complained about the woman who didn't spend time with your newborn son."

She ignored his observation. "Ari does love Simon."

He nodded. "She cares more about him than herself. That makes it really hard to accept the injustice of what happened to her. Not really fair, don't you agree, Raquel?"

"Why would you ask me that?" she demanded. "I tell you I had nothing to do with what happened."

Mitch fought to control his fury toward this woman who had hurt Ari with her actions. "Do you have any idea what happened that night?"

"N–no." She stumbled over the word.

"How long have you been coming here, Raquel?"

She pointed to the folder in his lap. "You have my chart right there."

"I do. And do you consider me to be an intelligent man?"

"What do you mean?"

"Several years ago, you came to me, depressed and upset that your affair had ended and the man convinced you to give up your son for the child's sake." She refused to look at him. "You were angry, Raquel. Furious that the man you loved took your heart and your child and tossed you away without a thought."

"He didn't."

"You said he did. Why didn't you tell me you were once Charles Kent's assistant? Why would you leave such a job?"

"You have been talking to someone about me," she accused.

"I asked about Ann Radnor. Not Raquel Wilson."

"It was a step up the career ladder."

Her claim didn't ring true. "Was it, Raquel? Could a sales manager position possibly be more prestigious than assistant to the CEO of Kent Enterprises?"

"It wasn't fair," she cried out. "He said he loved me. He promised to take care of me."

Horror filled her expression as she realized the import of her revelation. She curled in a fetal position on the sofa, tears trailing along her cheeks. Her voice grew soft. "I never knew anyone like him. When we started working together, he praised and encouraged me, said he could see me going far in the business. I listened when he talked about his wife and how she never wanted more children. It broke my heart to see how sad that made him. He wanted a son. He loved Ari, but she was young and didn't show any interest in the company."

"What did you do, Raquel?"

She became defiant. "I loved him. And he loved me."

"Are you Simon Kent's mother?"

She didn't speak for several minutes, and then she nodded. "I didn't mean for it to happen. Charles didn't seem at all upset when I told him. Said we'd handle the situation. I was afraid he meant an abortion, but he wanted me to have the baby. Said if it was a son, he'd bring him into the business and make him as successful as himself. I wanted my son to have all the opportunities in life I couldn't give him. That's why I agreed to the private adoption."

"Did Michelle Kent know you were Simon's mother?"

She shook her head. "I don't know what he did, but I suspect Charles begged her forgiveness and asked her to raise my son."

"Why would he do that?" Mitch asked.

"Divorce would have taken everything he'd worked so hard for over the years."

"Did she agree to raise your child?"

"Not right away. Charles stayed in the hotel for a couple of weeks before he sent for him. He told me it would be better if we didn't see each other again and returned home. He paid my living expenses until I was able to return to work and helped me find another job. Then he said I shouldn't ever contact him again."

"And you did so willingly?"

"What·else could I do?" she cried. "My son needed his father. Charles could give him so much more than I could."

"You could have loved him. You could have given him everything he needed to grow into a successful man in his own right."

"Do you think I don't regret my decision? Once I signed those papers, it was too late. I couldn't go back. Charles would have dragged me through the courts, and they would have granted him custody because he'd tell them I wasn't stable and had already given away my son. If I'd changed my mind, it would have destroyed us both."

"Why did you go to his home that night?"

Her expression grew stony, her tone cool. "I went with my fiancé. I've moved on and thought he had, too."

After the times she'd cried over the man telling her to stay out of his life, Mitch found it difficult to accept her response. He leaned more toward a need to see the man or force him to acknowledge her existence. "What did he say to hurt you?"

"He was so cold," she said almost sadly. "I complimented him on the art. We'd often visited galleries. Liked the same artists. He looked at me strangely and then invited me into the office to see his latest acquisition. I didn't know he would be so cruel. Demanded to know what game I was playing. Said I wasn't welcome in his home. I told him not to make a scene. Pointed out that he had as much to lose as I did. There was a photo of my son on his desk. I said he must be proud of this handsome boy. That's when he said he wouldn't allow me to disrupt their lives. Disrupt his life," she jeered. "His life was never disrupted. Mine was destroyed." She paused before speaking again. "Then he said, 'I'm not having this discussion. You signed the papers. Stand by your agreement and I'll stand by mine.'"

Her cheeks turned red against a pale face. "I never had any intention of doing anything to harm my son," she declared.

"What else have you done, Raquel? Did you see Simon at church?"

Her downcast gaze provided Mitch with his answer.

"He was so precious. I volunteered in his Sunday school classrooms."

"Did Charles know?"

"I don't think so."

"Was that enough for you?"

"I tried to move on with my life. I got really depressed. That's when I came to you. Charles paid your fees. He knew my problems were his fault. But he didn't care about me. He had everything he wanted. I had nothing."

"And?"

"Then I met Todd and had this crazy idea that if I married a successful man, maybe when Simon was older, I could tell him I was his birth mother. I hoped that he wouldn't hate me for giving him up."

"Does Todd know the truth?"

Raquel sighed. "I never stopped loving Charles. No matter what he'd done to me, we shared a child. He cared for that child and in my mind that meant he cared for me. He had to love me. I'd given him a son."

"How does Todd feel about that?"

"He hated Charles. Said he loved me far more than Kent ever would. When I got really sad and cried, he said he'd make him suffer. Todd knew I'd never love him like I loved Charles, but he still wanted to marry me."

"But you never married him. It's been two years, Raquel."

She stood and walked over to the window, her back to Mitch. "I couldn't promise to love and honor Todd when another man already occupied my heart."

"The man who cast you aside? Took your child? He used you, Raquel."

She whirled around. "I'm not stupid, Dr. Ellis. I know all that in my head, but my heart told me differently."

Mitch understood the need to listen to the heart. When he'd first met Ari, his intention had been to protect her, but somewhere along the way that intention had shifted to something far different. He still needed to protect her, but his feelings for her were much stronger.

"Ari doesn't know."

Raquel shook her head. "It was between Charles and me."

"Does Langan know the entire story?"

"Most of it."

"Why was he so determined to find Ari when she and Simon disappeared?"

"What do you mean?" Raquel demanded.

"What about the board?" Mitch asked. "Was the attempted takeover his idea?"

"Todd never said anything about a takeover."

"Did he plan to use you to take control of the board?"

She covered her mouth as the realization hit. "He did it all for me."

"And Simon."

She nodded slowly. "When I came back into the room, he could see that I was upset. He demanded to know what had happened. He said we'd get Simon back. Raise him together."

"Did you believe him?"

She shook her head. "It was too late. I wasn't about to rob Simon of the only security he knew, no matter how much I wanted to be part of his life.

Todd was furious when I refused. I said I'd never speak to him again if he didn't leave it alone."

"What did he do, Raquel?"

"Nothing."

Dawning realization suddenly filled her expression. "You think he. . . No. He wouldn't."

Suddenly she grabbed her purse and ran toward the door.

Mitch hurried after her. "Raquel? Come back."

She was gone. He grabbed the phone and dialed. "Who's the detective for the Kent case?" he demanded when Gary answered.

"Mitch? What's going on?"

"Call him now. Tell him to look into Todd Langan as a person of interest."

"Why? What do you know, Mitch?"

"I can't tell you, Gary. Make sure Ari and Simon are safe. I have a feeling something bad is about to happen."

Mitch disconnected and dialed Ari's cell number, planning to leave a message. She surprised him by answering the phone. "Where are you?"

There was a slight pause, and then she said, "At home. Simon has the flu."

"Don't leave the house. Get Tom inside and lock up tight. I'll be there in a few minutes to explain."

"But Simon has a doctor's appointment in an hour."

"Please, Arianna. I'll take care of everything. Promise me you'll stay there."

Mitch held the phone to his ear as he ran upstairs. He removed the pouch from the nightstand drawer, sliding out the gun and clip. "And whatever you do, stay away from Todd Langan and Raquel. . .I mean Ann Radnor."

"Todd called a few minutes ago," she said. "He wanted to come by and discuss my decision not to work with him. I told him Simon has an appointment. I really don't want to deal with him. I'll ask Erik George to—"

"Stay away from Todd Langan," Mitch interrupted. "I don't have all the facts, but I'm fairly certain he's involved in your parents' murder."

She gasped and cried, "No, Mitch. You're wrong. He wouldn't do that."

"You have no idea what Langan can do. Please trust me."

"Tell me why I should trust you."

Her plea touched that part of him that knew he had to be honest if he ever hoped to have a future with her. She wouldn't accept anything less from him. "Sometimes I hear things. I shouldn't tell you. It involves a patient. Someone you know. This is bad, Ari. Please believe me."

"Okay, I'll call Dr. Graves and cancel the appointment."

Relieved, he promised, "I'll tell you everything. The minute I get there. Stay safe."

Mitch ran downstairs and locked up the house, going out through the kitchen door into the garage.

His cell rang as he got into his car. "Mitch, Gary here. The detective says they already have Langan as a person of interest."

He hit the gas, barely waiting for the garage door to clear. "He called her, Gary. Wanted to come by to discuss the reason she won't continue working with him. She told him Simon had a doctor's appointment."

"You think he's at the townhouse?"

"I'd say he's fairly close. He's not stable. She promised to stay put, but you know Ari."

"I'll call Tom. Where are you?"

"In my car. Hold on. Something's not right." He climbed out of the car and fought back his anger. Why now of all the times in the world? "My tire's flat."

"Want me to send someone over?"

"No!" he shouted. "Keep Ari safe. I'll call a cab. See you soon."

"Okay, calm down. More men are on the way. We'll surround the place. I'll tie her to a chair if I have to."

"Do whatever you have to do to keep her safe."

Chapter 15

Mitch exited the cab and surveyed the police presence in the neighborhood. He tried to ask questions, but an officer instructed him to move on.

"He's with me," Gary called as he exited the building. The officer shrugged and turned his attention back to crowd control.

"What happened?" Mitch demanded. Thanks to the flat tire and an accident that blocked a major intersection, it had been well over an hour since he talked with Ari. He'd tried to call and gotten her voice mail.

"Tom came down to check the perimeter and spotted Langan's silver sports car parked over there." Gary pointed to the far end of the street. The car was still there. "The idiot was watching the townhouse through a rifle scope."

"A rifle. . ." Mitch broke off and Gary nodded.

"You don't think he planned. . ." Mitch shuddered at the thought of what might have happened if Ari and Simon had left the house. "Where's Ari? Is she okay?"

"Tom called the police. They found a high-powered rifle in the car. At first he tried to pretend he was concerned for their safety but they already had the story. Ann Radnor called the police. Evidently she convinced them Langan was a danger to Ari. Then she called Todd and broke off their engagement."

"Gary, answer me. Is she okay?" Mitch demanded.

"They're both fine. I've got so many men in that condo Langan couldn't have found her if he'd gotten inside."

Mitch wanted to know everything, but he needed to see Ari. Needed to keep his promise.

"The police arrested the man who killed the Kents three days ago. He was in a bar bragging about killing those rich people. He said their attorney had paid him well for the job.

"Even told how Langan let him into the penthouse the night of the dinner party. He hid out until everyone was gone. Said Langan made his job easier by drugging the Kents. The man has a rap sheet as long as your arm. Likes knives. Hurt his girlfriend pretty badly when she tried to get away from him. She lived to tell the story."

"But Ari. The gun." Mitch couldn't formulate a complete sentence if his life depended on his doing so.

"Langan told them everything. He's obsessed with Ann Radnor and hated Charles Kent. He promised to get her child back and believed that would convince her he loved her more than Kent ever had. When everything started falling apart, he decided to kill Ari so Ann could get Simon back. He must have been desperate to come here himself."

"Does Ari know?"

"The detective is with her now."

He couldn't bear another minute of this. "I've got to get up there, Gary."

"Come on. I'll get you in."

Mitch paused and grimaced. "Simon has the flu. I promised Ari I'd take care of him."

"Go see Ari. I'll call Dr. Graves and ask him to call in a prescription."

"Thanks, buddy. I owe you one."

"Nah, we'll call it even. You sent me the love of my life. Why shouldn't I return the favor? Ari's over there," he said, indicating the sofa, "with the police."

"Mitch," Ari called the moment she spotted him. She held out her hand.

He hurried over and sat next to her on the sofa. Taking her trembling hand in his, he asked, "Are you okay?"

"Todd. . . Did you hear?" Her gaze met his.

He nodded. The detective sat on the chair opposite them.

"Will you stay?"

Mitch tightened his hold on her hand. Nothing short of dynamite was going to move him from her side.

The detective flipped his pad open. "Todd Langan has admitted to contracting the murder of your parents."

"Todd?" Ari's voice broke slightly.

"Yes ma'am."

"No!" Ari's keening wail broke Mitch's heart. She clutched his arm. "It can't be. Why would he do that?" She stared at the detective.

"I'm sorry, Ms. Kent," the man began, unable to disguise his discomfort. "Ann Radnor contacted us about Langan. She informed us of her involvement with your father."

Ari's mouth dropped open.

"Langan's obsession pushed him to eliminate your father from the picture."

"My father?"

"He believed that if he eliminated you and your parents, they could regain custody of the child. Your brother."

"Simon?"

He nodded. "Ann Radnor is Simon's mother."

"No." Ari's head moved from side to side. "He's my brother."

"Charles Kent is his father."

Ari's eyes closed and she breathed deeply, her distress evident. "What are you saying?"

Mitch slipped an arm around Ari's shoulder and pulled her close.

"Langan believed the estate would go to Simon as the last remaining Kent heir. We think he planned to help Ann regain custody of her son and take control of the company."

"But surely he knew he would get caught." Ari turned her head into Mitch's shoulder. "He had my parents killed out of unrequited love?"

She sobbed softly, her tears wetting his neck. Mitch rubbed his hand gently across her shoulders. "It's over, Ari. He's been arrested."

She jerked up, her face pale. "It's only the beginning, Mitch. This will go to court. The media will be all over us. How do you think Simon will handle learning his birth mother's boyfriend had his parents killed?"

He squeezed her hand in his. "I'll help him work through this. Ann has no rights. You're his guardian."

"Poor Simon. He's so sick. This will make things worse."

She couldn't bear seeing this small child who meant so much to her harmed. Mitch couldn't either. "We'll protect him, Ari. If we have to move to the ends of the earth to keep him safe, that's what we'll do. No one is going to hurt him. Let's go check on him now," Mitch suggested. He looked at the detective and asked, "Can we continue this later? I need to check on my patient."

The man nodded. "We can talk later."

"Thank you," Ari said.

Together they walked down the hall to Simon's bedroom. The boy slept fitfully, the bedcovers hanging over the edge of the bed. She pulled the sheet and blanket back over him.

Mitch sat on the edge of the bed and touched Simon's forehead. "Have you given him anything for the fever?"

She nodded. "It's not helping."

"Mitch?" Simon mumbled as he came awake.

"Hey, buddy, how are you feeling?"

"Lousy."

"Let's see what we can do to make you feel better. Have you eaten today?"

"Not hungry."

"You need to eat. How about some soup and crackers? Or a Popsicle. Think you could eat that?"

"I'll try. I heard people talking. Who's here, Ari?"

"Security," she said, unwilling to upset him further. "Here, take a couple of sips of juice."

Mitch supported Simon against his chest as he sipped through the straw and then laid him back on the bed. He tucked the covers securely about him. "Go back to sleep. We'll get your medications and food."

"Okay," he mumbled weakly.

They turned out the light and stepped into the hallway, closing the door behind them.

"Do you think I should call Dr. Graves?"

Mitch grinned. "Don't you trust me? I went to medical school, too, you know."

She leaned lightly into him, tilting her face toward his. "I trust you, Mitch."

Relief greater than he could have imagined filled him. "Thank you, Ari. I've been so afraid you wouldn't ever trust me again."

"Why didn't you tell me?"

"I wanted to be there for you and Simon. You wouldn't have let me stay if you'd known the truth."

"And you can't tell me what you know?"

He shook his head. "You're smart though. You'll put it all together."

The shock held her immobile. "I don't want to think about it. I want to close my eyes and wake up to find things like they were not so long ago. I want my parents back."

The tears came in earnest. He pulled her into his arms, his hands smoothing her shoulder. "I know, honey. But you can't go back. You have to move forward. For yourself and for Simon."

"Will you help us?"

"You know I will. I'll be there every step of the way." He cupped her face in his hand and kissed her. "I love you, Ari."

She nodded, brushing her hand along his jaw. "I love you, too."

Chapter 16

As Ari predicted, the next few days were a paparazzi nightmare. She depended on the security staff to fight them off and did everything in her power to keep the truth from Simon.

Ann Radnor called often, and Ari refused to talk to her. Every voice mail message was a plea for forgiveness and a request to know how Simon was holding up under the siege of the press.

While Ari knew it was her Christian duty to forgive, she found it difficult to do so. She'd prayed and asked God to help her find forgiveness for their father and the woman who had brought so much harm to her family.

Healthwise, things were looking up for Simon. He recovered from the flu and just the day before had his cast removed. Ari needed to talk to her brother and didn't feel she could face this alone. Remembering Mitch's promise, she called to request his help.

"You're sure you want to do this now?"

"I have to. It's all over the news. What happens if he reads about it on the Internet or hears from someone else? He'll be upset that I didn't tell him the truth."

"Around seven thirty tonight?"

"Thanks, Mitch. Come for dinner."

⟨≈⟩

He arrived right on time. Dora Etheridge had returned to Ari's that afternoon after Ari called to tell her what they planned to do. Ari prepared Simon's favorites. The dining table had been set with place mats and everyday china. A huge bowl of spaghetti sat in the middle along with cheese bread.

Ari led the way, indicating Mitch should sit next to her. Simon sat across from Ari, with Nana next to him.

He sensed Ari's internal struggle over what she had to do. Reaching over, Mitch squeezed her hand in his and whispered, "It's going to be okay, Ari. Simon knows you love him."

Her gaze focused on him for a long time before she answered, "It's so hard, Mitch. No child should have to deal with something like this."

"We'll work it out," he promised. "Let's pray." Taking her hand and Simon's, he waited for them to bring Nana into the circle before he blessed the food and asked for God's guidance.

After dinner they went into the family room. Ari asked Nana to join the group.

"Simon, I have something to tell you."

The boy looked from one adult to another and then back to Ari. "That I'm adopted?"

Shocked, she demanded, "Who told you?"

"This guy at school likes to pick on the little kids. He heard it on the news and texted me."

Mitch witnessed her despair, saw the way her eyes drifted closed. Knew she blamed herself for not acting quickly enough. How could he help her fix this?

Simon stood and came over to wrap his arms around her neck. "It's okay, Ari."

Her arms tightened. "Oh Simon. Why didn't you tell me?"

"I wanted to, but I was afraid."

Tears leaked from Ari's eyes and trailed along her cheeks. The sins of the father had come to bear on this small brave boy. "I love you, Simon. Please don't ever be afraid to talk to me."

"I love you, too, Ari. I'm glad you're my sister."

"I am, you know. Dad is your father, too."

Simon rested against Ari. "I miss Mom and Dad."

"Me, too," Ari told him. "But we're family, Simon. You and me. You can always trust me to be there for you. I want to see you grow up healthy and happy. I want you to tell me everything. I'll be there lots of times when you'll wish I weren't."

"I'd never wish that," Simon said, a mischievous grin touching his face as he added, "You're my favorite sister."

"Rascal," she said, tickling him before she said with an affected tone, "I'm your only sistah."

The boy laughed and she hugged him.

"We're a team, Simon. No matter what happens in the future, it's you and me."

"Is Ms. Ann my mom? That's what Tony said."

Mitch wanted to have a chat with this bully.

"He said they called it a love triangle. Said Mr. Langan had Mom and Dad killed because Ms. Ann was in love with Dad. They said Mr. Langan wanted her to have her son back. Did he really do that?"

Mitch glanced at Ari and back to Simon. "Yes, that's true."

"Am I going to have to live with her now?"

Horrified, Ari exclaimed, "No. Never. You're staying right here with me."

A frown carved its mark on Simon's forehead. "But what if Ms. Ann wants me back?"

"She can't have you. We're family, Simon. Ann gave up her rights. One day when you're older, you may decide you want to have a relationship with her. When that time comes, we'll consider it, but for now she has a lot of personal issues to work through and won't be involved in your life."

"Where is she?"

"She left Chicago."

"Do you know where she went?"

Ari shook her head. "I haven't talked to her."

"You're mad at her, aren't you?"

This child was too perceptive for his own good.

"Yes, I'm angry with a lot of people for what they've done. They were adults, Simon. They should have known better."

"We need to pray that God will come into their lives and change them like He changed us."

"Yes, sweetheart, we do." Ari hugged him close for several seconds.

"If you ever want to talk about this, I'm there for you," Mitch said.

"Thanks, Mitch, but if you don't mind, I think I'll talk to Jesus first."

Mitch bumped fists with the boy. "I think that's a pretty smart thing to do."

"You do?"

He nodded. "I accepted Jesus into my heart when I was eleven years old, but then my parents died in a fire, and I didn't talk to Him after that. I thought I was a smart guy, but I wasn't really."

Simon smiled proudly at his sister. "Ari introduced me to God."

"And you and Ari reintroduced me to Him. You're disciples, Simon. You lead people to Jesus and He does the rest."

"That's awesome."

Mitch grinned at the boy's response. "Jesus is awesome. I want to get to know Him better than I did when I was eleven. And now that Ari is talking again and can go to Bible study, I'm hoping she'll invite me."

Simon glanced at his sister.

She smiled at Mitch. "Anytime you want."

Mitch winked at her. "Are you okay with all this, Simon?"

"I don't understand everything. Mom and Dad shouldn't have been killed like that. Killing is wrong. It's a commandment. Like those ones we saw written on the mountain."

"Yes," Ari agreed. She could have told him there was another commandment regarding adultery. "I want you to promise that when you hear things you find confusing, you'll come to me and ask questions. I'll tell you the truth. And when people say hurtful things, I need you to talk to me about what they said."

"Do what Ari says, Simon. Don't think you're being brave when you bottle it up inside."

"But Dad always said real men don't cry like babies."

"Real men are human," Mitch declared. "They hurt and that hurt needs an outlet. Maybe your dad believed he had to be tough to earn respect."

He looked at Ari and then back at Simon, trying to gauge how to continue. He hadn't known their father and what drove him.

"It's good to talk to adults about the things that bother you. Sometimes when you talk problems out, you realize they really aren't that important in the first place."

"Okay. Can I go watch my show now?"

Ari smiled and nodded her permission. The boy darted away to his bedroom.

Nana rose to follow. "I'll check on him."

Mitch knew she wanted to give them some privacy. "Simon will be fine. He knows you love him," he told Ari.

"Thanks for being here, Mitch." She looked at him, her eyes filled with a deep, curious longing.

Her tender regard was his undoing. "I realize we haven't known each other that long, but I love you. I'd like it if we could spend more time together. Get to know each other. I love the sound of your voice, but I loved you when you couldn't utter a word. I want to hear that voice every day for the rest of my life."

A cheeky smile flashed on Ari's face. "Are you asking for a date, Dr. Ellis?"

Mitch grinned in return. "More than one, Ms. Kent."

"Good. I'm ready to take this first step of the journey to learn God's plan for our future."

"Me, too," he agreed, cupping her face in his hands and kissing her softly.

The sweet kiss filled her heart with joy. Ari smiled at him, her gaze holding his as she sent up a silent thank-you to God.

JUST ONE TOUCH

Dedication

To those who suffer with sleep disorders.
Thanks RealCutie for your input.
To our heavenly Father—thank You for the
opportunity to write for Your glory.
To Heartsong Presents—thanks for allowing me to see my work in print.

Chapter 1

Surely she wasn't sleeping.

Jacob Greer could not believe his eyes when he stepped into the office of the chief financial officer and found Lauren Kingsley asleep in her chair. Obviously deep sleep since she did not respond to his throat clearing and other efforts to make her aware of his presence. No wonder Sleep Dreams needed a management consultant.

Ashleigh Fields, Lauren Kingsley's administrative assistant, entered the office carrying a salad and bottle of water. "Mr. Gre–Greer," she stuttered, looking horrified. "I'm sorry, sir, but you shouldn't be in here."

Obviously Sleeping Beauty didn't object to his presence. He eyed the young assistant, noting her extreme discomfort. "I plan to stay until Ms. Kingsley wakes."

"But sir. . ."

"Go back to your desk, Ms. Fields. I'll deal with this."

"But you don't understand."

From the way she wailed the words, Jake thought maybe she feared losing her job. He took her arm and urged her out the door. "I appreciate your loyalty, but this type of behavior is precisely why I'm here."

She gasped and covered her mouth. "Oh sir, no. It's not what you think. I've never known anyone to work harder than Lauren."

Obviously she admired her supervisor. Perhaps Ms. Fields aspired to one day nap anytime she wanted as well. His brow wrinkled with the contemptuous thought, and the administrative assistant scurried from the room without another word.

Jake turned back to the slumbering woman. He'd never witnessed such flagrant abuse of a position. Prepared to wait her out, he took the seat facing the desk, leaned back, and crossed one leg over the other.

He would be the first person Lauren Kingsley saw when she woke. Then she would hear exactly what he thought of her sleeping on the job. Her father had hired him to help turn things around here at Sleep Dreams and that was what he planned to do.

Jake allowed his eyes to drift over her serene expression, feeling a stirring of appreciation. He couldn't see the color of her eyes, but long black eyelashes brushed her cheeks. Her long golden brown hair was parted down the center and lay about her shoulders. Her skin was a flawless ivory that rivaled that of a baby. She even slept like a newborn, he thought. But she needed to pay less attention to her social life and more to her job.

After several minutes, Jake glanced at his watch and back at the woman behind the desk. Suddenly it occurred to him something wasn't right here. Was she sick? Unconscious? It was ridiculous that she'd still be sleeping.

Greg Kingsley rushed into the room. "Jake, I'm sorry. I meant to tell you..."

Lauren's eyes fluttered open. Jake noted her surprise as she took in the two men in her office. "Daddy? Is something..."

"Everything's okay, honey," her father comforted, hurrying to her side. He patted her shoulder gently.

"No, it's not." Jake's earlier concern evaporated. She might be the Kingsleys' daughter, but she owed her parents for giving her this key position in their company. "What kind of example is she setting by sleeping on the job? I've been in this room for"—he paused and studied his watch for effect before he said—"ten minutes and she didn't know I was here."

Greg's voice grew stern as he said, "Now wait a minute..."

"No," Jake interrupted. "No more excuses. There's no room at Sleep Dreams for anyone who doesn't carry their share of the load."

Lauren's face turned pink. *She should be embarrassed*, Jake thought. But he saw something else. Surely she wasn't pretending to be hurt.

A sad smile curved her lips. "It's okay, Daddy. Go back to your office. I'll explain."

Greg Kingsley appeared highly agitated, his ruddy complexion growing redder by the minute. "I should have filled him in before now."

She touched his arm and pleaded, "Go back to work. Please, Daddy. Let me deal with Mr. Greer."

Deal? Jake stared at her. Did she think they were going to negotiate her right to sleep on the job?

Greg Kingsley kissed her forehead. "I'm sorry, Laurie."

Even though he didn't want to, Jake experienced that same rush of fatherly affection he felt for his own child. These two loved each other.

"It's not your fault. It's not anyone's fault. It just is." She squeezed his arm. "We'll talk later."

After he'd gone, she looked Jake straight in the eye and said, "It can't be helped."

"Sure it can. A little less social life and more rest at night and you won't require naps to get you through the day."

"I do hope all your decisions aren't based on snap judgments." Her soft tone admonished as her hazel eyes pinned him in place. "And for the record, my nap had nothing to do with late hours."

His brows lifted, questioning her comment. "Looked that way to me."

She shrugged. "I can understand your assumption, but things are not always as they seem."

Jake leaned back in the chair and waved his hand imperiously. "By all means, share your reasons for disrespecting your parents and abusing their trust in you."

He couldn't abide the spoiled rich kids who took their positions with family businesses for granted. Lauren Kingsley was in her mid to late twenties.

She knew her father would never fire her. He'd strain the company budget further to hire someone to do her job. And in typical fashion of a spoiled brat, she'd take advantage of that knowledge.

"The situation happens to be. . ."

Both heads turned as Greg Kingsley burst into the room. "She can't help it. She's sick."

"Daddy! I said I'd handle this."

Jake saw frustration in her expression and heard exasperation in her tone.

Greg Kingsley's gaze focused on his daughter. "I won't have anyone criticizing you because of your problem."

Jake knew this man would fight the world to defend his child. He looked from one to the other. What did he mean by sick? She didn't look sick to him. A little tired maybe but if she was sick, why hadn't she stayed home to recuperate? Why bring her germs to the office to potentially risk infecting others? "You shouldn't come to work sick."

She smiled at that. "Don't worry. It's not contagious. I have narcolepsy. I'm sure you understand that it's not something we discuss openly. In fact, very few people within the company are aware of my disorder. My assistant generally keeps everyone out when I have an attack. She must have been away from her desk. The attacks often occur rather quickly."

"Bu–but. . ." Jake found himself stuttering this time.

"I won't have you berating her," Greg Kingsley emphasized, pinning him with his glare. "Lauren works rings around everyone in this company. No one works as many hours as she does."

Lauren rose and stepped around the desk. Jake took a moment to appreciate her long curly hair and curvy figure before giving her his full attention.

"It's okay, Daddy," she said softly, taking his arm and urging him toward her chair. "Perhaps we should explain and let Mr. Greer draw his own conclusions."

She chuckled and the hazel eyes brightened. "You have to admit that after watching me sleep for more than ten minutes he's entitled to feel I take advantage of your love for me." Lauren glanced at Jake and asked, "Don't you find it ironic that Sleep Dreams manufactures one of the most comfortable sleep systems in the world and the owner's daughter suffers from a sleep disorder?"

"I didn't realize," Jake choked out finally.

"It's okay," she offered, looking almost sympathetic. "I live with my problem. I hope you can do the same."

❧

Lauren wanted to sink through the floor. She'd asked her father to let her handle this, but in his usual overprotective manner, he'd raced to her rescue. Lauren had debated the situation for days, trying to determine the best plan of action. Her preference would have been to gradually ease into the truth with Jacob Greer. But today's incident had pretty much destroyed any possibility of that happening. Now they both dealt with the emotional fallout.

"I'm so sorry," he said for the fourth time since her father finally left. "I should have learned all the facts before jumping to conclusions."

"It's not a problem, Mr. Greer."

"Jake, please."

"I'm Lauren."

"I am sorry, Lauren," he repeated, the blue-green eyes pleading his case. "We're going to be working together closely over the next few weeks. I hope you won't hold this against me."

"Believe it or not, I completely understand your reaction. If I'd walked into an office and found the boss's daughter asleep and had no idea why, I'd have made the same call."

Well, maybe not. He probably considered her a spoiled woman who took advantage of her parents and in that, Lauren couldn't deny there was a hint of truth. At an age where most young women had moved on in their lives, had their own apartments and homes, careers, friends, and relationships, Lauren lived with her parents, worked for the family business, and pretty much depended on their support for her day-to-day existence.

It wasn't so much that she was unwilling to give those things a try. It required finding people who weren't scared off by her neediness.

She drew in a deep breath and sat down at her desk. "Let's start over. Tell me why you stopped by."

"Your father said you'd be able to provide me with the relevant data I'll need for my analysis. I want to go over the figures and do some charts and graphs to see if the situation relates to the economy or started further back."

"It shouldn't be any problem. All our records are computerized." She named a popular accounting program.

Jake nodded with satisfaction. "I'm familiar with that, so once I have computer access I should be able to pull the data for myself. I will need your expertise though."

Lauren leaned forward and said, "I'm willing to do everything possible to help my parents improve and expand their business."

"Which will one day become your business," Jake pointed out. "Your father indicated he wants to keep the company going for you."

A wry smile touched her lips. "My great-grandfather started the company, and I'd love to see Sleep Dreams become a legacy for the future generations." The double-edged sword was that there was no one to continue Sleep Dreams after she was gone.

He stood and Lauren did the same. She shook his outstretched hand. "It's been a pleasure meeting you, Jake."

They assessed each other for several seconds before he spoke. "I look forward to working together."

Strangely, despite her earlier embarrassment and humiliation, Lauren felt the same.

After he left, Lauren settled back in her chair. She'd been doing so much better, hadn't suffered an attack in a couple of days. And now she had to deal with Jake Greer's knowledge of her condition and his discomfort over calling her out, not to mention her own embarassment.

Lauren should be used to it by now, but she didn't think she'd ever overcome the shame of being imperfect. Despite counseling sessions too numerous to count, she'd been unable to get past the pain caused by people thinking her lazy and unmotivated.

She was different but wanted to be normal. Not someone people avoided because they didn't know how to deal with her medical condition. She desired the same things as other women, and God willing, she hoped to one day have some semblance of a life. But on days like today, her condition made that nearly impossible. She had a good idea stress had brought on this attack.

Earlier in the year, her father had surprised them with his plan to solicit proposals for an efficiency study of their company. His friend had recently done the same and convinced Greg Kingsley he would benefit from the experience. Out of the six proposals received, he'd chosen Jacob Greer. As he shared information on the man he hoped would shift their financial picture deeper into the black, Lauren fought her body's natural reaction to the overwhelming onslaught of emotions.

Three generations of the Kingsley family had owned and operated Sleep Dreams, each improving product and profits. As chief financial officer, she looked at their financial dealings every day. Profits were down a small percentage, but she attributed that to rising costs and a drop in sales that had to do with the economy. Of course, some items her father mentioned were outside her control, such as the need to replace equipment and a possible expansion into a larger nearby city. Had she missed some key factor that impacted their business?

Lauren knew her father believed Jacob Greer could provide a fresh vision for their company. He certainly seemed dedicated to the cause. Enough to call her father on a daughter who slept on the job. She couldn't help but smile at that.

Her father's choice in a consultant intrigued her. From his proposal, it seemed he preferred challenging jobs where he could utilize his education to make the most impact for the company. Based on the references they'd received, he'd unerringly done that without fail for a number of satisfied customers.

And he wasn't hard on the eyes either. Though Jake wore his executive suit with style, he appeared to be a man more at home in casual clothes. Tall and broad in the shoulders, he couldn't claim washboard abs. Like her, he could afford to lose a few pounds, but not doing so wouldn't stop women from finding him attractive.

She guessed that like her, he was in his late twenties. He wore his dark hair in a short cut that required little attention. The dark beard made it appear he sported a five o'clock shadow all the time.

Her father had mentioned he planned to bring a child with him. A little boy named Teddy. What was the story behind that? Why did Jacob Greer travel alone with his son? Where was his wife?

Jake had hoped she wouldn't hold his snap judgment against him. She on the other hand hoped he wouldn't hold her condition against her.

~

That afternoon Jake left the office in time to pick up Teddy and Yapper from their respective day cares. Now that he knew the lay of the land and felt comfortable with the job he'd signed up for, he really needed to find a home and a nanny. His job often required hours of overtime, and he needed to know they were safe and content. And he knew it would be cheaper than shelling out to the individual care facilities not to mention the hotel.

When the request for a proposal for this job came in, Jake thought about how he could make this work. He wasn't about to leave Teddy behind. Not while they were grieving Gwen's loss. His son needed his remaining parent.

After Gwen's death, his mother and stepfather had stayed at the house with Teddy while he completed his contract. When that wrapped up, he refused a couple of jobs until he could make some decisions about their future.

At first the idea of coming to North Carolina's Crystal Coast for a job hadn't seemed right for them. Then he'd gone onto the Internet and learned about the area. He'd accepted the job and brought his son and their dog to Morehead City in late July.

He collected Teddy and Yapper and headed for the hotel. Luckily, he'd found a place that allowed pets even if he did have to pay an extra fee. He really should pick up something for dinner. Did he have sufficient diapers for Teddy? Food for Teddy and Yapper? Formula?

Jake missed Gwen even more on days like this. When she'd been alive, he'd felt comfortable in the knowledge that their family was well cared for at home by a mother who loved them. Now he depended on the kindness of strangers for their care and faced an entirely different set of chores after work.

After stopping to pick up a burger, Jake drove to the hotel and parked. He found the room card, and then gathered baby, diaper bag, dog carrier, briefcase, and fast-food bag. Jake thanked the woman who held the elevator door for him. At the room door, he juggled everything and inserted the key. He left Yapper in her carrier and placed Teddy in the borrowed hotel crib while he changed into shorts and a T-shirt.

"Hey buddy. Ready for dinner?" His son babbled agreement, reaching out to him. "Give me a minute." Jake went into the bathroom and washed his hands before coming back out to sort through the small jars on the countertop. He brewed a pot of coffee and carried the cup along with the baby food to the table.

He secured the bib and lifted Teddy from the crib, settling him in his lap. "Daddy might have messed up today," he told his son. "I upset the boss's daughter."

Teddy babbled "*dadadada*" in return.

"Yeah, it was stupid of me," he agreed, his thoughts drifting as he fed his son.

242

Lauren Kingsley had said she wouldn't hold it against him, but Jake knew he'd have to earn their respect back and that wasn't going to be easy. Why hadn't they told him? Surely they'd known something could happen.

After Teddy finished eating, Jake put him back into the crib while he ate his dinner. He considered the things he needed to do, like take Yapper for a walk and get Teddy ready for bed and go over some files he'd brought home. He rubbed one hand over his face, already bone weary.

By the time he went to bed that night, he was exhausted. Teddy slept and for once Yapper was quiet. Jake turned off the lamp and lay there, his thoughts a jumble of all that had happened that day. Sleep would not come and he tossed and turned, angry at himself for getting off on the wrong foot with the Kingsleys.

He called himself a troubleshooter, but today he'd been a troublemaker.

Chapter 2

After a restless night, Jake called to request a meeting with Lauren. She welcomed him and asked Ashleigh to bring him a cup of coffee. She had a bottle of water.

"I think we need to address this elephant in the room."

"Excuse me." She looked stunned by his bluntness.

Jake forged on. "Let's talk about what happened yesterday."

"Why?" Lauren bracketed the question with the spread of her hands. "You didn't know and now you do. I don't hold grudges, Jake. I've lived with this long enough to understand how senseless that would be."

"Tell me about narcolepsy." He truly wanted to know.

"It's a neurological sleep disorder, triggered by the brain's inability to regulate sleep-wake cycles normally. Third most frequently diagnosed sleep disorder."

"How does it affect you?"

"I suffer from overwhelming daytime sleepiness. As for sleeping on the job, I do take brief naps, which help me stay more alert. Yesterday was a full-blown sleep attack. I think the stress of your arrival and my underlying fear that the company is in trouble might have triggered the situation."

"Your dad is being proactive, Lauren. He brought me in to help him look at the bottom line, to find ways to improve the operation. I hate feeling I got off on the wrong foot with Greg. Being a parent myself, I should have known better."

"Than to address a concern with the heir apparent?" she mocked, a smile curving her lips. "We discussed this last night. Daddy says we're at fault for not filling you in."

He placed his cup on the desk. "And I was equally at fault for jumping to conclusions."

Jake had noted Lauren talked with her hands. Now she lifted her palms out toward him. "So let's put it behind us and move on with business."

"Can we do that?" Jake asked. "I mean. . .I don't know much. . . . Actually I don't know anything about narcolepsy."

"Wish I could say the same." Lauren sounded morose.

"It's bad?"

"Life altering. At least my father is an understanding boss."

Jake paused for a minute and said, "I saw your emotional battle yesterday."

"Chaos and anguish," she joked. "That's my life."

Jake appreciated her attempt to bring humor into what must be a devastating situation. "I'm sorry I added to your worries."

"Don't be. Believe it or not, I'm blessed and I know it. I have loving parents who work hard to help make a difference in my life."

"You were born with this?"

She shook her head. "The symptoms started when I was around ten. Eventually the doctors did a sleep study and I was diagnosed. I'm the one in two thousand."

He waited for her to continue.

"Narcolepsy steals your life and your dignity. Doesn't matter what you're doing when the episodes occur. Having people laugh at me or comment that I'm lazy doesn't help."

Jake felt sufficiently chastened. He'd lost sleep over his insensitive behavior. "I'm sorry."

"I didn't mean you," she told him. "The medication and scheduled naps help me function as normally as I can."

No doubt the disorder caused her great anguish. He made a mental note to do research. He wanted to know more.

Jake hoped she didn't take his inquiry the wrong way. "Is there anything I should do if you have an attack while we're together?"

Lauren shrugged. "Do what you can to help me avoid injury."

"I appreciate you telling me this."

Her brow creased with worry. "Please keep the information to yourself. It's not common knowledge within the company."

Jake nodded agreement.

"Daddy tells me you have a little boy."

Jake pulled out his wallet and handed her a photo. "That's Teddy. He's eight months old."

"Oh how sweet. He's precious."

He noted the way she stared at the photo with something like longing in her gaze before handing it back.

"Thank you." He glanced down at the baby with his big grin and his mom's silky blond hair. Jake knew the color would probably change over time, but for now it was very blond. "He can be a handful at times."

"From what I've heard, they all are."

"We lost his mom this past February."

"I'm sorry."

He appreciated her obvious sincerity. "It's been difficult but we're getting by."

And they were. Some days were more difficult than others, but their routine fell into place and Jake found it comforting.

Jake felt more in control when he left Lauren's office. And true to her word, the Kingsleys didn't hold his gaffe against him. In fact, Jake found Lauren's disorder had very little effect on the work she performed. She came in with her father every morning and stayed until after six or seven most days.

She was a fount of knowledge regarding the company. More often than not, Greg Kingsley sent him to Lauren for answers.

He hadn't witnessed any further sleep attacks when they were together, but then Lauren spent the majority of her days sequestered in her office. Was she so concerned about others witnessing her attacks that she would imprison herself rather than risk someone finding out? While curious, he wouldn't ask.

*

"Hey Mom, what's up?" Lauren caught the phone between her shoulder and ear as she replaced the ribbon in her calculator.

"I invited Jake and Teddy to dinner tonight. Make sure you and your father get home on time."

Lauren held back a sigh. Wasn't it enough that she spent numerous hours of each day with Jake? Now her mother expected her to entertain him as well.

She liked him, but he made her feel unsettled. She had reached a comfort zone with her problem and contented herself with the life she had. Evidently Jake found the subject interesting enough to do his own research, and at times she felt like a bug under a microscope. He watched her so closely that she wondered if he was waiting for the next attack.

"Laurie, did you hear me?"

She could hear kitchen sounds. "Yes, Mom. I'll make sure we're home before six. You say he's bringing Teddy?"

"And their dog. He can't leave her behind because he's afraid her barking would cause problems at the hotel. He actually refused for that reason, but I told him to bring Yapper, too."

The name brought a smile to Lauren's face. She wondered who named the animal. Certainly two faces of Jake—father and furry little pet owner. He'd told her the dog was a teacup Yorkie Terrier. Not exactly a man's dog.

Despite her mixed feelings, Lauren looked forward to meeting his son and uncovering another facet of Jacob Greer. "We'll be home in plenty of time." Then another thought popped into her head. "Mom, has Jake ever said anything about what happened to his wife?"

"She drowned. Really sad, her dying like that and leaving behind a tiny baby. Jake explained the situation to your father when he called to offer him the job."

Lauren replaced the receiver and went to wash the ink from her fingertips. Back at her desk, she tried to concentrate on the work at hand, but her mind wandered.

She wished her life had more facets. There were two—daughter and CFO for her father's company. Actually there was another more important one—child of God. She loved the Lord and knew He would take care of her no matter what happened. That was one truth she could rely upon.

Her childhood had been a normal one. She'd been an adored only child and grandchild. Like any child's, her life had its ups and downs, bumps and bruises, but for the most part she'd been happy. She did all the normal kid stuff, attended school, played with her friends, and had sleepovers. And then everything changed.

The narcolepsy had been diagnosed, and they had come to accept things would never improve for her. She took medication and learned what would help her stay awake. And told herself her life was the best it would ever be.

At seven on the dot, Lauren opened the front door to find Jake juggling his son, pet carrier, and diaper bag. Teddy immediately threw out his arms toward Lauren. She smiled and touched his hand. "Hey there, cutie. Here, let me help you with that."

Taking the pet carrier that looked more like an expensive purse from Jake, Lauren noted his surprise. She knew he expected her to take the baby, but she was too inexperienced with children to take the risk.

She set the carrier on the floor and unzipped it. A tiny excited ball of fur exited and ran from the entry hall.

"Yapper," Jake called. "Come here."

His stern tone yielded no response.

"I didn't mean for her to run free." Jake placed the diaper bag on the chair and took a step in the direction Yapper had gone.

"She's okay." Lauren grabbed the diaper bag and took his arm. "Fred's in the family room with Daddy. Come on back."

Jake frowned. "Who is Fred?"

"Daddy's dog."

They walked into the open plan kitchen, dining, and family room to find the old bloodhound on his feet growling at the little dog.

"Fred, quiet," her father ordered.

Her mother chuckled as the little dog stood her ground against the larger and older bloodhound. She glanced at Jake. "I take it this is Yapper?"

He nodded. "Yes ma'am. I'll put her back in the carrier." Jake shifted Teddy and reached for the dog that remained just out of his grasp.

Seeing his frustration, Lauren looked at her mom and said, "I told him she's okay."

"Let her be," Suzanne dismissed with a wave of her hand. "Fred's bark is worse than his bite. I'm sure they'll be best friends before the night is over." She held out a hand. "I'm Suzanne."

He shifted Teddy and reached out. "Jake."

With all the excitement, Teddy bounced in his father's arms.

"Hello, sweetie," Suzanne said. She reached for him and then asked, "May I?"

Jake handed over his son. "He's absolutely adorable," she exclaimed. Teddy gave her a big grin. "How old are you, pretty boy?"

"*Dadadada.*" The baby pointed to his father.

"Eight months."

Lauren watched her mother with Teddy. Lauren had never been around babies. She'd missed out on babysitting in her teens, and there had been no siblings or cousins to practice on. Her mother's necklace caught his attention,

247

and he reached for the twinkling diamond. Her mother took the delicate chain from his fingers and dropped it into her shirt. The baby searched for the hidden object, and he worked his fingers indicating he wanted her necklace.

"Isn't he sweet, Laurie?"

She nodded. "Yes ma'am. He's quite the handsome fellow."

The pasta pot boiled over, and Lauren hurried over to handle the situation. After dinner was under control, she found treats for the dogs.

"Here you go, Freddie." She tossed the treat, and the dog barely moved as he snapped it up.

Lauren broke the other treat into smaller pieces and offered them to Yapper who ate more daintily. Soon the two dogs stretched out together on the cool hardwood floor.

When his son started to cry, Jake stood. "I need to feed him. I planned to do it before we came over but ended up making a grocery run after I picked them up."

Suzanne held Teddy while he washed up and pulled jars of peas and applesauce from the diaper bag. He added a spoon and bottle of formula. "Seems no matter how much of this stuff I buy we're always running out."

"Let me have that." Suzanne passed the baby over and took the bottle. "I'll warm it for him."

Jake sat at the island and tied a bib about his son's neck before he opened the jar of peas.

Lauren noted things like the food was cold and there was no plate. He must feed the baby straight from the jar. "Would you like me to heat those up for you?" She indicated the peas.

He pushed the jar in her direction. "Sure. Not long though, or it'll be too hot."

He popped the seal on the applesauce, and the lid clattered on the island. The baby devoured half the container before she returned with the warmed peas in a bowl. Teddy made faces when the food changed.

"Not the same is it, buddy?" Jake asked when he spooned the warm peas into Teddy's mouth.

"He's a good eater," Suzanne said.

"We do lots of food testing. There's some stuff he won't eat. Hates mixed peas and carrots."

Lauren noted her mother's nostalgic expression. "Remember those sessions with Laurie?" she asked her husband.

He smiled and nodded.

"She wasn't picky at all. The problems started when she decided to feed herself. She rubbed food all through her hair and tossed the bowl onto the floor when she'd had enough. I had to bathe her after every meal."

Jake glanced at Lauren. "You wild woman, you."

Suzanne winked at her daughter. "Thankfully, her table manners have improved by leaps and bounds."

Jake gave Teddy his bottle and he soon fell asleep. He cradled his son comfortably in his arms.

"Dinner's ready," Suzanne announced as she placed the platter on the table. She turned an oversized armchair toward the table and folded a throw from the sofa. "Lay him here, Jake. We'll use this chair to block him in case he rolls."

Over the meal, the conversation turned to Jake's first impressions of their business. "You have a quality product and the custom mattresses are a good idea. You need more promotion."

Greg scooped spaghetti onto his plate and added the chicken Parmesan. "Laurie suggested that awhile back. A local channel wanted to do a segment, but I never got around to scheduling it."

"Getting yourself out there in the public eye will make a difference," Jake pointed out. "A mattress is an investment. The public wants the best. You have to show them it's your product."

"Suzanne's better at that kind of thing."

"You could do it, Greg."

Jake cut into the chicken breast and took a bite. "Delicious," he told Suzanne. "You should check with them and see if they're still interested. Free publicity is good."

Lauren grinned when Yapper came over and jumped up, her paws resting on Jake's leg.

"Guess you forgot to feed somebody."

He frowned and nodded. "I got food for her, too. She'll have to eat out of the can."

No feminine touches for the Greer family, Lauren thought. She placed her napkin on the table and went to rummage in the utility room off the kitchen. Lauren returned with a bowl. "This should work."

"That's real china," Jake protested, pushing the fragile saucer back at her.

"Old set we don't use anymore," she explained. "I managed to break most of the pieces, so we got new dishes."

"If you're sure?" His expression told her he wasn't.

"Where's her food?"

He retrieved a small can from the diaper bag and popped the lid. He plunked it into the dish and added a little dry food from a plastic bag. Dismayed by the glob of food, Lauren asked, "Don't you cut it up for her?"

He shrugged. "She eats around the edges until it's gone."

Lauren used a plastic spoon to make the food more appetizing. "There, that's better." She set the bowl on the floor and patted Yapper's tiny head. She barked and nibbled daintily at the miniature dog-sized bites.

They washed their hands and returned to the table.

"I knew we'd be trouble when you invited us to dinner," Jake told Suzanne.

"Not at all. It's been a pleasure meeting your family. What do you do with Teddy and Yapper during the day?"

"Day care until I make other arrangements. I hope to find someone to keep them both."

Greg helped himself to a second serving of cheese bread. "You could bring Teddy to the office."

Jake shook his head. "He demands my attention when we're together. Hard to accomplish anything with a crying baby in tow." He turned the conversation back to plans for the business. "How's employee morale? Have the employees had a recent raise?"

Lauren sipped her tea. "We managed a longevity percentage last Christmas. It was based on their years with the company."

"What was their reaction?"

She glanced at her father and back at Jake and shrugged. "I think they were happy. Most have been with us long enough that it was a decent amount. Enough to offset their Christmas expenses."

"What other perks do they have? Do they promote Sleep Dreams to their family and friends?"

"Regular benefits. Vacation and sick leave. Good health care plan. And most of them have purchased a mattress from the company." Again Lauren glanced at her dad for confirmation. He nodded. "They get a discount on any mattresses they purchase. And a twenty-five-dollar bonus for any referrals that result in a sale if the purchaser gives their name."

Jake nodded. "You say they've been with you for a while?"

"Oh yes," Suzanne said. "A number of them worked for Greg's father. Some have retired and now their children work for us."

"Have you addressed succession planning?"

Greg nodded. "We do considerable cross-training. Older employees work with the younger ones on a regular basis."

"Do their benefits include retirement?"

"We match up to three percent of what they're putting into their plans. Most take advantage of the offer," Lauren said.

Greg smiled at his wife. "Delicious meal, Suze." She patted his hand.

Suzanne stood and took her own and Greg's plate to the sink.

"Finished?" Lauren asked, taking Jake's when he nodded.

Her mother picked up the cake stand from the counter. Lauren brought over the dessert plates.

"A number of small companies have been forced to reduce benefits to help their profit margins."

"We've had to pass on some increases to our employees," Greg admitted, thanking his wife for the slice of cake. "Mainly health insurance, but we'd like to avoid cuts if possible."

Jake took the plate Lauren passed him. "What about layoffs? Have you considered the possibility if sales drop?"

"We'll consider our options if the worst happens," Greg said without hesitation.

"You need to review those options now, Greg. See how benefits figure into the bottom line. You can't wait until you're in trouble."

Greg sighed heavily.

Lauren felt for her father. His generosity would have far-reaching effects on the company's bottom line. If someone didn't act as the voice of reason, he'd give the workers the shirt off his back.

"Lauren has an idea for an advertisement," Suzanne told Jake. "She wants to set up a bed on the beach, one of those iron canopy beds with sheer curtains blowing in the breeze. There's a couple asleep on a Sleep Dreams mattress with peaceful smiles while the waves roll in and out." She looked at Lauren. "What was your slogan?"

"Make every night as restful as a tropical vacation," she offered tentatively.

Jake's brows shot up with approval. "I like it. Let's see what we can do with that."

Teddy woke, and her mom rose from the table and took him into the family room. From his laughter, Lauren knew the baby was happy.

Jake insisted on helping with the dishes. They loaded and started the dishwasher. Jake wiped the dinner table, pushing the crumbs into his hand. Rinsing the dishcloth, he folded it over the sink divider. They picked up their tea glasses and joined the others.

Yapper tormented Fred until he snapped at her.

"He's going to eat her alive if she keeps that up."

"He won't hurt her," Lauren said. "Fred knows she's a puppy."

Jake shook his head. "She's three years old."

"But she's so little," Lauren said, picking Yapper up and cuddling her. "The perfect size to carry around. She can't weigh more than four or five pounds."

"She fit into the palm of my hand when we first got her. One of Gwen's girlfriends had a pup and she had to have one."

Lauren pulled the hair about the dog's face up into a little ponytail. "You should tie it up with a pink bow."

Jake grimaced. "I don't think so."

Lauren grinned. "She's a girl. We like pink. Don't we?" The dog yipped in agreement.

"All that hair is a pain. I have to brush her several times a week or it gets matted. Honestly, it's like having two little kids to care for. At times, she demands more attention than Teddy.

"You should see her wardrobe," he continued. "Gwen insisted clothes were a necessity because Yapper got cold easily."

That surprised Lauren. She thought of the times she'd played dress up with her dolls. His wife had done the same with their dog. "You dress her?"

"No way. I left them in a box in my uncle's garage. Yapper's going au naturel with me."

The conversation picked up again and around eight thirty, Jake said it was time to go. He packed up and took Teddy from Suzanne.

"Thanks for the wonderful dinner. Best meal I've had in a while."

"Thank you. Come again soon. I've enjoyed spending time with you and Teddy. And Yapper."

Lauren stood and said, "I'll help you get everything to the car."

She carried Yapper and paused in the kitchen to pick up the bag of goodies her mother had packed for Jake to have later.

In the entry hall, Lauren gave the dog a final pat before placing her in the carrier. She grabbed the handle and led the way to his vehicle.

She opened the back door and secured Yapper's bag with a seat belt as Jake fastened Teddy into his car seat. Lauren set the food on the floorboard. "Don't forget this."

Jake grinned and said, "It probably won't make it into the fridge."

She looked at him and asked, "Is Sleep Dreams in trouble?"

"That's why I'm here," Jake said. "To ensure it never is."

Chapter 3

G ood morning."

Jake entered her office at eight a.m. on Monday morning carrying two large cups of coffee. "Caramel mocha," he said, placing one on her desk. "Do you have time to review a couple of reports later this morning?"

Lauren looked at the cup with longing before she smiled and pushed it back at him. "Sorry, only water or decaf coffee and tea for me. I'm available around eleven. Will that work?"

He pulled up his calendar on his phone and nodded. "Looks good. We can have lunch in the cafeteria."

"Ashleigh can have them bring something to my office," Lauren offered.

Jake shook his head. "You need to eat with the employees whenever possible. Open a dialogue with them, improve operations and morale."

"Daddy does. . ."

"Greg, too," Jake interrupted. "It's a family business, Lauren. Make them feel like part of your family and you'll reap the benefits."

Unconsciously her brow furrowed. "What if I have an attack? They'll be uncomfortable and so will I."

"You need to let them know about your condition."

Startled, Lauren declared, "No way. The fewer people who know, the better."

"It's nothing to be ashamed about."

"You don't understand. People look at you differently when they're aware of weird medical conditions." Poor, pitiful Lauren wasn't the way she wanted to live. "I don't want anyone feeling sorry for me. Particularly the people who work here. I have an image to uphold."

Jake stared at her. She wanted to turn away but couldn't.

"You're too proud to accept that someone might care you have this condition that forces you to hide yourself away from life?"

It had nothing to do with pride. She wanted people to care about her as a normal person.

Lauren glanced down at her desk, her voice low as she said, "People get weirded out when they witness others losing control. They don't know what to do so they turn their heads and later whisper about this pitiful woman who shouldn't be out in public."

He frowned. "Don't you just fall asleep?"

If only it were that simple. Maybe she should explain the variables associated with her condition. "Tell me it wouldn't freak you out if I fell asleep in

253

the middle of this conversation. Maybe kept on writing or using the calculator while I appear to be asleep?"

"You can do that?"

Lauren nodded. "I've seen pads where I kept writing until it became illegible."

Her gaze shifted over the powerful set of his shoulders. How would he deal with the life she lived on a daily basis? Not much differently, she decided. Narcolepsy could drop a man his size as easily as it did her.

"Before I knew, maybe," Jake admitted. "Knowledge is power, Lauren. Making these people aware would offer you more protection. They wouldn't let anyone hurt you."

There were very few people she trusted with the knowledge that she wasn't always in control. She didn't fool herself that every employee relished the opportunity to help the boss's daughter through her sleep attacks. "How can you be so sure of that? People with narcolepsy have been taken advantage of when they were at their weakest. When I'm having an attack, I'm as helpless as Teddy. Would you hand him over to a stranger and expect them to take care of him?"

"No," he conceded.

"I have trust issues. Blame them on the school friends who fell into fits of giggles when I had an attack. Or to the guy who invited me to his prom and then deserted me. His girlfriend told him he was insensitive, and he got it into his head that inviting me to the prom would make her see him as more sensitive. I had to call Daddy to pick me up."

Jake grimaced. "I'm sorry, Lauren, but hiding yourself away from hurt isn't the answer. When you work through fiscal problems here at the plant, do you stop after one try? Or do you keep going until you find a solution?"

"I keep going."

He nodded. "You have to do the same with your life."

"I'm not sure I'm that strong. It hurts too much."

"So you'd rather have no life?"

She took a shaky breath. "I have a life, Jake."

"Do you really? You limited your world. Denied yourself the things you wanted. Told yourself you couldn't have them. What if you could?"

"And what if I can't?" The hazel eyes fixed on him. Challenging him to answer.

Impasse. He didn't understand her world. And she couldn't explain.

"You could take short jaunts into the cafeteria. Pick up the food yourself. Make a point of speaking to a different group of people each time."

Frustrated, Lauren asked, "Why don't you conduct a survey on their perception of our family? Of me?"

"And what if they think you feel you're too good to associate with them?"

"That's not fair."

He sighed. "They don't know why you hide from them."

"I don't hide."

Even with the strength of her denial, Lauren knew she lied. She might tell herself that was the case, but she couldn't put herself out there for the world to point fingers at and mock. She'd experienced people laughing at her when she was at her most vulnerable. She never wanted to hear the sound again.

"Okay, Lauren. You have to decide when you're going to stop secreting yourself from the world. I'll be back at eleven."

He rose, took the second cup of coffee, and walked out, closing the door behind him.

That hurt. Despite the short time she'd known him, Lauren couldn't believe Jake would say that to her. He acted as though he understood, but he didn't. He'd never walked in her shoes, lived with her condition. He couldn't begin to understand the necessity of protecting yourself from hurt.

Hadn't her disorder destroyed her childhood friendships? Parents didn't want their children playing with kids who were liabilities. They didn't want the responsibility, and no matter how often her mother reassured them Lauren was the same girl she'd always been, they avoided her.

Over the years, Lauren and her mother had become best friends. They had done so much together. Her mom even accompanied her on the few trips she'd taken as an adult. Lauren sometimes wondered if her dad had felt pushed out of the relationship with his wife or accepted it had to be this way because she was his child, too. She worked hard not to come between her parents. Mostly she felt like a third wheel. She was always there, in the midst of their lives; everything they planned included her, just as it had when she was little. They wouldn't do anything without assuring themselves she was safe.

Perhaps she should go to the cafeteria with Jake, Lauren thought. What he'd said about secreting herself in her office hurt, but it was true. She was too afraid to risk divulging the truth about herself.

When he returned, Jake said nothing of their earlier discussion. Lauren went over the reports in great detail, and they wrapped up their meeting a few minutes after noon.

"Thanks for your help. I needed to be sure I was interpreting the data correctly." He glanced at his watch. "Did Ashleigh order lunch?"

Lauren shook her head. "We're going to the cafeteria."

His penetrating blue-green gaze fixed on her. "Are you sure?"

She wished she felt as confident as Jake. "No."

"If you feel an attack coming on, let me know and I'll get you out of there."

"If there's time." Lauren left the comment open-ended. Though she usually recognized the signs of onset with an attack, she had no idea whether she could manage an escape once it started. "Look after me if it happens."

Jake appeared less confident.

She rose and walked around the desk. "Come on. Let's get this over with."

"You make it sound as though I'm doing something terrible to you," Jake protested.

Ashleigh was not at her desk. Lauren paused to write a note and stuck it on the phone.

"It's my decision," she told him.

"Because I pushed you?"

She didn't respond.

As they walked into the cafeteria, Jake said softly, "Remember, these people care about you and your family. They depend on you for their living. You need to learn to depend on them."

She sensed Jake appraising her interaction with the employees.

"These seats taken?" he asked the two men sitting at the large table.

"No," the older man said. "Help yourself."

Jake set the tray on the table and pulled out her chair.

"I'm Jacob Greer. I'm working with the Kingsleys to improve company production. You know Lauren Kingsley." The two men nodded in her direction. "We'd like to hear anything you'd care to share about the company."

It took a few minutes, but the two men eventually opened up. Mostly they sang praises for Sleep Dreams. "Best job I ever had," the man named Wade announced. "Fair salary, good working conditions, and people who care. Jimmy here had some health problems earlier in the year, and Mr. Kingsley called to check on him regularly. Asked if he needed help. Not many bosses willing to do that."

The men's comments boosted her spirits. When morale was low, the workers groused about their working environment. Her father preferred they be happy and content. Sometimes he went too far in his efforts to help them, but that was her dad.

The men stood and picked up their trays. "Need to get back to work. Nice meeting you, Mr. Greer. Good seeing you, Miss Lauren."

"Good seeing you, too, Wade, Jimmy."

The lunch break had passed quickly. When Jake opened her office door, he asked, "That wasn't so bad, was it?"

Tell that to my pounding heart, Lauren thought. "It wasn't bad."

"It gets easier with practice," Jake told her.

"Let's hope so."

"I've been thinking about the television program. Why didn't you offer to do the show?"

"Oh I couldn't," Lauren protested.

"Why not?"

"The stress. . ."

She couldn't begin to imagine how her condition would react to her doing something so out of line with her normal practices.

His brows lifted. "Are you afraid?"

"I'm not exactly the best spokesperson for Sleep Dreams."

His gaze shifted over her face. "You're attractive, personable, and well-spoken. I think you'd be the perfect person to do the show."

While she appreciated his compliments, Lauren couldn't believe he couldn't see the truth for himself. "It would be too stressful. Mom can do it. She's good at things like that."

Jake shrugged and said, "Someone should. Any promotion is good for your company."

"I plan to call and ask if they're still interested."

He nodded. "Do you have any customer testimonials on file?"

"We have mail. And the comments on the website. They're positive for the most part. A couple of disgruntled customers, but that's to be expected."

"I'd like to see them."

"I'll have Ashleigh bring the file to you." She walked into her office, thinking Jake would leave. He stuck his head back inside and asked, "Can you stay late tonight? I need your help with the accounts."

"What about Teddy?"

"I made arrangements for him to stay late at day care. Yapper's overnighting at the doggie care place."

"Sure. How late? I'll tell Daddy so he can pick me up."

"I can drive you home."

Lauren smiled. "I'm sure he'll appreciate not having to come back out. It's times like this when I wish I had my license."

"What's stopping you?"

The question hammered at her. She told him the truth. "I never learned to drive."

"Would they give you a license?"

"If a doctor signed off that I'm okay to drive."

"I'll teach you if you like."

Stunned, Lauren said, "I'll pray about it."

He nodded. "Good idea. Where do you attend church?"

"Peace."

"I'd like to find a church home for Teddy and myself."

It pleased her that Jake was a believer. "You're welcome anytime. We have a large nursery. Teddy would be happy there."

"Give me the address," he requested.

❧

"Jake offered to teach me to drive," Lauren announced when she came into the family room that night.

Her parents looked at each other and back at her.

Lauren held up one hand. "I know what you're thinking, but I checked and I can have a driver's license as long as my narcolepsy is under control. I think I might like to give it a try. Daddy, will you help me find a cheap used car to drive? I don't want to risk damaging Jake's vehicle."

"Use my old truck," he suggested.

"Are you sure? You love that truck."

"I love you more. So don't dent yourself."

Lauren chuckled. "That's the plan. Jake says we'll find a secluded road so I can get plenty of practice."

"You could drive around the farm," her mother said. "I learned on those dirt roads surrounding the fields. I doubt you'll find anywhere more secluded."

Lauren hadn't visited the farm since her grandmother passed away a few months earlier. "That's perfect. Jake says he'll find a babysitter. I told him I'd pay."

"Have him bring them over," her mother said. "I'll babysit in exchange for your driving lessons."

Lauren met her mother's smile with one of her own. "I will. I invited him to church. Told him I needed to pray over learning to drive, and he said it was a good idea. Even if I master driving, I have to consider what could happen if I experienced an attack while behind the wheel."

"Why haven't you ever told us you wanted to learn to drive?"

She shrugged. "I suppose this is one of those times when I thought why not instead of no way."

Chapter 4

On Saturday, Jake drove them out to the farm. Lauren directed him to the shed where her father parked his old truck. When he'd gone to trade vehicles, the dealership hadn't offered him much in a trade-in and he opted to keep the truck. Her mother used it occasionally for work, and they loaned it to friends when their vehicles were out of service.

As she stood in the farmyard, memories of the times she'd spent here flooded Lauren. She'd played with the cats and dog in this yard, swung in the old white swing in the garden, and climbed the old tree by the house, though she'd been too afraid to climb back down. She'd ridden the fields on her grandfather's tractor and wandered the farm in exploration.

Later, when fear kept her closer to home, the adults encouraged Lauren to come see the new farm animals and explore. She missed her friends and didn't understand the changes, but they did everything they could to make her life as normal as possible.

"You ready?"

She turned back to where Jake stood and nodded. Once in the truck, he followed Lauren's directions, and they bumped along the dirt and grass track running alongside the field. Jake parked underneath the big tree Lauren knew had shaded farmers for many generations.

"First, I need to teach you the basics."

He unhooked his seat belt and leaned closer to remove the manual from the glove compartment. As Jake covered the various components of the truck, Lauren grew impatient. "I know all this."

He appeared doubtful. Lauren wondered if his behavior would be stereotypical of parents teaching their children to drive.

"I do," she repeated. "I read all the time. I read the manual years ago while waiting on Daddy."

"That's good, but we're doing this my way. Sometimes manuals are not clear, and I want to be sure you understand."

She frowned at him and Jake laughed. "Stop that or I'll think you're not old enough to learn how to drive."

Lauren paid attention and repeated the information to his satisfaction. Jake opened the door and climbed out.

"Okay, slide behind the wheel. Adjust the mirrors and seat so you're comfortable."

Suddenly her palms grew moist. "Ah, Jake, maybe. . ."

"Come on, Lauren. Don't chicken out on me now. You can do this."

She slipped across the seat and sat stiffly behind the steering wheel. Was she doing the right thing? She looked at Jake again. He wasn't going to let her back out. He told her to fasten her seat belt, and went around to the passenger side. He settled in the middle of the bench seat.

Very aware of his presence, Lauren mumbled, "There's no seat belt there."

"We won't get ticketed back here."

"True, but I'd feel better knowing you're secure."

His eyes were gentle, understanding. "And I need to be able to take the wheel or hit the brake pedal if you lose control. I can't do that over there."

She pulled a face. "Okay, but hold on."

Their arms brushed and Lauren drew in a deep breath, so aware of him she could hardly concentrate.

"Check your mirrors and turn your head to look behind you. It never hurts to walk around the vehicle to check for kids and pets. Okay, turn the ignition key."

The truck started up immediately.

"Now place your foot on the brake pedal and pull the gear lever into drive."

He leaned closer and pointed to the *D* indicator on the column. Lauren drew a deep breath. If he came any closer, he was going to push her out of the vehicle.

"Now give it some gas." Jake's soft command seemed to brush her ear. The vehicle surged forward.

"Lightly," he yelped.

Lauren jammed the brake pedal, jerking them forward again.

Jake touched his neck and said, "Slow and easy, Lauren."

Calm down, she told herself. *You can do this.*

She gripped the steering wheel and focused on keeping the truck on the road. A thrill of excitement filled her when they crept along the grass and dirt track.

Their journey moved from slow to fast as she struggled to adjust her foot on the accelerator. Driving and ignoring Jake took every bit of Lauren's concentration. One time he grabbed the wheel when she hit a rut and bounced out of the tracks and into the edge of the field.

"Okay, let's turn around. See that layby up ahead? When you get closer, pull over and turn around."

She did as he instructed. Jake seemed as surprised as Lauren when the wheels sank into the sandy soil. He groaned and climbed out to find the rear tires buried.

"Let's see if we can free ourselves. I'll push. You drive forward."

Lauren drew a deep breath and pressed the gas. The tires slung sand everywhere, and Jake yelled for her to stop. She jerked her foot from the pedal.

He stepped back, brushing sand from his face and hair. "Put it in reverse. Let's see if we can rock it back and forth."

Lauren was terrified. "I've got my phone. I can call Daddy," she yelled out the open window.

"Come on, Lauren. Trust me. We can do this," Jake shouted back.

Determination raised his chin and fired his gaze. This sand wasn't about to stop him. His tenacity came as no surprise. It had been so long since she trusted anyone but her parents. Lauren pressed the gas pedal and moved the truck backward.

"That's good. Do it again."

She clutched the steering wheel, the tips of her fingers white with strain. The truck moved a bit farther.

"Okay, put it in drive and gun it."

The engine strained as if bound by some mighty force. Jake jumped clear of the truck.

"Good job," he yelled after she drove several feet down the road before stopping.

Lauren shoved the gear into park, released her seat belt, and climbed out. Jake grabbed her close, and her feet left the ground as he swung her about. "You did it. You got the truck out."

"You pushed."

He shook his head. "Not that last time when you reversed and then went forward. You shot out of there like a rocket. Ready to continue?"

Wobbly from the experience, she shook her head. "I think I've done enough for my first attempt."

"You have to get back into the driver's seat when something like this happens. I'll turn the truck around and you can drive back to the end of the road."

She drove all the way back to the house and stopped in the driveway.

He touched her shoulder. "Good job, Lauren. You're a natural."

She didn't believe that for one minute. Right now, all she could think was that she'd not had an attack during a stressful situation.

Jake studied the small frame house and asked, "Who lives here?"

"No one. It was my grandparents' home. Gramps died a couple of years ago and Gram a few months back."

The house gleamed white with the fresh coat of paint it had received at the first of the summer. The trim was crimson red. Her mother planned to fix the house up and rent it out. The land had been leased to another farmer earlier in the year by her grandmother.

"Nice place."

"Come on inside. There's soda in the fridge."

Lauren opened the door with a key on the ring she carried. They stepped into the sunny kitchen. Boxes littered the room where her mom had attempted to begin the process of going through her parents' possessions.

Taking two bottles from the ancient fridge, Lauren passed him one and twisted off the cap of the other one. She pulled a chair about and sat down at the table.

"Mind if I look at the rest of the place?" Jake asked.

She stood. "I'll give you the nickel tour."

The house was small by most people's standards. An eat-in kitchen, living room, den, two bedrooms, and a bath and three-quarters. Her grandfather had converted a section of the wraparound porch into a combination mudroom/bathroom for them, leaving the original bathroom for their daughter.

"Mom's room," Lauren announced, indicating the small room. "You should have seen it before she had it painted. It was a very rich, royal purple. Her favorite color. I slept in here when I stayed with them. I liked the color, too."

"Perfect size room for a kid." He glanced around again. "You think your mom would consider renting the place short-term? It would be great for us. And I could help with the renovation. I'm a good painter."

Lauren studied him closely, realizing he was serious. "You could ask. Though I think it might be awhile before she sorts through everything. Mom's finding it hard going at this stage. I suggested she leave the house empty or let us put their things in storage until she's ready."

"I think I will ask. I could see us fitting in here. We can live with things just as they are."

They locked the house, and Jake parked her dad's truck back in the shed. They didn't talk much on the ride home. Lauren unlocked the door to her parents' Front Street historical home, and they went inside. Her mother was in the family room.

Suzanne looked up from the house photos on her laptop. "How did it go?"

"She did great," Jake enthused.

Lauren pointed out somewhat dryly, "I got us bogged down in a field."

"But we got out," Jake said.

"Optimist," Lauren muttered.

Suzanne laughed. "I'm glad it went well. Fred and Yapper need to be walked."

Lauren went to get the bloodhound's leash and met Jake at the door of the family room. "You want to take Teddy?"

"He's asleep," Suzanne said. "Poor little guy had a miserable afternoon. He's teething."

Jake grimaced. "Sorry."

Suzanne nodded. "I gave him an ice cube in a cloth and it seemed to help."

"Really? I'll pick up a teething ring. And some baby acetaminophen. That reminds me. I need a pediatrician. Any suggestions?" He took the leash from Lauren and knelt to secure it to Fred's collar. He patted the dog. "Come on, fella. Time for a walk."

Everyone chuckled when the old dog's expression seemed to be something less than approval.

"Laurie's pediatrician is still practicing. I can give you the name and number."

"This parenting stuff is a challenge. Gwen handled everything."

"You're doing fine," Suzanne said. "Parenting is a learn-as-you-go process. No manuals for kids."

Jake feigned surprise. "Don't tell me that. I get all my development stuff off the Internet."

Suzanne burst into laughter. "Just don't get paranoid if he doesn't do something when the experts say he should. Kids develop at their own pace."

Lauren felt an overwhelming desire to have her mother share information with her regarding a grandchild. A child she might never be able to provide. Yapper barked and Fred growled.

"Come on, Jake. We'll be back soon, Mom," she said, feeling suddenly anxious to escape their conversation.

"Want to stay for dinner?" Suzanne called over her shoulder.

He paused and grinned back at her. "You know I can't turn down a home-cooked meal. If I never saw another container of takeout or fast food, I wouldn't care."

"We'll throw together a meal when you get back."

They let themselves out the side door and walked around to the sidewalk. Jake studied her parents' two-storied house with two porches and a widow's walk. "I like this house."

"It's been said Beaufort architecture was influenced by that of the Bahamas. Planters built their summer homes here to escape the heat and conduct their sea-related endeavors. Mostly wooden construction and white paint. The houses were often built by shipwrights. They knew how to build a house to stand up to the weather."

Across Front Street, past the sidewalk and piers, Taylor Creek sparkled and flashed like diamonds in the sunlight.

"Here," Jake said, passing her Yapper's leash. "You take her. I'll take Fred."

"You worried that good old Fred's gonna drag me down the street?" Lauren chuckled at the thought. "Or that someone will challenge your manhood because of your sissy dog?"

"Fred needs a stronger hand than Yapper."

This time Lauren roared with laughter. "Fat chance. He ambles along without a care in the world. A fifteen-minute walk takes an hour if I don't keep him moving."

Jake knelt and rubbed the dog's head. "I like Fred. He's a real man's dog."

"Yeah, we love him. He's getting on in years. Daddy brought him home as a puppy about eight years ago."

The afternoon was gorgeous, not a dark cloud in the sky as the sun beat down on them. They laughed about the cold front that moved through and dropped the temps from the high to low nineties. There was a slight breeze as they strolled along the sidewalk.

Dressed for the summer heat, Lauren wore knee-length shorts with a sleeveless print blouse and sandals. Jake wore cargo shorts with a golf shirt and flip-flops. A cap bearing the embroidered Sleep Dreams logo hid his dark hair.

Homes gave way to the business district, and they passed a number of shops filled with tourists.

"There's the North Carolina Maritime Museum," Lauren told him. "They have classes and build boats."

Jake nodded. "You ever gone on the Ghost Walk?"

"No."

"I was reading about it last night. They go to Blackbeard's home?"

"Yes, Hammock House. It's the oldest house in Beaufort."

They strolled in silence for a while before Jake asked, "Aren't you charged by your first driving lesson? I remember feeling like I could take on the world after my first time."

She glanced at him. Obviously Jake thought she'd show more enthusiasm for their adventure. "Yeah. Sort of."

He stopped walking. "It's a beginning, Lauren. What other things did you want to do?"

She hesitated, wondering why she felt compelled to share facts about herself with him.

"Come on, tell me." Jake nudged her playfully. "Surely there's more you want to experience in life."

Could she even begin to list all the things she'd considered? "Well, I'd like a place of my own," Lauren admitted. "A house. Not an apartment."

Jake nodded. "What else?"

"Maybe take more online college classes. And make some friends," she admitted shyly. "Mom and Dad are great, but I haven't had friends my age since I was diagnosed with narcolepsy."

"What happened to them?"

"I told you. It's too much for some people. Mom home-schooled me and we did some group things, but mostly it was just us."

He captured her hand. "Do you go anywhere to meet people?"

"Church and even there I keep to myself."

"Do the people at church know about your condition? Pray for you?"

"The pastor knows."

"What do you think people are going to do if you tell them the truth?"

She'd walked this path too many times not to know the answer. "They'll be afraid to hang out with me. I don't want to make people feel uncomfortable or have them making fun of me over something I can't control."

"You really worry that people will react negatively if you have an attack?"

She knew it to be a fact. She'd lived with this disorder long enough to know what reactions to expect. People might show genuine concern in the moment, but later when they recapped the experience, it became a joke. "I've met a few people online who have narcolepsy and we e-mail and chat. They understand."

"How does Ashleigh treat you?"

Yapper shot underneath Fred's leash. Lauren handed over the leash and moved to Jake's other side. He handed it back. "Like her boss. She's respectful and polite but keeps her distance."

Jake paused while Fred investigated a tree. "She wasn't happy that first day when she said I shouldn't be in your office. She called your dad. If Ashleigh didn't care, she'd have gone back to her desk and kept her mouth shut. Not risked getting me in trouble."

That didn't surprise her. "Could be she didn't want to get into trouble with Daddy. He made it clear that her job is to help me do my job." Lauren tugged the leash gently to bring Yapper back from her wandering. They passed two women who grinned at her and said, "Cute dog."

Lauren smiled back at them. "I like Ashleigh. She's a fun person. Keeps something going all the time. She volunteers and organizes lots of events at the office, and she's very popular with the other administrative staff. I often see them going to lunch together."

"How old are you? Twenty-five or so?"

"I turned twenty-seven on July first."

"Maybe you should suggest having lunch sometime. You're closer to her age. You have to give people a chance," Jake encouraged, "or you'll never find those you can trust."

"It's scary." She couldn't begin to explain how she dreaded activities outside the norm.

"I'm sure it is. Think about this, Lauren. If something happened to your parents, who would you depend on? You have to learn to be self-sufficient. They aren't doing you any favors with their coddling."

Offended, Lauren protested, "I do my part."

"I like your parents, but I think maybe they've protected you from too much."

In that instant, she wanted to tell Jake to mind his own business and stay out of her life. He couldn't begin to understand. "They do what they feel is best. You do the same for Teddy."

"Teddy's a baby," Jake said, coming to a halt. "That's something else. Why won't you hold him?"

Where had that question come from? Lauren flushed and glanced down at Yapper. "I don't know anything about children. I've never been around them."

"Kids adapt pretty quickly. If Teddy doesn't like something, he'll let you know."

She looked at him. "You should be afraid he could get hurt. Or left unsupervised if I had an attack. We need to head back. Mom expects us to help with dinner."

Upon realizing they were going home, Fred picked up his pace. Lauren considered what Jake had said. She'd watched movies and read books that gave her a glimpse of what other women experienced, not what she herself would feel. She prayed that God would send her someone to love, but as each day passed, it became more difficult to believe her knight in shining armor would ride into her world and make everything perfect.

In a very short time, Jake had pushed his way into her life and seemed to want her independence more than she did. He came off as a good friend who cared about her, but Lauren questioned his motivation. Why did Jake want her to be independent of her parents?

She opened the door and they stepped into the cool house.

Jake scooped up Yapper, disconnected the leash, and started to place her in the carrier.

"Don't do that." She took the little dog from him. Yapper lapped kisses of joy on Lauren's face. "We don't mind her running free."

"She'll irritate Fred. Besides, she's so tiny she could get hurt if someone doesn't realize she's there."

"Maybe he needs to be irritated. And she makes sure we know she's there. Do you have food?"

"In the car. I made a grocery store run earlier."

Lauren rolled her eyes. This man must spend his paycheck at the grocery. Seemed he shopped every day. "You should buy case lots. It would save you a fortune."

He flashed a wry smile. "Definitely cheaper than those late-night runs to the convenience store."

Lauren gasped. "You don't."

Sheepish, he admitted, "Sometimes. We run out of stuff. The convenience store is closer."

"You could use our membership at the wholesale club in Jacksonville. I'd be glad to go with you anytime. It's important to save money when you have a family."

"Thanks, Lauren. I might take you up on your offer."

"And thank you for what you did today," Lauren said.

"You did really well. I think we should get you a manual so you can study for your driving test. You can get a permit and once you're more comfortable driving on the highway, you could drive with your parents or a licensed adult."

"I found the manual online last night," she admitted.

They went into the kitchen, and her mother started issuing tasks like a drill sergeant. "Jake, the grill is hot. Throw those steaks on. Laurie, you can prepare the salad. Make that honey mustard dressing we like. I have potato wedges with olive oil and herbs roasting in the oven, and I prepared some of the corn we picked up over the weekend."

Her mother had fed Teddy, and now the baby played on a blanket in the family room.

Over dinner, they talked about her first driving experience and getting stuck in the sand. "She wanted to call you," Jake told Greg, "but we kept trying. You should have seen her. She handled it like a pro."

Greg glanced at his daughter. "Did you like driving?"

"For the most part. There was a time or two when I wasn't so sure."

There was reassurance in the smile her mother shared with her. "We've all been there. Learning to drive has its ups and downs, but it's quite an accomplishment once you master it."

Jake nodded and bit into an ear of corn. Afterward, he asked, "Did Lauren ever tell you she wants to fix up a little place of her own? A house?"

Suzanne looked dumbfounded. "No. Why haven't you told us this before?"

Lauren glared at Jake. Why had he done that?

"He asked about my life goals," she defended, emphasizing, "and it's a dream, a hope for one day. Not something I plan to rush out and do tomorrow."

"I suppose we could have converted the carriage house into an apartment for you," her mother said a couple of minutes later.

Lauren loved her bedroom. The large room had its own bath and closet with a window seat overlooking the waterfront. She'd spent hours curled up there, reading, watching television, listening to music, working on her laptop, even watching the waterfront.

"No." She glanced at Jake, giving him a silent *Look what you've done.* "I wondered what it would be like to have a place of my own. A small house where I could change the color or rearrange the furniture every week if I wanted."

Her dad harrumphed. "You obviously never painted. It's one of those less-is-better tasks. Right up there with rearranging furniture."

Lauren laughed. "You know what I mean, Daddy."

"You can repaint your room anytime you want."

She and her mother had redone the room a couple of years before. "It's fine, Mom. Really it is."

"What about one of the rental properties? There's that cute Victorian a couple of streets over. The tenants gave notice and will be moving by the end of September."

Lauren shook her head. "No. I wouldn't take advantage of you that way. If I thought I could manage, I'd have you find something I could afford."

"The house will be yours one day, Lauren. But if you prefer, you could pay rent. Let's see how you feel over the next few weeks and if things go well, your dad and I will help you paint the interior of the house any color you like."

She didn't know what to say. For years she'd fantasized about having her own place, thinking it an impossibility, and now all of a sudden everyone seemed to think it had become an achievable goal. Did she want to be alone when the attacks happened? It wasn't like having her own place would change anything. She would talk to her parents after Jake left. Make them understand her insecurities when it came to living on her own.

"Speaking of houses," Jake said to Suzanne, "Lauren showed me your parents' place today. I was wondering if you'd consider renting it short-term. I want to find a home and hire someone to stay with Teddy and Yapper while I work. You don't know anyone, do you?"

Suzanne nodded. "I might. A friend at church lost her job last year and hasn't been able to find anything. She's going stir-crazy and wants something to occupy her days. I could give you her number. You remember Mrs. Hart, don't you, Laurie?"

She remembered the woman well. Geraldine Hart had been her Sunday school teacher when she was a little girl. Lauren played with her daughter and stayed overnight in their home. Her friendship with Melissa Hart ended after Lauren's diagnosis. "She makes great cookies."

"I'll give her a call. So what about the house? We could live with it as it is."

Suzanne reached for her husband's plate and stacked it on top of her own. "I planned a few upgrades. I need to paint the kitchen and den and the porches and rockers. I'd also like to replace the appliances and tile the bathrooms."

"I could help with the renovation. I can paint," he added, sounding enthusiastic. "You buy the supplies and I'll provide the labor. I have some experience with tile, but you'd probably be better off with a professional."

"You've got a deal," Greg said quickly.

Suzanne laughed at her husband's eagerness to escape his most hated chore. "You're not getting off that easily. You can help."

"How much rental property do you have?" Jake asked.

"Five houses. I inherited my parents' place and two houses that belonged to my mother's aunts. I ran across the other two houses in the course of my work. As long as I keep the right tenants in place, they provide a good income. That's why I check references and require a security deposit."

Jake grinned broadly and said, "Well, you know where to find me. And we would take good care of the place. Yapper's housebroken, but I can restrict her to certain areas."

"Oh, don't do that," Suzanne said. "Mom and Dad had a dog. A retriever named Goldie. He slept in front of the fireplace." She chuckled and said, "If possible, he was lazier than Fred."

Lauren listened to their exchange as she chewed the final bite of her steak. It seemed her mother was giving the idea serious consideration. She doubted her mom could refuse Jake's hopeful expression.

"So you'll consider renting to me?"

"I need to do something with their things, but I don't see any reason you couldn't live there. In fact, I'll rent it fully furnished with the kitchen stuff and linens if you want."

"Perfect. We travel light. After Gwen died, I decided we didn't need the house. We moved what little furniture I kept into my uncle's loft apartment in New Mexico."

Lauren wanted to ask if he ever thought of settling down someplace but decided that was too personal. Obviously he'd eschewed the home his wife had made for their family in favor of practicality.

"I'll clean it out so you can move in next weekend," Suzanne said.

"Lauren mentioned that you were taking your time sorting through stuff," Jake began. "Teddy and I can live around anything you want to leave."

"That's sweet of you to offer, but there's a lot of stuff in the house that needs to go. I plan to donate their clothes to the church clothes closet. And they wanted Lauren to have their dining room table and china cabinet and the bedroom furniture. It's been in the family for generations."

"No sense putting it in storage when Jake can use it now," Lauren said.

Her mother nodded. "I'll pack up the china and Mama's bird collection. . ."

She choked up and Lauren quickly said, "I can do that. Daddy can take me over tomorrow after work."

"I'll take you," Jake said. "And I can use a broom or vacuum and dust. Let us handle this for you."

Lauren rested one hand on her mother's shoulder. "Yeah, Mom, we won't throw out anything."

"I'm their executrix, Laurie. I have to go through the papers and handle the legal stuff."

She remembered her mother doing the basic things required of the estate when her grandmother died. "I could box up everything and bring it here. I'll even organize it."

Her mother's warm smile encompassed them both. "I have to do it. I'll get started Tuesday."

Lauren glanced at her father. "Everything's under control at work. Okay if I help Mom?"

He nodded.

"Only if you have the time," Suzanne cautioned. "Don't get behind on my account."

Lauren glanced at Jake, wondering if he was going to object to her absence. He didn't say anything.

"We should have thought about you needing a place to stay before now," Suzanne said. "Living out of suitcases is a pain. I'd offer you Lauren's old crib, but I doubt it meets today's standards."

"Teddy had a nursery when Gwen was alive. The loft apartment wasn't big enough for his furniture. I'll get a crib for the house."

"Are you okay with the other furnishings? There might be some pieces here if you wanted something different."

"Everything looked good to me," Jake said quickly. "I'm going to call your friend and see if she's interested in caring for Teddy and Yapper at the house. Thank you all. I can't tell you how much this helps."

"We're glad to have you with us," Greg told him as Suzanne served the chocolate silk pie she had made that afternoon.

Chapter 5

S ure you're up to this?" Lauren asked as her mother unlocked the door.
        "Putting it off won't help. Plus, once we give Jake access, he'll do some of the work, which will save us money. I should let him stay rent free in exchange for his labor."

Lauren felt sad for her mom. She knew this would be difficult for her. "I don't think Jake would agree. Maybe you can charge him rent and no deposit instead."

"Maybe," her mother murmured thoughtfully.

"Where do we start?"

"We need to attack this room by room. I want Mom's china and bird collection out of the dining room. We'll leave the everyday stuff in the kitchen for Jake. Chuck those old pots and pans. You know how Mom was about holding on to everything."

"That new set is probably still in the box."

"They were expensive, too. Wonder what kind of cook Jake is? Maybe we should find him a cheaper set and you can take those for your place."

"Mom, I..." The urge to smack Jake grew stronger with each reference to her moving out. She hadn't gotten around to talking to them yet.

"I know, Laurie. It's not my intention to rush you, but we're willing to help if that's what you want. In fact, take anything of your grandmother's you'd like to have. We can put it in storage until you're ready."

"I'm in no hurry."

They moved systematically through the kitchen, sorting plasticware, recycled bags, dumping the junk drawer, sorting through the dish towels and other items.

"I never understood why Mom didn't toss this stuff," Suzanne said. "She had better."

Lauren shrugged. "I'm sure she planned to bleach out the stains, and you know everything in the junk drawer always has a purpose."

Her mother opened the cabinet and loaded the dishes into the dishwasher. She ripped the paper from the emptied shelf and tossed it toward the trash can. "We need new shelf liner. This hasn't been replaced recently."

Then she removed a handful of mismatched stainless silverware from the drawer. "I think this will be okay. Mom's silver chest is in the dining room. Don't let me forget that." The utensils clinked as she dropped them into the silverware basket.

They wrapped items in bubble wrap and pulled pieces of furniture into the living room to be moved into storage.

"I should take the file cabinet."

"What about the boxes in the attic?" Lauren asked. "They kept every financial document they've ever had."

"I'll check, but we can get a shredding company to handle those. I don't need to keep everything."

"There's no telling what's hidden in this house. She might have a fortune hidden up there. You know how Gram was about keeping money everywhere."

Suzanne patted her jeans pocket. "I'm several dollars richer."

"Me, too," Lauren declared.

"Let's see who collects the most."

"You're on."

Her mother sighed. "I don't think this is going to be a one-day task."

The keep, toss, and donate boxes turned into piles as they pulled out the elderly couple's treasures. When they filled the last of the boxes they'd bought, her mother said, "I'll call your dad to bring more."

Greg Kingsley arrived around noon bringing lunch, boxes, and Jake. "We're here to help."

"You could haul that pile to the dump."

Her father's eyebrows rose. "What do you plan to do with the rest of it?"

Suzanne shrugged. "Storage, I suppose."

"Hey Mom, check this out." Lauren climbed down the stairs from the attic and drew to a halt at the sight of Jake.

Self-consciously, she brushed back the hair that had come loose from her braid and brushed at the jeans shorts and T-shirt that were smudged with dust. "Hi. I didn't realize you were here."

"I came to help."

"Who's running the plant?"

Greg chuckled. "Same people who do it every day. They know where to find us."

"What did you find, Laurie?" her mother asked.

She handed over a stack of towels. "There are trunks of new stuff up there."

Greg looked at his wife. "We can't keep everything, Suzanne."

"I don't plan to. Laurie will take anything she wants, and we'll leave some for Jake's use, and the rest will be donated." She waved toward the piles. "You can see we've been sorting and tossing, but the attic's full to overflowing. There's a lifetime of memories up there."

"You could install a lock on the attic door and leave it for now," Jake suggested.

"A lock?"

Lauren noted her mother's curious look.

He shrugged. "I thought you'd feel more comfortable knowing it was secure."

"I trust you, Jake. I wouldn't let you live here otherwise."

Jake nodded. "Better to take your time. You're always hearing about the finds people make because someone didn't know they had a treasure. I spoke with Mrs. Hart, and we're going to see how Teddy responds to her."

Suzanne piled the towels on the table. "Will she cook and clean?"

Jake shook his head. "I didn't include that in the job description. I need someone to make sure Teddy's safe and to keep Yapper out of trouble. I can handle the chores."

"I'm sure Gerry wouldn't mind," Suzanne said. "She could put something in the Crock-Pot or stick a casserole in the oven."

"We'll see. If Teddy likes her, I don't want to risk running her off."

They continued the conversation over lunch at the kitchen table.

"Hey Jake, let's haul this trash to the plant Dumpsters."

The screen door banged behind them, and the women returned to their tasks.

"Trash is gone," Jake told Lauren when he walked into the living room later. "What else can I do?"

"Sort through those magazines," she said, indicating piles underneath the end tables and in a magazine rack. Lauren handed him a pair of scissors. "Remove the address labels. We'll donate them to the hospital."

He set to work and soon had the magazines sorted. "There's some mail I found. And this."

Jake held the birthday card she'd given her grandmother, a fifty sticking out of the envelope.

"She looked for this everywhere," Lauren said, a sad smile on her face.

Her parents came down from the attic, and her mom dropped onto the sofa. Her face was pink with her exertion.

"Look what Jake found in the magazines." She held up the card.

"She felt so bad about losing your present."

"I'll donate it to the church in her name."

"Good idea." Suzanne swiped at a tear that trailed along her cheek.

Greg reached for her hand. "You're not doing this too soon, are you, Suze?"

"No, sweetie. I'm fine."

The washer buzzer went off.

Her mother stood. "That's the towels. I'll hang them on the clothesline. They smell so much fresher when air-dried."

"I'll do it," Lauren offered.

"No. Keep sorting. I need fresh air."

Lauren went back to the books. She found a photo of her very young grandparents tucked inside one and studied it closely. They had been so in love. Marriage longevity was a given in her family. "Until death do us part" had been the case with both sets of grandparents, and her parents had recently celebrated their thirtieth anniversary.

"Who do you have there?" Jake leaned down to take a look.

"My grandparents."

"Nice-looking couple."

"They'd been married over fifty years when Grandpa died."

She laid the picture aside. If her mom didn't want it, she'd keep it for herself. Or maybe she could put a collection of photos into a digital frame for her mom's birthday.

Her parents left to take a load to the charity resale shop. Lauren and Jake continued working, and by late afternoon they had sorted through the items in the living room. Lauren went outside to collect the towels, and Jake followed. He lifted them to his face and breathed deeply. "They smell like sunshine."

"Could be the fabric softener," Lauren teased.

He folded the towel and laid it in the basket. "Nah. Too fresh. Your mom doesn't need to do all this stuff. She's got enough to do already."

"Mom's a homemaker at heart. She'll do everything she can before you move in."

She reached for another towel. "I meant to tell you, there are lots of toys in the attic. You might want to check them out for Teddy."

"Yours?"

She nodded. "I was the only grandchild."

"He might break them."

"It's okay, Jake. I don't mind sharing my toys."

He carried the basket into the laundry room. The Kingsleys entered a few minutes later.

"I need to pick up Teddy and Yapper. I can get pizza and salad for dinner if you want to keep working."

"Let's stop for the day," Suzanne said. "We've made good progress."

Jake appeared bothered by the situation. "I feel I'm pushing you. I can find another place."

"Don't. Mom would be happy knowing you and Teddy will be living here. You have plenty of household stuff, and the new fridge and stove will be delivered tomorrow. Once you buy groceries and we pick up shelf paper, you'll be in business."

"I can do that," Jake said.

Suzanne nodded. "Greg's going to have them bring over a new mattress. You need to decide which one you want."

"It's not necessary," Jake objected.

"Ah, but a Sleep Dreams mattress makes you a better employee," Suzanne teased.

"I'd have to write a testimonial."

Lauren grinned broadly as she set four bottles of water on the table. "And then you can star in the commercial."

Jake opened his and chugged half the bottle. "You don't think people will feel I'm paid for my opinion?"

"No more so than they'll think we are. Hey, we could put Teddy in a crib and let him cry, and then put him on a Sleep Dreams bed and watch him go off to sleep right away. Sales for new parents would skyrocket."

"Or parents might be discouraged if they thought their kids would have to sleep with them. Maybe you should develop a crib mattress line."

"Never thought about that," Greg said.

"Do you purchase booths at the home shows? I've been meaning to ask."

"We haven't."

"Might want to check into it this year." Jake glanced at his watch and frowned. "I need to go. See you tomorrow."

She watched him walk out the front door and climb into his vehicle. Lauren didn't doubt Jake would have worked into the night if they had been willing. He was certainly eager to get out of the hotel.

Chapter 6

Sleep eluded Lauren as her mind filled with all she'd done that day. After their fast-food dinner, she showered and lay in bed thinking of the time she'd spent with Jake.

Was today an example of what it would be like to create a home for a husband and family? A time or two she had fantasized that they were setting up their own home, choosing the bits and pieces that would surround them.

When had she started thinking of Jake like that? Just because he'd been nice to her didn't mean he had any interest beyond that of work. Sure, he'd encouraged her to make friends, but somehow she didn't think that included her falling for him.

The next morning she dressed and went to the office with her father. They discussed the day on their drive in and decided Lauren would go back out to the farm after handling a couple of things that needed doing.

She read her e-mail, returned a few phone calls, and gave Ashleigh a to-do list. Lauren called her dad to say she was ready. "Let's pick up lunch on the way," she suggested.

They met Jake coming up the hall.

"I was on my way to see you," he told Greg.

"Let me run Lauren out to help her mother. I'll be back within the hour."

"Give me a call." Jake glanced at Lauren. "Back to the sorting, huh?"

She nodded. "Mom's determined, and we don't want her doing it alone."

Jake's chest heaved with his mighty sigh. "I hate putting this extra stress on her."

Lauren's head tilted in her dad's direction. "Mom's not stressed. He's trying to figure out what to do with the stuff she's bringing home."

"House was already full to overflowing," he muttered.

Her father would be labeled a minimalist. He hated clutter and while her mother tried to please him, she insisted she needed a certain amount of frills in her life.

Lauren squeezed his arm. "Don't worry. We'll get it all put away."

"I'll come over later and help," Jake volunteered.

"I'm sure there will be plenty to do."

"And I'm taking a delivery truck over tonight," Greg said. "Why don't you choose a mattress, and I'll take it when I go."

"You don't have to do that," Jake objected.

Lauren wanted to laugh. He was getting a firsthand view of her parents' generosity.

Greg clapped him on the back. "Sure we do."

They arrived to find her mother had washed the curtains and they fluttered in the slight breeze.

"Here you go." Lauren passed her the food bag. "We ate ours on the way over. What's on today's agenda?"

"Mom's bedroom."

Lauren groaned. "Did we save the worst for last?"

"Probably. I bought more boxes. We're donating her things, but I thought maybe I'd offer a few of her nicer pieces to Miss Bessie."

Bessie Shaw had been her grandmother's best friend.

Lauren nodded. "Go put your feet up and eat your lunch. I'll get started."

In the bedroom, she looked at the line of boxes her mother had hauled into the room and knew they would need them. Gram loved clothes.

She tugged on the pulls for the first drawer and wasn't surprised when her action met resistance. Lauren used one hand to push down the contents and the other to pull the drawer from the dresser. Settling it on the bed, she picked up the first piece. Clean but shabby. She shoved it into a trash bag.

Lauren couldn't bring herself to discard the pieces Gram had worn often. As she stroked the colorful shirt, she decided to ask the ladies at church to make a memory quilt for her mother.

There were rolls of dollar bills and containers of pennies tucked into the drawer. Lauren smiled. This new haul would push her over the top in their competition. She assumed the plastic flower in the squashed gift box had some sort of sentimental meaning along with the empty body powder container. "Sorry, Gram," she whispered as she slipped them into the trash.

She had emptied three drawers by the time her mother came into the room. Suzanne pulled out another.

"Jake's really concerned that he's stressing you with all this."

"He's sensitive because he's gone through the same thing recently. I should consider this a lesson not to put you through this when I go."

Lauren never wanted to consider life without her parents. "Daddy's not happy. You know how he is about clutter."

Her mother folded clothes and tucked them into the donation box. "He doesn't have a lot of stuff from his parents' estate. They disposed of most of their possessions when they went into assisted living. Letting go is difficult. I know I'll do a more extensive disposal after I've had time to work through the loss, but for now I'm keeping what needs to be kept. I went through her Christmas decorations this morning." She smiled at Lauren. They shared a love of all things Christmas. "I kept the things you made for her."

Lauren looked up from her sorting. "You didn't keep those paper cups wrapped in aluminum foil, did you?"

Suzanne nodded. "Her joy bells. They're precious, Laurie."

"Promise they won't end up on our tree at home."

She shook her head. "Can't do that."

They were both thinking memories. "Okay, Mom. Whatever you want."

They soon had the dresser and chest emptied. Lauren opened the closet door and looked at her mother. It was packed tight. They pulled blankets and old purses from the top shelf, jumping back when things Gram had hidden underneath clattered to the floor.

Suzanne pulled a handful of papers from the first purse. "We'll have to go through these."

Lauren picked up a small box and set it on the bed. "Secondary filing system?" They laughed and dumped the papers inside, adding the handbags to the growing donation pile.

Later they surveyed the boxes and bags.

"Gram will help a lot of people today," Lauren said.

"What about those?" Her mother indicated the pile of older pieces on the bed.

Lauren quickly swept the clothes she'd reserved into a bag.

"Let's get this stuff out to the porch."

Her mother dragged a plastic bag toward the door. Lauren waited until she was out of sight before shoving the keeper bag into a dresser drawer.

They had loaded the last box in her mother's car when her father arrived. Greg kissed his wife and said, "Jake will be over as soon as he picks up Teddy and Yapper."

"Ride to the church with me. Lauren can wait for them." She glanced at her daughter. "The bedroom could do with a dust and vacuum."

They had already lugged out the old mattress and dismantled the double bed that matched her grandmother's antique furniture in preparation for the new king-sized bed. "I'll take care of it."

And then she'd hide those clothes in one of the boxes she planned to take home with her.

~

Jake unbuckled Teddy's car seat and removed him from the vehicle. He reached for the pet carrier and placed Yapper in the shade on the porch. The screen door bounced slightly with his tap.

A vacuum roared to life, and he doubted anyone could hear him over the noise. He glanced at his son. "What do you think, Teddy? Should we let ourselves in?"

It occurred to him that their unannounced presence might frighten who-ever was inside.

"Come on, buddy, we'll wait here in the swing."

Jake slipped off his sport coat and rolled up his shirt-sleeves. He couldn't get over the feeling that he'd come home. They were going to be happy here in the country. He filled Yapper's water bottle at the outside faucet and returned it to the bag before settling in the swing.

The vacuum shut off, but before he could announce his presence, Lauren came out of the house with a couple of throw rugs.

"Hi."

As feared, she screamed and the rugs went flying. "Sorry." Jake stood and picked up his son.

Lauren rested a hand against her chest. "I didn't know you were here."

"Only five minutes or so. Didn't want to scare you."

"Too late for that." She bent to pick up the rugs. "We finished downstairs. You can move in any time you like."

Jake's gaze widened. These Kingsley women were something else. "You mean like now?"

"The curtains need to be ironed and rehung and your new mattress brought inside."

"Would you watch Teddy while I run to the hotel for our things?"

Lauren all but cringed, and Jake knew she was afraid to be left alone with his son.

"Mom will be back soon. Could you go then?"

"Yeah. Maybe it's best to move in tomorrow." He pointed to the truck. "Do you have the key? I'll bring the new mattress inside."

"You can't move it alone," she protested. "Mom and I had a time getting the other set out."

"I'll back the truck closer."

She shrugged. "The keys are on the counter."

"Here, take Teddy."

She held the grinning baby tightly when his father charged into the house. "Your dad doesn't take no for an answer, does he?"

"I heard that," Jake yelled from inside.

Teddy blew a spit bubble in response.

"Got 'em," Jake said, jangling the keys as he ran down the steps. "Yell when I get close enough to pull the ramp out."

She called out when he neared the porch steps. He jumped out and came around to roll up the truck door and slide the ramp from underneath onto the porch.

Lauren glanced at Teddy. "How do I maneuver a mattress and hold him at the same time?"

Taking his son, Jake went inside and settled him on the carpeted floor with a couple of toys.

"Will he stay there?" While he wasn't exactly crawling, she'd seen Teddy scoot about on his bottom.

"Yeah. For a few minutes. Let's do this before he starts crying."

Lauren lifted one end of the first twin box spring that would serve as a foundation for the new king mattress. The screen door creaked as they entered and worked their way toward the bedroom.

After they finished doing the same with the second box spring, the mattress proved unwieldy and it shoved Lauren back against the side of the truck when Jake picked up his end. "Hey, watch it," she called in protest.

"Sorry." Together they carried it into the living room.

"Jake, look," Lauren said at the sight of Teddy holding on to the sofa.

"That's a new trick he's picked up recently. Mom said I walked early."

"You need to childproof that hearth. Once he starts walking, he could fall and hit his head."

"Let's put this in the bedroom, and I'll come back for him."

They leaned it against the dresser. "Whew," Lauren declared, blowing her bangs out of her face. "That's one heavy mattress."

"Made to last. I need sheets."

She pointed to the top of the chest of drawers where a set of crisp, clean white sheets waited. "Mom brought over a new set she had at the house. She even washed them for you."

"Air-dried, too?"

"Of course. Mom insists everything needs to be aired out. She even opened the windows and doors and refused to run the air conditioner for a while today. Do you know how hot it was?"

He shook his head in wonder at the Kingsleys' generosity. They seemed determined to do everything possible to set him up for housekeeping.

"Let me grab Teddy, and you can hold on to him while I put my bed together."

He returned to find Lauren pulling the bed frame from the cardboard box he'd brought in earlier. Jake took over as she took Teddy and lounged in her grandmother's comfortable armchair.

Once he had the frame assembled, she placed Teddy on the carpeted floor and helped Jake slide the box springs and mattress into place. Lauren dropped the fitted mattress cover on the bed. "Mom had this, too. It's waterproof, which will be a plus if you plan to sleep with Teddy."

They stood on opposite sides working together to make the bed. Once the fitted sheet was in place, Jake flapped the top sheet, laughing each time it fluttered from Lauren's grasp.

Exasperated by his play, she grabbed the sheet and jerked it down onto the bed, tucking the edges underneath the mattress. Jake fell backward across the bed and lay spread-eagled. She stared and he saw her cheeks flush.

"Pillows." She hurried off to find them.

Teddy cried out in protest, and Jake rolled off. He scooped him up and bounced him on the mattress. "What do you think, buddy? You like our new bed?"

The baby jabbered. Lauren returned. "Here they are."

She slipped cases on the pillows and placed them at the head of the bed. "Mom found a bedspread at home and took it to the dry cleaners. You have clean towels and washcloths in the bathroom and dish towels in the kitchen."

"I got the shelf liner last night."

"You want to start on that?"

He smiled at her and shook his head. "Not right this minute." Jake picked Teddy up and headed for the living room. There he sat in an armchair, holding the baby in his lap. "I can't tell you how much I appreciate this. This house and a yard will make a big difference for Teddy and Yapper."

Lauren and her parents had become very important to him in a short time. His first impression of Lauren had been so off base. She deserved so much more out of life than she had gotten.

After a few minutes, he handed Teddy over and said, "Show me the boxes. I'll start loading them, and we can decide what to do about dinner when your parents get back."

She pointed to the stacks over by the built-in bookcases. "Those are books." She indicated the half dozen or so marked "fragile". "These have breakable things."

"Better not pack them underneath the books," Jake teased.

She smiled back. "No, let's not."

"You watch my little man, and I'll load your boxes without breaking anything." Lauren nodded agreement, and he sat Teddy on the floor with a small collection of his toys. She picked up an old wooden block she'd told him she'd played with and handed it to the baby. Jake watched for a while as Teddy dropped it and waited for her to hand it back. He was very familiar with this game.

Jake walked out to the porch to retrieve the cart. Back inside, he loaded the first box of books. He wheeled it into the truck and returned to the living room.

As he moved through the room, Jake glanced over and stopped suddenly when he saw Lauren sprawled on the floor next to the end table. He moved quickly, calling her name. Teddy sat close to her, patting her arm and calling, "*Lalalala.*"

Blood oozed from her forehead. She must have hit her head when she fell. Panicked, he grabbed a tissue box from the table and pulled out a handful. He dabbed at the area, thankful when he found it to be more of a scratch.

Jake did what he could to make her more comfortable and sat there with her and Teddy, waiting for Lauren to wake. He wanted to shake her, see those hazel eyes, and know she would be okay. It worried him that he hadn't been there for her when she needed him.

A few minutes later, Lauren came awake, looking at him in surprise.

"Does your head hurt? Can you hold this while I get a bandage? You're bleeding."

"Bleeding?"

He shrugged. "You were sitting on the sofa when I went out. I found you here."

"Teddy decided to practice his throwing arm. He bounced a block off the end table. I suppose I had an attack when I stood up to get it. How long?"

"A few minutes."

Their gazes met, and she saw the concern in his eyes as he looked down at her. Emotion swelled in Lauren when she realized Jake hadn't run away from the situation.

"Help me up?" she implored.

He took her hands and pulled her to her feet. "Does your head hurt? I don't think you need stitches. It's more of a scratch." Jake didn't let go as he helped her over to the sofa. He glanced back to make sure Teddy was close by.

His touch was comforting, almost tempting Lauren to cling.

"Here, hold these," he said, placing her hand over the tissues. He took Teddy and went into the bathroom to search for first-aid supplies. He returned with a thumb bandage and gauze. "This was all I could find."

He pulled the backing off, his fingers gentle as he probed the area and then affixed the small piece of gauze with the bandage. "Not bad," he murmured. "You think we need ice?"

She shook her head. "I'll be okay."

Her parents returned and everything reverted to normal. Her father and Jake carried out boxes while her mother took the bedspread she'd picked up from the dry cleaners into the bedroom and came back. "You two have been busy." Her expression looked puzzled. "What's that on your forehead?"

"All Jake could find in the way of first aid. I fell and hit my head on the end table."

Her mother's gaze fixed on her. "Everything okay?"

Lauren nodded. "Just a scratch. I hoped. . . The last couple of days. . ."

Her mother knew what she was trying to say. "You've been pretty active."

Activity did help stave off the attacks, but not today. She shrugged. "I hope Jake understands the danger in leaving Teddy alone with me."

"Laurie. . ."

"Please, Mom. I know what you're going to say. It never changes. We all have to accept that."

"No," Suzanne declared with a shake of her head. "Every day without an attack is a good day. You've been attack-free for longer periods lately. That's wonderful."

For Lauren, wonderful would be never having another sleep attack.

Jake and her dad came back inside.

"I'd like to take everyone out tonight."

Suzanne flashed Jake an apologetic smile. "I'm sorry. We invited Pastor and Mrs. Bell to dinner. It's their anniversary. Laurie could go with you."

She mumbled, "I need to go home."

The elephant was back in the room, and Lauren didn't want to deal with him.

"I wish you'd stay," Jake said simply.

She pinned him with a serious stare. "So you can babysit me while Mom and Dad are away? I've been alone after attacks before."

The dark brows slanted in a frown, an edge to his voice when he said, "You shouldn't let these attacks get you down."

She glared at him. "Don't you think I know that?" Lauren tried to accept her lot in life and live with the complications of her condition. There were many—depression, difficulty in concentrating, extreme exhaustion, increased irritability, and the list went on. Then Jake Greer had come along, and she'd somehow gotten it in her head that maybe she could be normal for a change.

"Come on, Laurie," he pleaded, using her parents' name for her. "Join us for dinner. We want you to stay, don't we, buddy?"

As if to voice his agreement, Teddy looked over from where he had pulled himself up on a chair, grinned, and bounced up and down.

"Say yes, Lauren," he pleaded, a strange, faintly eager look in the blue-green gaze.

She wanted to. Why not? No sense in going home and sitting alone, moaning and groaning about her pitiful life. "Okay."

"I'll bring her home," Jake said.

"We won't be late," Lauren said. "Jake can't keep Teddy out past his bedtime."

"We could run by and pick you up after dinner," Greg suggested.

"That would be even better."

"Are you staying here tonight?" Suzanne asked Jake.

"I thought maybe we'd run by the hotel." He glanced at Lauren and said, "If you're okay with that?"

"Sure."

After they left, Jake changed Teddy and carried him out to the car. He gave the baby a bottle. Teddy leaned back in the car seat, sucking down the formula with obvious enjoyment.

He started the vehicle and said, "Oh man, I forgot Yapper."

"Done," he said as he climbed back in the car minutes later. Teddy had fallen asleep. "I walked Yapper and set her up in the bathroom. If she has an accident, she won't hurt the tile floor."

Jake drove over to the hotel, parked, and looked at Lauren. "Let's check to see if you're still bleeding." His fingers were gentle against her forehead as he peeled the bandage free. "It's stopped. I'll take it off so people don't look at you funny. I have a little first-aid kit in the room if it starts back."

They took a luggage cart up to the room where he and Teddy had been living. "I started packing last night. We've amassed a lot of stuff in a very short time."

Jake laid Teddy in the crib and picked up two boxes. He set one on the small kitchen counter. "If you pack this stuff, I'll take care of the bathroom."

Lauren admired the neat array in the small cabinet space. Jake had organized their instant food packets in plastic bins. She placed them in the cardboard box.

"That's it for the bathroom." He glanced around once more and flipped off the light.

He carried a shaving kit and the box contained very little.

"Can I put some stuff in that box?"

Jake pulled out a drawer and used a plastic bag for the items. Handing it over, he opened the small fridge and loaded the items into a cooler while she finished up. Then he stacked the cooler, boxes, and his luggage on the cart.

"Can you carry Teddy down to the car?"

Lauren shook her head. No way. He could be hurt if she had an attack and fell. "I can steer the luggage cart into the elevator."

Lauren watched his attempt to analyze her fear. He'd never witnessed her drop during an attack. Had no idea what could happen if she did.

"I'll do it. Will you stay here with Teddy?"

Apprehension filled her as Lauren recalled her earlier failure. She didn't want to disappoint him.

"Are you afraid you'll have another attack?"

She nodded.

"It won't take long to unload this stuff. I'll stop by the desk and come back."

Teddy woke while Jake was gone. Lauren tried to console him as he cried and called for his dad.

"He'll be right back," she said softly, jiggling the baby in hopes of calming him. She looked around and spotted the colorful fabric toy tucked under the pillow. "Here's your truck." She rolled the stuffed vehicle over his legs and up his chest.

He took the toy and pounded it up and down on the bed.

Lauren bounced playfully and said, "Rough ride, huh, Teddy?"

The baby grinned.

She glanced up to find Jake watching from the doorway. "Here's your daddy," she declared, sounding more relieved than she intended. Teddy all but threw himself from the bed.

"Dadadada."

"Words to steal a man's heart," he murmured, swinging his son into the air. "Ready?"

He tossed the keycard on the desk along with a tip for the housekeeper. Jake held the door as Lauren gave the room a final search and picked up a couple of toys that had fallen off the bed.

"What are your plans for tomorrow?" Jake asked as they walked down the hallway.

"The usual. Laundry and chores around the house."

"You have time to go crib hunting with us?"

Surprised, she said, "I don't know anything about cribs."

"I thought maybe we could work out the mystery with the help of a sales clerk."

She hit the DOWN button for the elevator. "Let's ask Mom. Maybe she knows someone who has one you can borrow."

The door slid open. "Okay. Feel up to a grocery store run?"

Lauren had never pushed herself after an attack. She generally took it easy but not tonight. She stepped into the elevator. "Sure."

They drove to the nearest grocery store. Jake parked and got out, taking

Teddy from his seat. "This isn't our favorite chore," he said as they walked toward the store.

"I don't know many people who enjoy grocery shopping."

Jake pulled out a cart and settled Teddy in the seat.

"You need to wipe those things down," Lauren declared. "They have so many bacteria."

"Mom says a little dirt never hurt anyone."

"Let's not test that theory." She pulled wipes from the canister next to the door and cleaned the cart handle. Teddy rewarded her effort by grabbing the stainless steel bar.

In the produce section, Jake bagged items. She noted he chose one or two of some fruits but opted for a big bundle of bananas. "Our favorite."

He bought staple items along with baby food and diapers. They checked out.

"Ouch," she said when the cashier announced his total. He grimaced and pushed the cart toward the door. Lauren helped unload the groceries into the trunk.

Back at the house, they reversed the process. While Jake set up the small grill he'd purchased, Lauren unpacked the perishables and formed the hamburger into patties. Teddy sat on the kitchen floor. Good thing her mom insisted on mopping it earlier in the week.

Jake came in from the deck and washed his hands. "Charcoal's on."

He opened the fridge and removed a packet of hot dogs. "You want a dog and a burger?"

Lauren shook her head. "A hamburger is plenty. Are we having chips?"

Jake nodded. "And lettuce, tomato, cheese, and pickles on our burgers. I'm a ketchup and mustard fan. What about you?"

"Me, too."

He dropped two hot dogs on the plate with the burgers and rummaged around until he found the seasoning he'd purchased along with a bottle of steak sauce, a small bowl, and a basting brush.

Jake sorted through the baby food and picked up two jars. He reached for Teddy. "I suppose a high chair would be another worthwhile purchase."

Lauren rinsed her hands and dried them with a paper towel. "There's one in the attic. Why don't you get it while the charcoal heats up?"

The wooden chair had been in the family for years. Lauren sprayed antibacterial cleaner liberally and wiped it down with a clean cloth. "There, good as new."

"Let's see how he likes it." Jake placed Teddy in the chair and pulled the wooden tray over his head. "What do you think, buddy?"

Lauren used a damp cloth to wipe the baby's hands. Teddy pounded boisterously as Jake sliced a banana onto a paper plate. The baby attacked the small bits.

"Be right back. I need to check the grill."

Lauren heated the baby food and picked up the small spoon. "Hey Teddy, let's say grace." She whispered, "God is good, God is great, and we thank Him for our food. By God's hand we must be fed, give us Lord, our daily bread. Amen."

Teddy pounded the tray.

She took a little food on the spoon, and Teddy consumed it almost faster than she could shovel it into his mouth.

"He was hungry," she said when Jake returned.

Jake seasoned the burgers and picked up the plate. "If you finish feeding him, I'll get these started." She nodded and he disappeared out the back door.

Lauren felt she'd accomplished a major task when she wiped Teddy's hands and face after his meal. She pushed the screen door open and asked, "Did you want to get him ready for bed?"

He glanced up from flipping the burgers. Flames shot up, and Jake used a spray bottle to knock them back. "I take him into the shower with me in the morning."

"He takes showers?" she asked curiously. How did Jake manage a shower with a baby in his arms?

"Yeah. He likes them."

"He'd probably love a tub bath more," Lauren said.

"We'll have to give it a try. Did you give him a bottle?"

"Not yet." She started back inside and paused. "Did you feed Yapper?"

He grunted. "Not yet."

"I'll get her."

Lauren opened the door, and the tiny dog raced into the kitchen, barking and joyous over her escape.

"Cut that out or I'll put you back," Jake commanded when he came in for a clean plate.

"It's just her way of letting you know where she is. Where's her bowl?"

"Bathroom. I gave her water before we left."

She retrieved the dishes and filled them with fresh water and food. Yapper ate almost as greedily as Teddy. She supposed it was later than their usual mealtimes.

Jake toasted the buns on the grill and brought the food into the kitchen. They sat at the kitchen table. Jake said grace and stacked his burger so high Lauren wondered how he would get it into his mouth. He did so without difficulty. She shook her head in disbelief.

Much later, after they consumed what Lauren thought might have been the best burger she'd ever eaten and Teddy was asleep and Yapper had settled down, they sat contented and happy.

"You want dessert? I bought ice cream."

"Maybe later," Lauren said, so stuffed she doubted she could eat another bite.

Jake stretched out his legs before him and laid his hands over his stomach. "I like this house. Feels like home."

Lauren noted his new air of contentment. "It does. Gram always said it had a lot of heart. Gramps offered to build her something bigger and she refused. Said this house was perfect as far as she was concerned. She let him make improvements, like redoing the kitchen and bathrooms and replacing carpet and flooring, but the rest stayed the same. They were happy here.

"Gram missed Gramps. We tried to get her to move in with us, but she didn't want to leave her home. I offered to stay here, but she said she'd be okay and she was. After she got sick, Mom stayed most nights."

"It would have been hard for her to leave."

Lauren nodded.

"Are you feeling better?"

As his gaze swept over her face, Lauren felt embarrassed. "I'm good. Sorry I snapped at you, but I get frustrated."

"You're entitled."

She shook her head. "No, I'm not. It's not your fault. And my situation could be worse."

Jake's gaze rested on her. "You said your mom home-schooled you?"

She nodded. "She handled the company finances at the time and took me to work with her. She would work with me on my assignments and then leave me to read or do my math problems."

"Why didn't you stay in school?"

"The system wasn't equipped to handle my condition. Mom insisted I was intelligent and capable of learning. She didn't want me labeled because of my problem. I didn't graduate with my class, but I finished school about the same time. Mom trained me to take over the job. She wanted to get back into real estate."

"Where was your dad in all this?"

"Running the company. Teaching me what he could. They're great parents. At times I feel I've destroyed their lives, but they never complain."

"They love you," he said simply. "Nothing can change that."

"I resent burdening them. I follow my routine faithfully and then when the attacks happen, I'm disappointed because it failed. I pray all the time that God will relieve me of this thorn in my side, but it's never gone away."

"Did you want to become the company CFO?"

She had thought about what she would have done with her life if she'd been normal. "I wanted to support myself, and this was a job I could handle."

"You're afraid to go after your dreams."

She let out a choked, almost desperate laugh. "It's not the dreams that make me afraid. It's the reality. What if I fall and hit my head? Or I'm cooking and have an attack? Or if I drive and cause an accident? If someone gets hurt or even killed, how do I live with that?"

Jake shrugged. "But what if none of that happens?"

Lauren didn't have an answer.

Their gazes met and held. "We all have to accept our lot in life. I never imagined I'd become a single dad. Most mornings I don't think I'll get Teddy and Yapper out of the house, but I do." He held up his hand and admitted, "I know mothers do it every day. But I had no experience."

She used a paper napkin to wipe the moisture from her glass. "Have you considered that you will have to settle down when Teddy starts school? Kids need stability. I don't see that happening with him in a new place every few months."

"You live with what you know. If that's the life Teddy lives, he'll adapt."

"What about marriage? More kids? Have you completely ruled out the possibility?" Lauren wanted to hear Jake's answer to that.

"No. Not at all. If the right woman comes into our lives, we'll adapt, too."

"Adapt?" Lauren considered that a strange response.

"Sure. Couples adapt in marriage or it doesn't last. Gwen and I had our problems because we couldn't. I suppose I sound like a jerk for admitting that."

Lauren shrugged. "I can't judge you. Only you know what went on between you and your wife."

"Our family and friends considered me selfish for refusing to give up the job I loved to come home and be a full-time husband and father."

"Like people consider me selfish because I still live with my parents?"

He frowned. "But you're justified in what you do."

"They don't know why I live my cowardly existence. I'm sure there's more than one person who wonders why I live in my parents' home instead of living my own life."

There was a flash of lights as her parents' car pulled into the driveway. She glanced at the kitchen clock, surprised to find it was after nine. "My ride's here," she said unnecessarily.

"You're not a coward, Laurie," Jake said. "Thanks for joining me for dinner tonight. I've enjoyed it."

Lauren picked up her purse from the end table. "Me, too. I'll ask Mom about the crib. Thanks for dinner, Jake. Sleep well."

"On my new mattress?"

They laughed and he reached for her hand. "Thanks, Lauren. You and Suzanne worked so hard to make this happen. I owe you."

"You do. Take care of Gram's house for us. And be happy."

He kissed her cheek. "I'll talk to you tomorrow."

Jake pulled open the door for her, and Lauren walked onto the porch, raising a hand in greeting to her parents. He followed and did the same.

She climbed into the backseat of her father's car. Her mother looked back at her. "Are they all settled in?"

"Getting there."

Suzanne smiled at her daughter.

Chapter 7

Jake showered and made his way into the bedroom. He removed the pillow bumpers and settled next to his son who sprawled contentedly in the middle of the bed. *Comfortable,* he thought, as the mattress conformed to the contours of his body.

He owed the Kingsleys for making this house work for him and Teddy. Jake planned on renting an apartment, but that day when he'd come here with Lauren, the place called out to him. She was right about one thing—it was a home. He didn't blame her grandmother for not wanting it changed. The house was perfect.

Yapper came to the bedside and barked. "Go get in your bed," he ordered softly.

After Yapper settled down, Jake thought about how upset Lauren had been over her attack.

Jake considered what Lauren had told him about her fear of reality. He'd never meant to stress her with his suggestions. Why had he come on so strong in encouraging Lauren to strike out on her own? He'd pushed the lesson immediately when she voiced a desire to drive and even brought up the subject of a house to her parents. That had upset Lauren. Jake knew he shouldn't have done it, but it seemed right at the time.

He liked Lauren. He wouldn't deny her condition frightened him. He couldn't help but see her as another needy female. Was that why he'd pushed so hard for her to become more independent?

Surely not, he thought, giving himself the benefit of the doubt. Still he found it difficult to be 100 percent certain his intentions weren't self-motivated. Could be he needed to stop meddling in a situation he didn't understand.

Across town, Lauren lay in her own bed thinking about her life. Jake was right about one thing—she'd hidden from the world for years. They had sought answers only to find there weren't any. While medications helped regulate the frequency of her attacks, she had been forced to exist in the safe world created for her.

She couldn't pretend the problem didn't exist or that it would go away so she could live a normal life. Now was as normal as it was going to get for her and while she'd accepted that as a truth, she knew Jake thought there was potential for change.

But Lauren knew her limitations, and she wouldn't allow him to make her feel even more discontented with her boundaries. Feeling at peace with her decision, she fell asleep.

She called Jake the next morning. "Mom found a deal for you. Her friend has a daughter with a crib and changing table/dresser combination she wants to sell. It's a mahogany wood set she's selling for two hundred dollars. Her grandson is getting a big boy bed. He's the last child her daughter plans to have, so she wants to find a new home for the nursery furniture now. You interested?"

"Yes ma'am."

"Hang on." She asked her dad a question. "Daddy says he'll go with you to pick it up. And Mom says we'll shop for Teddy's new room if you want."

"I'd appreciate that," he said without hesitation. "No cartoon characters though. Trucks, cars, or animals are okay."

Lauren decided he must have had some sort of experience with the restricted items that he didn't care to repeat. Or else he intended to expose his son to a more masculine design.

They went to a big toy store and while they didn't find anything they liked, Lauren found a musical toy for Teddy's crib and a safety bath seat. They visited three more stores before finding the perfect nursery decorations. A few more must-have items made their way into the cart at each place.

Back at the house, Jake met them at the door, taking in the number of bags.

Jake studied the seat contraption that fell out of the bag Lauren carried. "I thought we agreed to nursery decorations."

"Teddy will love playing in the tub." She nodded to the item. "This will keep him safe."

"What else?" Jake asked.

"A little push car and a child swing to hang in a tree or off the porch."

Jake sighed and reached for his wallet. "I should have known better. I forget how much women love to shop."

Lauren grabbed his arm. "These are gifts for Teddy."

"I'm paying for the nursery items," he insisted.

Suzanne came up the steps carrying more bags. "You can pay for what you expected us to buy, but I warn you now these aren't going back." She held up a carrier bag. "I never got to buy clothes for little boys. Teddy will be so cute."

"Cute?" Jake teased with sudden good humor. "Shouldn't he be handsome?"

"Maybe when he's an old man like his daddy," Suzanne quipped. She pulled a pair of short denim overalls from the bag. "Look at these. They're a necessity now that he lives at the farm. I got a couple of different styles."

Jake laughed at her reason for the purchase.

"Teddy outgrows his clothes almost as fast as I buy them, so I'm sure he can use whatever you bought. Though I think we can guarantee he's all but on the best-dressed list if the number of bags counts for anything."

Greg came out onto the porch. "Where have you been? We've been back for hours."

Suzanne kissed him. "Our assignment was more complicated. We had to find our items, which involved visiting more than one store. Wait until you see these clothes, Greg. They are adorable."

"There's another of those words," Jake said.

Suzanne eyed him. "Well, he is cute and adorable, and I think if a woman told you the same thing, you'd preen a bit, Jacob Greer."

"You think?" he asked with a broad grin.

"I know. Is the crib set up?"

Greg nodded. "They had it in the garage but hadn't taken it apart." He grinned. "I thanked Scott for being too busy to handle the chore. We put it in your old room. It's good to go."

Suzanne shook her head. "Lauren, get those antibacterial wipes from the car. You two do what you were doing while we ready the nursery for our little guy."

Jake started to follow. "I'll help."

"Leave it to us. You'll like what we bought. If not, I will personally take everything back."

He waved his hand in invitation to continue.

"Oh, there's a bag of sub sandwiches in the car."

"I'll get them," Greg volunteered. "I'm starving."

Suzanne patted her husband's ample waistline. "I doubt that, but go ahead and eat. We'll have this finished in no time."

Two hours later, Lauren looked around the room and announced, "Instant nursery. That's really nice furniture."

"I'm so glad I remembered Doreen saying they planned to move Scottie to a big boy bed."

"Certainly Teddy's gain." Lauren eyed her mother. "You think Jake will like this?"

"What's not to like? It's got everything a boy's room should have and more. I love that glove beanbag chair."

Lauren nodded. "I can see Teddy crawling into it for naps. Hopefully Yapper won't decide it's a doggie bed."

"I don't think Jake will allow Yapper in here when Teddy's playing. He's too little to know how to play with her. I've noticed Yapper keeps her distance from Master Teddy's little hands." She stuck her head into the hall and called, "Gentlemen, come tell us what you think."

Jake carried the sleeping baby in his arms. His gaze moved around the room and he nodded approval. "I like the sports theme."

Lauren pulled back the comforter. "Here, lay him down."

Jake settled his son in the crib.

"We loved every minute of it. I hung his new clothes in the closet." Suzanne pulled open the door and lifted out a little dress outfit. "I got this for church."

He'd told them he planned to attend their church the next day. "Thanks to you two, Teddy will have to beat off the girl babies in the nursery."

Lauren couldn't help but think Teddy's dad might have to beat off some of the single church ladies. She found the thought rather disconcerting. The idea made her feel almost territorial. She'd spent entirely too much time with him in a different environment these past few days.

Chapter 8

Jake and Teddy showed up at Peace Church a few minutes early. He found Lauren sitting in her dad's car and asked, "Can you show us where the nursery is?"

"Sure."

"I left Yapper in the kitchen. I hope that's not a mistake. I walked her and made sure she had water."

"Chew toys?"

"Yes. Her own and one of Teddy's that she's mangled."

"I'm sure she'll be fine. Hey Teddy," Lauren whispered as she touched the baby's stomach. "You look mighty handsome in that outfit." The oxford shorts and polo shirt were a perfect fit. He wore little rubber-soled sandals.

"I had a time getting him dressed. He wanted to play with all those new things in the nursery."

That pleased Lauren. "How did he sleep?"

"Woke once around four. I heard him on that baby monitor your mom bought. Then he went back to sleep and didn't wake again until seven or so."

"Is that a different schedule?"

"Oh yeah, the two of us spent restless nights in the same bed. Even though I pushed it up against the wall, I slept light to make sure he didn't roll off, and we woke each other during the night with our movement.

"We'll both rest better, though I think I might have one up on him with that new mattress. I can definitely give a testimonial to how comfortable it is. I'm going to have to take a set home with me. Give me a good reason to get home more often."

Lauren chuckled. "Let's take Teddy to the nursery, and you can come to the singles class with me today."

~

She knew from Jake's participation in the study that he had a good understanding of scripture. He obviously read and studied his Bible regularly, and it showed in his thought-provoking comments.

"Good to have you with us, Jake," their teacher, Conrad Little, said after class. "Come again."

The men shook hands, and the teacher moved on to speak with someone else. As Lauren expected, several women hurried over to welcome Jake. From her vantage point, she noted the way he smiled at them.

She wanted to push the other women out of his path and keep him completely for herself. She'd never experienced this before. *Don't be ridiculous*, she thought as he checked his watch and took her arm. They walked toward the sanctuary.

"Should I check on Teddy?"

"If he needs you, they'll post that number they gave you on the screen so you can come to the nursery. I'm sure he's enjoying himself."

They settled next to her parents. Suzanne leaned forward and patted Jake's hand. "Good to see you."

The music minister directed them to open their hymnals. Lauren sang but not loudly. She didn't fool herself that she had any musical talent. Her mother's voice had a beautiful lilting quality, but unfortunately she'd inherited her dad's vocal abilities.

After the song, the director indicated they should be seated. The pastor stepped up to the podium. "I see we have a number of visitors with us today. Welcome. Everyone, please extend the right hand of fellowship to those visitors."

The church erupted with people moving about to welcome visitors and speak to those whom they hadn't seen for a few days or a week. Several of her parents' friends came to be introduced to Jake. And other single women in the church took advantage of the opportunity to welcome him as well.

"You're a popular guy," Lauren said as they returned to their pew.

He opened and closed his hand. "Can't recall the last time I shook hands with so many people."

"Your church doesn't do that?"

He shook his head. "I visit churches wherever I am when my work schedule allows. I usually arrive in time for preaching."

She nodded, thinking how much she'd miss going to church each week.

"We have special music today," the music minister announced. The song was "One Touch." The Nicole C. Mullen song had always held special meaning for Lauren. She knew about being ostracized for something you couldn't control.

The service continued, the choir sang another song, they collected the offering, and the pastor stepped to the pulpit.

"I've had a number of requests for prayer this week," he began. "Members of our congregation are facing hardships and we've prayed for release from their pain and miracles for those who need them.

"If you'd like to open your Bibles and read along with me, starting with Matthew 14:36. 'And besought him that they might only touch the hem of his garment: and as many as touched were made perfectly whole.'

"We all pray for healing for loved ones." He paused and looked around the congregation. "And when those prayers seem to go unanswered, we feel let down, but I tell you our God is in the miracle business. We see them every day.

"This week I had a sister tell me she's been praying for a miracle for her friend. He's disabled and suffering great hardship, and she wanted nothing more than for him to be healed, to have his life back.

"As age goes, he's a relatively young man. Lots of life ahead of him. But she felt the prayer had gone unanswered until he told her the doctor said he's a walking miracle, that most people in his condition are wheelchair-bound. So you see she got her answer. Not the one she sought but still a miracle.

"An acceptable miracle? Better than nothing, you say. A gift from God, I tell you. He's given this young man mobility. Yes, he has this thorn to live with, the pain he suffers from, but he's also a believer. He attends church and reads his Bible and worships the God of love. And he knows that one day he will be freed of his pain because God promises him that.

"Our God is in the miracle business."

Cries of "amen" filled the room.

"Do we have the faith to believe in Jesus' ability to heal us? Listen to this, Matthew 17:20 says, 'Because of your unbelief: for verily I say unto you, If ye have faith as a grain of mustard seed, ye shall say unto this mountain, Remove hence to yonder place; and it shall remove; and nothing shall be impossible unto you.'

"Ask yourself this question. Do you have mountain-moving faith? Is your belief that you can be healed strong enough to remove that mountain of pain? That burden you bear? Will you glory in God's miracles in your life, or will you declare yourself destined to live with the affliction you bear?"

Did she? Had she stopped praying? Seeking God's healing? When had she lost hope?

Jake glanced at Lauren and she smiled wanly. Jake covered her hand with his. His touch made her feel so warm. Safe.

She turned her hand over and clasped his. Their hands remained entwined as the service continued.

God must have intended this sermon for her today. She couldn't claim faith that strong when she doubted her own ability to accomplish the dreams she'd revealed to Jake. Could she overcome her fears and live a full, contented life?

The service ended and Jake got to his feet. "Guess I'll head on home. Feed Teddy and check on Yapper."

"Can you find your way back to the nursery?"

He nodded. "Thanks for inviting me," he told Suzanne. "I enjoyed the service."

She hugged him. "I'm glad you came. We're going out for lunch. You want to come?"

"Not today. Thanks for asking."

He glanced at Lauren. "What are you doing later? I thought we might go exploring."

She had no plans. She could laze around the house, read, or watch television, but that didn't appeal. Nor would she ask her dad to take her over to the plant to catch up on the work she'd left undone while working on the house.

"We could take the ferry service over to Carrot Island," Lauren suggested.

"Check out the beach, look for shells, and see the wild horses."

"Sounds like fun."

"They leave you on the island for a couple of hours so bring whatever Teddy needs for that time. I'll bring a beach sheet and water."

"What time?"

"Around one thirty? The ferry is just down the street. Be sure and put sunscreen on Teddy. We don't want him getting sunburned."

Both elected to wear shorts and sneakers. Lauren wore a knit top and Jake wore a T-shirt. He had dressed Teddy in a sunsuit and sneakers.

They arrived at the ferry service and when Lauren went to pay, Jake said, "My treat."

She shrugged and stuck the money back into her pocket. They walked along the wooden deck and down a steep plank to the dock where the ferry-boat waited. Lauren climbed in, and Jake passed Teddy to her. She sat on the bench seat in the middle front. Jake joined her, placing the bag between his feet.

The captain told some people to shift to the other side of the boat and then backed around and headed slowly out to sea. "If you look over to your right, you'll see the dolphins."

They were rewarded with the view of a fin or sometimes a bit more of the dolphins at play.

They moved slowly through the wake and then picked up speed. Lauren held on to the silver bar along the side, feeling the splatter of water as they rode the waves.

The trip only took minutes. Lauren felt ungainly as she climbed off the front of the boat and stood on the beach. Jake passed over their things and then Teddy before following.

"The shells are over that rise and the horses are in the middle of the island, doing horse things," their captain said, adding a final warning. "Be back here in two hours when we return to pick you up."

Jake carried Teddy as they walked the area, keeping their distance as they watched the horses and then looked for shells.

Later they rested on the beach sheet at their drop-off point. Lauren placed a couple of nearly perfect shells she'd found on the sand next to her, planning to keep them as a reminder of their day together.

"Now I know what a castaway feels like," Jake said.

Lauren giggled. "Hey, maybe one day we can take the three-hour tour." They both remembered the old sitcom.

While they were not alone, the place had a feeling of isolation. The island rose out of the water, a mountain of sand with no beach, wild grasses, and trees.

"Do you do a lot of sightseeing when you travel?"

"I usually find a hotel close to where I work and then visit the nearby restaurants. I tried to go home every other weekend, so on the weekends I stayed, I would get out and visit the tourist sites that were recommended to me."

She used a shell to scoop and pile sand next to where she sat, her legs stretched out before her. Teddy sat between them. "I've traveled a few times. Mom and I took a cruise once with church ladies and there were training sessions for the computers at the plant. I don't dare fly on my own. Heaven knows where I'd end up."

Jake smiled at that.

When Teddy tried to stand, Jake took the baby's hands in his, letting him sink his feet in the warm sand. He flopped on his bottom and grabbed handfuls of sand and cried when the wind tossed some into his face.

She dug through the bag for the wipes and handed the packet to Jake. "Did he get any in his eyes?" Lauren moved to help.

"I don't think so."

She handed him a bottle of water. "Here, wash his face just to be sure."

Afterward, Jake swung his son up on his shoulders. "Let's walk until the ferry arrives."

Teddy's hands tangled in Jake's hair. He winced. "Easy there, buddy. Don't yank your old man bald."

Lauren walked alongside, enjoying the feel of the warm sand beneath her bare feet. "You live in New Mexico?" At his curious look, she said, "I saw the address on the proposal. What about your family?"

"I have a brother who lives in Seattle. Dad died after a stroke, and Mom remarried a couple of years later. She and my stepfather split their time between Florida and Arizona. I don't see her as often as I'd like."

Lauren looked at him. "She doesn't want to see Teddy?"

"Every chance she gets. Mom visits when I'm home."

"What about your brother? Does he have a wife and children?"

"Ryan's had a couple of wives and has two boys with his second wife. Ryan Jr. and David are four and five. I haven't seen them in a while. We talk and threaten to visit each other, but it rarely happens."

"Threaten?"

"We aren't the closest brothers in the world. He's a few years older than I, and we defined sibling rivalry. Fought about everything."

Lauren felt a degree of sadness for this family that was so distant from each other. She loved her parents and couldn't imagine life without them. Even if she didn't live in their home, she wanted to be in the same area. If she'd been blessed with a sibling, she liked to think they would have been close as well.

Teddy yawned widely.

"Time for somebody's nap," she said.

"Yeah, he'll probably fall asleep right about time for the boat to pick us up."

They managed to keep Teddy awake until they arrived back at the car. Jake drove Lauren home.

"I'll be late in the morning. I want to see how Teddy and Yapper do. If everything works out, I'll be in. If not, I'll take the day off and drop them at day care on Tuesday."

"They'll like Mrs. Hart."

Jake looked hopeful. He'd met the woman briefly at church and she seemed nice. "Didn't you say you were friends with her daughter?"

Lauren nodded. Long ago, before the diagnosis, she'd been good friends with Melissa Hart, but that had ended when the girl decided she didn't want to be the freak's friend anymore. She couldn't blame her. School was hard enough without having your peers question your friends.

"I'll send up a prayer that all goes well. Thanks for this afternoon. It's been a nice change."

Chapter 9

She needed friends. Lauren came to that conclusion as she showered and changed into knit shorts and a top and went downstairs. The time with Jake and Teddy left her feeling energized and alive, ready for more fun.

Her mother looked up from her book. "Did you enjoy yourself?"

"I did. Jake plans to stay home in the morning to see how things go with Mrs. Hart. He's nervous. I hope it works out for them. He's very happy about the house."

Her mother nodded. "He wanted a home environment for his family. He'll have that at Mom's. I need to pick up the paint. He wants to get started. I told him there's no big rush. He's going to be there for a while."

"He's contracted for six months?"

"Mid-January, I think."

Much too soon, she thought, considering how much time had passed already.

After dinner, Lauren went to her room to read e-mail and play computer games on her laptop. She read her Bible for a while and then reached for her iPod.

She took it outside to the upper deck and sat in a rocker, enjoying the nice breeze. The moon glistened off the water and boats clanked in their moorings. She pushed the buds into her ears and started the mystery she'd downloaded from the library.

All too soon her eyes drifted closed. She gave up and went inside to prepare for bed.

◉

Ashleigh looked up and greeted her with a big smile. "Good morning. Your mail's on your desk. There are a few things that need to be signed. I put in some requisitions for Jermaine on Friday for some items that need to be ordered. If you'll approve them, I'll call in the orders."

"I'll take a look." Lauren started for her office and almost as if she heard Jake whispering in her ear, turned back and asked, "How was your weekend?"

The young woman didn't miss a beat. "Pretty good. I had a blind date Friday night, but he's not going to work out. He was all about himself."

"I'm sorry."

Ashleigh grinned. "I'm not. Believe me, to know this guy was not to love him."

Lauren chuckled.

"What about you? Did you finish at the house?"

She nodded. "Mr. Greer and his son moved in Friday night."

"How old is his son?"

"Nearly nine months. A real cutie." She could see Ashleigh had more questions but wouldn't ask them. "Do you recall the name of that lady who wanted to do a feature on Sleep Dreams?"

Ashleigh thought for a moment and shook her head. "Want me to make some phone calls?"

"Check with Mrs. Ava and see if she remembers. Daddy got the inquiry, so she probably has the name in her message book."

"Are you thinking about doing the show?"

Lauren nodded. "Mr. Greer thinks the publicity would help sales."

"It can't hurt. Seeing how mattresses are made is pretty interesting."

Lauren started toward her office and stopped. "I need you to pull the time sheets for the past couple of years. Mr. Greer wants to review them."

Ashleigh grimaced. "Last year is in storage. I have the printouts here in the office. I can ask some of the guys to pull them."

"Hold up until I ask if he can use the printouts. Easier than combing through the time sheets."

Lauren spent her morning catching up. She checked and filed production reports, keyed payments, prepared the deposit, and gathered data Jake had requested.

Midmorning, Ashleigh came in with the name and number of the woman who had asked them to do the program. "Like you said, Mrs. Ava had the number logged into her message book."

"We should all be that organized." Her father had a true gem in the secretary who had worked for him since Lauren was a little girl.

She smiled up at her assistant. "Looks like I may get my fifteen minutes of fame doing promotion for Sleep Dreams."

"You don't sound very excited."

She eyed the paper and asked, "You ever dreamed of being a star?"

Ashleigh stifled a giggle. "Maybe when I was a teenager. No adult aspirations."

"I'm not excited," Lauren admitted. "Daddy's not about to do the program, and if I can't convince Mom, it's me. And I'm not television material."

"You'll do fine."

"If I don't have an attack."

"Don't think about it," Ashleigh advised.

"Hard not to but if I have to do this, I will."

Since his arrival, Jake had sent her thoughts off on all kinds of tangents. This television program for one. He'd been very encouraging. And basically all she had to do was talk about what she knew. Hadn't she run these floors since she was a child? All she had to do was answer questions and be personable while they filmed.

"I'm sure there won't be a problem," Ashleigh said.

"You may have to tag along with a really cold drink, but I'm going to call and see if they're still interested. If so, we're going to be on television."

Within an hour of her arrival, Jake knew Mrs. Hart would be a good addition to their family. Teddy hadn't shown any of the stranger anxiety he'd been experiencing lately, and she thought Yapper was the cutest little thing she'd ever seen in her life.

Jake picked up his briefcase and keys. "I need to get to work. My cell and office numbers are on the fridge, and I've shown you where to find Teddy's things."

Mrs. Hart settled Teddy on her hip. "Does he have any food allergies?"

They had gone over his feeding and nap schedule. "None that I know about. He eats pretty much everything except mixed peas and carrots."

"Oh, but carrots are good for his eyes."

"He can eat carrot sticks when he's older. It's not worth the fight to get them in him now."

The woman looked to be about the same age as Suzanne Kingsley. Attractive, thin, and appreciative of the job. "Thank you for giving me this opportunity."

"Thank Suzanne Kingsley. She referred you."

"I have."

"Call if you need anything. We moved in Friday night so most of our stuff isn't unpacked."

"Would you like me to handle that for you? I'd be happy to work on it during Teddy's nap."

"How do you feel about laundry?" Jake asked, not yet comfortable with the scope of the job he had to create for the woman.

"I don't mind."

"Teddy's dirty clothes are in plastic bags in the utility room. I planned to do them at the hotel but never got around to it."

"Do you have an iron?"

Jake shrugged. "I'm not sure what the Kingsleys left."

"Suzanne probably left an iron and board."

"I usually send my shirts out to the laundry."

"I did my husband's shirts. He always said I did a better job than the dry cleaner."

Jake wondered what had happened with the husband. The woman took a deep breath and answered his thought as though he had spoken it aloud.

"I suppose the new wife sends his stuff out. He traded me in for a younger model after the kids left for college."

"I'm sorry."

"Oh, don't be," Mrs. Hart said, waving her hand to negate the issue. "She didn't get any prize. He was a hard man to please. I suspect he was the reason my kids attended colleges across the country and took jobs so far away. Not having my kids close is much more difficult. Besides, I don't mind having no one to please but myself. Makes life easier. Oh, that's probably something I shouldn't say to my new employer. I'm sorry. TMI."

Jake grinned. "I appreciate anything you feel like doing. Of course, Teddy is your primary concern."

"Oh, no doubt about that, Mr. Greer."

"Call me Jake."

"You can call me Geraldine. Or Gerry. I answer to either one."

"Okay, Gerry, I'm off. Call if you need me. I'll be home around five thirty or so."

Jake went out to his car, glancing up to see them standing in the door. Gerry and Teddy waved good-bye. Jake waved back.

He paused in the driveway, pushing back his concern, but then he remembered the Kingsleys' recommendations for Gerry Hart and felt reassured.

At the office, he stopped by to see Lauren. She waved him in, holding up a finger to indicate she would be another minute on the phone.

"Okay, Sarah, I look forward to seeing you on the twenty-fifth. I appreciate the opportunity to tell the Crystal Coast about Sleep Dreams."

Lauren wrapped up the conversation and hung up the phone. "I just made arrangements for them to come out and talk about what they want to cover on the show."

"That's good. It will make more people aware of what we have to offer."

"How did this morning go?"

"Gerry Hart and Teddy clicked right off. She even asked about doing other chores before I brought it up. I told her Teddy was her priority, but she could do anything she felt would help around the house. By the way, is there an iron? She asked and I didn't have a clue."

Lauren nodded. "In the laundry room. In the built-in ironing board cabinet."

"Okay. Good," he said, turning toward the door.

"Jake, hold on. About those time sheets. Ashleigh has the printouts where they were entered for computer payment, but the cards are in storage. Do you need the actual cards?"

"The sheets are fine. If she has any current time sheets, I'd like to take a look. We need to discuss the way the timekeeping is done."

"I'll have her bring them to your office."

"Anything else?"

"Ashleigh thinks I'll do okay on television. I'm still not sure."

"You'll never know if you don't try. Don't look for problems."

Chapter 10

Lauren's confidence level skyrocketed when she managed to get through the stressful event without an attack. Not that she'd been totally attack-free during the time leading up to the program, but she had survived what she thought would be the worst situation ever and felt proud of her accomplishment.

As first experiences went, it hadn't been as bad as she feared. Her mom had a scheduling conflict, and Lauren ended up on the other side of the microphone talking about Sleep Dreams. She'd taken Sarah Warren through the factory, showing how their mattresses were manufactured, even giving tips on how to care for mattresses.

Sarah had sent over a copy of the program, and Lauren watched it with her parents and Jake in the conference room.

"Good job, Laurie."

"Thanks, Dad."

"Very good," Jake agreed. "We need to look at doing some commercials to follow up on this."

"Well, now that we've got our own Miss Hollywood," her dad all but drawled, "I agree wholeheartedly."

"No way," Lauren cried. "You can peddle your wares just as well as I can."

The program aired a couple of days later.

"We saw you last night. You did a great job," Ashleigh enthused the next morning when she greeted Lauren with a big smile.

"Thanks." Curious, Lauren asked, "Who is *we*?"

"I had some friends over and when I told them they were doing a piece about Sleep Dreams, they watched with me. You have an admirer."

Lauren did a double take.

"I told him you were out of his league, but he wouldn't let it go. I finally said I'd ask. I can tell him you're busy or something."

"What kind of guy is he?" She surprised herself with the question.

"He's okay."

"Just okay?" Not much of a recommendation for her new fan.

"I never considered him dating material," Ashleigh admitted. "He's not my type. We're having a pool party this weekend. If you thought you might want. . . You're welcome to come to the party."

You have to start somewhere, Lauren told herself. Why all of a sudden did she feel driven to make friends?

"I'd be there," Ashleigh continued. "I wouldn't let anyone. . . You know what I mean."

Lauren smiled at her assistant. "I appreciate that you look out for me. I probably don't tell you often enough, but having you outside my door helps me function in my crazy world."

"I don't really know what it's like to live with. . .the narcolepsy. It can't be easy."

"It's not unless you adapt to the situation." *Adapt.* She'd used Jake's word. "I pray a lot. And lately I've realized how deep I have my head buried in the sand. I don't have friends because I'm afraid of what they'll think when I have an attack. And we both know it's always when, never if."

"If they're good friends, they'll be concerned about you, not your problem," Ashleigh said without hesitation.

"Not everyone can handle it. Some people freak out. Some laugh. I need people who don't mind my problem. I know me being your boss makes our relationship different, but I thought maybe we could have lunch sometime. Or we could go out to dinner. Maybe even see a movie, though I don't know how long I'd last in a dark theater."

She grew quiet, and Lauren realized she'd put Ashleigh in a difficult situation. "It's okay. You don't want to deal with me in your off time."

Ashleigh frowned. "It has nothing to do with your condition. I like you, and what's more I respect you and all you've accomplished. I don't know that I would be as strong as you've been."

"I don't think of myself as strong." Lauren felt like a coward who hid out and limited her life.

If Jake hadn't asked those questions and shared some pretty brutal personal observations, she probably wouldn't be doing this now.

"Maybe we can eat lunch in the cafeteria. Jake says I need to socialize with the staff."

"Sure. Anytime."

"Thanks, Ashleigh." Lauren picked up her purse and lunch bag and walked toward her office.

"You should come to the pool party," Ashleigh called.

Lauren looked back and shook her head. "Too dangerous. People start playing around and next thing you know you're in the pool. I could drown."

"It can get rowdy. I hate it when they shove me in. Uh, Lauren," she began hesitantly, "Austin said he'd fix me up with this friend of his that I like if I introduced him to you. So if you want to meet him, we could double-date. See if these guys are worthy of us."

Ah, an ulterior motive. "Why do you think he wants to meet me?"

"He kept saying how pretty you were and asking why he'd never seen you before." She paused again. "I told him you were way too classy for him. I always tease the guys about being classless. They're not at all dignified like your dad and Mr. Greer. They're into partying and sports and acting stupid. I can't believe how juvenile they can be at times."

Her comment gave Lauren pause. She wasn't into any of that either.

"Daddy likes sports. Of course he's much older than your friends and has Mom to keep him in line."

Ashleigh laughed. "Yeah. Behind every good man there's a good woman."

Lauren nodded. "What's that old saying? Something about kissing a lot of frogs before finding your prince?" Not that she planned to do any kissing anytime soon. She'd need to know the guy really well before that happened.

"Yeah, and some of them are big, old, ugly toad frogs with attitude."

"Where do you meet guys?"

"Mostly at clubs and on the beach. I met Austin Danforth at college. We take the same night class."

Well, that said something for him, Lauren thought.

"He plans to get his degree and move out of sales. He said with the economy being like it is now, car sales are tough."

Times were difficult, but they had to hold firm and believe things would get better.

Then her thoughts shifted to Jake and the way he encouraged her to make friends. Did that include dating? What would it hurt to meet this guy?

"If you don't mind double-dating, I'd like to meet your friend."

"Okay," Ashleigh declared enthusiastically. "Is there a night that's better for you?"

"Friday or Saturday?"

"Should I tell him about your condition?"

Lauren shook her head. She didn't want total strangers aware of her situation. Later, if things worked out, she'd fill him in herself.

"Probably best until you get to know him. Things might not work out, and that's not the kind of information you want him sharing. Would you like for him to call or e-mail you?"

"Let's do the double date. I'll meet him then."

"I'll get back to you with a date and time."

"Meanwhile you can tell me everything you do know about him. Do you have pictures?" Lauren covered her mouth. "That sounds superficial."

Ashleigh shook her head. "Not at all. Seeing him might answer some of your questions. I'll bring one."

Safe in the privacy of her office, Lauren considered the step she'd taken. Driving lessons, the discussion over the house, and now a date with a stranger. Yep, her parents would think she'd lost her mind. And she wasn't so sure they wouldn't be right.

She wanted to say Jake Greer was her motivation for making changes in her life but thought perhaps voicing her desires had been the motivator.

Ashleigh came in around noon the next day with an invitation.

"Let's go to lunch and I'll tell you what I know about Austin."

"I brought lunch today, but there's enough for both of us." Lauren didn't share that she'd thought maybe Jake would stop by so she'd added an extra cup of soup to the thermos and packed a sandwich for him.

"Want me to run to the cafeteria for iced teas?"

"Sounds good. Unsweetened decaf for me."

After she left, Lauren moved a pile of folders from her small conference table and found two mugs for the soup. She spread the food on the table and pulled a roll of paper towels from the cabinet.

"Looks good," Ashleigh commented as she settled opposite Lauren.

"The soup is Mom's specialty. She watches the Food Network when she can and is always trying some new recipe." Lauren bowed her head to say grace and picked up her spoon.

Ashleigh took a taste and nodded. "Do you cook?"

Lauren smiled at that. "With supervision. I don't dare try it on my own. I could burn the house down. I do like to bake. Which I'm sure accounts for the fifteen pounds I can't lose."

"I don't cook much," Ashleigh said. "It's easier to eat out."

She unwrapped the cold-cuts sandwich and offered Ashleigh half. "We probably wouldn't cook as much if it weren't for Daddy. He's not likely to let a night go by without meat and potatoes on the table."

"I suppose a husband motivates a woman to prepare meals."

Lauren laughed outright at that. "Love motivates women to do a lot of stuff. Brings out the homemaker in us."

"None of the men I meet make me feel the least domestic."

They ate for a few minutes before Lauren asked, "What brought you here?"

"Former boyfriend was in the military. I followed him to North Carolina and liked the area enough to stay when the relationship fizzled. Sometimes I miss my parents and Savannah, but I like the area and my work. What about you? Do you like your work?"

Lauren considered the question. "I do. Though I doubt I could find another company that would tolerate my condition."

"You work so hard. I did some reading about narcolepsy after coming to work for you, but it's hard to understand."

Hard to live with, too, Lauren thought. "None of us understood what was happening until the doctors diagnosed the problem."

"And they don't know why you developed it?"

"There's no definitive answer. I live with it. I suppose you could call what I do living. Some might say I exist."

"Don't say that, Lauren. You have impressive accomplishments given what you face on a daily basis."

"Thanks." They had worked together for a couple of years now, but she'd never seen this aspect of her assistant. Lauren scooped some of the veggies from the mug.

Ashleigh pushed the photos across the table to her.

Lauren wiped her hands before accepting the pictures.

"He's six feet tall with brown hair and brown eyes. He has a pretty good build. Jogs five miles every morning. Claims he feels lousy if he doesn't."

"Uh-oh."

They grinned at each other.

Lauren wasn't a morning person nor did she jog. She didn't do much exercise for that matter. Like most people, her greatest motivation came around the New Year when she resolved to do better but quickly slid back into her old ways after a few days. She did walk Fred occasionally, but that hardly qualified as exercise.

"He tries to get us to run with him, but no one is interested."

"What else?" Lauren prompted.

"He's a transplant like me."

"From where?"

Her forehead creased. "California, I think."

That caught Lauren's attention. "He's a long way from home."

"He came here for a girl he met online. Found out all was not as it seemed."

Both Ashleigh and Austin had changed their lives for another person, and it hadn't worked out for them. Would she give up the life she knew and leave her family behind for the possibility of love? In her case, leaving her world behind could cause serious problems if she couldn't depend on the man she chose.

"Why didn't he go back home?"

Ashleigh shrugged. "Same as me, I think. We like the beach. He's a nice guy, Lauren. A good friend."

She wouldn't mind a good friend. "I look forward to meeting him."

Lauren rose and took their cups into the bathroom to rinse and dry them with a paper towel. Ashleigh swept the crumbs into the palm of her hand and disposed of them along with the sandwich wrappers.

"This has been fun," she said. "Let's do it again. Next time I'll bring lunch."

Lauren grinned and said, "Anytime you want."

Chapter 11

Teddy and I were talking, and he thinks it's time for another driving lesson now that I've got your grandfather's Jeep running again."

Lauren's eyes widened at his words. When Jake stepped in her office that morning, she'd expected nothing more than business as usual.

Over two weeks had passed since Jake and Teddy moved into Gram's house. The past week had been hectic with regular work and meetings with Jake and her dad to discuss company improvements. And then today, out of the blue, he'd come up with this. "And how did Teddy say that?"

His grin did all kinds of things to Lauren's heartbeat.

"Well, actually I suggested it and he clapped his hands. He thinks we should make plans for this weekend." Jake spoke in a casual jesting way.

"You got Gramps's Jeep running?" When had he found the time? Her mom said he'd painted the rockers and swing, too.

"Yeah. Suzanne said it was okay. We'll throw Teddy's car seat into the back and go cruising."

Horror filled Lauren at the thought. "No. That's too dangerous."

Jake ignored her comment. "We can picnic under that big old tree."

"Are you listening to me?" She didn't like being steam-rollered, and that was exactly what Jake was doing. And even worse, he expected her to fall in with his plans without argument.

The blue-green gaze pinned her. "If I doubted your ability, I wouldn't suggest this."

She stood up, surprised and more uncertain than ever. "My driving is too erratic. It can't be good for him."

"Don't you intend to drive anyone else around?"

The printer stopped and she reached for the pages. She glanced over the numbers, avoiding his question.

"Lauren?"

"I don't know." The truth gushed from her. "I have mixed feelings. Hurting myself would be bad enough, but harming others would be devastating."

He looped his arm about her shoulder, giving her a gentle squeeze. "If you don't believe in yourself, no one else will."

Jake's comment cut deep. "It's only with God's grace that I've accomplished anything in life."

The realization struck hard. Had she asked God to help her with these plans she was suddenly fast-tracking? And why wasn't she doing that? She'd always prayed first.

She needed to be certain she was doing what Jesus wanted for her. He'd helped her accomplish all she had in life and if this was His intention, He'd help her through.

Jake's encouragement and her parents' responses to her shared dreams had been wonderful. And she'd be the first to admit the idea of driving herself anywhere was fantastic. But where would she be when she got there? She didn't like being alone when an attack occurred. "I'm not comfortable with Teddy in the car."

"What about me?"

"I shouldn't risk your life either." Lauren watched him as she said, "Perhaps I should drive myself around the farm until I feel more comfortable."

"No way."

The words exploded from him and Lauren wondered why. "Are you afraid I'll fall asleep and hurt myself?"

"No, I'm not."

"You should be."

Jake sighed. "It's important that you have someone there to help when things happen and you don't know what to do."

"Like getting stuck in the sand on that first driving lesson?"

"Exactly. I pushed and you drove. You can't do both."

He had a point. "Okay, but I'll find a babysitter."

"Don't ask your mom. She already has so much to do."

She hadn't thought about whom she'd ask. Maybe no one and then she could put off the driving experience. "I could ask Ashleigh. We ate lunch in the cafeteria today."

He nodded approval, and she debated telling him about the plans. What would he think? Oh why not. Hadn't he encouraged her to get out there and meet people? "The television program had more results than expected. One of my fans wants to meet me."

A strange expression fleeted across his face. "What do you mean by 'fan'? You're not seriously considering meeting with a complete stranger, are you?"

Lauren shrugged. "Yeah, you meet strangers and sometimes they become friends. Actually this guy is a friend of Ashleigh's. We're going on a double date. She promised to stay nearby."

"Be careful. Some people aren't what they seem."

"I won't take any chances."

"Let me know about the driving lesson. Maybe Sunday after church. I thought we'd pick up a bucket of chicken and sides. Teddy can eat mashed potatoes."

After he left, her thoughts went to how carefree Jake sounded. Just the idea of having Teddy in the back of a vehicle while she drove scared her senseless. At least Jake could react in the event of an accident. Teddy wouldn't stand a chance.

❧

Lauren had a date. The words repeated themselves in his brain as Jake moved down the hall to his office. As he flopped down in his chair, it hit him that he didn't like the idea at all.

Sure, he'd encouraged her to make friends, but this wasn't what he meant. He particularly didn't care for the idea of her risking getting her heart broken by some guy who might not understand her problem. But what right did he have to interfere?

In a short time, he and Teddy would move on to the next job. He liked Lauren and if things were different, he could be interested in pursuing a relationship with her, but she needed more than he could give.

Still, he didn't have to like the idea. Maybe they could discuss it this weekend, and he could determine how comfortable she was. Was she taking the step because he'd pushed her to expand her horizons? Had he done the right thing?

He couldn't be sure. The worst thing would be for her to become discontented and depressed with the life she had because of something he'd said. Yes, he definitely would talk with her.

Jake smiled when he found Lauren waiting by his vehicle after church services on Sunday.

"I still don't know why I let you talk me into this."

His brows lifted. "Because you can't refuse really good fried chicken."

She laughed as she pulled her seat belt into place. "Yeah, the chicken motivated me."

"And the driving experience will, too."

"I didn't find anyone to watch Teddy."

"I've got it under control."

He'd asked Gerry to come over that afternoon. She'd be there by two thirty. That would give them time to change and have lunch.

Jake understood Lauren's concern and appreciated that she cared enough not to endanger his son. He stopped at the restaurant and ran inside to pick up the order. After stowing it behind his seat, he drove toward home.

He parked and Lauren carried their lunch bag inside. Jake carried Teddy with the diaper bag slung over his shoulder. She placed the bags on the counter and moved to take Teddy from his arms.

"He needs to be changed," Jake said. "We'll be right back."

He moved the guard blocking the doorway and carried Teddy down the hall to his room. After changing his son into the overalls, Jake left him in the crib while he exchanged his suit for jeans shorts and a golf shirt.

Back in the kitchen, he found Lauren had changed into capris and a print top.

"You are so cute in those," Lauren cooed to Teddy.

Teddy grinned and reached for her. Lauren took him. Jake noted that as she'd become more familiar with the baby, she'd grown more comfortable in handling him.

"Hey buddy." She hugged him close. "Did you have fun in the nursery today?"

Teddy chattered nonsense for a few minutes before he chanted, "*Dadadada*." Lauren glanced over her shoulder to where Jake worked at the counter. "Your son's calling you."

"I hear." He screwed the top on a sippy cup and handed it to Teddy.

"I thought you planned a picnic?"

"Change in plans." He took Teddy's bowl from the drain tray and scooped mashed potatoes, added a little gravy, and asked, "You want to feed him?"

"Sure."

Jake pulled the high chair over to the table, and Lauren settled Teddy and tied on his bib. When she bowed her head to say grace, Jake did the same and listened to Teddy babble along with her.

She scooped potatoes into his mouth and smiled when Teddy decided he liked the food and reached for the spoon. "You want to feed yourself?"

"Not potatoes and gravy," Jake warned. "Last time he rammed his hands in the bowl and had them all over everywhere."

She chuckled. "Did he get any into his mouth?"

"That might have been the only place he missed."

Lauren fed the baby more potatoes. "He's growing so fast. When's his birthday?"

"November twenty-fourth."

She nodded. "So tell me about this change in plans."

Jake eyed her before he spoke. "I asked Gerry to come over. But not because I don't trust you," he added.

Lauren touched Teddy's cheek. "He's so precious. I'd die if I hurt one hair on this head."

"What about my head?"

"Yes, you, too. There's no guarantee something won't happen."

He shrugged. "There's no guarantee for anyone who drives. I suspect you'll be more attentive than most."

"I'd like to think so, but then I know I can get sidetracked as easily as the next person."

"We're safe here, and you'll become more confident as you develop your skills."

"I hate to waste your time. Take time away from this little guy." She used Teddy's bib to wipe a bit of mashed potatoes from his chin.

He glanced at his son. "We'll go during his nap and have some fun after he wakes up. I think he wants you to push him around in that little car you bought him. It's killing my back."

"I should have gotten a wagon." Lauren placed the bowl on the table, out of the baby's reach. "That's all the potatoes he's going to eat."

Jake took a banana from the fruit bowl, deftly sliced it in half, and then cut that into bits, which he spread on the high chair tray. Teddy demonstrated his pincer grasp and pushed the banana into his mouth.

"Fruits and veggies. You start them out eating right and all too soon they're existing on junk food."

Jake tapped her arm. "Stop being philosophical and come fix yourself a plate."

Lauren peered down into the box and chose a chicken breast. After scooping potatoes and cole slaw onto her plate, she opted to skip the biscuit.

They sat at the kitchen table. Teddy ate a few more banana bits before he grew tired and started to cry.

Jake wiped Teddy's face and hands and settled him on the living room carpet with a couple of toys. He waited to see if his son was content before returning to the table.

"This grilled chicken is actually pretty good." He held the drumstick in the air. "I eat way too much fast food, but every now and then I get the urge to eat right. Actually I have the urge pretty often but can't summon the enthusiasm to cook.

"At least Teddy has a decent diet now. You're right though. I need to clean up my act before he starts eating regular food. Nutritionally balanced meals won't hurt either of us. So are you excited about your date?"

He could see his sudden change of subject startled her.

"I don't know much about the guy."

"You didn't know me either," Jake pointed out. "And here we are, two friends sharing Sunday lunch. Think of the date the same way."

Lauren dropped her fork on the plate. "It's not the same." She dropped her gaze. "You don't have expectations at the end of our lunches or dinners."

He felt his jaw tense. "He shouldn't either."

"Ashleigh says he's nice."

"I hope you have a good time." Did he really? He hoped she wasn't going too fast.

"No expectations, no disappointment if it's not what I hoped for." She glanced around and asked, "Where's Yapper?"

"Good question." He'd left her in the kitchen. Jake noticed the lower corner of the guard he'd used to block the laundry room was pushed back. He spotted the tiny dog curled up on the pile of laundry he'd planned to wash the previous evening.

"Yapper," he called, moving the guard. She jumped up, coming over to dance about his feet as they walked back into the kitchen. "I'm surprised she didn't hear us. Must have worn herself out playing while we were gone."

The tiny dog barked nonstop as she made a wild dash into the living room. Yapper dodged Teddy's hands as she lapped at his face and then ran into the kitchen to jump up on Lauren's leg.

She wiped her hands and patted the dog's head. Her greeting served to excite the dog even further and she began to bark.

"Yapper, stop that," Jake demanded. "That yippy little bark drives me crazy."

"Poor baby can't help how she sounds," Lauren crooned as she patted her once more. "It's how she communicates."

"Quiet, Yapper," Jake snapped.

The dog looked at him with her big sad eyes.

"Why does her barking bother you so much?"

He was transported back in time to the day Gwen died. As usual, they argued over his refusal to give up his consulting job, and he had retreated to his home office and closed the door. Gwen had gone to swim in their heated pool while Teddy napped. Yapper's constant barking served as the impetus that forced him outside. He found the dog paddling furiously to keep her head above water while Gwen floated facedown in the pool.

He'd tried to resuscitate her, but it had been too late. The determination had been accidental death by drowning. The police thought she'd probably tripped over the dog, knocked herself unconscious when her head hit the pool coping, and drowned when she fell into the pool.

Jake felt a tremendous load of guilt. Not only had he been angry with his wife, he'd possibly provided the weapon that killed her.

"Jake?"

"She never stops."

"Teddy cries continually at times. Does that bother you?"

"No," he admitted gruffly.

The dog ran off. Lauren glanced into the living room and saw Teddy and Yapper engaged in a war over a stuffed toy. She laughed as the two waged battle. Like every tug-of-war, one would get ahead and then the other, until Teddy shook his head and yelled, "No."

That surprised the animal, and Teddy yanked his toy back to safety. Yapper danced around out of reach.

"Those two are quite a pair."

Jake nodded grimly. "You'd think Yapper would be afraid Teddy would grab her. He's got his hands on her a time or two, and she howled like he was killing her."

Yapper grabbed the other toy and ran off. Teddy crawled after her in hot pursuit.

"Look at him go."

The dog abandoned the toy in favor of dancing from side to side and barking at the baby. Teddy waved his arm and told her no again.

"He learned that from you." She started to laugh when Teddy chanted, *Nonono.*

Jake joined in and their laughter turned into deep belly laughs. The glass she'd been drinking from hit the floor.

He grabled her arm to keep her from falling off the chair. The attack passed in a couple of minutes. Lauren could hear Jake, felt his support as he kept her from falling out of the chair. It only lasted a couple of minutes.

"What happened?" he demanded, his arms wrapped about her.

"They call it cataplexy."

"Has it happened before? What caused it?"

"Yes. Probably caused by the laughter."

"Laughter?"

"I haven't laughed like that in a long time."

He could see she was angry at herself for being embarrassed. "Lauren, I'm sorry."

"It's not your fault. Laughing is an ordinary everyday activity."

"Do you need a doctor?"

"No, but I won't try to drive today."

"We can do something else. I'll call Gerry and let her know we don't need her. We can go for a drive. I know. Let's go see the Cape Lookout Lighthouse."

"We need to plan that for when we have a full day. We would have to catch a ferry over."

"I could take you home to rest."

"Yeah, I really need more rest."

Her sarcastic response bothered him. "I'm sorry, Lauren."

"Stop saying that. You didn't do anything," she snapped. "Sorry. I don't mean to be hateful. The experience still scares me."

"You've had these attacks before?"

"Not often. They're generally brought on by emotion."

"Should you call your mom?"

"There's nothing she can do."

He watched her closely. "Then what do we do, Lauren?"

"Next time I don't laugh so hard when I find something funny. See, there are reasons I subdue myself. Obviously I can't handle anything more."

Sadness touched his face. "Tell me you're okay. That this hasn't caused any harmful side effects."

"It's over, Jake. Let me clean up this mess before Teddy or Yapper gets into it."

"I'll handle it."

Withdrawn, she muttered, "Maybe you should take me home."

He grabbed a handful of paper towels and wiped up the tea. Jake stepped on the can lift and tossed the towels into the trash. "No. Your parents aren't there." He knew they had gone out for lunch with friends and planned to play pinochle that afternoon. "Teddy and I like having you around, so if we don't do anything but sit in the porch swing, we want you to stay."

"You have better things to do."

"I spend my Sunday afternoons doing what I like and today that's spending time with you."

She jumped up from the chair. "Don't do me any favors, Jake."

He caught her shoulders. "Stop it, Lauren. Did you take your medication today?"

"I don't know. I'd have to check my pillbox. Maybe it was relief in not having to drive with Teddy in addition to the laughter."

"So you think I caused your reaction?"

She wouldn't look him in the eye.

He didn't hear Teddy's babbling and glanced over to where his son pulled magazines from the rack. Yapper chewed furiously on Teddy's toy.

Lauren's gaze followed Jake's. She rose from the chair and went into the living room. "Bad dog," she chastised, taking the toy from him. "This is not yours." She picked Teddy up and moved to the sofa. "You should call Mrs. Hart."

"Sure you don't want to try driving?"

"I don't know what happened, and I'm not about to get behind the wheel of a vehicle and see if it happens again. That would be like playing Russian roulette with a fully loaded gun." Lauren's quiet but firm response left Jake with no doubt to her feelings on the matter.

Jake lifted Teddy from her arms. "I'll put him down for his nap and give Gerry a call. We'll hang out here. Maybe even go for ice cream later if you're up to it."

"Oh, I'm always up for ice cream."

~

After Jake left the room, Lauren went into the kitchen. She put away the leftovers and wiped down the table and high chair, pushing the chair back into the corner of the room. Teddy's bib lay on the floor. She picked it up and flaked off a bit of dried potato.

There were spots on the wall and cabinet where the tea had splashed. Finding a sponge underneath the sink, she wiped them off and debated cleaning the floor, which felt sticky. She located a mop in the laundry room and used it to clean the floor.

Had her fear brought on the attack? The laughter? She had been terribly afraid that Jake would insist on carrying through with his plan. What was he thinking? They'd had one lesson. Things had gone well, but that didn't mean every time would be the same.

Unbidden tears tracked along her cheeks. There were no guarantees in her life. No certainties.

Lauren understood the same could be said for everyone, but the balances didn't always make sense to her. Here tiny Teddy had lost his mother and Jake his wife, and yet she with all her flaws lived on. A misfit in a world that would never understand her.

At her feet, Yapper whimpered as if she understood Lauren's pain.

Tired of the maudlin thoughts, she swiped her eyes with the back of her hand. While her purpose might not be clear to her, it was clear to God. He had a reason, and it wasn't hers to question.

She picked up the little dog and pulled her to her chest, feeling comforted by her closeness.

~

After Teddy sprawled comfortably in the crib, Jake stepped out into the hall. He pulled the cell from his pocket and dialed.

"Gerry, Jake here. Hope I caught you before you left."

"I'm still at home."

"Good. There's been a change in plans. You don't need to come after all. I'll pay you for this afternoon."

"You will not."

He leaned against the wall. "It's the least I can do for changing your plans."

"I didn't have plans. I went to church, picked up lunch, and came home."

"Well, now you can relax and prepare for next week with the terrible twosome."

She laughed. "They're not terrible."

"They keep us on our toes."

"That they do. See you in the morning."

Jake found Lauren on the sofa, thumbing through the Sunday paper he'd left on the coffee table.

"She hadn't left yet."

Lauren laid the paper down.

He sat next to her and sprawled comfortably on the sofa. She had picked up the magazines, put the toys in a basket, and straightened the kitchen. They sat in silence for a minute or so before Jake asked, "Lauren, do you feel I'm pushing you to step outside your comfort zone?"

There, he'd said it. Put his concern out there for consideration. He could see from her expression that she was uncomfortable with the question. "You do," he announced glumly.

"No, Jake. You encouraged me when I opened up to you about my dreams. And you've done what you could to make them happen. I don't understand why it's so important to you, but I appreciate the encouragement you've offered."

Why was it important? What purpose had he served by offering to teach her to drive? Revealing her secret desires to her parents? Pushing her to do the television program? Suggesting she find friends?

She wasn't Gwen. Lauren's decisions weren't based on being a healthy young woman who could do anything her heart desired. Not only was she forced to consider the ramifications of how narcolepsy affected her life in every decision she made, but she had to consider what could happen to her if she chose wrongly.

He had even suggested she rip herself from the safety of her parents' home. The one place in the world where she could feel secure. Why had he blinded himself to that? Needy women. He'd dealt with that with Gwen. He liked Lauren and didn't want to see her fall into the same trap. He'd encouraged her to pursue her dreams. Was that so wrong?

"Jake?"

"Sorry," he muttered, shaking himself from his reverie. "I was thinking about what you said earlier. You told me you weren't comfortable, but I insisted. I should have realized the stress wouldn't be good for you. I'm sorry,

Lauren. That was wrong of me."

After a few minutes, Lauren spoke, "Sometimes the faith others have helps us to try a little harder. I think maybe I, along with Mom and Dad, reached a consensus that my life is the best it can be. I contented myself with the status quo even though I have dreams and aspirations. Maybe not as big as some people's, but I do have hope for the future. I don't see myself leaving Sleep Dreams, but you're right. Mom and Dad aren't always going to be there. I need to be practical and think about the future."

"No, Lauren. You don't. Both of your parents are healthy, active people who will be around for years. You don't need me pushing you to change your life."

"Is this because of what I said earlier? About the driving?"

He shrugged. "That and the feeling that I came on too strong. I don't live your life, Lauren. I have no right to say what you can and can't do."

She stared at him and then recited, " 'Doing what you've always done gets you what you've always gotten.' Isn't that what you told us?"

He had said that and he'd meant it from a business perspective. Companies had to change constantly or become stagnant. He supposed people did as well.

"I think you're a great encourager, but then improving quality of life is what you do."

Was it? Jake wondered. He certainly hadn't improved his family's life. Doing what he'd always done hadn't helped his marriage, and he knew it wouldn't help his son either. As Teddy grew older, he would need roots. A steady home environment where he could develop properly.

Not now, Jake thought. Teddy was a baby. It would be years before he would be forced to make a decision that would keep him in one place.

"I placed added stress on you," Jake said. "You need to tell me when it's too much. You did such a great job with the television program that the newspaper wants to do a feature. Your dad suggested you do the interview."

He felt her shiver with a frisson of fear.

"I'll do it. We have to keep the Sleep Dreams name out there to increase our profit margin."

"Tell me about the Christmas in July sales event," Jake suggested, hoping to distract her from their earlier conversation. "Greg said it was your idea."

Lauren rested one foot up on the old coffee table. "People fix up their homes for the holidays. The ad promotion had to do with getting new bedding before the guests arrive. We offered six months same as cash and promised their custom-made mattresses would be in place before the holidays. Sales were good. Some people elected to take warehouse inventory while others wanted custom. We're about two-thirds complete on the custom purchases."

"Well in advance of the deadline. Any other ideas?"

"I thought we might have a Snuggle sale in October."

"Snuggle?"

She laughed. "Winter is coming and people like to be warm and cozy in their beds. We could offer flannel sheets or a duvet with every purchase."

"What about Valentine's Day? Give your sweetheart a mattress."

Lauren's mouth widened with her smile. "Now that would be very different from flowers and candy."

Teddy cried out. "Nap's over," Jake said. "Ready for ice cream?"

"Let's go for a walk," she suggested. "I'm sure Yapper could use one and I know I could."

"Okay, we'll be right back. Yapper's leash is in the laundry room."

Chapter 12

Lauren sat at her desk considering the previous afternoon. The walk had been fun. Jake explained that Yapper had a tendency to chase after wild animals, and he kept her on a leash to keep her out of trouble.

"She's got the heart of a lion," Lauren defended.

The little dog pranced and prowled as they walked along the dirt road that bordered the perimeter of the farm. Later, they went for ice cream and ate their favorite flavors from bowls. Teddy smacked his enjoyment of the icy treat.

She considered Jake's concern that he'd pushed too hard. She needed that push. Shove, actually. She wouldn't have reached out to Ashleigh nor done any of the other things she'd tried since meeting him.

Her assistant tapped on the door and came into the office. "You have plans for Friday night? The guys want to take us to dinner."

"I'm free."

"What if I come over and they pick us up at your place? Or we could meet them at the restaurant."

"Have them come to the house. Will he be weird about meeting my parents? I know they'll want to meet him and know where we're going. I don't think they'll show up at the restaurant, but you never know."

Ashleigh giggled. "I promise to look out for you. I'll stick by you like glue."

"And they'll bring us home pretty quickly."

She shrugged. "If they don't understand, too bad."

Lauren smiled at her. "Just remember, they don't know the whole story."

The week flew past and all too soon, Lauren was fighting back the butterflies in her stomach as she waited for her date to arrive. Her mother had taken her shopping the previous evening.

"Mom, I have plenty of clothes."

Suzanne shook her head. "You need something new. It's not every day a girl goes on her first date."

She groaned. First date. She sounded like a teen, not a twenty-seven-year-old woman.

"Where are they taking you?"

"Ashleigh suggested Clawson's 1905."

It was just down the street from her parents' home, and they loved to eat at the beautifully restored restaurant.

Lauren tried on a pile of clothes and came away with a cute top to wear with her black dress slacks and a pair of wedge heels. She refused to wear stilettos.

"Men like heels on a woman. Particularly when they wear a skirt."

Her mother was determined to get her into a dress. "Well, I don't plan to show him my legs or my teeth."

Suzanne roared. "Okay, I know when to shut up."

Now Lauren tugged at her clothing, which suddenly seemed not to fit properly.

"Stop that," her mother chided, slapping at her hands. "You look fine."

She glanced over into the family room where Jake and Teddy sat talking to her father. "What are they doing here?"

"Jake brought over some papers for your dad. I invited him to stay for supper."

Lauren rolled her eyes. Wasn't it bad enough that her parents had to sanction her blind date? Now Jake would be here watching. She bit the inside of her lip and steeled herself to deal with the situation.

The doorbell rang and Ashleigh breezed in, dressed in a short black dress guaranteed to impress her date. Lauren felt frumpy in comparison.

"You look great," Ashleigh declared.

"Thanks," Lauren mumbled.

"She does, doesn't she, Mrs. Kingsley?"

"Yes, Ashleigh, she does. Of course she didn't believe me when I told her."

"You look very pretty, Laurie." Jake stood in the doorway.

She blushed and offered him a self-conscious smile.

Teddy bounced in his father's arms, a smile on his face as he reached for her. *"Lalalala!"*

"He wants to say hello," Jake said as they came closer.

"Hey sweetie," she said, taking him into her arms. She sat in the armchair and bounced him on her legs. "Did you have a good day with Mrs. Hart?"

Teddy jabbered. He reached for the decorations on her shirt and tried to pluck the tiny beads with his fingers. She patted them and asked, "Do you like my beads?"

He patted them with his hands.

Lauren pointed to the embroidery on his overalls. "Puppy."

Teddy touched it and chattered something that didn't sound like *puppy*.

In all the commotion, she didn't hear the doorbell and looked up to find Ashleigh standing there with two men.

She smiled shyly and got to her feet. Jake reached for his son. "Go get him," he whispered softly.

She grinned at him.

"Austin Danforth, this is Lauren Kingsley."

"Hello, Lauren," he said with a huge smile as he engulfed her smaller hand in his. "It's a pleasure to meet you."

"You, too." She quickly introduced her parents, Jake, and Teddy. He shook hands with her mother and father and nodded at Jake before smiling at the baby.

319

"Hi there, little guy. I have a nephew about your age."

Teddy continued to chant his version of Lauren's name and struggled to reach her.

"No, Teddy," Jake said, pulling the baby up in his arms. "Laurie has to go."

He wailed inconsolably. Suzanne took him. "Come on, sweetie. Let's check on dinner."

She paused to kiss her daughter's cheek and said, "Have fun, Laurie. Nice meeting you, Austin."

"You, too, Mrs. Kingsley. Ready?" he asked Lauren.

She nodded and paused by the entrance hall table to unplug her phone and tuck it into her purse.

Austin walked next to her on the sidewalk. "I've been looking forward to this all week."

He paused to open the passenger door and pulled the seat forward so the other couple could climb into the back.

"Me, too," Lauren said. His easy chatter made her comfortable.

Austin helped her inside and closed the door. He climbed into the driver's seat.

"Ashleigh tells me you're the CFO for your father's company," he commented as he drove the short distance to the restaurant.

"Among other things. It's a small company. We all wear a number of hats."

"You did a great job on the television program. I'm thinking of ordering a custom mattress."

"I'd never done anything like that before. The interviewer was really good. I followed her lead, and the time flew by. I didn't want to do the program, but Jake said it would be good publicity."

"Jake? The guy at the house?"

"Yes. He's working with us to improve operations."

Austin glanced at her and moved his gaze back to the road. "The little boy belongs to him?"

"Yes," Lauren said.

"He really likes you."

"I'm fond of him, too," she admitted.

His look became a little speculative. "You spend a lot of time with him?"

"Not a lot." She didn't want to talk about how often she saw Teddy or Jake. Lauren changed the subject. "Ashleigh tells me you're a car salesman."

"Yes." He named the dealership where he worked. "I've been there for about two years now. I'm working on getting my BA so I can pursue a different field. Maybe something in banking."

She nodded. "Ashleigh said you met at the college."

"We did. Do you have a degree, Lauren?"

"No. I have some college credits but no degree."

"I don't suppose it's necessary since you already have a good job. You like working for the family business?"

Why did that question always seem to arise? "I do. My mom trained me to take over when she went back into real estate."

"How's that working for her? Her sales down?"

"Mom does well. She's been selling real estate for years. She's well-known in the community and gets lots of referrals."

"Definitely nice to have regular clientele."

Lauren could hear Ashleigh and the man she'd introduced as Seth Green getting acquainted in the backseat. "So how do you like our area?"

He glanced at her and said, "I really like it a lot. I enjoy the beach in particular."

"I rarely get to the beach," she admitted. "Between work and my other responsibilities I never have time. Jake and I went over to Carrot Island recently, but that's the first time in forever."

She noted that look again.

"I spend every Sunday at the beach."

"We went after church."

He didn't pursue her mention of church, and Lauren knew he didn't attend. "What else do you like to do?"

"Hang out with friends. Sometimes we have pickup games at the apartment complex."

Everyone had friends.

He waited for a car that was leaving and angle-parked right in front of the restaurant. "Meant to be," he said with a big grin.

Austin's hand brushed her back now and again as the hostess led them to a private table in the front of the building. They placed their drink orders.

"Anyone interested in an appetizer?" the waitress asked. The men conferred over the menu and ordered wings and cheese fries.

"I'll be right back with your drinks."

"Hey, you can be the designated driver," Austin announced.

"Sorry. I don't drive." Lauren had chosen ice water. It struck her that it was a good thing her home was only blocks from the restaurant.

His head bobbed backward, and he looked at her with disbelief. "You don't drive? I don't think I ever knew anyone who didn't drive. Except for my grandmother."

Lauren knew she was a dinosaur in the modern world. She shrugged.

"I was going to ask what sort of car you drove."

So far he scored zero on the sensitivity scale. Lauren twisted uncomfortably in her chair. She glanced at Ashleigh who rolled her eyes.

"No car." She studied the menu.

"Do you know what you want for dinner?"

Lauren laid the menu on the table and rested her hands on top. "I'll have the Salad Sampler Trio."

"Sure that's going to be enough?" Austin asked. "You look like a girl with a hearty appetite."

Lauren couldn't help but feel insulted. "It's more than enough."

"Not that you're fat or anything."

His attempt to backpedal his way out didn't do much to soothe her ruffled feathers. "It's enough," she said succinctly.

"So what kind of music do you like?"

"Contemporary Christian. You?"

"Oh. I'm more into rock. Some rap. What about movies?"

Lauren unwrapped her silverware and laid it on the tabletop, pulling the napkin into her lap. "I suppose you'd call me a PG kind of girl."

With that, their conversation ground to a halt. Lauren supposed he was trying to come up with a topic. This wasn't going well. So far they had nothing in common.

The appetizer arrived. "Careful," the waitress warned as she slid the platters on the table. "Hot." She took the plates and more napkins from another waitress. Lauren took a couple of fries and a wing. "I love these," Ashleigh commented as she placed wings on her own plate.

Of course she did. Ashleigh was skinny.

Lauren wiped the sauce from her fingers and asked Seth, "What do you do?"

"I work for my dad. We have a furniture store. Green's Furniture."

Another longtime family business. "I know that store," Lauren said. "My mom has bought furniture there."

Austin waved his fork at Seth. "That's how we met. He sold me my recliner and my flat screen."

Seth grinned at Ashleigh and said, "I'm trying to get him to replace that pitiful excuse for a sofa."

"But he couldn't offer me as good a deal."

Ashleigh glanced at Lauren and said, "That sofa is the reason we never go to Austin's apartment. I'm pretty sure he sharpens those springs when no one is looking."

"What springs?" Seth joked. "Sit down on that thing and you'll never find your way back."

"Pretty heartless of you guys to demean my sofa like that," Austin declared with mock offense.

The couple laughed, and Lauren felt as though she were on the outside looking in. They lived in their own world and while she could possibly fit in, she didn't feel any strong desire to try.

"Yeah, Lauren, don't ever sit on his sofa," Ashleigh said. "Make him give you the recliner."

"Oh, I'll share with pleasure," Austin said with a grin that bordered on a leer. Why did she suspect that if he'd had a moustache he would have twirled the ends?

"I'll remember that." Not that there was any possibility she'd ever visit his apartment.

"After dinner, let's go back to my place and watch television. There's a game on tonight."

"No way," Ashleigh and Seth said together.

Austin fixed his puppy dog gaze on her. "What about you, Lauren? You interested in seeing my place?"

She looked at Ashleigh and the young woman answered for her, "We're not going back to your apartment."

"What did you plan to do after dinner?"

Go home, Lauren thought wistfully. She liked Austin okay but didn't feel the same connection she felt with Jake. She wasn't being fair. She'd known Jake longer.

"So, Lauren, why didn't you ever get your driver's license?"

"Austin! That's none of your business."

Ashleigh's angry outburst surprised them.

"I was making conversation," he defended.

"And if she'd wanted you to know she would have told you when you brought it up earlier."

Not wanting to cause controversy between the friends, Lauren said softly, "Health reasons."

Under lowered lashes, she watched him attempt to puzzle that one out.

"Do you run?"

She shook her head.

"I do five miles a day. My day stinks if I don't get my run in."

She tried to look impressed.

"I run all year long." He nodded toward his friends. "I tried to get them to go with me, but they're not interested. What about you, Lauren? You want to come along?"

She chuckled. "I wouldn't last through the first quarter mile."

His eyes drifted over her again. "Wouldn't be long before you could run a mile."

"I really don't have time, Austin. I'm usually at work by seven and most days I don't get home until after seven in the evening."

"Well, if you change your mind, give me a call. I'd love a partner."

Their food arrived, and the conversation veered off to other subjects the three of them had in common. Lauren listened, wishing herself elsewhere.

"Anyone leave room for dessert?" the waitress asked.

They all groaned and shook their heads.

When their bill came, Austin pulled out a credit card and slid it on the tray. Lauren felt she should pay her own way. She hadn't been much of a date.

"Well, ladies, what would you like to do next?"

"Let's ride down to Atlantic Beach," Ashleigh suggested. "That sound okay to you, Lauren?"

"Sounds great." They climbed into the vehicle and Lauren reached for her seat belt. She fought the familiar feeling of an attack as Austin backed out of the parking space.

He put the vehicle in drive and said, "That place has some great food."

"It does."

She wanted to say more, but the movement of the car added to her overwhelming sleepiness.

Lauren came out of the attack several minutes later with Austin demanding, "What's wrong with her? Why did she flake out like that?" There was laughter in his voice.

They were parked near the beach access.

"Shut up, Austin," Ashleigh snapped. She sat on the edge of the seat next to Lauren, holding her hand. "You okay?"

She managed a slight nod. Why had this happened tonight of all nights?

"Did she pass out?" Austin demanded from where he stood outside the passenger door.

In her head, Lauren could hear Jake urging her to share the truth. He didn't understand her narcolepsy was not something to be shared randomly. It required people who cared and wanted to help her, not those who would be turned off by her attacks.

"I'm sorry but I need to go home," she said, finding she couldn't open up to this man who stared at her with confusion in his brown gaze.

"Sure," Austin said.

He pulled up the seat for Ashleigh to clamber into the back. Lauren sensed Austin's gaze on her as they rode in silence. She wouldn't look at him. She could hear Ashleigh and Seth talking low in the back. Probably making plans to see each other again.

"I'll walk her inside," Ashleigh said as soon as Austin pulled into the driveway.

He made no effort to leave the car. Lauren opened the door and climbed out. She pulled the seat forward, and Ashleigh and Seth followed her from the car.

When Seth told Austin he'd catch a ride home with Ashleigh, Austin looked from one to the other, confused over the sudden change in plans.

Lauren leaned down and said, "I'm sorry about how the evening ended. I enjoyed meeting you." She rooted through her purse and pulled out a twenty. "Here. For my dinner."

He looked at the money and shook his head.

"No. I insist," Lauren said, pushing it into his hand. "It hasn't been a very fun evening for you. There's time to watch your game or meet up with friends and do something fun."

Austin shrugged and took the money, dropping it on the console.

"It was nice meeting you, too, Lauren." The unhappiness in his expression told her he'd hoped for a different ending to his evening.

She smiled and waved good-bye before turning to go inside.

Ashleigh followed. "Are you okay?"

"I'm fine."

"Not your Mr. Right?" Ashleigh giggled and whispered, "I've known guys who put me to sleep, too."

"I feel bad."

Ashleigh shrugged. "He wasn't your type."

"Not sure I have a type but if I do, he wasn't the one. We didn't have much in common. But then I didn't give him much of a chance."

"It only takes seconds to form your first impression," Ashleigh reminded. "You knew from the moment you met whether things would click and they didn't."

"You and Seth really hit it off."

"He's so nice," she said dreamily.

Lauren nodded toward where Seth stood. "Go on. I'll see you Monday."

Ashleigh hugged her. "I'll find someone for you."

Lauren wanted to tell her not to bother. She'd already found someone, and he wasn't interested in anything but friendship. She had the feeling no one could ever measure up to Jake Greer. "Have fun." She called to Seth, "Nice meeting you."

"You, too."

She let herself into the house and found her parents and Jake sitting at the dining table. Teddy slept on the sofa.

"Back already?" her mother asked, looking dismayed.

"I had an attack when we got into the car after dinner. I asked him to bring me home."

Jake looked past her. "And he didn't escort you inside?"

"Ashleigh walked me to the door. She and her date left in her car."

"So what happened to him?" Jake demanded.

"I suspect he's finding someone to help him complete his evening."

"Not your type?"

She shook her head. "We didn't have much in common."

Did he look pleased or was it her imagination? Jake wouldn't be happy about her failed attempt at making friends. Not after he'd encouraged her to get out and meet people. He'd think she hadn't tried hard enough.

"How was dinner?"

They talked about the restaurant, and Lauren refused dessert when her mother indicated the punch-bowl cake on the buffet. "Maybe later. I'm going to change."

She removed the new blouse and hung it in her closet, knowing she'd never wear it again without thinking of that failed first date. Lauren pulled on shorts and a T-shirt and dropped down onto her bed. She considered the way they had abandoned Austin and felt guilty.

There was a tap on the door. The door opened and her mom stuck her head inside. "You okay?"

"I don't feel good about the way the evening ended."

She came into the room. "Would you feel better if you'd stuck it out?"

Lauren shook her head. "He wasn't a Christian. Every time I mentioned God, he changed the subject."

"That is an important consideration. You need a man of faith. Love has its own problems, and your condition requires someone to stand by you in prayer when things get particularly difficult."

"I still feel bad," she said glumly. "I repaid him for my dinner. I thought that was fair."

"What happened?"

Lauren told her mother about their conversation. "We were going to ride down to Atlantic Beach. I woke up to find Ashleigh next to me and Austin asking what was going on. He laughed."

"You didn't tell him?"

She shook her head. "I can't tell everyone, Mom. Jake believes it would afford me more security, but I think information in the hands of the wrong people could be dangerous."

"I agree. There's no reason for everyone to know."

"But it seems unfair to pretend nothing happened. Maybe I should have explained."

"You think he would have asked you out again?"

Lauren pulled her leg under her on the bed. "Probably not. All I could think was this is not my crowd. I love Ashleigh, but I don't see me hanging out with her friends. They like to party and have fun."

"Most young people do, Laurie."

"But there's no way I'd put myself out there in the clubs."

"Did they lead you to believe that's where they hang out?"

"I think they party in each other's homes more. Not Austin's apartment though. His furniture must consist of a really bad sofa, a recliner, and a big-screen television. He did say he was thinking of ordering a mattress from us. Guess I can forget that sale."

Her mother chuckled. "Your dad would probably furnish this place the same way if he didn't have me around." Suzanne took her daughter's hand. "Come on. I'm sure your dad has run out of conversation by now."

They settled in as if nothing had happened. Jake challenged Lauren to a game of Wii golf and the older Kingsleys joined in. Her parents had been surprised when Lauren gave them the game system for Christmas, but they played often. Her mother particularly enjoyed the fitness program.

They tried to keep their voices down as Teddy slept on the sofa. The four adults took turns and Lauren was the victor.

"See, Suzanne," her dad said. "I need to spend more time on the golf course."

"There's nothing stopping you, Greg. In fact, I suggest you get it out of your system while Jake is with us."

He frowned. "Let's don't talk about Jake leaving."

Lauren felt the same way. She knew their time together was growing shorter. It was already mid-September.

"This has been fun, but I need to get Teddy home to bed. I'll have those graphs for you on Monday."

The two men shook hands. Jake hugged Suzanne and then Lauren. "Want to go see the lighthouse tomorrow?"

Was he offering himself as a consolation prize? "It's supposed to be a nice day. I'll pick you up around eight and we could spend the day."

She nodded.

"Since we're going over to work in the attic, we could watch Teddy and Yapper for you," Suzanne volunteered. "I know Greg would be happy to have an excuse not to go up there."

"They'd probably be happier at home," Jake agreed.

"We'll see you in the morning then. We'll bring Lauren to your place."

Chapter 13

Over coffee early the following morning, Jake thought about Laurie's date. They hadn't clicked. Why exactly did that please him? Lauren needed someone who considered her special and would protect her from harm.

And that person couldn't be him. Right now, Teddy was as needy as he could handle. He'd learned his lesson with Gwen. No more women with unrealistic expectations.

Still, he hadn't liked that Austin guy. Everything about him had been too much. Too handsome. Too polished with the ladies. He wasn't her type. And the jerk hadn't even helped her to the door after she'd suffered the attack.

She deserved better. Much better. He filled the thermos with coffee and dumped snacks into the backpack he'd picked up last night.

Jake heard the Kingsleys' car pull up outside and opened the door. "Teddy's still asleep."

"Rough night?" Suzanne asked.

"I changed him into his pajamas and put him in the crib. He slept all night. You think something's wrong?"

"We all need more sleep at times. You two go ahead. We'll dress and feed him when he wakes."

Jake drove Down East toward Otway and Harkers Island and the Cape Lookout National Seashore. "Greg won't be much help with Teddy underfoot."

Lauren laughed. "Mom won't let Daddy near the attic."

"But she said. . ."

"He'd toss it all without a second thought. Mom has no intention of letting that happen."

Jake sighed almost dramatically. "That makes me feel better."

She smiled at him, and he suddenly felt wonderful.

They drove to the visitor center and went inside to study the displays, pick up literature, and watch a film entitled *Ribbon of Sand* before heading out to find a passenger transport ferry.

They parked and Jake carried the pack with their supplies. "Have we got everything?" he asked, glancing around. Lauren had the camera and binoculars. "I don't know how to act without Teddy."

"We could have brought him."

"He's happier at home. He's not a sun and sand fan."

They boarded the ferryboat, a flat-bottom skiff that would deliver them to the south-side beach. The captain welcomed them and told them where to sit. The other three passengers smiled at them. The ride across the open water was exhilarating, the spray splashing back on them now and then.

They wore jeans and carried lightweight jackets to ward off the chill, though the sun seemed determined to handle the task alone.

When they arrived at the island, the captain advised everyone of the pickup time. Jake clambered off the boat and offered his hand. Awareness shot through him as Lauren took it.

"There you go," Lauren said, pointing to the Cape Lookout Lighthouse. "Built one hundred and fifty years ago to help mariners safely negotiate the dreaded Lookout Shoals, aka Graveyard of the Atlantic."

"I heard the locals call it the Diamond Lady."

Lauren nodded. "The painted diamond pattern aids in direction, black north-south, and white east-west. One hundred sixty-three feet tall with two hundred and one steps and a three-hundred-sixty-degree view of the Crystal Coast from the observation deck."

"Can we climb it today?"

She shook her head. "Season is mid-May through mid-September."

Jake sighed. "I meant to come sooner."

They toured the area, Jake taking photos of her in front of the lighthouse and her doing the same for him. And he handed over the camera when another couple offered to take one of them together. They also saw the Keeper's House and the former US Coast Guard Station.

Later they boarded the skiff again and went to Shackelford Banks to see the wild Banker ponies. The free-roaming Spanish horses were said to have descended from horses that swam to the island four hundred years before.

They had quite a walk before they located a group of horses. They kept their distance as Jake raised the camera and snapped a number of photos.

Lauren sat reading the flyer she'd picked up from the park service. " 'They divide themselves into harems and bachelor bands. Each dominant alpha stallion guards a harem of mares and foals. Sometime between a year and a half to five years the young fillies and colts leave the harem. The females join other harems and the males form loose bachelor bands.' " She laughed outright at that. " 'Bachelor band life gives the colts a chance to spar and mature into stallions so they can challenge the existing alphas.' "

Just like human bachelors, Jake thought.

"You want to go shell hunting?"

He brushed sand from her arm. "I'll pass. I don't need shells to remember this day."

Her gaze met his as she said, "Me neither."

<hr/>

After that day, life shifted into high speed. The days disappeared as September slipped into October and all too soon Thanksgiving loomed in the very near future.

"What are your plans for the holiday?" Lauren asked Jake over lunch in the cafeteria.

"We're going to Arizona to see Teddy's grandparents. I promised I'd bring him, but I've been so tied up that we haven't seen them since July. Afterward, we'll go to my brother's home in Seattle for Thanksgiving."

Lauren frowned, feeling suddenly sad. "You'll be gone for Teddy's birthday."

He nodded. "That's why we have to go. They insist on spending his first birthday with Teddy."

She would have loved throwing a party for Teddy, but it was only right that he be with his grandparents. "What about Christmas?"

Jake shook his head. "It's too soon to go back. We'll do our celebrating over Thanksgiving and come back here to finish up the contract."

Lauren refused to think about them leaving forever. "Did you see the article in Sunday's paper?"

"I did. Great job," he enthused. "Nice photo of you and your dad. How did you get Greg to participate?"

Lauren grinned. "Mom laid out his best suit that morning, knowing the reporter and photographer would be here. And then I dropped in with them and he had to talk."

"Any feedback yet?"

"I haven't checked with sales."

"I see they have the television program playing in the sales area."

She grimaced. "I think Daddy might be behind that. Though he's not admitting to anything."

"Of course not." Jake enjoyed this playful side of father and daughter. "You have time to sit in on an employee meeting this afternoon?"

Lauren shook her head regretfully. "Doctor's appointment."

"Can you reschedule?"

Though tempted, she needed to get her blood test results. "I've put it off too long already."

"I'll ask Greg to sit in."

"Don't let him make any promises he can't keep."

"He understands he can't be so generous and stay in business."

She sipped from her water bottle and returned it to the table. "I hate that for him. He gets such joy from doing for others, but he's got to draw the line somewhere."

Jake stood and gathered his tray. "I'm out of here. Hey Laurie," he said, pausing next to the table. "Want to go Christmas shopping with me?"

"Won't hurt to get a head start now that I have a few more people on my list."

He groaned. "Please don't buy a lot of stuff for Teddy, or I'll have to hire a moving company."

She shook her head. "You can get your things in a U-Haul trailer."

"Nah, we'll need a truck. I'm buying mattresses and Teddy needs his bed, too."

That made her smile. "As fast as he's growing you can invest in a twin mattress for Teddy. For that matter, we'll give you the company discount for everyone on your Christmas list."

"Imagine wrapping that kind of present," Jake said with a shake of his head.

Later that afternoon Jake walked down the hall with Greg Kingsley.

"That went well," Greg offered, apparently pleased with the meeting outcome.

"It did. Making them aware they'll benefit as the company benefits is good. I think they'll be inspired by the improved bonus plan. Every person in that room knows people who need new bedding."

Jake studied the man who had brought him there. "Greg, you know I'm close to accomplishing what you set out for me to do. Our contract is up in January, and I'm sending out proposals for my next job."

"You don't have to go. I've been thinking, and you could make a big difference here at Sleep Dreams. I'm not getting any younger, and Lauren can't handle it alone. She does a great job, but the stress would be too much for her. I'd like to reduce my hours and spend more time with Suzanne. Maybe travel a bit."

"You'd leave Lauren alone?"

Greg hesitated and said, "If she had someone to call on when she needed help."

Jake felt the pressure building in the back of his head and reached to massage his neck. "I can't do it, Greg."

"Can't or won't?"

"I'm a problem solver. You no longer have a problem."

"I wouldn't say that."

"Laurie's doing well."

"I worry about her. Who will take care of my little girl when I'm no longer around?"

A huge knot formed in Jake's throat. He felt Greg's pain, understood his fear. "She's not a little girl, Greg. She's a woman who can handle what life throws at her. She will take care of herself. Laurie wants you and Suzanne to enjoy your lives. You should do those things you mentioned. She can handle things here."

Greg Kingsley looked resigned. "We've lived with this for so long. It's changed our lives."

"Lauren won't give up. You and Suzanne taught her that."

"Suzanne did all the hard work. I kept this place going and provided the money."

"That's important, too, Greg. Don't ever doubt the role you play in your daughter's life. She loves you very much."

"We keep praying research will find the cure."

"Strides are being made in medicine every day."

"She's going to miss you and Teddy. We all will."

"We'll miss you, too, Greg. Our time here has been great, but it's time for us to move on. You could always hire a manager to help Laurie. She would look after your interests."

"If you change your mind, you're always welcome here."

Jake detected a slump to the man's shoulders. He made his way back to his office, thinking of the offer and what it could mean to him and Teddy. A long-term position would require him to settle down and would give Teddy a home. Stability. If he were listing positives and negatives, there would be a lot of positives.

But what about Laurie? He didn't want to put her in the negative column, but Jake knew that's where she'd end up if she got involved with him. Gwen had told him he was a terrible husband often enough that Jake knew she was right. Laurie didn't need a selfish man in her life.

⁓

Lauren flipped the page in her calendar book. Five days since Jake and Teddy left for Arizona. She fingered Yapper's ears. "You miss them, too, don't you?"

When Jake asked if she'd mind checking on Yapper, Lauren suggested the dog would be lonely without them and it would be easier if she were at their house.

"Gerry said she'd keep her, but she's going to visit her kids for Thanksgiving," Jake said.

"Good for her. I don't think she's ever left Beaufort."

"The kids can't come and she wants to be with them. Are you sure Yapper's no problem?"

"She will be fine with us. Yapper and Fred get along great."

Jake sighed with regret. "Seems senseless to take time now when we'll be wrapping up the contract in a few weeks."

Lauren ignored the obvious. "I'm sure your family wants to see you before then."

"It's not that long before we leave, Laurie."

"But it's not now," she offered resolutely. "You'll be back for Christmas and the New Year."

Lauren found herself holding on to that fact, wishing it could be longer. She was determined to make the best of their last days together. She'd deal with the fallout after they left. Hopefully she could fight back the depression that she felt building about the edges of her life.

Chapter 14

Jake and Teddy returned, and they worked and played together and prepared to celebrate Jesus' birthday.

When Jake said he didn't plan to have a tree, Lauren felt bad for Teddy and urged him to reconsider. She and her mother insisted he needed to celebrate the holiday for his son's sake. They shopped for the tree and decorations and even picked up stockings for the mantel.

Tonight she'd come home with him after work to decorate. He looked on with doubt. "I don't know who will tear it down first—Teddy or Yapper."

Lauren thought she detected a mischievous glint in the little boy's eyes as he toddled among the decorations in the room. No doubt he couldn't wait to get his hands on the tree.

"I should have a tabletop tree."

She shook her head. "No. This is better. We'll secure it to the wall so Teddy doesn't pull it over on himself."

"What about the ornaments? He could get cut."

As if to prove a point, Teddy pulled a box from the coffee table. The ornaments rolled about the floor, still intact. Teddy picked up a bright red ornament and offered it to her.

Lauren tapped on it. "That's why I bought the nonbreakable kind."

Jake looped an arm about her shoulder and pulled her close. "You're so smart."

She grinned. "I know. We need to finish up. Mom said she'd pick me up around eight."

"I could have taken you home."

"No sense in taking Teddy out into the cold."

The weather had turned unseasonably cold for the past few days, and she didn't want to risk him getting sick.

Soon the tree lights winked at them with beautiful abandon among the mixture of children's ornaments they had chosen and the plastic candy garland.

"Teddy will try to eat this," Jake told her as he fingered the candy garland.

"Stop being such a Scrooge."

Lauren went to hang the wreath on the front door. She'd placed electric candles in the windows earlier. Back inside, she draped garland over the mantel and added red bows. "I love Christmas."

"I saw."

She looked at him and laughed. The Kingsley family had decorated their home the previous weekend, and he'd showed up at one point when it looked like an explosion in a Christmas factory.

"It came out beautifully," Jake said.

Lauren opened the box they had picked up earlier and studied the memory quilt. "Isn't it beautiful?" she asked, running her fingers over the bits of fabric that had been her grandmother's.

"Your mom will love it."

"It's going to make her cry." Lauren knew her mother would treasure the quilt but hated the thought of making her sad. "The Christmas cantata is this Sunday night. Are you going?"

Jake grumbled as he sorted tangled ornament hooks. He pulled out two and hung ornaments on the tree. "Yes. I finished my shopping over the weekend. Had some wrapped in the stores and bought bags and tissue paper for the rest."

At least he wasn't shopping at the convenience store on Christmas Eve, Lauren thought.

"Don't forget the company Christmas party is Friday night. We distributed the longevity checks at the end of November."

Jake looked perplexed. "I thought you intended to give them a cost of living raise instead."

"Daddy ran the numbers and says we can do both."

"Lauren. . ."

She held up a hand. "I know, Jake. Daddy's not going to relent. He wants them to have this, and you're not going to change his mind. I will say they've brought in a number of new customers lately. We've issued a lot of bonus checks for referrals. Ashleigh even sold a mattress to Austin Danforth."

Lauren enjoyed the holidays more than she had in years. Jake and Teddy joined their family for dinner, and the future was forgotten as they concentrated on Christmas Day. Her mother adored the quilt and became quite emotional when she saw what Lauren had done.

A surprise snowstorm the day after Christmas forced them to close shop for the day. Lauren sat in the window seat, watching the snow fall and wondering what Jake and Teddy were doing. She wondered if they were out playing in the snow. Wished she were there with them. Around two, she checked her e-mail and found a photo of Teddy with a child-sized snowman next to a man-sized one. " 'Wish you were here,'" she read.

Her parents held their annual New Year's Eve party and Jake and Teddy attended. The toddler slept on the daybed in the guest room as they rang in the New Year together.

As she marked the days off on her calendar, Lauren thought about what would happen soon.

Yet no matter how often she told herself to stop wishing for the impossible, the hope refused to be stayed. Her dad had said he offered Jake a long-term job. Maybe he'd change his mind and decide to stay.

They spent the workdays wrapping up, discussing the process, finalizing plans for how they would continue. Every night, she came home tired and feeling as though her heart would break. Then three weeks later they were saying good-bye to Jake and Teddy. The going-away party was held in the company cafeteria. Jake had made a big impression on their workers, and they showed up in force to wish him well for the future. He held Teddy in one arm and shook hands with the other.

"I'm going to miss you so much," Lauren said when her turn came, cradling Teddy's cheeks in her hands as she kissed his forehead.

"We'll miss you, too." Jake boosted his son with his arm. "He's become attached to your family and Gerry. He's not going to understand."

Lauren took Teddy and cuddled him close. She looked up at Jake. "Promise you'll come back for a visit."

"You know how it is, Laurie. I promise with good intentions, but life gets hectic and we never make it back. You see how it is with my parents and in-laws."

She did understand. People came and went in her life and while she was blessed for knowing them, the good ones were very much missed.

"There's something else," Jake began almost tentatively. "Say no if you want, but I feel it's the best thing for all involved. Would you be willing to take Yapper?"

Lauren's mouth dropped open.

"Teddy's too young to have a pet," Jake said. "And now that he's walking, poor Yapper spends all her time looking for places to hide."

"But you'd. . ."

"We would miss her, but I'm terrified she's not going to survive Teddy. I cringe every time he gets her in his clutches. I try to make him understand, but he drags her around like one of his stuffed animals."

She knew Jake was right. Yapper would be no competition for the toddler's affections. "You know I love Yapper."

"Then she's yours. I feel better knowing she will be with someone I trust and she'll be happier, too. If I were fair, I'd find a permanent home for Teddy, but I can't leave him behind."

"No. Don't do that." She visualized Teddy when he started his *dadadada* chant the moment he laid eyes on Jake. "He needs you. Have you considered finding a job that keeps you in one place?"

"I'm good at troubleshooting, Laurie. I enjoy change."

She looked him in the eye and said, "You're good at a lot of things. You'd find a challenge in any job you took on."

Later that afternoon, Lauren hid her tears as she waved them off.

He'd turned back to her after placing Teddy in his car seat in the cab of the large rental truck and pulled her into a hug. "You're a special person, Laurie. Promise me you'll never forget that. And that you'll keep trying to do those things you dream of doing."

She nodded. The way he'd touched her heart in these months was not something she could easily forget. He and Teddy had given her so much, helped her understand how narrow her world was without love. She could have friends who were trustworthy and understood what she was going through. The parameters of her almost solitary world had changed thanks to Jake and she had to be thankful. "I can't thank you enough for all you've done."

He stared at her for several seconds and then kissed her gently before turning away to climb into the rental truck.

Her hand came over her mouth, holding back the sobs. She'd known saying good-bye would hurt. Jake had made a major difference in her life. He awakened her to life's possibilities, and for that she'd always be thankful.

She stood in the parking lot, staring after the rental truck long after it disappeared in the distance.

"You okay, Laurie?" Her mother's arm curved about her waist, comforting her in the way only her mother could.

"I'm going to miss them."

"We all will. They made quite an impact on our family."

Lauren nodded, swiping away the tear that spilled down her cheek. "I owe him, Mom. Jake changed my world."

"Do you love him?"

She met her mother's gaze and nodded. They shared too much history for her not to tell the truth.

"Does he know?"

Lauren suspected that deep down inside Jake did know, but not because she'd voiced her feelings or tried to change his mind. "I wouldn't do that to him."

"What do you mean wouldn't?"

"I'm not the woman for him. I can't give Jake what he needs."

"I'm not so sure Jake knows what he needs. I suspect he's running from his past."

Lauren's gaze jerked up to her mother's face. "Why do you think that?"

"Why would he want a transient lifestyle, particularly with a small child? Most men are ready to settle down at his age. I hope he realizes Teddy needs permanence in his life soon."

"Jake provides permanence."

Suzanne's head moved slowly from side to side. "Too many people coming and going in Teddy's world. Eventually he'll stop bonding for fear everyone he loves will leave."

"Do you think Jake knows that?"

Her mother shrugged. "He's Teddy's father. I'm praying for God to open his eyes. Teddy has already lost too many people in his young life." Suzanne touched her cheek gently. "I'm praying for you, honey. God will get you through this."

Lauren reached up to squeeze her hand. "He always has. I'd better get back to work."

"Why don't we go out to dinner tonight? Take our minds off this."

She wasn't in the mood. "You and Daddy go."

"No. I'll fix something at home."

"See you later."

Dinner that night was a solemn affair. They ate in silence and worked together to clear the table. Her mother had made an extra effort with the meal, but the events of the day stole their appetites.

The glasses clinked together as her mother picked them up and headed for the sink. "Laurie, do you still want your own place?"

Did she? She hadn't given the idea much thought lately.

"I was thinking. Now that Jake's gone, you could move into Mom's place."

She couldn't. There were too many memories of Jake and Teddy there. She couldn't live with a constant reminder of their absence.

"Laurie?"

She shook her head quickly. "I don't want to move. Not now."

"That's fine, sweetie," her mother said. "You can stay right here for as long as you like."

Lauren had professed to desire a change in her life. With Jake by her side, that had been easy to consider. Without him, she couldn't imagine how she would survive, much less make major changes in the life she'd always known.

A box arrived a few days later, and Lauren smiled when she opened it to find piles of little doggie outfits. She read the note Jake had included, "Checked the weather and thought Yapper might appreciate these."

The new year continued. As she'd known it would, the depression hit her head-on like an eighteen-wheeler running over a subcompact. Despite taking her medication, Lauren suffered more frequent attacks.

Ashleigh came up with another blind date, but Lauren refused. "I won't do that to someone else. I'm not what your friend is looking for."

"You don't know that. This guy's ready to settle down. He's not into party-ing or chasing women. He's a one-woman kind of guy. It's Seth's older brother, Chase."

She glanced at her assistant. She knew Ashleigh and Seth had been a couple for months now and she had admitted to her hope that he would ask her to marry him. "Has he proposed yet?"

Ashleigh shook her head and sighed. "No, not yet. Chase retired from the military and came home to join the family business." Then she frowned. "Though he's nearly forty."

Ancient to this younger woman, Lauren thought. "I appreciate you thinking of me, but things aren't going well right now. I'm having attacks all the time, and I'm afraid if I don't get my life back to some semblance of normalcy, it's only going to get worse."

Concern filled her assistant's expression. "Is there anything I can do?"

"Be my friend and pray for me," Lauren told her.

"I am your friend, but I'm not so sure about the praying part."

Lauren knew that some people would feel her next question a violation of their rights, but as Ashleigh's friend she needed to ask. "Do you know Christ as your Savior?"

"We weren't a church family."

"Jesus loves you, Ashleigh. If you'd like to talk or even go to church with us, let me know."

The young woman nodded. "If you'll sign these, I'll get them in the mail this afternoon."

Lauren wrote her name with a flourish and handed over the letters.

❧

Jake glanced down at Teddy. "Ready for lunch, buddy?"

"Lunch." His son's vocabulary was growing.

In the days since he'd been back at his apartment, he'd sent out more proposals but had no responses. What was going on? Why the delay? He'd worked steadily since he'd gotten his degree and now it seemed no one wanted him. Businesses were in trouble. The economy was bad. Why wasn't anyone calling?

He should have stayed at Sleep Dreams. No, he'd been right in moving on. It wasn't right to take the Kingsleys' money when he'd done what they'd hired him to do.

Almost as if he read his mind, Teddy looked at Jake and chanted, "Laurie."

Jake had heard it several times a day since they'd left North Carolina. He shifted his son to his lap and said, "Yeah, buddy, I miss her, too."

He missed her bright smile when he walked into the room, her teasing and funny little jokes. The way she played with Teddy and Yapper. He even missed Yapper.

"Want Laurie, Daddy?" Teddy's little forehead wrinkled.

"Sure, why not." Jake reached for the cell phone on the table and dialed Lauren's office number. It was after lunch there. She'd be at her desk this time of day.

It rang four times before her voice mail picked up. He listened to the message. Weird. He hit the one and listened again. "You've reached the office of Lauren Kingsley. I am temporarily out of the office. If you have concerns that require immediate attention, please hang up and call. . ." He recognized Ashleigh's extension.

Jake disconnected and shifted straighter in the chair before dialing Greg's private number. The man sounded harried.

"Greg, Jake here. Where's Laurie? I got her voice mail."

"Oh Jake, it's terrible. She fell last Tuesday after work. Broke both her wrists."

Stunned, he demanded, "What's going on? I thought she had her narcolepsy under control."

"She's been having problems," Greg admitted. "Laurie's really struggling with the attacks right now."

Not what he wanted to hear. "Both wrists?"

"Yeah. She wanted to go into a rehab center until the casts come off.

Suzanne refused. Laurie's not doing well."

"I'm sorry. Is there anything I can do?"

Greg paused and then he said, "Maybe a call would brighten her spirits. Her mother and I haven't been able to help much in that area."

"I'm sure that's not true," Jake discounted. "She's depressed because she hurt herself so badly."

"I don't understand why it was so bad this time. She's had more than her share of bumps and bruises. Laurie's fallen over on her head a time or two and on the street, but she usually crumples into a heap. This time she pitched over the parking barrier."

"Teddy was chanting her name today and I thought I'd call so she could hear. I'll give her a call at the house. Can she answer the phone?"

"She has a speaker phone in her room. I think Suzanne had a client this morning so Lauren's probably still in bed. Her mother doesn't want her wandering about while she's casted. She's afraid Laurie will suffer an attack and hurt herself worse."

"I'll call her now."

She sounded far from her usual happy self when she said hello.

"Laurie? It's Jake. I spoke to your dad. He told me you'd hurt yourself."

"Jake?" she repeated almost in disbelief.

"Yeah. Teddy was calling for you. I had no idea."

"How is Teddy?" Her voice grew softer with the question.

"He's okay. We're at our apartment."

"You don't have a job?"

"Not yet. It's the first time I've been out of work since college."

Teddy burbled, "Laurie, hi."

Jake tilted the phone so she could hear.

"Hey buddy."

Jake chuckled as he fought the baby for the phone. "He's bouncing up and down and trying to take the phone from me."

"I miss you, Teddy. Yapper misses you, too."

"Where Yap?"

"He's developed quite a vocabulary."

"Mostly no and the names of his favorite people. So how are you managing?"

"Not very well. I can't do anything for myself. Mom and Dad feed me, and I have an aide who comes in to help me bathe and dress."

She sounded near tears.

"What happened? Did you have an attack?"

"I wasn't paying attention and tripped."

"Is there anything I can do?"

"Pray. I'm glad you called. It's good hearing from you."

They talked for several minutes, catching up on the time they'd been apart.

"The trip went okay, but I don't think I want to drive pulling a vehicle too often."

"I still say you could have gotten the stuff in a trailer if you'd dismantled the crib."

"Nothing ever goes back together the same way. I lugged the mattress upstairs to my bedroom and put the rest in storage in my uncle's garage. Don't tell your mom, but Teddy and I are sleeping together. There's nowhere in this apartment for his crib."

"Maybe you should have kept your house."

"Too many memories and a waste when you consider how little time I spent at home." There was a pause, and Jake wondered if something had happened.

"What about Teddy?" she asked finally. "Don't you worry that he won't become attached to people if he's always on the move?"

He did worry about separating his son from the people he loved, but what choice did he have? "I'm not going anywhere. Teddy will always have me."

At least Jake hoped that would be the case.

Life didn't come with guarantees. Accidents and sickness took loved ones every day. Jake often thought about what would happen to Teddy in the event either of those affected their lives. His mother was growing older, and he wasn't so sure his stepfather would welcome a child in their home. Gwen's parents would take him, but they were getting on in years. He supposed he could trust his brother to take care of Teddy, but he didn't like thinking about it. Too morbid.

"Tell me what to send to cheer you up."

"Short of a miracle cure, prayers and the occasional phone call would be most appreciated. Poor Mom is picking up my slack at the office as well as handling her own work and taking care of me. I feel so bad about putting more on her. I'm trying to fade into the background and not complain. Ashleigh's been a great help. She's taken on a number of things I usually handle and doing a great job."

"How are the attacks?"

Her pause gave him the answer.

"They're worse. My medications are off schedule. When Mom's not here, I can't open the bottles. Forget childproof caps. Mine are cast-proof."

"Why don't you ask your mom. . ."

"She already has too much to do. I'm stuck here in bed anyway, so what does it matter if I have an attack." The self-disgust in her tone was palpable.

"Laurie, I'm so sorry this happened to you."

"I wouldn't wish it on my worst enemy."

"Like you'd have one." Teddy started to whine. "It's time for his lunch."

"No peas and carrots for my buddy."

"Call me if you want to talk."

She sighed and he said, "You can't push the buttons."

"I'll have mom put you on speed dial."

Teddy started to wail.

"You'd better go. Thanks for calling, Jake. I'm glad you did. Kiss Teddy for me."

He kissed the top of his son's head and said, "Laurie's hurting bad, Teddy."

"See Laurie?" His son appeared puzzled as he looked around the room for her.

"Yes, Laurie," he said, bouncing Teddy on his knee as he allowed his thoughts to drift. How terrible it must be to have both hands in casts. He wished he were there to help her.

What if he went back to Beaufort? What could he do? Put her in a chair next to Teddy and shovel food into both their mouths? Lauren had more adult needs.

He thought of the pain in her voice when she spoke of the burden she'd placed on her mother. At one time, he'd suggested her parents were overprotective, but he now understood they were motivated by love for their child. It didn't matter how old she was. Lauren needed them and they'd be there for her always.

Jake considered how much of her pain he'd caused with his crusade to convince her she needed to change. He carried his son into the kitchen. The back door opened to admit his mother, who had been shopping.

"Hey Mom. I didn't expect you back so soon."

Stella Greer Simmons piled the bags on the counter. "I gave up. Couldn't find anything that appealed." She reached for her grandson and nodded toward the bags. "I picked up the food and diapers you had on the grocery list."

Jake frowned. "You didn't have to do that. I planned to go out later."

"Now you don't have to. Want me to feed him his lunch?"

"I can do it."

She hugged Teddy close. "Go do something else. I want to spend quality time with my grandson."

She'd been like this ever since she arrived Sunday afternoon, taking over Teddy's care every chance she got. She'd insisted she needed a grandbaby fix, and he hadn't argued. Except for their brief visit at Thanksgiving, it had been months since she'd seen her grandson.

Jake used the time to follow up on job leads. He pulled out his laptop and checked his e-mail. Nothing. Why wasn't anyone responding to his proposals? Sure, it hadn't been that long, but he usually had a job waiting when he wrapped up the previous one.

He typed in the link for the Sleep Dreams website. Lauren had gotten the site redone and it looked great. He considered her reluctance to take over certain tasks and to be in the limelight, but whatever she did she did well. She'd carried out every plan he'd outlined.

Jake searched online for a local florist. He placed an order for a rainbow bouquet of roses, hoping their beauty would boost Laurie's spirits.

After a while, he went back into the living room. Teddy toddled about the room, chasing his ball, and his grandmother's gaze followed him.

An afternoon talk show played on the television. Jake sat down next to his mother. He watched for a few minutes before he asked, "How can you watch this stuff?"

"You should pay attention. You might learn something."

He doubted that. Jake reached for the magazine he'd placed on the coffee table earlier and thumbed through the pages. He couldn't tune out the woman on the television as she talked about her failed marriage.

"He expected me to ignore my needs and focus on his. He could be so selfish. After a while, I hated him."

"Their marriage was probably already in trouble," he muttered.

His mother glanced at him and said, "A man can't expect a woman to give up everything and be happy with love. It doesn't work that way."

"We don't expect that."

She flashed him a pitying look.

Teddy came over and patted his tiny hands against Jake's legs. "Play, Daddy?"

He swung him up and caught him. "Hey buddy."

Teddy stood with his bare feet planted against his father's chest, holding on to his fingers as tightly as possible. His son offered him a grin. Jake looked on with pride. "You are something else, Teddy Greer."

The television program served as white noise for his thoughts as he held his son. In the months since Gwen's death, he'd become attached to Teddy to a degree he'd never imagined possible. Would that have happened if she hadn't died? Or would they have eventually gone their separate ways, citing irreconcilable differences? Would he have lost this opportunity to bond with his son like this? Jake feared the latter might have been the case.

"Mom, if you fell in love with someone who had a serious medical problem, would you stay?"

Recognizing his need to talk, she used the remote to lower the volume. "You spoke the vows yourself, Jake. In sickness and health. Once said, they were a vow to God as well as your wife."

"No. I mean before proposals and marriage. In the getting-to-know-each-other/dating stage. Would you walk away?"

She looked puzzled. "How could you walk away from love?"

Jake thought maybe that was exactly what he'd done. "I met this woman in North Carolina. Her name is Lauren. She has narcolepsy."

He shared how the disorder affected her life, talked about his erroneous accusation, how he'd encouraged her to reach for the things she wanted in life, and even how happy he'd been when her blind date had been unsuccessful.

"Teddy liked her from day one, but she wouldn't hold him out of fear that he could be hurt. By the time we left, she and Teddy were very comfortable together."

"She's the Laurie he calls for?"

Jake nodded. He'd thought Teddy would forget in time, but he hadn't.

"What does this problem mean to you as a couple?"

"When she takes her medication regularly, Laurie functions fine. She's a CFO for the company and has a wonderful support base in her parents. At first, I thought they were overprotective and urged her to become more independent, but now I realize they're a team. They work together to keep Lauren's life from being unbearable. But she still has the attacks, trusts very few people, and lives in fear of strangers."

"Seems she's won your heart. What will you do?"

Jake sighed heavily. "She's very easy to love. But I vowed no more helpless women."

His mother's eyes widened. "You saw Gwen as helpless? I always admired her strength."

Shocked, he repeated, "Strength?"

Stella shrugged. "I couldn't have done what Gwen did. She was alone in that big house with a baby and a tiny dog."

"I had to work to support my family," Jake said. "I couldn't be at her beck and call. She knew how things would be when we married, but that didn't keep her from nagging me at every opportunity."

"Perhaps her needs changed as she matured," his mother suggested. "She needed her husband around more often. We marry for companionship, Jake."

"At first, I asked her to travel with me, but she refused. Then she had Teddy and Yapper and her family."

"But you weren't there, Jake. Husbands fill a special place in a woman's heart. We need you more than you realize, and it's not all about the honey-do list. I think you have some praying to do. Ask yourself if you're man enough to take Lauren on."

Her comment pricked his masculinity. "What do you mean 'man enough'?"

"You have to be sure this is what you want. You can't decide it's too hard and walk away later."

"I wouldn't do that to her," he muttered.

Teddy worked his way across the sofa into his grandmother's arms. She pulled him close. "I would hope not. I raised you better than that. You need to seek God's plan in all this. Would she be able to give you more children?"

He lifted one shoulder. "She wants a family but worries about caring for them. We would need help. I had this great woman caring for Teddy and Yapper while we were there."

"If it's right, you'll make it work."

"Is it too soon?" he asked. "It's barely been a year since Gwen died."

"That's a personal choice, Jake. You'll know when you're ready to marry again."

That night, he lay on the sofa, his back hurting as his mom and Teddy shared his comfortable bed.

Though he tried to convince himself differently, Jake realized that in a way he'd expected Gwen to sublimate her needs for his. And then he'd gotten angry when she wouldn't. Couldn't. She wasn't nagging. She was asking for what she needed from him.

And his way of dealing with it had been to stay away even longer periods of time. He expected the house, a dog, and Teddy to be enough for her. His mom was right. She'd married a man, expecting him to keep the vows he'd spoken on their wedding day.

He could tell himself he'd done it for Gwen, but Jake knew he'd been selfish. He hadn't cheated on his wife, but he'd lived like a bachelor. He stayed in hotels, ate out, watched sports, and did his own thing until guilt forced him back home to his role of husband and father.

Then after a few days, when he decided he couldn't bear another minute of the arguing, he'd pack up and take off for the next adventure, leaving her behind to hold down the home front until he returned.

Gwen hadn't planned on a solo marriage, but that's what she'd gotten. He'd been the selfish one. Putting his needs first and expecting her to pretend everything was wonderful.

What had Lauren said today? Something about Teddy not bonding with people. Would Teddy suffer from disassociation because of him? No, Jake decided. That wouldn't happen.

"Lord," he called softly, "please tell me what You would have me do. Should I pluck Lauren from her safe haven and take her away to a new environment that would be alien to everything she knows? Would my love for her be enough? Does she love me? Is she the one You intend for me?

"Teddy and I need love in our lives, and You provided us with such a wonderful loving group of people while we were in Beaufort that we're spoiled. Take care of her, Lord. Heal her hands as quickly as possible so that she can have her life back. Help her get her medications back on schedule so the attacks occur less frequently.

"And as always, Lord, thank You for Your love and grace. Without You, I am nothing."

Only God knows the answer, Jake thought as he concluded his prayer. He tossed and turned for another hour before falling asleep. He dreamed of Lauren and her broken wrists.

"You're up early," his mother said the next morning when he came into the kitchen.

"Tough night."

"You want coffee?"

He nodded, and she poured the fresh brew into a mug and set it on the table before him. "Breakfast?"

Jake grimaced and said no. He reached for the cup and took several fortifying gulps before he spoke again.

"I'm going back to North Carolina. Greg Kingsley offered me a job managing the company."

"Is this what you want or are you nervous about not hearing back from the RFPs?"

"It's about Lauren. And the life I hope we can share."

"So you made a decision?"

"I did as you suggested and prayed over the matter. Then I tossed and turned until everything came clear."

"So she's worth the effort?"

"The boss's daughter," he offered with a wry smile. "I said I would never do that again, but we plan and God laughs."

Stella smiled. "But what sort of wife will she be?"

"I don't even know that she'd consider marrying me," Jake admitted. "But I feel strongly enough for her that I'm willing to help take care of her now and hope for a future."

"What about dependent women?"

"I wasn't fair to Gwen, Mom. I loved her and I don't regret marrying her, but I never explained what our lives would be like. I expected her to accept my plan without complaint. We both suffered as a result of my immaturity. That won't happen again. Besides, Teddy needs a stable home and people who love him as much as he loves them. People who won't disappear from his life every few months."

"What do you need?"

"A woman who loves me."

"When are you going?"

"After your visit. Will you come see us in North Carolina?"

"You know I will."

He nodded satisfaction with the plan that had suddenly come clear to him. "You'll like the area." He rubbed his bristly cheeks. "I'll shower and shave. How about two of your favorite guys taking you out to lunch?"

"I'd love that."

His mother stayed the remainder of her two weeks and during that time Jake spoke to Lauren several times. She'd loved the flowers and seemed cheered by their chats. He longed to be closer to her.

Laurie told him she felt more useful when her mother brought work home for her to complete.

"She says she doesn't remember how to do some of it," Lauren told Jake. "I suppose things have changed. Feels good to do something besides feel sorry for myself."

He called Greg Kingsley the day after his mom left for home. "Hello, Greg."

"Jake," he called, sounding happy to hear from him. "How are you? And Teddy?"

"We're fine. Mom left for home yesterday, and we're getting used to not having her around to spoil us. And I'm glad to get my bed back."

Greg chuckled. "Laurie's doing better. I didn't realize how much she does around here. Suze is serving as Lauren's hands, and they're working together to handle the office paperwork."

"I talked to her earlier. She's happy to have something to occupy her time."

"What's on your mind? I know you didn't call to check on Laurie since you've already talked to her."

"I wanted to ask if the management offer is still on the table."

"You thinking of coming back?"

"I've been praying about my life, and it seems God is leading me home."

"I think you'll be a fine addition to the Sleep Dreams family."

Maybe even the Kingsley family. Jake didn't talk about his feelings to her father. He needed to talk to Laurie first.

"When should we expect you?"

"I'll get things in order here and hopefully be back there in two weeks. Will you ask Suzanne if the house is still available? Should we tell Laurie or keep it a surprise?" He paused and then answered his own question. "We should tell her. A surprise might bring on an attack."

"You know, Jake, if I had any doubts, that comment pretty much reassured me that you'll be good for Laurie. You care about her, and that's the most important thing in the world to her mother and me."

"We miss her."

"Come home, Jake."

Chapter 15

And home was exactly the way it felt, Jake thought as he walked through the front door of the little house. He'd missed the place. His apartment lacked the same feel.

He'd called Gerry Hart, and she was ready to report the next morning when he started back to work.

Jake dragged in their stuff, considerably more since he'd emptied the garage apartment and loaded the rental truck for their return.

"Get used to it, buddy," he muttered as he looked around the crowded room. "No more nomad life for you."

After he'd stacked the items in the house, he went to turn in the truck. At the truck rental place, he unhooked his car from the tow bar, took the car seat from the cab of the truck, and returned it to the backseat of his car.

"You ready to go see Laurie?" he asked Teddy as he settled his son in the car.

"See Laurie?" The child looked excited.

Jake smiled at his son's question. "Come on, buddy. Time to work on getting me a wife and you a mom."

Suzanne had invited them to dinner when he called earlier to tell her when they would arrive. Greg was parking in the driveway and they walked into the house together, Jake's arms filled with Teddy and two bouquets of flowers.

"You trying to make me look bad to my woman?" Greg teased.

"Hostess gift."

Greg led the way through the house, Yapper welcoming them with her excited barks.

"Jake," Suzanne called. He managed a hug and handed her one of the bouquets. He looked around. "Where's Laurie?"

"In her room." She reached for Teddy. "Why don't you go say hello?"

Lauren rested on the bed, her legs covered with her mother's memory quilt. It pleased him that Suzanne had shared her treasure in Laurie's time of need. Her earbuds were in place and her eyes closed. When she didn't respond, he sat on the side of the bed and leaned forward to kiss her cheek.

Her smile was all the reassurance he needed. Jake kissed her, his lips lingering as the impact of the connection filled him with confidence. "I'm home."

The hazel gaze fixed on him. "Where's Teddy?"

"With your mom. I brought you these."

She cradled the roses in her casted arms. "They're beautiful. Thank you."

"How are you feeling?"

"Okay. They replaced the casts yesterday, and the doctor says I'm healing well."

"Good. I'm going to need your help at the office."

"What made you change your mind?"

Lauren's eyes never left his face, and Jake considered his vow to give her time, but he needed to know if she cared for him. "There's this beautiful woman who haunts my dreams. I came back to see if she feels the same for me."

Her eyes widened. "You love me?" She put a casted hand over her mouth.

He grinned broadly. "I do. But I need to explain why I left."

He propped against the headboard, and she leaned against his chest. Jake wrapped his arms about her and felt a contentment he'd never experienced before. "I once said I'd never become involved with another needy woman."

Jake could see from her crestfallen expression that she'd misunderstood what he was trying to say. He explained about his marriage to Gwen.

"You're not needy," he corrected quickly. "Neither was Gwen. I was the selfish one. That same selfishness is why I held back even though I knew I cared for you. I told myself I couldn't give you what you need."

"You're afraid of my problem," Lauren whispered.

Jake tipped her face up and looked into her beautiful face. "Actually I'm more afraid I won't do the right things, but I promise to try. Mom suggested I pray over the matter, and I felt God leading me to come back. I won't blame you if you don't want to try," he said finally. "I understand completely."

Her features became more animated. "There are things in life that are as necessary as the air we breathe," Lauren told him. "There's no way I'd walk away from what we could have, though it won't be easy."

"It wouldn't be anyway," Jake said without doubt. "Your narcolepsy is one more thing we'll have to work our way around."

"I feel like the selfish one right now," she told him. "I know I should tell you to find someone else. But I can't let you go."

"I don't want to. We're going to take this slow, Laurie. I'm going to show that love I've been hiding from you and in time, I want to make you my wife. We'll work together in your company and raise Teddy. Happiness will be ours because God will direct our paths and answer our prayers and we will be content in our love."

She looked down at her hands, obviously frustrated by the casts. "You know these are your fault."

"Mine?"

"I was thinking about you and not paying attention to where I was going."

Jake hugged her closer. "What were you thinking?"

She shrugged. "About what you were doing. Wondering if you were happy. That kind of thing."

He smiled. "I'll gladly take the blame. But you have to promise not to let it happen again. We can't spend our married life with your hands in casts because you were daydreaming."

Lauren's head moved from side to side. "Oh, never again. Next time I fall, I won't use my hands to stop my fall."

"Come on," he urged, swinging his feet off the bed. "You've got to see Teddy. He's growing so fast."

They went into the family room and found Teddy running after Yapper.

"Oh Jake, he's gotten so big. Hey buddy."

The child looked up and a beatific grin split his face as he raced headlong toward her. "Laurie, Teddy back."

Lauren fell to her knees and reached for him, beaming as she hugged him close.

Tears wet Jake's eyes, and he smiled sheepishly at Suzanne as he reached to wipe them away. She did the same as she mouthed a thank-you to him.

One year later

Lauren glanced up when the back door opened and Jake stepped inside. She finished stirring the contents of the Crock-Pot that held their dinner and grinned up at him.

"There's my beauty." He piled his things on the table before tugging her into his arms for a hug and long kiss. "Missed you."

His words thrilled her as much as his touch. While she still suffered from attacks, Lauren knew God had healed her in a way she never imagined. He'd sent her someone to cherish, and she felt healed by Jake's wonderful love. "I was only gone for the afternoon."

He looped his arms about her waist and looked into her eyes. Gerry Hart had picked her up at the office and driven her to the doctor's office that afternoon. The woman continued to stay with Teddy and Yapper and help around the house. They had grown closer and just that afternoon in the doctor's office Gerry apologized to Lauren for the pain they had caused her all those years ago.

"You don't need to apologize. I understand."

"I don't," Gerry said. "There was no reason for us to be afraid. Melissa said the same thing when we talked at Thanksgiving. She said you didn't deserve it. I think she understands even more since her little girl was diagnosed with Down syndrome."

"I'm sorry." Lauren hugged her.

"How did the appointment go?" Jake's question pulled her back to the present.

"Good." She leaned away slightly and called, "Teddy, Daddy's home." She turned back to Jake. "He's been looking for you ever since we got home."

The two-year-old made his way into the kitchen doing double-time, his arms raised into the air. "Daddy."

Jake grinned and grabbed him up, swinging him about before giving him a big smack on the cheek. "Hey buddy."

A flurry of words poured from the toddler's mouth, some understandable, others nearly unintelligible. He patted his chest and said, "See shirt."

Lauren grinned. She'd wondered if he would do what she'd taught him.

"You got a new shirt?" Jake asked, holding him out slightly so he could read the writing. "Lauren?" he began, his gaze widening when he read I'M GOING TO BE A BIG BROTHER.

She nodded. "It's going to be scary, Jake. I'll have to go off my medication until after the baby is born."

He jerked out a chair and urged her to sit. "Are you okay with this?"

"I'm happier than I ever dreamed possible. Mom and Dad will be over the moon."

"They don't know."

She grinned and shook her head. "Not before you. They'll be home from their trip this weekend. I thought we might have a special dinner."

"Sure. Whatever you want," he said.

"They never dreamed they would have grandchildren. Teddy is such a blessing to them." She touched her stomach. "And now this baby will add to their joy."

He set Teddy on his feet and dropped to his knees next to her. "And mine. I love you, Laurie."

Her arms went about his neck, her fingers smoothing his hair. "You've given me so much, Jake. Love I never dreamed I'd have in my life, my own home, a wonderful son in Teddy, and now this baby. I don't know how I ever lived without you. You're all those dreams I told you about rolled into one." She sniffed and giggled. "I think we finally found a reason to change this place."

He shook his head. "We can add on, but there's one thing this place has that will never change."

"The love?"

He nodded and held her tight.

They had fought past the fears of human nature and come out stronger for their efforts. Lauren prayed daily that their bond of love and faith would indeed be the mountain-moving kind.

Once she'd longed to touch the hem of Jesus' garment and be healed, but instead she'd been given the touch of this wonderful man who had made a difference in her life. His touch soothed, comforted, and conveyed caring in ways she'd never imagined possible, and because of his love, she'd learned to trust and reach out to others. Lauren knew without doubt that all along God had known Jake would be just what she needed.